JACK HIGGINS

THE KILLING GROUND

HARPER

Harper
An imprint of HarperCollins*Publishers*
77–85 Fulham Palace Road,
Hammersmith, London W6 8JB

www.harpercollins.co.uk

2

First published in Great Britain by
HarperCollins*Publishers* 2007

Copyright © Harry Patterson 2007

Harry Patterson asserts the moral right to
be identified as the author of this work

ISBN: 978-0-00-722368-8

Set in Sabon by Palimpsest Book Production Limited,
Grangemouth, Stirlingshire

Printed and bound in Great Britain by
Clays Ltd, St Ives plc

Mixed Sources

Product group from well-managed
forests and other controlled sources
www.fsc.org Cert no. SW-COC-1806
© 1996 Forest Stewardship Council

FSC

FSC is a non-profit international organisation established
to promote the responsible management of the world's forests.
Products carrying the FSC label are independently certified
to assure consumers that they come from forests that are managed
to meet the social, economic and ecological needs
of present and future generations.

Find out more about HarperCollins and the environment at
www.harpercollins.co.uk/green

JACK HIGGINS

Jack Higgins lived in Belfast until the age of twelve. Leaving school at fifteen, he spent three years with the Royal Horse Guards, serving on the East German border during the Cold War. His subsequent employment included occupations as diverse as circus roustabout, truck driver, clerk, and, after taking an honours degree in sociology and social psychology, teacher and university lecturer.

The Eagle Has Landed turned him into an international bestselling author and his novels have since sold over 250 million copies and been translated into fifty-five languages. Many of them have also been made into successful films. His recent bestselling novels include *Bad Company, Dark Justice, Without Mercy, East of Desolation, The Valhalla Exchange* and *Storm Warning*.

In 1995, Jack Higgins was awarded an honorary doctorate by Leeds Metropolitan University. He is also a fellow of the Royal Society of Arts and an expert scuba diver and marksman. He lives on Jersey.

Visit www.AuthorTracker.co.uk for exclusive updates on Jack Higgins.

ALSO BY JACK HIGGINS

For Henrietta with love

Now the field of battle is a land of standing corpses; those determined to die will live; those who hope to escape with their lives will die.

Wu Ch'i

THE AMERICAN EMBASSY

LONDON

1

Blake Johnson was received with courtesy at the American Embassy in Grosvenor Square, as befitted President Jake Cazelet's most important security adviser, the head of a secret White House operation known simply as the Basement. An aide took him to the Ambassador's office, a fine young Marine captain in dress uniform bearing medals from Bosnia, Iraq and Afghanistan.

'The Ambassador's hosting a cocktail party, mostly for those who weren't invited to Brussels for the conference.'

'And who would that be?' Blake asked.

'The dregs of every embassy in London, Major.'

'I know the feeling. And it's not Major – Vietnam was a long time ago.'

'Once a Marine always a Marine, Major. My dad was in Vietnam, and my grandfather was in North Africa and in Normandy on D-Day.'

'They must be proud of you. That Navy Cross speaks for itself.'

'Thank you, sir. I'll alert the Ambassador.' He went out. Blake helped himself to Scotch from a decanter on the sideboard and moved to the French window opening onto the terrace and looked into Grosvenor Square, the roads shining in the street lights, rain pounding down.

He stood under the canopy, inhaling the freshness, savouring his drink, and the door opened behind him. He turned and it was the Ambassador, Frank Mars, a friend of many years' standing. As little more than boys they'd served together in 'Nam. Mars shook his hand warmly.

'It's good to see you, Blake, but also a bit of a surprise. I thought you were in Brussels with the President.'

'Well, at first I wasn't going, but the President decided that his meeting with the

Prime Minister and President Putin might veer into my territory, so he decided he wanted me in Brussels anyway. I'm meeting Charles Ferguson tonight and we're flying over together.'

Ferguson was the head of the group of special operatives often referred to as the Prime Minister's private army. Blake had run many operations with him, and the tempo had only picked up of late.

Mars topped up their glasses and they stood there, looking into the square. 'All the years I've known this place and now I have to look down at those great ugly concrete blocks protecting us. The terrorists have accomplished what two world wars could not.'

'Not to mention the Cold War,' Blake said. 'Still, it all helped lead to this, those years of strife, the atomic submarines, the cancer of communism, East versus West.'

'We got it wrong with Berlin in 1945,' said Mars, 'allowing Russia to take the city. That's when they first sensed they could roll over us. I remember the first trip I made behind the Wall in Berlin. It chilled the soul.'

Blake gestured to the left of the square to the statue of Eisenhower on its plinth. 'What do you think he'd make of it? After all, it was he, Roosevelt and Winston Churchill who were responsible.'

'I'd remind you that Joseph Stalin had something to do with it,' Mars pointed out.

Blake nodded thoughtfully. 'And now we have Vladimir Putin. Think the Cold War is on its way back?'

Frank Mars put a hand on his shoulder.

'Blake, old friend, it's not on its way, it's arrived. From the moment Putin became President of the Russian Federation he had an agenda. We've seen it unfold bit by bit, and he's got the money to back it up, all that gas and oil. I think he's capable of anything. And there's something else about him that's very dangerous indeed.'

'And what would that be?'

'He's a patriot.' Mars swallowed his drink. 'But enough of that. Come and let me introduce you to my guests.'

*   *   *

Most of the guests were not too important, mostly minor attachés of one kind or another; the big fish were either in Brussels already or on the way there. After a little bit of talk, Blake stood in the corner, and soon Mars joined him.

'So, if you're flying off tonight you're not staying at the Embassy house off South Audley Street.'

'Right. My luggage is there, though, and I'm expecting Sean Dillon and Billy Salter to pick me up and deliver me to Farley Field to join Ferguson.'

'Ferguson's promoted young Salter to be an agent in the Secret Intelligence Service, I understand.'

'Yes. Mind you, Ferguson had to obliterate Salter's criminal records from the files to get him in. But he and Dillon make quite a team.'

'You could say that. An East End gangster and the most fearsome enforcer the Provisional IRA ever had. Quite a combination!'

As they talked, Blake noticed someone observing them, a man with Slavic features, an excellent suit and an eager smile. He was going heavy on the vodka, and, as Blake watched, took another from a waiter's tray.

Mars half-turned and murmured to Blake, 'Colonel Boris Luzhkov, senior commercial attaché for the Embassy of the Russian Federation. Of course, he's actually Head of Station for the GRU. They're all *something* else over there. Would you like a word?'

'If I must.'

Mars waved. Luzhkov gulped another vodka and rushed over, smiled ingratiatingly and shook hands. 'A great pleasure, Mr Ambassador.'

'Why, Boris, I thought you'd be in Brussels.'

'That is reserved for those more important than I.' He glanced inquiringly at Blake.

Mars said, 'Mr Johnson is on his way to Brussels this evening. It seems the President can't talk to your boss without him.'

'Blake Johnson? Mr Johnson, your reputation goes before you.' Luzhkov shook hands; his hand was damp and shook a little.

'Yes, well, just another day at the office,'

Blake said, and suddenly had had enough. 'You'll excuse me. I must thank you for the offer of the Embassy house, Frank. I'll stop over another time.'

'Of course.'

Luzhkov watched as Blake went to fetch his raincoat, then immediately went into a corner and called a number on his mobile phone. 'He's on his way now, to the Embassy house. Yes. Do it now.' He switched off and went down to the cloakroom.

Blake refused a car and accepted an umbrella, went down the steps into the square and walked towards South Audley Street. He made a brief call on his mobile and was answered by Sean Dillon in the passenger seat of Harry Salter's Aston Martin. Billy was driving.

'Where are you?' Sean demanded.

'Moving down to the Embassy house. I felt like the walk, the rain, all that stuff. The romance of a great city.'

'You damn fool. You know you're a marked man. Anybody special at the Embassy?'

'As a matter of fact, yes, a guy called Boris Luzhkov, Station Head of the GRU, apparently.'

'Idiot,' Sean said. 'You know the moment you landed here the GRU were on to you, don't you?' He switched off.

'Where is he?' Billy demanded, pulling his hat down.

'Near the Embassy house. Make it fast. Pass him, in fact. Go straight up that little side lane. Turn in there. Whoever's up to no good is probably parked by the house. I'll bail out fast and you can join me. Are you tooled up?'

'What do you think?'

Billy moved out to pass three parked cars and then Blake, the umbrella over his head. They ignored him, moved into the turning by the house and noticed a small sedan. Billy slowed, and Dillon pulled a Walther PPK with a silencer from his raincoat pocket, opened the door of the slow-moving car and rolled out. The car carried on. He pulled open the door of the waiting sedan and menaced the two men waiting inside. One of them was just clutching the driving wheel, but the other had a Browning, which Dillon wrenched from his hand. Billy arrived a moment later, opened the car door and relieved the driver of a Colt .25 from his waistband.

'Here, what is this?' The driver protested. It started, the usual bluster.

'I hate people being stupid,' Billy said. 'Don't you?'

'Absolutely,' Dillon told him, and at that moment Blake turned the corner and approached.

'What's going on?' he demanded.

'Just go and get your luggage and we'll be on our way, idiot,' Dillon told him. 'Get moving.'

'Did I have company? Ah well, I knew I could rely on you two.' Blake laughed and went to the front door of the house.

'Assume the position, both of you,' Dillon said, which they did with reluctance. Billy went through their pockets, did a quick check and found a wad of fifty-pound notes. 'Two thousand,' he said, counting. 'Must have been more originally. Had to be.'

Dillon stuck his pistol in the first man's ear. 'Who put you up to this?'

'Get stuffed,' the man said. He sounded cockney. The driver stayed silent.

'Stupid *and* arrogant,' Dillon said. 'A lethal combination.' And he shot half the man's left ear off.

The man cursed and moaned at the same time, and Dillon said, 'If you want the other one taken care of as well, that's all right with me.' He slipped the two thousand into the man's pocket. 'You can keep this. Just tell me who it was.'

'George Moon,' the man said, gasping. 'Runs the Harvest Moon pub in Trenchard Street, Soho. Farms out work.'

'And pretty dirty work, too, if that old sod's still at it.'

'And who was he representing?' Billy said to the driver. 'You might as well come clean.'

'Russian guy. Moon said he was called Luzhkov. He met us in a pub in Kensington across the High Street from the Russian Embassy.'

'And the gig was to kill off Blake Johnson.'

'Something like that.'

Dillon gave him his handkerchief. 'It's clean. Now piss off and find a hospital.'

They couldn't get in the car fast enough.

Billy said, 'Nice and generous of you, letting them keep the two grand.'

'It helped grease the wheels, Billy. A little pain, a little reward.'

The front door opened and Blake came out carrying a couple of flight bags. He put them in the back of the car. 'Anybody dead?'

'We wouldn't do a thing like that.'

Blake said, 'Who was it?'

'Couple of small-time hoods, hired by Luzhkov.'

Blake said, 'Interesting. He wouldn't have done that on his own.'

'Don't worry,' Billy said. 'We'll sort that lot out. It'll be a pleasure.'

They drove off. Dillon lit a cigarette and leaned back. 'Foot down to Farley Field, Billy. Ferguson won't be pleased if Blake's late.'

*　　*　　*

At Farley Field the rain fell relentlessly. Ferguson's pilots, Squadron Leader Lacey and Flight Lieutenant Parry, busied themselves with the aircraft, while the General drank coffee and a Bushmills whiskey and stood at the window of the small lounge staring out at the rain. He was indeed not best pleased.

'You're late.'

'Well, if you can be bothered to wipe the scowl from your face, General dear, I have news for you,' Dillon told him.

Ferguson's face became wary. 'And what would that be?'

'A couple of gentlemen of evil intent tried to hurry Blake into a better world.'

'Explain. Billy, I need another drink.'

He sampled the Bushmills and listened while Blake watched, amused. 'What I want to know,' said Ferguson, 'is what's with all this bloody game-playing? A third-rate colonel working for Russian military intelligence wants to shoot the President's key security man, and the best he can do is hire these incompetents? Somebody's head is going to roll.'

'All right,' Billy said. 'So where does that get us?'

'Well, obviously we're going to have to look into whoever put Luzhkov up to it, but that will have to wait until I return in four days. After Brussels, Putin visits Germany, and the Prime Minister and the President will be trying desperately to knock some sense into France.'

'I'll be glad to help with the France thing,' Billy said.

'Very funny. I've got something else for you to do. We've had a tip that some very bad actors may be flying in during the next twenty-four hours. Don't know who or from where, but it bears checking out. Sean, you know a lot of these people by sight – you and Billy, go to Heathrow and haunt passport control, see who's flying in from nasty places. We've got other men there, too, but they haven't got your experience.'

Dillon nodded.

'Meanwhile,' Blake said, 'we have to be off. Coming, General?' He boarded the plane, and Ferguson turned on the steps. 'I'll send the Gulfstream back in case of emergencies. Use it at your discretion if something comes up. You might also want to check in at the Holland Park safe house. Major Roper's just got in a new batch of satellite computer equipment. Very powerful stuff – you'll find it interesting. And Greta's there now – I thought it would be good experience for her.'

He was referring to Major Greta Novikova, once employed by the Russian army in Chechnya and Iraq. Circumstances had made it seem sensible for her to transfer allegiance to Ferguson.

The door closed, the plane started to move, and they walked back to the Aston and drove away. Dillon called Billy's father, Harry Salter, at his pub, the Dark Man.

'Are you on your own?'

'Roper and Greta are here, that's all. Managing a steak with all the trimmings, with Sergeants Henderson and Doyle eating fish and chips in a booth in their best blazers and flannels and trying not to look like military police. Can't say they're succeeding. Are you coming round?'

'No, but you can do me a favour.'

'Anything.'

'Tell Roper that Luzhkov was hanging around having drinks at the Embassy.'

'Huh. Light a match close to that one and the vodka would explode. What a clown.'

'Yes, well, that clown arranged for a couple of nobodies to take out Blake, who was rather foolishly walking down South Audley Street in the rain. Stupid because he knows it's open season on him.'

'Here, we can't have that. What's the game?'

'Oh, Billy and I sorted it with a little ungentle persuasion that left one of them with only half an ear. But it was Luzhkov who laid it on, and our old friend George Moon who did the hiring. Paid them two grand, apparently.' He gave Harry the rest of the details.

'George Moon? I didn't realize he was still breathing. Had a nice little wife, Ruby. She was straight, he wasn't. Right, it's taken care of. Are you coming to the pub?'

'No, Ferguson's got a job for us.'

'Well, enjoy yourselves.' Harry switched off the mobile and nodded across to his two minders, Joe Baxter and Sam Hall. 'I'll have a large Scotch, I'm thinking. Vodka, Greta?'

She was most attractive, wearing a black silk Russian shirt and trousers and knee-length boots. Her hair was tied at the nape of her neck.

'Why not?'

'A large one?'

'Is there any other one for a Russian?'

'Probably not. What about the Major?'

Roper sat in his state-of-the-art wheelchair wearing a reefer coat, his collar turned up to his bomb-scarred face. He didn't get a chance to say no because Dora brought the drinks on a tray and distributed them.

'Good girl, Dora,' Harry said. 'What are we going to do without you? She'll be leaving in a week. Australia. Got a daughter and two girls. Wants to test the water. Might never come back. Here's to her.'

Greta swallowed her vodka. 'Knock back that whisky,' she told Roper, 'because I know you're eager to get back to your machines.

That's all he ever does,' she said. 'Eats sand-wiches, drinks a bottle of Scotch a night, smokes, hardly sleeps, and plays around on those damn machines.'

'Yes,' Roper said. 'It's a wonderful life.'

'Let's move it, gentlemen,' Greta called to the military police. 'Take it easy, Harry.'

The policemen took the chair out to the special van, loaded it, and a few moments later drove off to Holland Park.

'Another one, boss?'

Harry shook his head. 'No, I've got a mind to see a bit of action. Remember George Moon?'

'And his boyfriend, Big Harold,' Baxter said.

'A couple of years ago they tried to run Roper into traffic in his wheelchair.'

Sam Hall laughed. 'I remember. The Major shot Harold in the side of the knee and Moon through the thigh. The word to the police was they'd been attacked by muggers. The cops didn't have much sympathy. They would have been only too glad to do it themselves.'

'So what's the point?'

'On behalf of a Russian geezer who is no friend of Dillon and Billy, George Moon produced a couple of low-lifes who tried to take out Blake Johnson for two grand.'

'Anybody damaged?' Baxter asked grimly.

'One of them left minus half his left ear, and the other one told Dillon the score.'

'So that leaves George Moon in deep trouble.'

'I'd say so.' Harry got up. 'So let's pay a visit to the Harvest Moon, home of the worst pint of beer in London. And make sure you're carrying.'

Trenchard Street was Victorian, and the Harvest Moon even more so. They drove in the Bentley over cobblestones to the pub, with its half moon over the door.

Harry told Sam Hall, 'Wait by the car. Anything could happen in a dump like this.'

Hall nodded, lit a cigarette and paused. At that moment the pub door swung open and a rough voice called, 'I told you to lock up.'

Ruby Moon stepped into the rain trying

to put on a mackintosh. Big Harold came out behind her and pulled her hair, making her cry out. 'Cry? I'll make you cry,' he said, and then slapped her twice across the face. 'You need discipline. I'll enjoy taking care of that.'

Harry turned to Joe Baxter. 'Look at that. Neanderthal man come back to haunt us from the Stone Age, and it slaps girls around, too.'

Harold pushed Ruby to one side and she burst into angry tears.

'Won't do,' Harry said and removed his smart military trenchcoat which he placed over her shoulders. 'Do you know who I am?'

Ruby stopped crying. 'Oh God, I think so.'

'Maybe you know my nephew, young Billy?'

'If he's who I think he is, I do.'

'That's good. Slip up to your bedroom. Find a few necessaries, put them in a suitcase and come back. Anything else you can get tomorrow. I'm losing Dora at my pub, the Dark Man at Cable Wharf, and you can take over the bar. Now hurry.'

'But this animal? What's he going to do? He won't let me go.'

'Dear me, I was forgetting.'

Harry offered his hand to Baxter, who passed him a .25 Colt with a silencer, and as Big Harold tried to step back Harry shot him through the fleshy part of the thigh and shoved him back on the step.

'Find him a towel in the gents,' Harry said. 'And you get upstairs, girl.'

She ran into the pub, and Harry and Baxter followed her.

Inside, George Moon was peering through a half-open door, and Harry could see a room lined with books behind him. Moon was small, balding and generally unsavoury and, just now, sweating profusely. He retreated to his desk and sank into a chair.

'Harry, my old friend, is that you?'

'Old friend? You must be bleeding joking.'

Salter put his gun on the table and walked to a sideboard. 'Whisky – a large one, and feel free yourself, Joe.'

'Certainly,' Baxter said.

Moon didn't have the nerve to reach into the desk for his gun. Harry said, 'I'm in a hurry, George, *old friend*. A couple of geezers tried to knock off an actual friend of mine tonight, but Dillon and my boy Billy managed to turn things around.'

'On my life, Harry, I swear . . .'

'Nothing. You pain me in my backside. Just confirm that a Russian named Luzhkov approached you for two hard men.'

'All right. It's true. It was for two grand, and I gave him two men – good men. I was just brokering the deal.'

'For two grand? That's rubbish money these days. Give me the truth.' Harry slapped the Colt across the sweaty face. 'I'll do for you, I swear it.'

'Christ, all right, I'll tell you. They met me in a Daimler in Hyde Park. Luzhkov was driving. The passenger was also a Russian, smoking a cigar, drinking vodka out of a flask, laughing all the time. He had a bad scar from his left eye down to the corner of his nose. He gave me a briefcase with ten grand in it.'

'So you pocketed eight and gave those two guys only two? Very naughty.'

'Harry, I wasn't sure what to do.' He struggled for something good to say. 'I know who the other one was, though. I saw him in the Dorchester Bar one evening and got his name out of a waiter. Max Chekov.'

'Yes, ten thousand quid would make more sense.' Harry turned to Baxter. 'See if the safe works.'

Moon moaned, 'Please, Harry,' but the safe did work and there was even a key in the door. Baxter held up a briefcase. The contents spoke for themselves.

'Excellent. Ruby can buy some nice things. Go and get her into the car.'

'Yes, boss.'

Baxter went out. Harry made for the door, and paused. 'Dear me, I was forgetting. Ruby is leaving you.' He shot Moon through the right thigh. Then he said, 'It would be wise to get some medical help for that. These days terrible things happen – street robberies, guns. It's a shame.' He shook his head. 'Get me?'

He left, the room was quiet, then there was only the sound of the limousine driving away. Moon groaned and reached for the telephone.

* * *

In the Bentley, Harry passed the briefcase over. 'You'll need a savings account.'

Ruby examined it. 'My God, this can't be happening.'

'It is happening. You'll do a great job running the pub. I'm never wrong about people. Happy days, sweetheart.'

At Heathrow it wasn't busy, possibly due to the lateness of the hour and, though the customs and passport officers on duty regarded them with deep suspicion, they knew better than to object to Dillon and Billy's presence.

They'd been there a couple of hours, with no one particularly interesting coming through, when a new entry on the arrivals screen caught Dillon's attention.

'Well, look at that, Billy,' he said. 'An old friend. Hazar.'

Billy stopped smiling and shivered a little at the memory of the ordeals they'd gone through in that desolate Middle Eastern country. 'Dear God, Kate Rashid of blessed memory.'

'Is that how you remember her?'

'She was some woman.' Billy shook his head at the thought of the woman who had sworn to kill them, and almost succeeded. 'If I never see that place again I'll be only too happy.'

'A long time ago,' Dillon said. 'But thinking of her brings events flooding back, enough to want to take a look at who's doing night runs from Hazar these days.'

As the queues lengthened, a supervisor called over the loudspeaker for people travelling from Hazar to move to a special section, which they did with surprisingly little fuss.

Caspar Rashid was one of them. His was a tall, handsome man, comparatively light in colour, his chin and mouth covered by a beard that was almost blond. He had one piece of folding hand luggage and a briefcase.

Billy said, 'He looks like a Bedouin.'

'That's because he is, Billy. Let's join him.'

As they approached, the passport officer had already opened the passport and was examining it. 'Mr Caspar Rashid? Address?'

'Gulf Road, Hampstead,' Rashid told him.

'Country of birth?'

'England.'

'Would you like to have a look, sir?' The passport man passed it across, and Rashid waited impassively while Dillon stepped back and examined the pages.

Finally Dillon said, 'Fine,' and handed the passport to Rashid, who gave him a wonderful smile and walked away.

'He has, you would agree, a great smile,' Dillon said.

'Yes, I suppose so, but then he's a good-looking guy.'

'But that isn't why he's smiling. He's smiling because he thinks he's got away with it, and I'm smiling because I've caught him. He's hiding something, Billy. I don't know what, but he's hiding something. Let's go.'

Rashid was tired from the flight, and obviously beyond caution. His vehicle was a red hire car on the ground floor of the car park opposite the exit. Rashid unlocked the door, including the luggage compartment. They were close enough to get a good look when Rashid heaved out the spare tyre and started to lift up the carpet.

'Get him, Billy.' Dillon said. They moved fast, and Rashid turned to face them. Dillon produced his Walther. 'Hands behind your neck. See what you can find, Billy.'

Billy struck gold straightaway, lifting out a cloth in which were wrapped a few tools – and a pistol. He held it up.

'.38 Smith & Wesson automatic. Loaded.'

'Cuff him.'

Billy did as he was told. 'Do we take him in?' he asked.

'No. He interests me.'

'Why?'

'You didn't need to be Sherlock Holmes to know he was up to no good. His passport indicates that he arrived in Cairo last week by plane from London. Took a train to Mombasa, then a ferry from Mombasa to Hazar. He didn't even stay a full day before flying back to London. Why did he do all that? Why not fly from London to Hazar and back?'

'I see what you mean.' Billy nodded. 'Probably because he didn't want to be noticed.'

'And there was a better chance of that by the roundabout route.'

'So why didn't you want to be noticed, Mr Rashid?'

'Because,' Rashid said, his face twisting with emotion, 'I couldn't be. They might have killed me. They might have killed her. I had no choice.'

'Wait a minute,' said Billy. 'Who are we talking about here?'

'Al-Qaeda. And the Army of God.'

A chill ran through them at the mention of the two terrorist organizations.

'What did they want with you?' asked Dillon.

'They called me. The man spoke excellent English and perfect Arabic. He told me I was under surveillance and could be killed at any time. He said I had to think of him as the Broker. He gave me no connecting number, but said they wanted to talk to me in person. That's why I went to Hazar, that's why I took such a roundabout route, they told me no one must know. The gun was given to me in London. It appeared in my desk drawer, but I didn't know what to do with it, and I just wrapped it up in the cloth and stuck it in the car. I'm not a terrorist, you must believe me.'

'But why did they call you?'

Rashid's face contorted again. 'To talk about my daughter. My beautiful thirteen-year-old daughter, Sara. They were – they were brought in by my father. He is very wedded to the old ways, and when he told us he intended to marry Sara to a cousin, someone we hardly know – a thirteen-year-old girl! – we refused, my wife and I. She's English too, a doctor. We refused – and then he just took her. Took her away. And now Sara is in Iraq.'

'Bloody hell,' Billy said.

'Please, I don't know who you are, but you must be with the government in some way. Can you help me? I'm not a terrorist, but I've learned a lot about the Army of God. I can tell you everything I know if you only help me get my daughter back. Please.'

'Take off the handcuffs.' Dillon lit a cigarette. 'Leave his car. We'll use the Aston Martin.'

Billy did as he was told. 'Where to?'

'To see Roper.'

LONDON

BRUSSELS

2

At Holland Park they were admitted by Sergeant Doyle, who was on night duty.

'Unexpected guest,' Dillon told him. 'Get Henderson out of bed. Billy, you stick Rashid in the interview room and wait. I'll see if Roper is still up.'

Which he was, roaming cyberspace as usual, Cole Porter sounding softly from a player. He was humming, perfectly happy, with Greta in a nearby chair, browsing through the *New Statesman*.

'Come into the viewing room, both of you.'

They assembled quickly, watching through the glass as Billy left Rashid alone in total silence.

'This is Caspar Rashid, a doctor of electronics at London University. He's forty-two, born in London, and his wife Molly is a medical doctor. Hope you're getting this, Roper. I'd like a full flow analysis as you record details of the interview. Assist by all means.'

'Of course. Let's keep it friendly,' Roper said and brought the lights up on both sides of the glass so Rashid could see them as well. 'Dr Rashid, we're a mixture of military and intelligence personnel. My name is Roper, the lady is Major Greta Novikova of the GRU, and Dillon and Billy Salter you already know.'

'I'm impressed,' Rashid said.

'We belong to a group personally authorized by the Prime Minister. Normal rules do not apply to us, so your complete honesty will be required.' That was Dillon.

Billy laughed. 'The only rules we have are not to have any. It saves time.'

'I understand,' said Rashid.

Greta suddenly said in Arabic, 'What nonsense is this? The analysis on Major Roper's flow machine fits no Arab I ever knew. It's there now.'

Rashid said in good Russian, 'Oh, I'm Arab enough, although I prefer Bedouin. I'm a member of the Rashid tribe, based in the Empty Quarter.' He continued in English. 'My father was a London heart surgeon from a wealthy family in Baghdad. Money meant nothing to him.'

'And you forswore your faith? Renounced Islam?' Greta asked. 'I can't believe it.'

'My parents moved back to Baghdad nearly thirteen years ago. My marriage to a Christian was a terrible shame for them. Unfortunately for them, I had been left a fortune by my grandmother, so I was independent. She'd even left me the Hampstead house I'd been born in.'

It was Dillon who said, 'And all this without provoking any blowbacks from your fellow Muslims?'

'Many and often. I became what someone once called a Christmas Muslim. Once a year. The kind of electronic engineering I specialize in is linked to the modern railway. I'm well known in my field as an expert. I visit many Muslim areas. I've been subject to pressure from extremist colleagues on many occasions at the university and on my travels. I know of things happening in places that would probably disturb you.'

'Such as?' Roper said.

'I will not say. Not until my terms are met. I will only say that eight months ago, when I was in Algiers for a week and my wife was on a heavy operating schedule, my daughter was abducted from her prep school at lunch time, driven to a flying club near London and flown out of the country by agents òf the Army of God, backed by Al-Qaeda. She was delivered to my father's villa at Amara, north of Baghdad.'

'Good God, there's a war on,' Greta said. 'Why would he be there instead of getting the hell out of it, a man like him?'

'He's seen the light, is dedicated to Osama. He allowed Sara to speak to us on the telephone once, but said I would never see her again. Since then I've tried everything and I've got nowhere.'

'So that's where we come in,' Roper said.

'No one in any official capacity can help.

The place we call Iraq is an inferno,' Rashid said.

'I'm interested in why your father, a man of such wealth and influence, should stay in the war zone. The major has a point.'

'He has dedicated himself to the other side. That is the most I will tell you. What I know about the Army of God during the past months and related dealings with Al-Qaeda in many areas of the Middle East and North Africa would interest you, Mr Dillon, particularly as an Irishman.'

'Now you've got the pot boiling. What the hell is that supposed to mean?'

'Not now. You know what I want.'

'What about your wife?' Greta put in.

'She won't crack, she's too strong. A great surgeon. Children are her speciality.'

'And she never knew about your problems with the Islamic business and the Army of God?'

'I thought I was protecting her from it, but the abduction of Sara changed all that. She has her work. That is her mainstay.'

There was a long pause.

Dillon said to Roper, 'Can it be done?'

'Well, there is the small matter of the war, but we'll just have to see what we can do. It's a good thing Ferguson's in Brussels, so we don't have to tell him. Allow Henderson to take this poor sod away for a shower.' He called to Rashid as he stood up, 'Your trip to Hazar. You thought it had a purpose, but those Army of God people were playing with you, was that it?'

'I've nothing more to say.'

'Good.' Roper said. 'Always nice to be reassured.'

Sitting in the computer room, Roper, who liked to think of himself as the planning genius of all time, had a large Scotch and smoked a cigarette for twenty minutes, but he wasn't taking it easy.

First, he checked on Molly Rashid's where-abouts. She was a professor of pediatrics at several hospitals, but that night she had performed heart surgery at Great Ormond Street and gone home at midnight.

He also checked the Rashids in Iraq. The villa on the north road beyond the village of Amara outside Baghdad was still intact, according to American sources, and inhabited by the head of the household, Abdul, aged eighty. There were two or three ageing females and five or six young men of the AK-carrying variety, and many refugees from the bombing. He was also pleased to see a mention of a thirteen-year-old girl named Sara. So she was still there. Roper had Rashid brought back to the viewing room.

'What now?' Rashid asked.

'Dr Rashid, we're now going to call your wife.'

'Can I speak to her?' Rashid had brightened.

'I insist on it. I'm afraid it has to be on speakerphone, and I suggest you tell her everything – which I suspect you haven't.'

There was the heavily amplified sound of a telephone and a woman's voice. 'Caspar? Is that you?' She was well spoken, a timbre to her voice.

Roper said, 'Dr Molly Rashid?'

'Yes, who is this?' She was uncertain.

'My name is Major Giles Roper.'

Before he could carry on, she said, 'Good heavens. I once met you at a charity lunch for the Great Ormond Street Hospital. You're that wonderful man with all the medals for dealing with bombs.'

She paused, and Roper carried on for her, 'The man in the wheelchair.'

'Yes. What on earth do you want at this time of night?'

'Dr Rashid, I'm here with your husband.'

Rashid broke in, 'It's true. Back from my trip to Hazar. Listen carefully, Molly, these people may be able to help us get Sara back.'

When he'd finished talking, everything was quiet. The exchange had been full and frank.

Roper said, 'What do you think, Dr Rashid?'

'I'm astonished. I knew more than my husband realized of the great pressures he's suffered from radical Islamic sources. He didn't want me to know about such matters, I'm sure, and I allowed him to think I was ignorant. It's what wives do. The abduction of Sara finished all that. The lack of any legal means to retrieve her from that dreadful war zone has been very hard.'

'Your husband offers us a bargain. If we can retrieve your daughter he will give us what he swears is incredibly valuable information touching on Al-Qaeda and the Army of God. Do you think I should believe him?'

'Major Roper, he has never lied to me. He is a Bedouin. His honour is everything.'

'It would mean him staying here in custody for the period the operation lasts. And you, Dr Rashid, perhaps you would be better in protective custody too. We live in a hard and dangerous world.'

'No, thank you. My operating schedule at the hospital would never permit it.'

'After what your husband has indicated about the people he won't talk about, I think I could suggest a compromise,' Dillon said. 'Major Greta Novikova, a valued colleague, is a highly skilled officer experienced in several wars. She could travel with you as security.'

43

Molly Rashid seemed to hesitate, and her husband said, 'Take the offer, please, Molly.'

'All right. Can I see Caspar?'

'Visit, by all means. Major Novikova will arrange to pick you up.' He hung up. 'That's it for this show. Take him to bed.' Henderson took Rashid out.

Afterwards they gathered to talk it out while Greta poured tea and vodka, Russian style. 'So this is the way it looks to me,' said Dillon. 'Roper, you'll handle logistics from here. Henderson and Doyle will mind Rashid. I know they'll tell me they can't bear the sight of any other military police sergeants in this place anyway. Greta, you'll guard Molly Rashid.'

'I liked her,' Greta said, handing out vodka.

'Which leaves you and me, Billy boy, to go to Iraq,' Dillon told him.

'Saving the world again.'

'The job of all great men,' Dillon said.

'Now, tell me how you see this gig going,' he asked Roper.

'Well, at some stage I imagine it would involve you or Billy kicking the door of that villa open, gun in hand.'

'Very funny, Roper.'

At that moment Roper's Codex Four, his secure mobile phone, rang, and he could see it was Harry Salter.

'Harry! What's up?' he asked.

'Is everyone there?'

'Not for long.'

'Put me on speakerphone and I'll tell you what's up.' He waited a moment. 'Remember George Moon and his thug, Big Harold?'

'I'll never forget them,' Roper said.

'Listen and learn, children.' Harry's voice floated out of the phone. By the time he had finished everybody was up to date on the events at the Harvest Moon.

At the end, Billy groaned. 'Ruby? Ruby Moon at the Dark Man?'

'She's safely tucked up in bed right now. It could be a lot worse, Billy. It'll make a man of you, old boy, isn't that what they say?'

'Not at the school I went to.'

'And it was one of the finest public schools in London, too. I wanted to make a gent of him, teach him how to behave. Look how it turned out.'

'Yes, you've created a gentleman gangster. A highwayman!' Roper laughed. 'It certainly suits Billy.'

'All right, let's have you home, Billy. I smell things happening over there. Make an old man happy, and tell me all about it.'

'I'll see you in twenty minutes.' Billy said and clicked off. He turned to Roper and Dillon. 'So, what's the deal?'

'We'll keep Ferguson out of it entirely,' said Roper. 'I'll arrange false papers – I think you'll play war correspondents again. I'll book a flight from Farley Field. Dillon takes the rap for telling Lacey and Parry it's an unexpected flight, highly secret and so on. The weapons will be supplied by the quarter-master at Farley. I know a firm called Recovery that'll help us in Baghdad. It'll just take a call to make sure. I can let you know tomorrow. Off you go.'

'Christ Almighty. Titanium waistcoats again.'

Billy left. Dillon walked Greta out and watched as Henderson let Billy out of the electronic gates. After he drove away, they went back inside.

'I think I'll sleep in staff quarters.' Greta said, and at that moment Ferguson's voice echoed out of Roper's computer, and he sounded annoyed.

'Isn't anyone there?'

Greta jumped, Roper placed a finger on his lips and Dillon poured Bushmills from a bottle on the corner table.

'I'm here, boss. You know us, we never close,' Roper said.

'How's Brussels?' Dillon put in.

'Bloody boring, but that's politics for you. As far as the Prime Minister is concerned, though, we're into another time of the wolf.'

'A second Cold War?' Dillon said.

'I think we've known that for a while. General Volkov never leaves Putin's side, and as for that fat fool Luzhkov at the embassy, we'll deal with him later. So things are quiet at the moment?'

'Absolutely, your honour, and boring with it.'

'The stage Irishman act is past its sell-by date, Dillon. All right, if that's all, I'll say goodnight. I'll check in with you tomorrow.'

He clicked off and Dillon said, 'I'm going to bed for a while. Knowing you, you're going to get started on the false papers.'

'Nothing like a bit of forgery to pass away my lonely nights. It's like something out of Dickens,' and Roper turned to his beloved computers. 'Sean – the mystery man from Al-Qaeda, the Broker. Do you believe in him?'

'Absolutely.' Dillon said.

Roper smiled. 'I'm so pleased. So do I.'

In the embassy in Brussels, Vladimir Putin sat drinking vodka with General Volkov, his most trusted security adviser, and Max Chekov.

'So, things are proceeding well with Belov International?' the President asked.

'Of course, Mr President. Thanks to Belov's untimely demise we control oilfields and gas pipelines from Siberia to Norway and over the North Sea to England.' Volkov shrugged. 'And we can stop most of those pipelines any time we want.'

'Stop, go, stop, go. Play with them,' Chekov put in. 'When you think of all the effort in the old days devoted to the threat of the atom bomb.' He shook his head. 'Now we can achieve more than we ever dreamed of by just turning off a few taps.'

'Yes,' Putin said. 'It was a wonderful gift when Belov ended up at the bottom of the Irish Sea, thanks to Ferguson's people.'

'What's happened to Belov's Irish estate?'

Chekov said, 'Drumore Place. I've visited it twice. It has been developed for light industry. There's a decent runway for light aircraft, and a helicopter pad. A nice little harbour. All in all, a useful property for us to have.' He smiled. 'And if you ever want to visit and have a drink, there's a great pub called the George.'

'Strange.' Putin, once a KGB colonel, knew his history. 'King George was the man who oppressed the Irish peasantry in the eighteenth century for being Roman Catholic. They hated him for this, so why call their public house the George?'

Chekov said, 'I asked the publican, a man called Ryan, that very question. He answered that it was their pub and they liked it the way it was. And let me note: they may all be Catholic by persuasion – but their real religion is the Provisional IRA.'

'Yes.' Putin sniffed at his drink. 'Those former IRA men, so violent – and so useful for certain jobs. Well!' He raised his glass. 'Let us drink to the future of Belov International.' He nodded towards Chekov. 'And to its chief executive officer.'

The vodka went down, and another, then Chekov excused himself. Volkov poured another couple of vodkas.

'What do you think of him?' Putin asked.

'Of Chekov?' said Volkov. 'He'll be fine. He's got a good tough army record. The kind who laughs and kills, you know? And he's so personally wealthy that he seems totally trustworthy from my point of view – he's unlikely to get too greedy.'

'Good. Now, Volkov, concerning this sorry business with Blake Johnson. You need to check the quality of your staff. Taking on such a prestigious target is only worthwhile if success is certain. Failure is not an option. And I keep seeing that damn Dillon's name popping up everywhere!'

'Of course, sir, I understand. As for Dillon – he's an exceptional man.'

'Are you saying we have no such individuals? Whatever happened to Igor Levin, for example?'

Volkov hesitated. 'He became unreliable, Mr President. By the end of the Belov affair he decamped to Dublin with two GRU sergeants, Chomsky and Popov. Chomsky, I believe, is studying law at Trinity College in Dublin now. It's difficult.'

'You're wrong,' Putin said. 'It's very simple. Tell them their President needs them and Russia needs them. And if that doesn't work – well, we have ways of dealing with people who "decamp", don't we? As for Ferguson and company, I'm sick of them. It's time to finish it once and for all. Every time we make headway towards our goal, they interfere. Disorder, chaos, anarchy leading to a breakdown in the social order: this should be our aim. Cultivate our Arab friends, let them do the dirty work. Their favourite weapon is the bomb, which means civilian casualties – that'll stoke the fires of hate for all things Muslim everywhere in Europe. You have my full authority.'

Volkov tried to smile. 'I'm very grateful, Mr President, for everything.'

'I'll have a vodka with you, then I'll let you go.'

'My pleasure.' Volkov went to the side table and filled two glasses, which he brought back.

'I've been thinking,' Putin said. 'This Arab you're running in London, Professor Dreq Khan, the Army of God man. He seems almost untouchable, all those committees he's on in Parliament, all those political connections. He could get away with murder.' He laughed. 'Don't you think?' He raised his glass. 'To victory and to Mother Russia,' and he took the vodka down in one easy swallow.

Called out at 2.30 a.m. to Warley General Hospital by an A & E department that was two general surgeons short, Molly found herself dealing with far too many drunks and victims of violent attack, many of them women. And some of the patients were scuffling among themselves.

On duty, too, was Abu Hassim, a general porter, not tall, but strong and wiry, and more than able to look after himself in that brawling crowd. Abu, born in Streatham, had a Cockney edge to his voice although his features were Arab.

He knew Molly, and she knew him enough to nod and say hello because he lived in a corner shop owned by his uncle and aunt half a mile from Molly's house.

She was hot and sweaty and deadly tired, and as she pushed through the crowd a man of thirty or so, hugely drunk, screaming and shouting and demanding a doctor, saw her.

'Who's this babe?' he yelled, and tried to kiss her.

She cried out, 'Leave me alone, damn you,' and tried to fight him off.

He slapped her on the side of the face. 'Bitch.'

The crowd surged, and a hand pulled her away. It was Abu Hassim, who said, 'That's no way to treat a lady,' took one step forward and head-butted the drunk with great precision. The drunk went backwards, and Abu grabbed him by the front of his jacket and eased him into a chair.

She wiped her face with a hand towel. 'That was definitely not in the book, but thanks. Abu Hassim, isn't it?'

'Yes, doctor. Sorry about that – good thing I was here.'

'It certainly was. But all in a day's work, I guess. Thanks again.'

'Don't mention it. I'll see you in the morning,' he said.

'Not me, I've got the morning off.'

'Lucky you.'

He went out into a windswept rainy road. There was no one at the late night bus stop. He waited. In a few minutes Molly drove out of the main gate at the wheel of a Land Rover. She pulled up and opened the passenger door.

'Get in. It's the least I can do.'

'Why, thank you,' and he accepted it with every appearance of gratitude.

'I've seen you coming out of that corner shop in Delamere Road,' Molly said.

'My uncle and aunt own it.'

'Where are you from?'

'Right here in good old London. I'm a Cockney Muslim.'

'I'm sorry.' She laughed uncertainly.

'Nothing to be sorry about. I like being what I am.'

She felt in deep water for some reason, 'Your parents . . .'

'Are dead,' Abu said. 'They were originally from Iraq. Two years ago they returned for family reasons and were killed in a bombing.'

She felt the most intense shock. 'Oh, Abu, that's terrible.'

'So far to go, and so little time to do it.'
His face remained calm. 'But as we say:
Inshallah, As God Wills.'

'I suppose so.' She pulled up outside the
shop. 'I'll see you soon.'

She was so nice and he liked her very
much. It was such a pity she was what she
was, but Allah had placed this duty on him,
and he got out.

'Sleep well, doctor. Allah protect you.' He
walked to the side door of the shop and she
drove away, more tired than she had ever
been. The electronic gates swung open and
she was home.

In the shop, Abu and his uncle embraced.
'A foul night and you are wet. Put this on.'
The old man handed him a robe. 'I'll make
some tea. Your aunt has been called to
Birmingham. Her niece has gone into labour.'
He busied himself with the kettle. 'Now tell
me what has happened.'

Abu held the offered cup of tea between his hands. 'Our quarry, Dr Molly's

husband, the Bedouin Rashid, arrived off the plane from Hazar, and was apprehended. We had two sweepers working close enough to the action. He was seen walking away pursued by two individuals, who turned out to be some kind of government officials. This was confirmed by one of our brothers working on a passport desk nearby. He said they were called Dillon and Salter. Another of our people saw them get into an Aston car with Rashid and drive away.'

'What then?'

'Nothing, except that our man got the licence number.'

'How do you know all this?'

'My control called me at the hospital to see what the situation was with the wife. Obviously the police will contact her.' He shook his head. 'I like Dr Molly. She's a good woman. Why does she have to be one of them?'

Instead of offering an explanation, his uncle said, 'Do you weaken in your resolve?'

'Not at all, not before Allah.' Abu

shrugged. 'I'm going to bed. She has the morning free, so it will be difficult to check the house then. We'll see.'

His uncle embraced him. 'You are a very good boy. Sleep well.'

The uncle found that with age he slept lightly, and he rested on the couch by the fire. He dozed, contemplating the current situation and how lucky he was, with the strengthening faith of age, to have such power from Allah. The phone rang.

'Ah, so you are still awake, Ali my brother.'

'What can I do for you?'

'Abu has done well to involve himself with the Rashid woman. Tell him to take the day off from the hospital tomorrow and observe her. One of my agents at Heathrow managed to follow Caspar Rashid to a place in Holland Park. There was a lot of security there.'

The man speaking was Professor Dreq Khan, whose field was Comparative Religion. He was a highly regarded academic in many countries, but especially in London, where he was on many government and inter-faith committees. His great secret was his fateful meeting with Osama bin Laden in Afghanistan years before, and the changes in his thinking that had led to found the Army of God.

'We'll find out what we can, but if I'm right it would be a waste of time trying to get in. My computer assistants at the university have come up with an owner for the car, who turns out to have been a rather famous criminal in his day, named Harry Salter. He is incredibly rich, but an informant tells me he still gets up to his old tricks. You know what he tells people? Smuggling cigarettes pays the same as heroin, but only gets you six months if caught.'

'London is truly an amazing place.'

'He has a nephew named Billy Salter, but the computer listing shows nothing for him. I'll put the word out, though. Perhaps the authorities have wiped his records. In any event, do what you can, and God be with you.'

Ali Hassim sighed, folded his hands and lay back.

An hour or so earlier, Billy had driven up to the Dark Man. He knew the front door would be locked, so he went through the side door and passed through to the lounge bar, and found Harry sitting by the fire being served coffee by Ruby. They both looked up and she managed to smile, for she had realized Billy might prove to be her greatest obstacle, but Ruby was Ruby and undeniably pretty.

'You were stupid to put up with it, Ruby. He was always a toad and Arthur about as appetizing as a corpse. Now, I'm about to break some bad news to my good old uncle Harry. You might as well hear it, too, because since you've become a member of the team and live here, you'd wriggle it out of any man wearing well-cut trousers anyway.'

'Do I take that as a compliment?' Ruby asked.

'Absolutely. Now shut up.' He turned to Harry. 'We're going to Baghdad again.'

'Wonderful,' Harry said. 'The troops are coming home, but my nephew and some wild Irishman have to do the exact opposite.'

'It's worthwhile.' He went through the details. 'The girl is just a kid, thirteen, for Christ's sake, so if Roper has worked a way we might pull it off, then I'm for it. Frankly, the more I think of that kid and what her future is likely to be, the more I'm inclined to go for it.' He got up. 'I'm going to bed now, before I fall down.'

He went out. There was silence, and Harry said, 'Very stubborn, my nephew. What would you say, Ruby?'

'I'd say he needs a good night's sleep.' She carried the coffee things to the bar. 'But I'd also like to say that I think he's marvellous, and on that note I'm going to bed, too.'

In Hampstead at six o'clock in the morning, Greta Novikova was moving through rain-soaked streets that were relatively empty. A

Mini Cooper, dark blue, a couple of years old, was what she preferred, the engine lethal. The house was easy enough to find, with its large, old-fashioned Edwardian railings. She called Roper.

'I'm here.'

'I'll give her a nudge,' and after a few moments she heard over a voice box, 'Gate opening.'

It revealed a fine driveway lined by poplars, a gracious Edwardian house standing at the far end, with terraces and french windows.

Greta had left her phone on. 'Fantastic. That's worth four or five million, easily.'

'Clever lady, four and a half. But when his great grandfather bought the place it went for one hundred and seventy-five thousand pounds. Gasp away, that's inflation on the housing market for you.'

Molly Rashid opened the front door at the top of the terrace steps, her hand outstretched. 'Major Novikova. Welcome.'

'It's so beautiful.'

'The house? Oh, we're very happy here.

My husband worships the place, and so does my daughter.'

It was as if everything was normal. Greta looked around, noticing dramatic paintings everywhere, and Yorkshire stone on the floor, which from the warmth was heated underneath.

'Kitchen's at the end of the corridor,' Molly said. 'I'll make us a brew unless you would prefer coffee.'

'I'm Russian, remember, a tea person.'

'It's so useful having a husband who is a Bedouin. Rashids are great tea drinkers. Go on, five minutes. Poke your nose anywhere. See if you can see why there's no bathroom in the main bedroom.'

Greta moved quite quickly from bedroom to bedroom, several bathrooms and dressing rooms, all beautifully decorated, a cheerful life-size stuffed bear standing on the landing.

Finally she reached the master bedroom, which was a work of art, with a superb dressing room next door. She returned to the bedroom and looked thoughtfully at the wardrobe's mirrored doors. She opened them one by one, and suddenly a section swung back disclosing a hidden bathroom, a joy in contrasting marbles. She went downstairs to find Molly sitting at one of the bar stools dispensing tea.

'How did you get on?' Molly asked.

'I found it, after a thorough search. It's a refuge, I presume?'

'Well, I've never had to use it in that way. The idea of needing it for such a purpose fills me with alarm. Why does it have to be us?'

'Your husband is a man of some distinction in the world, therefore of great use for the dark side of the Muslim world. Positive publicity would emerge if he went public supporting extremism. Instead, he turns away from his faith, spurns it. That makes him a traitor in their world. Fundamentalists, or many of them, do not wish to acknowledge their Britishness, even when born here.' She got up. 'I think we had better get moving.'

A few minutes later they were drawing out of the main gate. 'How far did you say it was to Abu's shop?'

'Five minutes, that's all. The traffic at that

time of night is very sparse. We'll actually pass it, so I'll show you.' She did, pulling to a halt on the other side of the road. There was a yellow painted van parked outside the shop, with a sign that said Cleansing Department. Two men stood beside it with Arabic features and yellow oilskins, not surprising because of the rain, and then a third man in a yellow oilskin appeared, pushing a yellow painted wheelie bin, spades and brushes falling out of it. They exchanged words, and the van drove away.

'Now that's strange,' Molly said.

'What is?'

'That third man was Abu. He's supposed to be on shift today.'

'Maybe he works a second job,' Greta said, but she didn't believe that for a moment. 'I'll call Roper.'

He returned her call fifteen minutes later. 'You're getting nervous, ladies. They've got half a dozen vans travelling the area and checking drains. It's a monthly exercise.'

'All right,' Greta said. 'We'll see you soon, then. What about breakfast?'

'Taken care of. Tony's Café round the corner in Arch Street. Takeaway delivery. Congealed scrambled egg, bacon, toast long since past its best. I'd like to take someone on to cook, but I haven't the authority. I also lack the genius that allows General Charles Ferguson, DSO, Military Cross, to select middle-aged women with rosy cheeks to run a successful canteen, like Mrs Grant did. Unfortunately she's gone to a better place, or wasn't that her funeral I went to three weeks ago?'

'You're mad, Roper,' Greta said.

'I have been ever since I met you, dear girl. It's a privilege to serve you. Until then . . .'

Greta was laughing hugely. 'He's such a fool.'

'All bluff,' Molly said.

'Oh yes, there's no hope. All those lives he saved, and what was his return? A burned face and severed spine. Shrapnel still in five places. A wife who dumped him. It's true. Dillon told me when we were drinking too much one night. Apparently she simply couldn't cope.'

'She was young, weak and vulnerable. It happens. To have done what he has is proof that Major Roper is a remarkable man. Don't think that beneath the surface there must be a man who is cursed by his suffering. He is a survivor.'

'Tell me about it. You're a nice lady with a good heart. I, on the other hand, served in Chechnya, Afghanistan and Iraq. I still haven't discovered what that means about me. When I have, I'll let you know.'

'I'm so sorry,' Molly said.

'Don't be. In a strange way I rather enjoyed it. I wonder what that makes me?' and she turned into the safe house and waited for the gate to open.

The breakfast from Tony's was delivered to Sergeant Doyle in a vacuum-packed carrying box, and he allowed Molly to join her husband in his cell. The others made do with the committee table in the conference room. After they were all done, Roper asked the Rashids to join them in the conference room.

'We'll finish our coffee in a civilized way and then I'll fill you all in,' he said. 'I'm expecting a couple of people who are essential if we're ever going to get off the ground.'

A moment later the doorbell sounded and Sergeant Doyle returned with two fit-looking men in leather bomber jackets. The RAF moustaches said it all. Greetings were exchanged and Roper made the introductions.

'Squadron Leader Lacey AFC and Flight Lieutenant Parry AFC. They'll be flying the Gulfstream. They specialize in operations for our outfit.'

'Anything and everything,' Lacey said.

Dillon, who had a flask of Bushmills in his pocket, took it out, unscrewed the cap and toasted them. 'There's just one small correction. It seems that our two distinguished pilots have not one, but two Air Force Crosses apiece.'

They both looked at him dumbfounded.

'Harry always reads *The Times*. It appears you've been gazetted in this morning's issue, something about covert operations. Can't imagine *where* they got that from,' Billy said.

Dillon said, 'To many more happy landings,' and raised the flask.

Many more congratulations followed, until Roper opened a briefcase and took out a document pouch. 'All right, Squadron Leader, this is for you. Flight details to Baghdad. It's rather like that job we did a year and a half ago. Your passengers are Billy and Dillon. The purpose of the trip is contained in that file. You'll wait for them, and on the return there'll be one other passenger, a thirteen-year-old girl being held under restraint in Iraq. Dillon and Billy will recover her and bring her back home.'

Lacey said, 'The situation in Baghdad is still very rough. In the last two weeks seven helicopters have been downed. Naturally we'll do our best, though.'

'We know you will.'

'When, sir?'

'I'd say within the next twenty-four hours.'

'Right, Major. Anything more?'

Roper put a little mystery into his voice.

'Squadron Leader, you will have seen many war films where the hero, being asked to do some deed of daring, is told it could win the war for us. Well, this is rather like that. There are security repercussions that would be hugely favourable for us if we can pull it off.'

They took that very seriously indeed. 'Just let us get on with it. We'll get straight up to Farley now.' They took their leave.

Dillon turned to Rashid. 'Caspar, you should know that Billy and I had dealings with the Rashid tribe ourselves the other year. With Paul, the Earl of Loch Dhu, and his sister, Lady Kate, both of them in turn the leaders of the tribe.'

'When they were still alive,' Billy put in.

Caspar stiffened. 'Did you have anything to do with that? The events were a huge shock to the people.'

'It nearly cost them a railway bridge,' Billy said. 'You probably know it – the Bacu? Spans a five-hundred-foot gorge, constructed during World War Two. The bridge almost got blown up.'

Rashid was most disturbed. 'The Earl and his sister were killed. That was you?'

'My friend, you're not telling us your secrets, so why should I tell you ours?'

'Incredible view from the bridge,' Billy said.

Molly said slowly, 'Are you trying to tell us you executed them?'

'Notice the interesting scar on Billy's face?' said Dillon. 'That was Kate Rashid, as well as two bullets in the pelvic girdle and another in the neck. I know the rights and wrongs of these things are difficult to handle, but that's the way it was. Believe me when I tell you they were very bad people. Perhaps you should retire to your husband's holding cell and try to come to terms with it.'

Roper said, 'And we *are* the good guys, Doctor. Confusing, isn't it?'

Doyle appeared to escort them and Roper said, 'You might as well sit in on this, Greta. The Rashid villa is north of the city in Amara, and thanks to the genius of my equipment I can show it to you now. Amazing what we owe to the satellite. Look and marvel, children.'

The villa was obviously the home of a wealthy man. There was no sign of bomb damage. It was surrounded by palm trees in clumps, and there was a sizeable orange grove, plus lemons and olives. Boats drifted along the Tigris. 'All very peaceful.'

'You'd never think a war was going on,' Billy said. 'Look carefully. Some women on the house terrace. Go through the orange and lemon groves. At least half a dozen male workers, and the main gate is fortified. Three men down there, and I'll bet those rifles they are carrying are AKs. A few tents in the grounds.'

'Tough nut to crack.' Dillon said.

'But not impossible.' On the river, a forty-foot speedboat flashed past. 'Because of the state of things in the city, the boat business is booming. It avoids roadside bombs. Ex-Navy guys, SAS, former Green Berets are all at it.'

'Who have you got?' Dillon demanded.

'A rogue named Jack Savage. He was a sergeant-major in the Special Boat Service, Royal Marines. Used to specialize in operations against the IRA during the Irish troubles, knocking off trawlers and the like running guns in the Irish Sea. I've negotiated an extremely large fee, for which he'll organize everything. You'll meet him in Baghdad.'

'Where?'

'A club down by the river. He owns it in partnership with a wife called Rawan Feleyah. She's Druse. He's named it the River Room. Tells me it reminds him of the Savoy. I've filled him in on the situation. He'll have the right sort of plan worked out.'

'You mean an approach from the Tigris?'

'He and other vessels travel up and down, particularly at night, on good business and bad.'

Dillon nodded and turned to Billy. 'Run me down to Wapping. Let's fill Harry in. You know he likes that.'

'He'll try and come, too,' warned Billy. 'He's done that before.'

'Tell me about it.' Dillon said to Greta, 'You'd better try to prise the good doctor from her husband.'

Greta went to their room, and Molly and Caspar rose to greet her. 'Time to go. You won't be seeing each other again until this whole thing is over. How do you feel about that?'

'As Allah wills,' he said.

'For a man who doesn't follow his religion, you reflect on Allah a lot.'

'You could be right, but we are all at the mercy of events. This will be a violent affair?'

'If things go right, it could go very simply.'

'And if they go wrong, people will die. Even Sara could die.'

'There are always risks. But let me tell you about the man you're dealing with, Sean Dillon. He was the most feared enforcer the Provisional IRA ever had.'

'And what went wrong?'

'During the war in Bosnia he flew a private plane into Serbia carrying medical supplies for children. He was shot down and facing death when Charles Ferguson arrived. Ferguson blackmailed Dillon into joining his organization, and then did a deal with his captors.'

'What kind of people inhabit your world?' Molly Rashid asked in a kind of horror.

'People who are prepared to do whatever is necessary. We must go. You said you were on call at the hospital.'

'Yes, I am.'

'Do you want to visit the house?'

'No, not really. I have everything I need.'

'Good. I'll drop you off, then check to see that all is well. I'll see you again at the end of the afternoon. I have your mobile number.'

The rest of the journey passed in silence. At the hospital, Molly Rashid took the umbrella she was offered, opened it and stood looking down. 'You must have killed people yourself.'

'Many times,' Greta said serenely. 'I'm in the death business – but then so are you. I'd have thought you'd have got used to it by now.'

Molly Rashid smiled sadly. 'I imagined I was in the life business, but it seems I was misinformed.'

She turned towards the hospital entrance,

and Abu came out and down the steps. 'Abu,' she called. 'Where are you going? I thought you were on duty.'

He smiled at them both. 'Ladies. No, I've got this afternoon off. A friend is picking me up,' and at that moment the yellow van appeared, carrying just the driver, an Arab with a pockmarked face. 'This is Jamal. I often help him in my spare time.'

Jamal, who looked like the kind of man who was permanently angry, nodded unwillingly. Abu climbed in beside him, and they drove away.

Greta said to Molly, 'I'll see you later,' and followed them.

The traffic was light at that time of the afternoon and, on a hunch, she drove straight to the Rashids' house, parked in the garage and locked the door. She went upstairs to the highest window in the house, and only a few minutes later she could see the yellow van stop across the road. Abu got out and came towards the house; the van moved away and parked under the trees.

Greta nodded. Better to let Abu make a

forced entrance. Information on Caspar Rashid? That must be what he was after. She listened to the sudden crash of a pantry window, then retreated to the master bedroom and concealed herself in the refuge.

She could hear him moving around and finally entering the bedroom. Then he used his mobile phone and spoke in Arabic to Jamal. Thanks to her service in Iraq, she spoke fair Arabic herself.

'There's no one here. No, wait for me, you have your orders. I'm going to search the study, see if I can find anything for Professor Khan. Just stay by the canal.'

Greta took her Walther from the waist holster and twisted the Carswell silencer on the muzzle. She stepped out into the corridor. He was towards the far end, a pistol hanging in his right hand.

'Surprise, surprise,' she said softly in Arabic. 'Nice of you to call. Dr Rashid is not at home, but I'm her minder.'

He swung round, thunderstruck, and for a moment seemed dazed. She continued in English. 'Caspar Rashid isn't at home either.

We've got him, which must make you Army of God people mad as hell. And who's Professor Khan?'

His face contorted, his hand started to lift, and she shot him between the eyes, a dull thud, and he fell backwards, dead instantly.

She followed procedure as she had been taught, got through to Roper on her Codex Four.

'Where are you? What's up?'

'I've got a disposal. I'm at the Rashid house, alone. The Abu boy broke in armed. I'd no choice.'

'They'll be on their way immediately. He'll be six pounds of grey ash at the crematorium in a matter of hours.'

'Should I tell her when I see her at the hospital?'

'If I judge her right, no. She's not like us. She's one of the good people.'

They were excellent, the men in dark suits, they might have been undertakers all their lives. Abu's head was wrapped, he was body-bagged, and one of the men cleaned the corridor, which luckily was varnished wood.

'You'd hardly notice, Major.' He produced a throw rug and laid it down. 'There you are.'

She saw them out, then walked down the track beside the canal. Jamal was sitting behind the wheel of the yellow van. She leaned down.

He started violently and she tapped the Walther on the van. 'Don't try anything,' she said in Arabic. 'The Army of God is one man down. I've shot Abu dead and my people have taken him away. If he's lucky, all those virgins are waiting in Paradise; if not, you've all been sold a bill of goods.'

'But who are you?' he asked in English.

'British Intelligence. And I've got a message for you to deliver. Tell your boss, Professor Khan, we're on to him. His little army is out of business, starting today, or you'll all be following in Abu's footsteps. Is that clear?'

Jamal said nothing, but his forehead was

sweating. Greta turned and walked away. The engine started up behind her and she heard the van race off, tyres squealing.

Her Codex went and Roper said, 'We're all set. We even replaced the window and swept up the glass, so there should be no sign of what went on. You OK at your end?'

'Yes. Tell me, Roper, does the name Professor Khan mean anything to you? It certainly did to Abu and Jamal the van driver.'

'No, it doesn't ring a bell.'

'I think if you put the professor through the wringer you might get a surprise.'

'I might just do that.'

When Molly Rashid came out of the hospital it was close to eight o'clock, and it was wet and miserable out. She slid into the car. 'I'm absolutely bushed.'

'Hard day?' Greta asked.

'Never stopped. One operation after another. Frankly, all I want is a sandwich and then bed. What about you?'

'Oh, the usual kind of day. Bloody boring.' Greta laughed as she drove away. 'Come on, let's get you home.'

BAGHDAD

3

The deal Roper had made with Jack Savage had been enough to make him sit up and take notice, especially as the payment would be in American dollars. They had known each other well during the Irish troubles, Roper up to his ears in bomb disposal work, Savage chasing gun-runners by night in the Irish Sea. When they had discussed Roper's requirements Roper had told him of Dillon and Billy, of Sara Rashid, and their intention of spiriting her away. Savage couldn't care less what they were up to, the deal was so good there was no way he was turning it down.

His wife, Rawan, saw things differently. A couple of years ago Abdul Rashid had used his connections to spirit her parents out of Iraq to Jordan after extremists had burned their houseboat on the river. She owed him one.

When her husband explained what their guests would be doing when they arrived, she made it clear she didn't approve.

'Listen,' he said. 'I'm not turning down a payday like this, and the connection with British Intelligence is likely to be worth even more in the future. Just get that through your head.'

'Bastard,' she said. 'Money – that's all you care about. You can sleep on deck tonight.'

'I'm not missing much. It suits me fine.' He grabbed a couple of rugs and a bottle of Scotch and went on deck.

The only major point that Roper had got wrong was that Sara Rashid wouldn't be running anywhere, because her grandfather had arranged to have her fitted with leg irons after her persistent attempts to escape.

She had been locked in a bedroom for most of each day. For exercise she was given the chance to walk in the gardens and orange groves, but there were guards with her armed with AK assault rifles, and her cousin

Hussein, who one day would marry her, was always one of them.

She was treated with due respect by the guards, in fact by all the servants, for her grandfather was not only rich, but powerful, his connections with Osama bin Laden and the Army of God well known.

His love for Sara was genuine and very deep, especially since the death of his own wife, one of seventy-two other people killed in a car bombing in downtown Baghdad. The fact that Sara was of mixed race he could accept, but his son forswearing his religion – that was an abomination.

Sara, mature beyond her years, sat in her room and, with little better to do, improved on her Arabic, and contemplated what her grandfather had told her, that they would eventually be forced to join the exodus of middle-class Iraqis from Baghdad. Hazar would be their destination, to join her grandfather's brother, Jemal, head of the family in that country. They were rich, and the Rashid Bedouins lived in the Empty Quarter, one of the most ferocious deserts in the world. It would be a guarantee of safety.

So that was the way things would probably work out. She was outside now on one of her walks, and the wind off the water played with the wonderful silk scarf that framed her face. She was pretty, and she knew it. Hussein adored her, and she took full advantage of that fact.

'Do you want to return to your room?'

'Not yet. Who is that?' She pointed to a shabby motor launch approaching. As it slowed and drifted in to the jetty she saw that it was a woman at the wheel, dressed in Western style, her hair tied back, wearing a khaki bush shirt and pants and a shoulder holster under her left arm. The woman tossed a line and one of the men caught it and tied up. The launch had an English name – *Eagle*.

'Hussein, how are you?' she said.

'I'd rather be doing my final year at medical school, but there you are. The war, the war, the bloody war. This is Sara. Sara, this is Rawan Savage.'

She turned to Sara. 'I've known you were here for some months, but we've never had an opportunity to meet. My, you are pretty, aren't you?' All this was delivered in English.

Sara said, 'Were you born in Baghdad?'

'Yes, but to a Druse family.' She turned to face Hussein. 'I need to see your uncle right away, Hussein. Can I go up?'

'Of course. He's in the orange grove.'

'Until I see you again,' she said to Sara, and started up the steps leading through the oranges to where Rashid was seated.

Rashid greeted her courteously, and leaned close to her while she spoke, and when she had finished he placed his hand on her head in a blessing. She stood up and returned to the boat. He called to Hussein.

'Wait for me here,' Hussein said and mounted the steps. 'Uncle?'

'See Sara goes to her room and I'll send women to help her pack.'

'Pack, Uncle?'

'I've prepared for this day for months. It is time for us to go. She'll need a woman – take Jasmine. We'll need two Land Rovers,

I think, three of the men to assist with security. You're in charge.'

'But where are we to go?'

'Kuwait. Only four hundred miles by road. The instructions are in the briefcase I'll give you. My people there will make all arrangements for your onward flight to my brother Jemal in Hazar.'

'But why, Uncle?'

'Rawan brought me disturbing news. Her husband is engaged in a plot with two men from England, named Dillon and Salter, to kidnap Sara and return her to my son in London.'

'This cannot be,' Hussein said.

'I have made what I trust will be a suitable greeting for them. She informs me they arrive later today.'

'Then I'll deal with them.'

'No – I hope I have taken care of it. Sara is my most precious jewel. You are the only one I can trust. Swear to me you will guard her with your life, always.'

'In the name of Allah, I swear it.'

'Go now, and Allah go with you,' and he

turned and went in, content, for Hussein Rashid was no ordinary man. Twenty-three years of age, dark hair but blue eyes, he could have passed as a Western European. He was slim but muscular, and hugely intelligent, and when anger sparked in his eyes he changed, became truly frightening, the warrior few people realized he was.

He'd been a medical student at Harvard when the Gulf War started, and had immediately packed his bags to go home, only to be arrested at Logan Airport in Boston. It was six months before lawyers succeeded in obtaining his freedom, and he had gone home to discover that his parents had been killed in a bombing raid three months earlier.

His uncle had kept him sane during the bad time, had provided him with money, set up accounts for him in Paris and London, had provided him with addresses, the right people to see, people who would pass him hand by hand until he reached the camp in the Algerian desert. There they'd turned him into the man known as the Hammer of God, and it was there that he'd grown the luxuriant long hair and the beard that became his trade marks.

He was not a religious fanatic, hardly religious at all, but he'd discovered his true calling there: to be a soldier. They'd taught him everything, and by the time he was finished he was an expert in weaponry, explosives, hand-to-hand fighting, vehicles and the fine art of assassination. His medical training was just a bonus. They even taught him to fly.

He had worked for what some people might call terrorist organizations in such places as Chechnya and Kosovo, but his speciality had been assassination, and he had become a master. In the mess that Iraq developed into, he had lived with his uncle, operating as a freelance sniper. His personal score was twenty-seven American and British soldiers and Iraqi politicians. It was all the same to Hussein. And then his uncle had kidnapped Sara, and everything had changed.

*   *   *

In London, Roper wished them well and grinned as Dillon and Billy made final preparations for departure.

'Got everything?' he asked.

'Of course,' Billy told him as he zipped up an aircraft bag. 'What would we bloody leave, for God's sake?'

'There's always your Codex Four.'

'Very funny,' Billy said.

'Never mind, Billy, you're going off to war, and you know from experience, there's nothing like a nice war. Try not to get your head blown off.'

'Yes, well, you've got Ferguson to think about. What if he phones up and tells you he wants his plane?'

'You mean I could get the sack? I doubt it.' Roper smiled. 'I inhabit a wheelchair and I've got medals. As for the Gulfstream, didn't he tell Dillon he was sending it back in case of emergencies?'

'So he did. Mind you, he might think Baghdad a bit of a stretch.'

'We'll worry about that when we have to. Now get moving. Sergeant Doyle's waiting with the Land Rover. Try not to screw up.'

'As if we would.'

They left, and ten minutes later Ferguson did come on the line. 'How are things going?'

'You mean at the coal face, sir?'

'Is that a reprimand, Roper?'

'Now would I imply that you weren't beating your brains out, General, taking care of world affairs?'

'Well, we *were* up half the night and I'm just about to join the conference again. Anything to report?'

'Not a whisper, sir. It's as if every terrorist in the land has rolled over and died. The chaps are all polishing their nails.'

'You're incorrigible, Roper.' A bell sounded faintly. 'Must go. I'll be in touch.'

'Yes, sir. I look forward to it.'

Roper poured a large Scotch, lit a cigarette and continued his investigation of the mysterious Professor Khan.

*   *   *

At Farley Field the quartermaster had loaded their supplies and weaponry. Two AKs, a couple of .25 Colts with hollow-point cartridges and ankle holsters, titanium waistcoats.

'Nothing left to chance, Sergeant-Major.'

'I don't believe it should be, Mr Dillon. That's not the way to operate. Good luck, gentlemen.'

At the top of the steps to the Gulfstream, Parry waited for them in flying overalls. A car horn sounded and the Aston came round from the entrance and pulled up, Harry at the wheel. He ran forward, and as Billy turned he flung his arms round him.

'Take care.'

Dillon said, 'I always knew you were a sentimentalist at heart.'

'You think what you like, as long as you bring him back.'

They went up the steps, Parry closed the door and joined Lacey in the cockpit. Billy and Dillon settled down, and a few minutes later the Gulfstream took off.

*　　*　　*

Roper came on line two hours into the flight. 'Is everything going all right?'

'Fine. What about you?' Dillon asked.

'Professor Khan is proving more than promising. Dreq Khan is his name, he was a clever young man who took a first degree at home in Pakistan, then earned a scholarship to Oxford. Totally Anglicized now, with an apparently unlimited supply of cash. He started as an Assistant Lecturer in Morality at Leeds University.'

Billy laughed. 'Sorry, I didn't know you could be one of those.'

'Apparently. Left after a year and moved to America, the University of Chicago, then a year later to Berkeley in California.'

Dillon said, 'You see, Billy, he couldn't resist the call of Hollywood.'

'Came back east for a post at the United Nations. Secretary to the International Committee for Racial Harmony.'

'Let me guess,' Dillon said. 'After that he finally made it back to good old England. Londonistan.'

'Right you are, and he's certainly made his

way in politics. The Committee for Socialist Values – that really made his bones in London, got him in good with a lot of well-meaning socialists. He's also on the Interfaith Committee at the House of Commons and is sponsored by various Anglican bishops. He's muted his support for the Army of God ever since three of its members were arrested in Yorkshire for that bomb in a bus station that killed three and injured fourteen. But he insists that those three were a splinter group, that the organization itself is purely spiritual and educational.'

Billy said, 'What do you think?'

'I think he's dangerous as hell, and all those committees just obscure what he really is.'

Roper said, 'I've never been so certain of anything in my life. But there's no proof of anything, not even a whisper of terrorist activity. There's nothing to spark an investigation by the police anti-terrorist squad.'

Dillon said, 'Except that when Greta raised the question of Professor Khan with that driver and told him she'd killed Abu, he was terrified.'

'And made no attempt to deny it,' Billy said.

'It's still not enough,' Roper said. 'But I'll keep at it. I heard from Ferguson, by the way.'

'What did you hear?' Dillon said.

'Only that he keeps going into conference with the Prime Minister and the great and the good.'

'Has he indicated when he's coming back?'

'Not exactly. I wouldn't give it more than a couple of days, so it's all up to you gentlemen. Keep in touch.'

He clicked off.

An hour out of Baghdad, with dawn coming up fast, they descended to 30,000 feet. There was considerable traffic, and Parry came back from the cockpit to fill them in.

'We're doing a night approach, which means the sods on the ground don't have as good a view – the ragged-arse brigade are good, unfortunately, particularly with hand-held missiles. A lot of helicopters get wasted over the city.'

'So what's the solution?' Billy asked.

'It's a trick the Yanks resurrected from the Vietnam War. We approach from fifteen thousand, then dive. Pull up only at the last possible moment.'

'That sounds pretty hairy to me,' Billy said.

'But it works. The RAF used it in Kosovo, too, and with larger planes. Now, as to what's facing you down there, I know you gentlemen have done this once before, so I'll only say it's even worse. There's an old saying: Hell is a city. Well, gentlemen, I doubt whether anywhere in the world could be worse than Baghdad. Take care at all times, and remember – in this town, you can't even trust your grandmother.'

'The last time we did this,' Dillon said, 'we were cared for by a Flight Lieutenant Robson. He was police.'

'Still at it. Squadron Leader now. He's already been on the radio. Everything's waiting.'

'And we had a safe car, with an RAF police sergeant named Parker. A really good guy.

He stood by us in a firefight,' Dillon said. 'Do we get him again?'

'Unfortunately not. He was killed by a roadside bomb last month. I'd better join Lacey now.'

'Jesus,' Billy said. 'What a bloody place.' As he looked down at the city below, there was an explosion, a mushroom cloud of smoke rising from the damage.

'Never mind, Billy, you've seen worse.' Dillon took out his flask, unscrewed the cap and swallowed a generous mouthful of Bushmills.

'No, Dillon, I don't think I have.' Billy leaned back and closed his eyes for the descent.

In Baghdad they were received in the mess by Robson himself, as a waiter in a white tunic arranged tea things. Robson said, 'So bloody hot in this hellhole. Tea's just the thing, as they discovered in the days of the Raj. Well, things have certainly been happening to you,' he told Lacey and Parry.

'Awarded a second Air Force Cross each. What are you doing? Trying to fight the war on your own?'

'Something like that,' Lacey told him.

As the tea was poured, Robson turned to Dillon and Billy. 'I won't ask what you two have been up to. I don't know, and I don't want to. Just like last time, the Gulfstream will stand by here ready for an immediate exit at any time. I have a red Security One tag for each of you. It covers everything. You must be hot stuff. Even the station commander doesn't have one of these.'

Dillon said, 'I'm sorry to hear of Sergeant Parker's death.'

'Most unfortunate. Happens all the time, I'm afraid. You won't need anything like that this time. A Mr Jack Savage is picking you up, I understand. We know him well.'

'Is someone taking my name in vain?'

They all turned and saw him standing in the mess doorway, medium height, roughly cut blond hair, a broken nose, a reefer coat over his arm.

'Come in, you old bastard,' Robson said. 'And that's an order, Sergeant Major.'

Someone once said that in Baghdad all the streets seemed to be some sort of market, although many of them seemed to be lucky to have any buildings left at all. And the peasants were still there, their donkeys carrying not just produce from the countryside, but everything from laptops to televisions, the detritus of war.

They moved through narrow streets down towards the river, finally turning into a courtyard outside an old colonial house, with a fountain that still worked. A sign over the door traced out *The River Room* with bulbs. They got out of the Land Rover leaving their luggage inside.

'The sign?' Billy asked. 'Does it still light up?'

'I'm missing half a dozen bulbs; they're hard to replace, but it reminds me of London, the Savoy, the old River Room.'

'Why do you stay?' Dillon asked. 'These

days it must be the ultimate way of living on the knife edge.'

'That's what I like about it. You can make money here like nowhere else on earth. Let's go in.'

They followed. It was shadowy, a floor of Arabic tiles, tables and chairs of cane. Even the bar was cane, with a mirror and what looked like every kind of bottle in the world stacked against it. The bartender, who stood polishing glasses, was big and fat, wearing white shirt and pants, a scarlet belt of some kind around his middle.

'What's your pleasure?' Savage asked.

'For Billy, nothing. He doesn't indulge. I'll have Bushmills Irish Whiskey.'

'Two, Farouk. Takes me back to Northern Ireland in the Troubles. So you're the great Sean Dillon.'

'And you're the bad Jack Savage.' Dillon turned to Billy. 'He had a lovely racket going. Chasing down gun-runners on the one hand, then selling the proceeds to the Provisional IRA on the other.'

'But not while I was in the Royal Marines,

not while I was wearing the badge. That wouldn't have been honourable.'

'He's big on honour.' Rawan Savage moved into the room. 'I'll have a large vodka – very large. God, it's hot in here.' She walked out onto a wooden balcony, and they followed.

A couple of minutes later Farouk was distributing the drinks. 'Cheers. To new friends.' Rawan raised her glass and in a way seemed to swallow it whole, but that was only an illusion. She held it out to Farouk. Without saying a word, he turned and went back inside.

The river wasn't particularly busy. Below them, tied to the jetty, was the motor launch *Eagle*. Rawan said, 'Just up there, a quarter of a mile, is Abdul Rashid's place. Do you want to have a look?'

'Shut up, Rawan,' Savage told her.

'Yes, sir.' She gave him a mock salute.

'Look, I won't tell you again,' Savage said. 'Drink up or shut up. Take your choice.'

'Is that so?' She turned to Dillon. 'Well, I know why you're here and I don't admire it.'

'Is that so?' Dillon said.

'Snatching a thirteen-year-old girl from her grandfather.'

'Let's keep to the facts,' Billy put in. 'The said thirteen-year-old girl was snatched from her parents in London in the first place.'

But she didn't want to listen and charged into the bar, where Farouk stood behind the counter, a strange threatening stillness to him. Customers, four of them, were there, one with an AK on the table close to his hand, another with one slung from his shoulder. The other two each had a hand in a pocket.

A woman slipped through the door, her clothes held tightly around her. She looked terrified and glanced anxiously about her. Rawan said, 'Ah, someone bearing ill news. Bibi, gentlemen, this is one of Sara Rashid's ladies of the bedchamber. What's wrong, Bibi? Have they gone without you?'

The woman cried bitterly, flung herself to her knees and a flood of Arabic ensued. Rawan said, 'Excellent. Someone seems to have spoiled the party and warned Abdul Rashid. Several hours ago he dispatched Sara with Hussein Rashid, her intended, in a small convoy to Kuwait by road. Once there, friends will forward them by private plane to Hazar, where the rest of the Rashid clan thrive. It is all true – Bibi heard it being discussed. You are dead men walking. Hussein will see to it.'

There was a silence. Savage said, 'But who told him?'

'Who do you think? I'm sick of you, Jack, have been for a long time. You can rot in hell.'

In the near distance there was a huge explosion, and everybody instinctively ducked. The sound of the aftershock drifted like a wave. The telephone on the bar sounded.

Farouk picked it up and listened, then held it out to Savage. 'Omar, the boy you had watching the Rashid villa. He saw the convoy for Kuwait leave two hours ago.'

'So?'

'Old Rashid had just driven out in his Mercedes, accompanied by two guards. It exploded as it went through the gate.' His face said it all. 'Because of people like you, who come amongst us and destroy everything you touch.'

There must have been something about his expression that gave warning, a twitch, a glint of determination, because Dillon, who had been sitting down, pulled on the ankle holster, yanked out the .25 Colt and shot Farouk between the eyes, the hollow-point cartridge wreaking havoc. In almost the same moment he pulled out the silenced Walther from his waistband under the jacket and shot the man who was reaching for the AK on a table.

Billy produced his Walther as a third man was trying to get a Browning out of his right-hand pocket and snagged it. Billy shot him instantly and the man was hurled against his companion, who shot him inadvertently in the back.

'Don't shoot, for God's sake,' the companion called in as Irish a voice as you could wish for, but as Billy hesitated, the Irishman's hand swung up to fire, and it was Dillon who finished him off.

'Don't do that again, Billy. It never pays.'

'Christ, I thought he was Irish.' Billy went down, felt in an inside pocket and produced a passport, brown, with the gold harp of Ireland on it, and a few papers.

'Bring them with you.'

Dillon turned and Rawan said, 'Damn you, damn you all and damn this stinking country, Jack.' She ran down the steps to the jetty, untied the line on the *Eagle* and cast off.

Savage clattered down the steps after her and jumped for the *Eagle* as it drifted out. 'Rawan,' he called. 'Just listen.'

'Not any more,' she said and pressed the starter.

It rattled a couple of times and then there was a huge explosion and the boat simply came apart.

Billy was hurled backwards over a cane chair. Dillon pulled him up. 'Let's get out of here, and fast. The military will be here in no time. We'll take that Land Rover Savage used to bring us from the airport. Our stuff is still on board.'

They were out in seconds and into the Land Rover, Billy at the wheel, and moved into the main street as two Scimitars came the opposite way. A sizeable crowd was already assembling, but the confusion of it helped them to make a rapid exit.

Dillon called Roper, who answered at once. 'Just listen,' Dillon said and gave him an account.

'My God, you have been in action. Why does this sort of thing always reach out to touch you, Dillon?'

'Just tell Robson to alert the boys to get us out of here. God knows where to. The mad side of me wants to pursue them to Hazar, but I don't think the General would approve.'

'No, he damn well wouldn't,' Ferguson cut in. 'Outrageous, finding my plane has been hijacked. Get yourselves back here immediately.'

At Baghdad airport they were admitted through a discreet security entrance, and found Lacey and Robson waiting in a Jeep.

'Just follow,' Lacey called to Billy, which he did, and found the Gulfstream waiting.

'Off you go,' Robson said. 'We prefer to think of you as never having been here.'

They went up the steps and Lacey locked the door. 'Thanks a lot, you bastards. The General was not exactly thrilled when he tried to book his personal plane for the flight from Paris and found it elsewhere. What in the hell were you playing at?'

'Didn't I tell you?' Dillon said. 'Trying to win the war.'

Dillon got his flask out as they climbed, but it was empty. He waited until they levelled off at 40,000 feet and peered out of the window.

'Goodbye to Baghdad, city of romance, intrigue and adventure.'

'Yes, everything you can do without,' Billy said. 'I can't figure it. So the Rawan bird is fed up with Jack and spills her guts to old Rashid – and he responds by having someone arrange to have the launch blown up?'

'Rashid was after the three of us – Savage, you and me. It was just too bad about her.'

'And what about the car bomb?'

'A daily risk. A man like him would have more enemies than he could count.'

Dillon got up and went to the rear of the cockpit, opened the first-aid drawer and helped himself to the half-bottle of brandy it contained.

'Purely medicinal,' he told Parry, who had glanced over his shoulder.

'Always is with you.'

When Dillon returned to his seat, he found Billy examining the Irish passport taken from the man he had killed in the bar.

'Terence O'Malley, age forty-two, an address in Bangor, Northern Ireland.'

'A nice place.' Dillon opened the brandy and poured some into a plastic cup. 'What else does it tell us?'

'Apparently he's a schoolmaster.'

'I'd bet he's not been that for a long time.'

'IRA?'

'I'd say so. We know many old hands have moved into organized crime. It's a very small step from what they were doing into the world of the mercenary, Billy. Wild Geese, that's what they've always been called, in Ireland or out of it. If you've been a Provo for all those years, it's difficult to turn your hand to something else when it's all over. What have you got in there?'

'A monthly rental bill from Dublin, a letter from a man named Tom, a please come home letter, signed "Your loving mother, Rose". Address in Bangor. Cash, five one hundred dollar bills, American.' He looked up. 'What do we do? About his mother, I mean?'

'I'd let it go, Billy. If she knows nothing, then it leaves her hope. Now I'm going to catch a little sleep,' and he dropped his seat.

On the road south from Baghdad to Kuwait it was a macabre situation, a landscape of burned-out tanks and trucks and civilian vehicles dating back to the original Gulf War, the Highway of Death they had called it, a landscape that also contained the remains of many thousands of refugees. And yet all the way along the highway at suitable intervals there were petrol stations open twenty-four hours, for fuel was the one thing they weren't short of, and places you could get coffee and short-order cooking, and the telephones worked.

In the first Land Rover were Hussein's three henchmen, armed to the teeth, veterans of the streets, men who knew their business, which was proved by the fact that they were still here.

In the second vehicle were Hussein, Sara and Jasmine, another cousin of Sara's, who was devoted to her. Fifty miles out of Baghdad the little convoy had pulled up in the car park of a petrol station. Hussein received a call on his satellite phone from the man he knew only as the Broker. He had been allocated to him by Al-Qaeda for three years now. They spoke on occasion in Arabic, but in English when appropriate, and on those occasions the Broker sounded like an Oxford professor.

Hussein answered at once. 'Where are you?' said the voice. Hussein told him. 'Good, you were in an impossible situation. Other contacts covered events for me. One of Rashid's men placed the bomb in the Savage people's boat.'

'And Rashid himself?'

'It was a local Sunni group who got him. An old score. How has Sara taken it?' He sounded strangely paternalistic and yet there was a certain concern in his voice.

'I'm just about to tell her, but I've further information. The woman who told Rashid of the kidnap attempt said the men involved are called Dillon and Salter. Are they familiar to you?'

'No, but they soon will be. I'll call you when I know more. Take care of Sara. I've made all the arrangements in Kuwait. A Hawk. You'll enjoy flying that.'

When Hussein returned to the group, they were waiting. 'You could have gone for coffee and a bite to eat,' he said.

'Not in my leg irons, cousin. Must I endure further humiliation?'

He didn't hesitate, extracted no false promises. 'Forgive me, cousin. So much has happened.' He produced a key and unlocked the chains, dropping them over the seat, then said, 'I have grave news from Baghdad.'

His words lingered, his people waited, so used to bad news they knew this must be special, and Hussein put an arm around Sara's shoulders. 'My uncle, Sara's grand-father, has been taken from us at the villa. It was a car bomb, as he was leaving in his Mercedes.'

Jasmine gave a short wail, then started to sob. One of the men, Hassim, said, 'Sunnis?'

'It would appear so.'

'May they rot in hell,' Hamid joined in. 'Cursed for a thousand years.'

'Two thousand,' said Khazid.

Sara stood there, saying nothing.

'Come,' Hussein said. 'We all agree, but we still have a long trip ahead of us. We must eat.'

She nodded, torn in her heart between her feelings for her parents and a stubborn old man who had wronged her terribly yet loved her deeply. 'Yes,' she said. 'Yes.' She took Hussein's arm and they walked to the café.

LONDON

DUBLIN

KUWAIT

4

At Farley Field, as the Gulfstream touched down, Dillon looked out and saw Ferguson standing under an umbrella smoking a cigarette.

'What do you think? Trouble?' Billy asked.

'Oh, I don't know. You might be surprised,' Dillon answered.

Parry opened the door and they moved out, followed by Lacey, who said, 'Dammit, Sean, we don't like our time wasted.'

'I'm not sure that's a correct description. Savage and his wife were blown up in their boat on the Tigris.'

'And some very unpleasant geezers tried to take us out in the bar at Savage's club. When we left, it looked like the Last Chance Saloon in a bad movie,' Billy pointed out.

'How many?' Lacey said slowly.

'Four,' Dillon told him. 'So your time wasn't wasted – and I suspect we're about to use your services again.'

'Where to this time?' Lacey said.

'You've been there before. Hazar.'

'Christ Almighty,' Parry said. 'You nearly left your bones there, Billy.'

'Well, I didn't, and I've no intention of leaving them there this time.'

They reached Ferguson, who said, 'All right, gentlemen, get in the back of the Daimler and explain yourselves. Your body count is beginning to rival Tombstone's.'

After Dillon sketched in the events, he said, 'After all, General, you did say we could use the Gulfstream in an emergency.'

'Yes, but I hadn't envisaged this.'

'And it all started with you,' Billy said. 'Last time you saw us you suggested we go to Heathrow and haunt passport control.'

'Which is where we came up with Caspar Rashid,' Dillon cut in.

'All right, all right.' Ferguson was getting testy as they coasted through London towards Holland Park. 'I'm the first to admit he could be very useful to us.'

'Have you told him we failed to get Sara?'

'Not yet. I thought his wife should be considered, too. She's operating now, but Major Novikova will tell her, and then bring her to us. Eleven o'clock should be about right.'

'Great,' Billy said. 'Time for a full English breakfast.'

'We don't have a cook,' Dillon reminded him.

'Who says so?' Ferguson frowned. 'All I had to do was telephone the Civil Service pool. A Mrs Hall appeared almost straight-away. Answers to Maggie. She's from Jamaica, though – I'm not sure about the full English breakfast.'

'For God's sake, General, they probably invented it.' That was Billy.

'So they failed?' At the hospital, Molly Rashid was very pale, no colour in her face at all, and weary suddenly in a way she hadn't been before. Greta noticed at once that her hands were shaking.

'You need a drink,' she said.

'No.' Molly ran a hand through her hair. 'I've got another operation this afternoon.'

'I don't think so. Your right hand is shaking like a leaf. You couldn't possibly operate in your present condition.'

Molly covered her face with both hands. 'What am I going to do?'

Greta got a glass, took a bottle of vodka from the fridge. She almost filled the glass. 'Come on, take it straight down. It numbs the brain.'

Molly hesitated, then did as she was told. She gagged, staggered to the sink. For a moment it was as if she was going to be sick, but she took a couple of deep breaths and pulled herself together.

'My God, that hit the spot.' She turned and smiled wanly. 'We'd better go and face it, I suppose.'

'Yes,' Greta said, 'I suppose we should.'

*　　*　　*

'What do you mean, you failed?' Rashid said, as he turned from the window to Dillon.

'We simply couldn't get anywhere near her.'

'Oh, dear, you couldn't get anywhere near her. My father will be pleased.'

'Mr Rashid, your father is dead.'

Rashid was stricken, aged visibly, took a step, stumbled, reached for a chair and grabbed hold of it to steady himself.

'I think you'd better sit down,' Dillon said.

Rashid did so. 'How did he die? Was it you?'

'No, I'd nothing to do with it. He was killed going out of the main gate of his villa with his chauffeur. Car bomb. The word is that it was a Sunni operation.'

'Were there any other casualties?'

'Yes, four men intent on killing us.'

He seemed to come alive again, not that it lasted. 'Since they obviously didn't succeed, I assume you managed to kill them.'

'That's correct. Your wife has been informed. Major Novikova went to give her the sad news and bring her back here for a conference.'

'A conference?' He said it slowly, as if he was finding it difficult to speak at all or to understand. He plucked at words, reaching in a futile way and running his fingers through his hair. And then he took an enormous deep breath, took out a cigarette, lit it and inhaled deeply.

'That's better, I think. Let's get to it and see if there's some way of sorting this out.'

They sat in the committee room, Ferguson at the head of the table, Rashid and Molly close together, holding hands. Greta was pouring coffee. Dillon and Billy stood together by the window, listening, and Roper, in his chair, was at the far end of the table.

'I'll come directly to the point,' Ferguson said. 'There was a bargain between you and my people.'

'Which was not fulfilled,' Rashid said. 'I don't see my daughter here.'

'That was due to circumstances,' Dillon

said. 'The body count makes that clear. The point now is what comes next.'

'Comes next?' Rashid asked.

'Of course,' Ferguson told him. 'Nothing has changed fundamentally. You want your daughter back, and so do we. And we know her destination – Hazar. It's a place we've all worked in before.'

'You were there yourself recently,' Dillon said. 'What for?'

Rashid didn't reply, his face showing great emotion. It was his wife who intervened. 'For God's sake, Caspar, talk to them. What happened wasn't their fault. We're not playing games here. People died. I want my daughter back, so tell them what they need to know to make that happen.'

Caspar sighed. 'I was fooled into believing that my Uncle Jemal in Hazar would act as a middle man between my father and me.'

'What made you think that?'

'Not what, but who. It was the Broker. He first spoke to me over a year ago when I was being pressured by Army of God fanatics to join their organization. A colleague at the university, Professor Dreq Khan, was the chief mover and shaker behind the Army of God, and at first they seemed harmless, just a charitable organization, but then, on my world travels, I started receiving approaches from a number of extreme groups. When I tried to withdraw from my involvement, Dreq Khan warned me that I would be considered a traitor, that I would be targeted by Muslim extremists. And then came my daughter's abduction.

'The Broker said that if I did what they told me, he would arrange for Jemal to act as a go-between with my father, so I felt I had no choice. I mainly acted as a bagman under orders, passing highly technical information on various matters to Khan, who obviously passed it on. Then the Broker told me I should come to Hazar, that they were ready to talk to me, but it was all a lie. They just wanted me to take a look at an old railway that Al-Qaeda wanted to update. I was near to despair – and that's when you found me.'

'So here we are,' Fergusson said.

'Here we are. And the Middle East wasn't the only place they sent me. They sent me to Ireland, too. I'm a visiting professor at Trinity College, Dublin.'

'Good God,' Ferguson said. 'Are you going to tell us that's a centre of Muslim radicalism?'

'Not at all, but in my bagman identity I had to act as a go-between for certain organizations there.'

'Such as?' Ferguson asked.

'Outfits claiming to be security firms. It's an open secret that with peace in Northern Ireland many former members of the Provisional IRA have found themselves on the scrapheap and don't much care for it. One way out for them is crime. I believe that in the last year there have been at least seventy shootings in the Dublin area that show evidence of having been committed by professionals.'

'So what?' Dillon said. 'What do you expect after thirty-odd years of their own war?'

'I accept that, but what I'm talking about

are firms claiming legitimacy in security affairs, but actually supplying what can only be described as mercenaries – people hired as instructors for terrorist training camps in North Africa, Algeria. One of them, for instance, is called Scamrock Security, run by a man named Michael Flynn.'

'And you have details of these camps?' Roper asked.

'Of some of them, yes. There are one or two in the Empty Quarter as well.'

There was a long silence while Ferguson drummed his fingers on the table. Finally he said, 'You've given us a lot to digest. While Roper's working on this information we have to consider our next step regarding your daughter, which would be to move the action to Hazar. Would you wish us to do that?'

It was Molly who answered instantly. 'Oh, God, yes. I want my daughter back more than anything. But can you do it?'

'As I said, we've operated in Hazar in the past. For the past three years my cousin, Professor Hal Stone of Corpus Christi College, Cambridge, has been diving on an ancient

Phoenician wreck on the edge of the harbour at Hazar. He works from an old dhow, using Arabs. It's a shoestring operation, but I happen to know his diving season is soon to start. Dillon and Billy are expert divers themselves, and he'd welcome us, I assure you. We'd pass as a perfectly acceptable group of mad English archaeologists. Would that be acceptable? You could come with us.'

'No, not that.' She shook her head. 'I'm part-way through some of the most important work of my life.' She turned to her husband. 'Caspar?'

'Of course.' He nodded. 'I must.'

'Isn't there the chance you'll be recognized?' Billy asked.

Caspar shook his head. 'I'll wear robes, a fold of cloth across my face, use the language. It will work.' Suddenly he looked fierce, determined. 'It must work.'

'Right,' Ferguson said. 'Things to do. I must contact my cousin. You, Dr Rashid, will oblige me by pouring your heart out to Roper. As for you,' he said to Dillon, 'see to the plane.'

Molly Rashid stood up. 'I'll get back to the hospital.'

Ferguson put an arm around her shoulder. 'Don't worry, my dear, we'll succeed, I promise you.'

Greta said, 'I'll take you back.'

They went out and Caspar waited until the door closed and said, 'There is something else of great importance I must tell you.'

'And what would that be?' Ferguson asked.

'Sara's cousin, the man who is to be her future husband when she is of age.'

'Hussein, isn't it?' Roper said. 'A medical student.'

'Does the Hammer of God mean anything to you?'

'Not that I know of.'

'When I last counted, his score was twenty-seven Allied soldiers and a handful of political assassinations in Europe.'

'Good God,' Ferguson said. 'Tell us about him.'

Which Rashid did.

When he had finished, Dillon said trimly,

'Well, at least we know.' He turned to Billy. 'Let's get moving.' As they left he said to Roper, 'Michael Flynn. Years ago he was IRA Chief of Staff till he ended up in the Maze Prison. Look him up.'

Sitting in his suite in Paris, Volkov went over in his mind the last conversation he had had with Vladimir Putin. The elimination of Ferguson and company made sense. It had already started with the murder of Detective Superintendent Hannah Bernstein the year before.

Igor Levin was a more difficult case, however, because he had a few million sterling tucked away in London. He could not be bought. Chomsky, the sergeant who had gone to Dublin with him, was a clever one, but irritatingly seemed to feel some sort of loyalty to Levin. Popov was the weak link.

Volkov took out his address book, found Popov's number in Dublin and phoned him. It was a mobile and found Popov strolling along Wellington Quay beside the River

Liffey. It was raining and Popov was holding an umbrella over his head, a young woman named Mary O'Toole at his side.

'My dear Popov,' Volkov said in Russian, 'Volkov speaking. How are you? It's been some time.'

Popov was shocked and replied with difficulty, 'General, I can't believe it. It's been so long.'

'Oh, I like to keep in touch,' Volkov said.

Popov and the girl were approaching a hotel he knew. He squeezed her waist. 'Mary, my love, you go in and get us a table in the cocktail bar. This is important.' She went, and he reverted to Russian. 'General, I don't know what to say.'

'Why, just say you're happy to hear from me. How's the job? Still at Scamrock Security? How *is* my old friend, Mr Flynn?'

Popov swallowed hard. 'My God, I didn't realize –'

'That I got you the job? Oh, yes. Flynn and I go way, way back, to the very early days of the Irish struggle. That he hasn't mentioned this to you shows how much he is to be trusted. I presume you find that your experience in military intelligence is of value in your work.'

'Absolutely, General.'

'You've heard about Belov International? That Max Chekov is the new chief executive officer? Did you ever serve under him?'

'I never had that privilege.'

'You may have that pleasure to come. I trust that I can still rely on you?'

'Of course, General.'

'Excellent. How is Chomsky?'

'He breezed through his law exams and works for a city lawyer as a leg man.'

'And Levin?'

'Enjoys himself. He is, after all, rich.'

'As I'm well aware. So, nice to talk to you. I'll be in touch. But, please: keep this conversation private.'

For some reason he couldn't explain, Popov was thrilled. 'Of course, General.'

The line went dead and he went up the steps to the hotel two at a time. The bar was half empty and Mary was seated in a booth by the window. She was a secretary at

Scamrock Security, and was used to hearing him speaking foreign languages, for he was proficient in German and French.

'Russian,' she said. 'That's a new one. You always surprise me.'

Popov had an English mother, and he'd been raised on the language as a child in Moscow. He was perfectly capable of passing himself off as an Englishman, and did.

'Business,' he said, 'you can never get away from it. Now, what would you like to drink?'

Chomsky was a different proposition. He had a first-class academic brain and a firm belief in himself. He'd completed his law degree in just over a year at Trinity, a phenomenal achievement, and working as a leg man for a top firm of barristers suited him perfectly. He much preferred to be out of the office, for he could handle himself and had a medal for bravery in Chechnya to prove it.

He was walking through Temple Bar, one of his favourite places in the city, with its bars, restaurants, shops and galleries, and was making for Crown Alley with its cafés and brightly painted shops. His intention was to meet Levin, enjoy a drink, go to the cinema, and eat afterwards.

When his phone rang and he heard Volkov's voice it did not affect him the way it had Popov. He was used to handling people, especially under the stress of legal and illegal situations. Nothing in life surprised him any more.

He dodged in a doorway to avoid the rain. 'General, what a surprise.'

'I thought I'd catch up. My spies tell me you performed magnificently in your law exam.'

'True, though I say it myself.'

'And your work for the Riley partnership. More than interesting.'

Chomsky laughed. 'Why, General, you've been checking up on me.'

'My dear boy, we do have an embassy in Dublin in which the GRU is well represented. Checking on your activities gives them something to do.'

'I can imagine.'

'And how is Levin?'

'Come now, General, I'm sure you are well aware how he is. He has a luxury apartment looking out over the Liffey, and more than one lady, and he enjoys his life completely.'

'But it's a bit boring for someone of his background, I should have thought.'

'On that, I can't comment.'

'This firm Popov works for, Scamrock Security, my information is that it supplies contract mercenaries to the trade. Now that there is peace in Ireland, there must be many members of the Provisional IRA seeking gainful employment.'

'Now if it was the police saying that to me, General, I'd have to say I don't know what you're talking about.'

'But of course. Nice to talk to you. Goodbye for now.'

'What was all that about?' Chomsky asked himself as he stepped out into the road.

Volkov caught Levin a few moments later, after he had stepped out of the rain into a quiet bar called Kelly's. It was an old-fashioned sort of place with comfortable booths offering privacy. He was greeted with familiarity by a barman named Mick who brought him a large Bushmills.

Chomsky entered the bar at that moment. 'Same for me, Mick.' He took off his raincoat. 'Guess who's just been on the phone to me.'

'Shock me,' Levin said.

'Volkov.'

At the same moment Levin's mobile rang. He answered it, smiled and leaned close to Chomsky so that he could hear it was Volkov.

'General, what a pleasure,' Levin said amiably.

'Ah, Chomsky has joined you. You are still close?'

'Siamese twins.'

'This is good. How are you?'

'In excellent spirits. Rain in Dublin is curiously refreshing, and the girls are more than beautiful, they have Irish charm. Life couldn't be better. Where are you? Moscow?'

'No, Paris. I'm with President Putin at the

Brussels Conference. He was asking after you, Igor.'

'Really?' Levin said.

'Yes. Charles Ferguson was in Brussels, too, with the British Prime Minister. It jogged Putin's memory. Ferguson's people have been an intolerable nuisance.'

'You could say that.'

'Plus Blake Johnson. My original order was to get rid of the lot of them, but we only succeeded with Superintendent Hannah Bernstein.'

The mention made Levin feel uncomfortable, as it always had in spite of the fact that all he had done there was chauffeur an IRA hit man to Heathrow airport.

'What's this all about?' he asked.

'Why, I miss your valuable services, you and the boys. The President wants you. I told him you'd decamped to Dublin and that it was difficult.'

'And what did he say?'

'To tell you that your President needs you and Russia needs you. Think about it. Good help is hard to find, and you're the best. It's amazing how frequently people let you down.'

'And what's that supposed to mean?'

'I'll give you an example. A few days ago Blake Johnson was in London, available to all, walking down the street. Luzhkov and Max Chekov arranged for a couple of would-be assassins to take care of him. Instead, Dillon and Salter took care of *them*. It was ludicrous. You would never have let that happen.'

'Like you said, good help is hard to find. Never mind, General. If at first you don't succeed . . . You know the rest.'

'My poor Levin, you must find life infinitely boring not being in the game. Just think about what I've said. We'll speak again.' He rang off.

'The old bastard,' Chomsky said. He waved to the barman. 'Same again, Mick.'

'Interesting, though,' Levin said. 'A piece of crap like Max Chekov in charge of Belov International. I've been following that one closely.'

'Nothing changes, it would seem,'

Chomsky said. 'I wonder . . . do you think he's called Popov?'

'A good point. Don't tell Popov about our conversations with Volkov. Just see if he mentions his. In fact, why don't you phone him now?'

Chomsky did, finding Popov still with Mary in the cocktail bar of the hotel.

'Hello. It's me,' Chomsky said in English. 'I'm just having a drink with Igor and then we're going to a show. Do you want to join us?'

Popov didn't even hesitate. 'Not tonight, thanks. I'm about to have dinner with Mary.'

'That's all right then. So, how are things with you? Anything new?'

'No, just the same old thing.'

'OK, just thought I'd ask. Have a good time!'

He slipped his mobile in his pocket. 'He's having dinner again with the girl from the office.'

'He's getting serious,' Levin said.

'No, I don't think so. Not if the way he's talked in the past is anything to go by.'

'But he didn't mention Volkov, did he? It's inconceivable that the General would have spoken to us and not to him.'

'Which shows he's stupid, then. Surely he would know that we'd assume that he had.' Chomsky shrugged. 'What does it prove?'

'That maybe – just maybe – friend Popov is in Volkov's pocket, has been since we left London. I knew one of you was. I'm satisfied it isn't you. Circumstances indicate otherwise.'

'Thanks very much. Is there any reason why it matters?'

'I think Volkov's approach indicates that there could be. But enough.' Levin got up. 'The delights of James Bond await. We'll dine afterwards.'

Michael Flynn was in his early fifties, almost six feet tall, a powerful figure of a man in an excellent suit of Donegal tweed, his face strong and purposeful, the face of a man who didn't waste time on anything. His office at Scamrock Security had panelled walls of oak, dark green velvet curtains at the windows, green velvet carpet, the desk and furniture speaking of a successful man who liked to be exact. In the great days of revolution he had been, for a while, Chief of Staff in the Provisional IRA, although prison had followed that.

Those days were far behind him. Now he was a successful businessman, head of a company offering its expertise in the field of international security.

He looked out of the window at the rain, but he was in a cheerful mood. Business was good, the death business – with all the wars and rumours of wars, it was the kind of world in which his business could only thrive. He returned to his desk, took the stopper out of a cut-glass decanter and poured whiskey into a glass, and then his mobile sounded, the special one he kept only in his inside pocket.

'Yes,' he said.

'Mr Flynn, this is Volkov.'

'Sweet Jesus.' Flynn swallowed the whiskey and poured another. 'It's been a while since I heard from you.' He sat on the edge of the desk. 'So what can I do for you?'

'Oh, I just wanted to keep you informed. As you know, I have a direct pipeline to Al-Qaeda.'

'The Broker, right?'

'Yes. He has informed me that an associate of mine, Abdul Rashid, was car-bombed in Baghdad. It was a Sunni operation.'

'So how does this touch me?'

'A man you supplied worked for him. His name was Terence O'Malley, a Provo.'

'The schoolmaster. A good man. Came from Bangor. What happened?'

'He was killed in a firefight with a man named Sean Dillon and a London gangster called Billy Salter. Have you heard of them?'

'You could say that. Dillon and I were comrades in the old days. Salter I know only by reputation. What was it about?'

'A personal matter. Old Rashid had kidnapped his granddaughter from England, a girl of thirteen. Apparently Dillon and Salter were trying to get her back. A good deed in a naughty world.'

'That sounds like Sean Dillon. Mad as a hatter.'

'Anyway, I thought you should know.'

'I appreciate it. Listen,' Flynn said. 'The new company, Belov International. Does it need security work?'

'As a matter of fact it probably does, especially at the Irish end, Drumore Place. That's a good idea, Flynn. We'll speak about it later. Goodbye for now.'

Flynn sat there thinking about it. A pity about O'Malley. A good comrade, and big for the Cause, but like so many, unable to handle a future without it.

He poured another whiskey and raised his glass. 'Here's to you, Terence. Rest in peace.'

He emptied his glass, put on a trenchcoat, and went out.

KUWAIT

THE EMPTY QUARTER

LONDON

5

Kuwait was Kuwait, the oil wells working away, the visible signs of war no longer in evidence. Desert Storm had been a long time ago. Hussein had checked on the satellite phone and before arrival had been given directions to a part of the airport some distance away from the terminals used for jumbos and other passenger planes.

The Land Rovers moved through a number of parked cargo planes and finally reached a place of separate hangars and private planes, parked with precision.

The one on the end was an old Hawk eight-seater, and a man in stained overalls came down the steps from the interior. He was American from his accent.

'My name's Grant. Mr Rashid?'

'That's me,' Rashid said.

'She's all yours. Are you familiar with this aircraft?'

'I'm familiar with many aircraft types. Have I anything to sign?'

'No, everything's taken care of.' He opened an envelope and took a document out. 'I'll return your pilot's licence.'

It was an excellent forgery, but Hussein made no comment on that. 'My thanks. Flying down to Hazar, how long would it take in such a plane?'

'Two and a half hours, maybe three. How experienced are you at desert flying?'

'I've flown many times in Morocco and Algeria.'

'This is the Empty Quarter. Winds of great force can come out of nowhere, so be careful.'

'I have flown in the area south of here and I'm familiar with the landmarks and the airport.'

'Good. Anyway, I photocopied a section of the map for you, just in case you need it – the route there and the airport between

Hazar town and the small coastal village of Kafkar on the bluff overlooking it.'

'Thank you. Right, let's get on board,' Hussein ordered Jasmine and Sara. They went up the steps, followed by Khazid. Hamid and Hassim, Hussein passed up the weaponry, several AK rifles, some Uzi machine pistols and assault bags loaded with ammunition and grenades, and three or four shoulder-fired missiles.

'Are you guys expecting a war or something?'

'I thought there was always a war of some kind in the Empty Quarter.'

'That's true.'

'My family is Rashid Shipping. As I'm sure you know, piracy is not unheard of.'

'Tell me about it. If you'd just sign the manifest, you can be on your way.'

Hussein was the last to board, heaving up the steps and closing the hatch behind him.

Jasmine and Sara had already discovered a large basket and were examining it. 'Plenty of food in here, and good bread,' Jasmine said.

Sara opened another one and took out a bottle. 'You can tell he was American,' she said. 'Wine, red and white, whisky and brandy. Hardly what the Prophet, whose name be praised, would recommend.'

'I've always found the Prophet very understanding,' said young Hamid, who had been an artist before taking up the gun.

'Well, each man makes his own arrangements.' Hussein eased himself into the pilot's seat.

He unfolded the map Grant had given him, and Sara said, 'Can I get in the co-pilot's seat?'

'Why not.' She did and he said, 'You can help navigate. Just follow the red line that the American, Grant, has drawn.'

'What's this?' she asked and ran her finger a good hundred miles or more along the line.

'St Anthony's Hospice. It's a Christian monastery that's served the trunk road across the desert since before Islam. There are only twenty or thirty men there now, Greek Orthodox in strange black robes. Fifty miles further on is the Oasis of Fuad with what's called St Anthony's Well. In ancient times they served travellers of all religions.'

He pressed the starter and the engines rattled into life, first the port, then the starboard. 'Fasten your seat belts,' he called as he boosted speed and they roared down the runway. Sara was excited and grabbed his arm.

'Oh, this is so thrilling.' She stared out at great mountains of sand dunes extending into infinity.

'A bit different from Baghdad.'

'Oh yes, very different. No war.'

He levelled out at 10,000 feet and put the automatic pilot on. Although there was air conditioning, on such an old plane it was not perfect. Hussein was wearing dark aviator's sunglasses and a tan suit of fine Egyptian linen. He removed the jacket and revealed a shoulder holster under his left armpit holding a Beretta pistol.

Sara looked upon him. Hussein had been very careful in his dealings with her during the months she had been at the villa. As far as he was concerned, she knew nothing of his background other than the fact that he'd attended Harvard to qualify as a doctor and the war had prevented it.

But she was a remarkably astute young lady, soon to be fourteen, as she was fond of pointing out to people, and could not fail to notice the enormous respect with which he was treated by other people, and not just at the villa. Even important politicians and imams treated him as special.

The truth was that she loved her father very dearly and he had been the most important man in her life. He had strong principles, you somehow took it for granted that anything he did was exactly the right thing for you. No argument needed. Hussein was exactly the same. By religion she had been baptized and raised as a Christian. She had no intention of changing that, although she had never argued about it with her grandfather, being perceptive enough to realize it would get her nowhere, and intelligent enough to understand she was embroiled in a complicated problem. She liked Hussein very much as her cousin, but the idea that at an appropriate age it would lead to marriage was something she had no intention of taking seriously. Her father would find a solution. All she had to do was wait.

The war, of course, was the war, but she was in a strange position. It was on the television every time you turned it on, and it was also on the streets, very real, and it wouldn't go away. Even the death of her grandfather had failed to shock her. Many members of the household staff had been killed on the streets one way or another during her time in Baghdad.

The young men were already sampling wine behind her. When they offered a glass to Hussein, he refused, pointing out that he was flying, but he accepted salad sandwiches in leavened bread and sat eating a couple with Sara, who noticed that when his right trouser leg slid up a little it disclosed an ankle holster containing a Colt pistol. When she asked what it was for, he made light of it, stressing that though it was hardly likely that anything would go wrong, there were

Arabs down there whose lives were hardly formal.

On the other hand, he omitted to mention that an ankle holster was the mark of the true professional.

For the moment she was content and quite thrilled, and gradually her head went back and she dozed.

Charles Ferguson's cousin, Professor Hal Stone, a Fellow of Corpus Christi College, Cambridge, and Hoxley Professor of Marine Archaeology, had what was common to most academics in his profession: an almost total lack of money with which to conduct any kind of significant research.

At Hazar a diving operation on a Second World War freighter had disclosed beneath it a Phoenician trading ship of Hannibal's era. He could only afford one or two annual visits using local Arab divers operating from an ancient boat called the *Sultan*. On a previous visit, Dillon and Billy, both expert divers, had been able to render him some assistance.

The phone call from Ferguson had sent the

good Professor into a frenzy of delight. When he wasn't there he employed his Arab foreman, a man named Selim, as caretaker. He phoned him with the news that he would be arriving, and packed hurriedly.

He hadn't felt so cheerful in a long time, and it wasn't only because of the prospect of diving. His dark secret was that as a young man he had worked for the Secret Security Services, and was well aware of the kind of thing Ferguson and his minions got up to. To be involved delighted him.

'Transport provided?' he asked Ferguson.

'Of course. We've got a Gulfstream these days. The boys will have to get rid of the RAF rondels. We'll call it . . . a United Nations Ocean Survey. That sounds good.'

'Absolutely. So – the reason your people are going there. What is it this time?'

'Come by my flat and I'll fill you in.'

Stone hung up and checked himself in the wardrobe mirror. The man who looked out at him was in his sixties, tanned, white bearded, wearing a khaki bush jacket, khaki shirt and slacks and a crumpled bush hat. He produced a pair of dark Rayban sunglasses.

'That's better,' he said. 'Not exactly Indiana Jones, but not bad. Here we go again then.'

He opened the door to his rooms, took a bag in each hand and left.

Roper had had a few problems running to earth the details of the charter plane flying from Kuwait with Hussein and party. The American, Grant, found himself visited by a Captain Jackson of Military Intelligence at the British Embassy, who was delighted to do Charles Ferguson the favour. The fact that just on the corner of the hangar was a security camera, which on inspection proved to have taken several photos of the entire party, brought Jackson's visit to a more than satisfactory conclusion. In no time at all everyone interested was able to examine them as much as they liked.

'The photos of Hussein Rashid are a real bonus,' Ferguson said.

'What do you think of the girl?' Roper asked.

'Typical of these cases, making the girl dress in that way. What about you?'

Roper poured a whisky. 'She has a calm sort of face, a face that doesn't give a great deal away.'

'I'm not sure it resembles the father to any great degree.'

At that moment Caspar Rashid hurried in with Sergeant Doyle. 'What's all this about photos?'

'Here they are,' Roper told him. 'Fresh in from our contact in Kuwait.'

Caspar examined them carefully, shuffling the photos several times.

Finally he said, 'It's amazing to actually have photos taken such a short time ago.'

'How do you think she looks?' Ferguson asked.

'I don't know, I really don't. I know I might sound strange saying this, but it's the clothes she's wearing. They change her personality so much, or so it seems. Can my wife see these?'

'Good heavens, yes. It's a real stroke of luck getting such excellent photos of Hussein and his merry men.'

Caspar examined a couple of them more closely. 'You know, I barely recognize him. It's been several years, and then there were those six months in that American prison. I recall him as a very nice boy when young.'

Dillon, who had come in quietly and was looking at the photos, said, 'People change, and circumstances change them even more. His mother and father killed in a bombing raid, that six months in jail. It must have seemed cruel and heartless.' He helped himself to a shot of Roper's whisky. 'God knows, I had enough experience in Ireland during the Troubles to see how people can change fundamentally.'

'Well, you would know, Sean,' Roper said. 'This Hussein, though, he's no ordinary one. Judging by his score, he's almost as good as you.'

There was a heavy silence, for there was not much left for anyone else to say.

Sara, engrossed with her map reading and following the red line, saw the palm trees and the buildings that was St Anthony's Hospice before anybody else. She pointed and called out, and Jasmine and the boys stood up and crowded to the windows to see. Hussein went down lower and lower, to no more than 2,000 feet. He circled. There was a parapet, several monks on it in black hats and black robes. They waved. Hussein waggled his wings and turned south.

It was perhaps ten minutes later that their luck ran out. Quite suddenly, smoke, black and oily, started to come out of the port engine. Jasmine saw it first and cried out, and there was a general disturbance, but no sign of flames, just that heavy black plume of smoke.

Sara, who's dozed off again, came awake with a start to hear him say, 'Calm down, all of you.'

He switched off the engine and turned on the extinguisher for the port engine. Spray mingled with the smoke, but there were still no flames. 'I think I know what it is. The oil seals have gone, leaking oil over the hot engine and creating all that black smoke. Everybody fasten their seat belts and we'll go down.' He said to Sara, 'Follow Grant's line on the map. We must be close to the oasis at Fuad and St Anthony's Well.'

He went down fast, the black plume of smoke flaring out from the wing, and Sara said calmly, 'Over there on the right,' and she pointed through the windscreen.

'Good girl.'

They went down lower and lower until they were only a few hundred feet above the sand, and the oasis seemed to be coming towards them fast. Sara saw a clump of palm trees, a small, flat-roofed building to go with it, the clearly defined line of the road marked by the feet of countless travellers over the centuries.

There was a large pool of water, six horses drinking from it, Bedouins in robes beside a cooking fire gazing up, hands raised to shade their eyes from the sun.

Of further interest was a man in black robes, his wrists tied above him as he hung from a pole beside the house.

Hussein dropped the Hawk down on the road and rolled to a halt some distance from the oasis. He said to his three men, 'Out you go. Rifles at the ready.'

One of the men by the pool was holding a riding whip. He turned as if ignoring them and slashed it across the monk's back. The monk's robe had slipped from his shoulders and they were already bloody.

Sara said, 'They can't do that. He's a priest.'

'Calm yourself.' Hussein reached for his phone, which rang as his men disembarked, and discovered it was the Broker. 'Good,' Hussein said. 'I was hoping you'd be available.' He explained the situation with the plane and detailed their position.

'I'll contact the airport at Hazar and arrange a recovery,' said the Broker. 'Probably by helicopter. I'll call you back when I know more.'

Hussein said, 'Let's get moving, ladies.' He smiled at Sara. 'Pass me my jacket, will you?'

As she handed it to him, she saw the maker's label inside and it said Armani, and she thought it was the most beautiful jacket she'd ever seen and suited him completely.

'Be ready for anything, boys,' he said. 'Some bad bastards here, I think. Remember your blood Rashid before anything else.'

'As one, cousin, we are with you,' Khazid said, and they started forward, Hussein with Jasmine on one arm and Sara on the other.

The six men by the pool watched them approach, cradling their rifles, wearing black robes and black-and-white headscarves. The leader, tall and bearded, waited, the whip dangling from his right hand.

'And who have we here?' he demanded.

'Who asks?' Hussein asked, and moved to the right where a pole protruded from a wooden fence, and sat on it.

'Mind your manners, pretty boy,' the man said. 'I am Ali ben Levi. I say who comes and goes here. I claim the well, and this one cannot gainsay me.'

He turned and slashed the priest across the shoulders again, and Sara cried out, 'No.'

'Learn your place, girl. He is only a Christian.'

'And I am Christian too,' she said in Arabic. 'Would you lash me?'

She ran at him, and he grabbed her wrist and laughed. 'To do so would give me great pleasure.' He flung her to the ground and raised the whip. Hussein's hand fastened on the Colt .25 in the ankle holster and he drew it and fired, catching ben Levi between the eyes, the hollow-point cartridge propelling him backwards into the pool and blowing away the back of his skull.

In virtually the same moment one of the men opposite started to raise his rifle and Hassim shot him with his AK. There was dead silence. Hussein gestured, the Colt still in his hand.

'On this occasion I allow you to live,' he told the rest of ben Levi's men. 'So take your dead and go. Go now.'

Hurriedly, they collected their horses, tied the bodies of the two dead men over the saddles of two mares and mounted. They waited for a moment, and Hussein spoke.

'I am Hussein Rashid. I am the Hammer of God. I welcome any man of the ben Levi tribe who seeks satisfaction.'

Which they did not, and left. Jasmine was trembling, but Sara was strangely calm. 'I'll see to the priest,' she said and went to him.

The satellite phone sounded, but there was heavy static. The Broker shouted, 'It's me. Is the static clearing?'

'I'm here.'

'They're sending a helicopter. Is everything OK?'

'A minor problem. It's been taken care of.'

'Good. We'll be needing you soon, Hussein. There's work to be done, you know that. Osama himself was inquiring about you when we last spoke. He sends you his blessing.'

'Tell him I thank him. Goodbye for now.'

By the pool, Sara and Jasmine tended the priest, Sara washing his back carefully with a cloth from the house.

'Are you truly a Christian, child?' he asked.

'My mother is English, my father Rashid. I am baptized.'

'And yet you wear the clothes of a Muslim woman.'

Hussein and his men sat smoking and listening, and heard her say, 'In the whole of the Koran there are only two mothers of prophets. The first, the mother of Mohammed, whose name be praised, and the second Mary, the mother of the prophet Jesus. There is good in all things. I think this is true of the Bible and the Koran.'

'So young and yet so wise.' He counted his beads and started to pray.

She stood up and went and sat on the ground beside Hussein, and the others stood up out of respect and moved away.

'I didn't know,' she said in English. 'About you.'

'Of course you didn't. You weren't meant to.'

'I thought I knew you. Now I see I never knew you at all. The Hammer of God.' She shook her head, repeating it in Arabic. 'The servants would speak of you and sometimes you were mentioned in newspapers. Strange.' She shook her head. 'I read the news to improve my Arabic and didn't realize I was sometimes reading about you and your doings.' She changed to Arabic. 'The great warrior. Never your face on television, but when you spoke on radio you always described yourself as the Hammer of God in English. Even the young children learned it that way, and some of the T-shirts also were printed with the English phrase. Why did you allow this?'

'Personal arrogance – to mock my enemies. In the English papers the wording would be rather different. Not great warrior, but terrorist, I think.'

'Yes, it's amazing how much it's a matter of the words one chooses.'

'How wise,' he said. 'Such wisdom in one so young.' In the distance a sound emerged, the unmistakable stutter of a helicopter. 'So, another stage on our journey.' He pulled her up. 'Say goodbye to the good father and we'll be on our way.'

The port of Hazar was small, with white buildings and narrow alleys, the vivid blue of the sea contrasting with the whiteness of the buildings. The harbour was well used, with coastal shipping of various kinds, fishing vessels, old fashioned dhows and motor cruisers.

They came in from the sea in a half-circle, and about a mile out from the town Sara noticed a big dhow, apparently very ancient. She said, 'That looks interesting.'

Hussein said, 'It is. It's really being used as a diving platform. They call it the *Sultan*. Some years ago, marine archaeologists discovered the wreck of a freighter about ninety feet down that had been sunk by a U-boat in the Second World War. When they dived on it they discovered Phoenician pottery from about two hundred BC. The freighter's been sitting on a much more interesting wreck.'

'Are they doing anything about it?'

'The Hazar government? They couldn't care less. A few years ago a professor from Cambridge University got a licence to dive it. He came back occasionally, but he never had any money to speak of. As I recall, he used local divers and treated it like a holiday.'

'It sounds lovely. Have you ever dived?'

'Oh, yes, many times when I was younger. It's a different world down there.'

They swung in across the town, circling the airfield complex to the left and beyond, and then they drifted to the right to what looked like a small village above a tiny port, and on the hillside above it was an extensive villa, obviously old and standing in gardens and terracing of great beauty.

'This is the pride of the Rashid family – the great house that has stood here for three hundred years. This is Kafkar.'

The helicopter swung down towards a landing pad, and there were people waiting there, many people, all in traditional dress, and standing alone in front of them was a very old man in a white linen suit, a Bedouin burnous on his head. From the look of him he had once been a man of great power, but he was leaning on a stick now.

As the engine stopped, Hussein said, 'Your Great Uncle, Jemal. You go first.'

He opened the door, sent out the steps, and she went down. There was silence. Then the old man beckoned to her. 'Sara – come to me, child.'

She started forward and the crowd broke into spontaneous applause.

Later they sat on a wide terrace above the garden, palm trees and exotic plants on every side. The sound of water was everywhere as it channelled from terrace to terrace in small waterfalls, and Jemal and Hussein sat and smoked. News of the shooting at the oasis had spread.

Jemal said, 'The ben Levi business is nothing. Ali was a bandit of low repute. There'll be no question of an honour killing in revenge. Don't worry.'

'I don't,' Hussein said. 'They needed a lesson, those people.'

'They received one. What of your plans?'

'I shall stay a few days, leave Sara in your hands and go. There is work for me to do – important work. I am in close touch with Al-Qaeda. Osama himself sent me a message only today.'

'Of course, you have been picked for great things, the chosen of Allah. The child will be safe here. What happened in Baghdad was a terrible thing. My brother's death was the will of Allah and the work of Sunnis, but the presence of these devils from London who would steal Sara – this troubles me.'

'And me.'

'My brother was disturbed that she was not happy.'

'Certainly she attempted to run away at first, so they tell me,' Hussein said.

'My brother and I discussed it. We made a decision to chain her. I'm surprised to see this is not so now.'

'I put her on her honour and she gave me her word. The travelling would have been difficult.'

'She is not travelling now.'

Hussein was on dangerous ground, needed to proceed with caution and knew it. 'For a young woman to be shackled so is at best awkward and difficult.' He played on his uncle's sense of what was fitting. 'After all, she is Rashid. For the world to see her shackled would be a great shame. There is your authority to consider.'

'You are right. To see her in public thus would shame us all.'

'Also a particular shame to you, Uncle.' He played now on the old man's vanity. 'That she was seen so.'

'This is true. There can be no question of the shackles. The woman Jasmine will accompany her at all times when she is outside. Two armed guards.' He looked up at the house. 'The blue room will be her living quarters. All the doors and shutters are fitted with keys. No telephone.'

'That should suffice.' Hussein inclined his head. 'Your wisdom, as usual, is boundless.'

At that moment Sara came down the steps with Jasmine behind her. They were both wearing fresh clothing.

'Ah, there you are, child. Come to me.' Jemal put out his hand.

She glanced at Hussein, who gave her a hardly visible nod, so she went and knelt at the old man's knee. 'It is good to see you, Sara.' He kissed her lightly on the head.

'It is good to see you, Uncle.' She took his hand and kissed it. 'I regret the passing of my aunt last year before I could have the privilege of knowing her.'

'A fault not of your making, but of your father's, but we will say no more of that sorry affair. Come – walk with me in the garden and tell me how it is in Baghdad.'

He pushed himself up on his stick and gave her his arm, and they moved along the path, stopping now and then for him to speak to gardeners. Hussein watched them go. She was a clever girl and would soon learn to handle the old man. He lit a cigarette and leaned back, looking a mile out to sea at the *Sultan*. It was all so beautiful, and he felt a drowsiness. But not for long. There was, after all, work to be done. His satellite phone rang. It was the Broker.

'Have you arrived? Are you settled?'

'Yes, thanks be to Allah.'

'Good. Now as I said, Hussein, we have need of you.'

'I know – I know. Give me some time.'

'That is what we do not have.' There was a pause. 'A week, then – one week, and I need you in London.'

'For a purpose?' Hussein shook his head. 'Ten days.'

'All right. There is a man who handles the British Prime Minister's personal security, General Charles Ferguson. I need to do the Russians a favour, and they want him dead. Can you do it?'

'If the will is there, it is possible to kill anyone.'

'Excellent. I'll talk to you again tomorrow. If you check on the computer there, you will find everything you need to know. I'll be in touch.'

The Broker poured a cup of green tea and leaned back in his chair. Every so often things came together. The will of Allah actually existed. Take this present business. Ferguson and the Prime Minister, Blake Johnson and President Cazalet, Volkov and Putin. Hussein Rashid and the whole nonsense of Sara Rashid. Dillon and Salter, Flynn in Dublin, Levin, Chomsky and Popov.

There wasn't one of them he didn't have a hand on. It was all very satisfactory.

LONDON

HAZAR

6

At Holland Park they all met for a final briefing. The Rashids, Harry and Billy Salter, Ferguson and Hal Stone, Dillon, Greta, Roper, Boyd and Henderson, Lacey and Parry.

'I'll turn you over to Roper,' Ferguson said. 'He's worked everything out.'

Roper swung round his wheelchair. 'If this is going to work, the greatest thing in our favour is speed. You all know about what happened in Hazar, the narrow escape with the plane and so on. Computer records indicate that a Lear Jet for Rashid Shipping has been booked in exactly ten days. I think it's a reasonable assumption it's for Hussein Rashid.'

'How can you be sure? It could have something to do with Sara,' Molly said.

'Not likely, my dear,' Ferguson told her. 'They've gone to such trouble to get her to a place of safety. Why would they disturb things now?'

'But such thinking works in our favour,' Roper said. 'She's only just got there. Who in their right mind would imagine her spirited away so soon?'

'So why are we wasting our time talking when we should be there?' Caspar Rashid demanded. He was restless, sweating a little.

Roper said, 'Our plane leaves at five in the morning. The flight takes ten hours.'

'And you would rather I didn't come?'

Ferguson cut in. 'On the contrary. Having the girl recognize her own father in the midst of the confusion when we snatch her back has considerable merit to it.'

'And your suggestion that you could wear robes, a fold of cloth across your face, to pass as a desert Bedouin speaks for itself,' Roper put in. 'Obviously Professor Stone has to go. After all, it's his gig. Billy and Dillon will pose as divers to explain their presence and give credibility to him. The two pilots will pretend to attend to maintenance on the aircraft.'

'What about me?' Greta asked.

'Continue to act as minder to Dr Molly, if you would, Greta.'

'Fine.'

Ferguson said to Rashid, 'Satisfied?'

Rashid, perhaps understandably, still appeared nervous.

Roper said, 'Let's examine the situation calmly. You aren't going to get your daughter back by presenting yourself at your uncle's house and asking for her. Frankly, getting our hands on her is likely to be completely opportunistic – strolling in a garden, walking in the street, swimming off a beach. Who knows?'

'I suppose so,' Rashid said reluctantly.

'He's right, darling,' Molly told him.

'All I can tell you is that when it does happen it will have to be damn quick. That's why we'll have the pilots hanging round the plane for a quick departure.'

'That's about it then,' Ferguson told them. 'Now our new cook has promised an early dinner, so let's get on with it.'

Roper said, 'Just one thing. Something I want to show you.' They all turned. 'I hope we're successful – I hope like hell – but the one unproven quantity is the Hammer of God himself, Hussein Rashid. Here he is.'

On a screen appeared a photo of Hussein taken from the security camera at Kuwait airport. In this one he'd taken off his black Rayban sunglasses for a moment and his bearded face was on show. He had, in a strange way, the look of a young Che Guevara.

'What's your point?' Ferguson said.

'It's this. The moment the Gulfstream leaves the ground at Hazar we release to the press this portrait of Hussein Rashid, Hammer of God, known associate of Osama bin Laden. Rumour has it he could be in Britain. It'll make it very difficult for him to follow us.'

'My God, you wonderful bastard,' Ferguson said. 'How in the hell could he cope with that?' He turned to Molly Rashid. 'And they may just be the end of your problem.'

The dinner bell sounded and he offered her his arm. 'Shall we go in?'

In Hazar the heat of the day was intense, and Sara was not happy. If things had been difficult at her grandfather's villa in Iraq, they were infinitely worse at the great house at Kafkar. To start with, her uncle had stipulated that not only Jasmine would have a bed in her room, but also two older family widows. Armed guards on the terraces made things no better.

'It's intolerable,' she told Hussein. 'I feel as if I'm being swallowed whole.'

'Let things settle down,' he urged her. 'After everything that's happened, he's feeling a bit paranoid.'

'I'm not even allowed to eat with you. I'm consigned to the women, and most of them are old enough to be my grandmother. I can't go for a swim in the pool unless I dress for it the way Muslim girls do. It's like going swimming at Brighton in Edwardian times.'

'But you are a Muslim girl, and before you waste my time arguing the point, I will remind you that your uncle is very old-fashioned.'

'Tell me about it.' She was furious and gestured down to the private beach and the sea beyond. 'It looks so normal down there. Tourists, waterskiing, jet skis, speedboats, and up here it's armed guards, a parallel world.'

'What nonsense.'

'Even you leave me for most of the time.'

'I have important matters to attend to.'

'I can imagine. Back to the war or something, everything a discussion. I've seen you, constantly on that satellite phone, arranging things with your friend, the Broker.'

He was shocked. 'What's this?'

'The pool at Fuad. I heard him shouting at you on the phone when the static was bad.'

He shrugged. 'He's simply an investment counsellor – a broker, just as I said.'

'Can I at least go shopping in the town or out on the bay in a motorboat?'

'We'll see.' He stood up.

'Or go to town to visit the mosque. Even your uncle can't say no to that.'

He smiled, aware of how much of a child she was when she chose, and was suddenly acutely aware of what he had promised her grandfather.

'It's all for your own good. It really is. I'll see what I can do.'

'And let Hassim and Hamid guard me. At least they're friends, as is Khazid. They know what war's about, not like the people here. Not like you.'

He was touched. She couldn't have pleased him more, which was exactly why she'd said it.

'I'll do what I can. Be a good girl.' And he left her to Jasmine and the other two women who'd been seated some little distance away.

Sara moved to the balustrade at the edge of the terrace and looked down towards the harbour. There was a life down there, things were busy. The old dhow, the *Sultan*, was picturesque and fitted the landscape. There was activity on deck: they were unloading a large rubber boat with what looked like gas cylinders. It was difficult to see at this distance. However, at that moment Hamid appeared with Hassim. They both wore camouflage trousers, green T-shirts and sunglasses, and carried AK rifles. There was no doubt they looked good and were much admired by the female staff.

Hamid said, 'Hussein has sent us, little cousin. He says you are bored.'

He delivered this in English, for he was trying to improve it and she knew that. He had a pair of Zeiss glasses slung around his neck.

She said, 'Excellent – you can start by letting me have your glasses.'

He handed them over. She raised them to her eyes, focusing on the dhow. There was an Arab on deck and another, a desert Bedouin, very dashing in black robes and black and white turban, a fold across his face leaving only the eyes uncovered.

Although she did not know it, her father was helping Selim, the caretaker of the *Sultan*, pull up air canisters as they were passed from the rubber boat by Dillon and Billy. At the same moment Hal Stone emerged from the wheelhouse.

'What are you looking at?' Hamid asked.

'The big dhow. Hussein told me all about it. It's used by a Cambridge University professor as a diving platform. There is a very ancient boat down there – Phoenician, I believe. You know about that?'

'Sure I do,' Hamid said. 'I learned about the Phoenicians in school. Let's look.' She gave him the glasses and he raised them. 'Yes, that's diving equipment they're taking on board. It must be fun. I'd like to try.' He passed the glasses to Hassim.

'If we were allowed to go out in a boat, we could take a look,' she said.

'That would depend on your uncle.' He accepted a cigarette from Hamid and they sat on a bench and smoked.

The Gulfstream had managed an uneventful trip, with no need to refuel. They had discussed things over and over again. Caspar

Rashid's recent trip to Hazar had been his first since boyhood. His face was not a familiar one, certainly not to the caretaker of the *Sultan*.

Each of them had photos provided by Roper. First, one of Sara in her school uniform with her mother and father taken earlier that year, then group photos of Dillon, Billy and Hal Stone taken with Molly and Caspar. These were all obviously to establish credentials with Sara, though they provided no solution to how they could make contact.

The first situation they encountered had to do with Selim. There had been a family death up country in the Empty Quarter. It required his presence, and he needed five days for the trip. If anything this made things easier, though, particularly regarding Caspar. Hal Stone provided Selim with his blessing and US$100, checked that he'd stocked up on everything needed in the galley, and ran him across to the jetty in the early evening. While there, Dillon and Billy hired jet skis from a hire shop, plus a battered station wagon, and returned to the dhow, where they found Hal Stone and Caspar looking across to the Rashid house through glasses.

There was plenty of tourist traffic around and Hal said, 'The jet skis made sense. There's a lot of that kind of stuff over there. You can blend in.'

'That's the idea,' Dillon said. 'Get a diving suit on, Billy, and we'll take a look. Hello,' he stiffened. 'There are two guys walking along a terrace over there with slung rifles.' He paused. 'Yes, two more, and a third above.'

'Place is a fortress,' Billy said. 'Come on, let's take a look.'

'OK, and remember we're just tourists. Do what everybody else is doing and nothing more.'

At the airfield it was bakingly hot, but as a shabby, unshaven police lieutenant had told them, it wasn't a busy time of year for them. The BA flight was their main connection to

London, and that was only three times a week. The rest of the traffic was made up of smaller aircraft, private jets owned by the rich or local firms. The lieutenant's name was Said, and they gave him cigarettes and Lacey slipped him $500, the direct result of such munificence being the empty hangar he had allocated them. It was a damned sight cooler than being outside, and there were even crew quarters with four truckle beds, a shower room and a toilet. Everything was broken down and shabby, but as Lacey had said, with luck, it wouldn't be for long.

The first task was to refuel, which they did, and then they returned the Gulfstream to the hangar and removed the port engine's cowling. Said appeared and watched them for a couple of minutes.

'Are you sure you want to sleep here? I could send you to a good hotel. My cousin –'

Lacey cut him off. 'This engine wasn't its usual happy self, so we're going to check it out.'

'Working for the United Nations is good,'

Parry told him. 'We not only get excellent wages, but very good expenses. We'll spend it later in a better place, Dubai.'

'Or the South of France.' Lacey smiled. 'You get a better class of girls there.'

'I see your point. I see from the files that you were here before.'

'A couple of years ago,' Lacey said calmly.

'The United Nations again?'

'Well, for Professor Stone, really,' Parry said. 'The United Nations Ocean Survey funds him.'

'All for the sake of some old boat ninety feet down. In the old days there were sponges down there. As a boy my father was one of those who dived to the boat. He and his friends jumped holding big rocks and the weight took them straight down.'

'Jesus,' Parry said. 'Hadn't they heard of the bends?'

'They would snatch a sponge and go straight back to the surface. Such youths were much admired for their bravery.'

'Well, they would be,' Lacey said dryly.

'The café in the terminal keeps going even

when business isn't good. Her cooking is to be recommended. She is a cousin of mine on my mother's side.'

Lacey said, 'I'll see how the engine goes, but I'll need to test fly it. Will that be OK?'

'Of course. Whenever you want. You can see what it's like here. A graveyard.'

He turned and walked away. Lacey said, 'I think you can say that's sorted. I vote we check out the café.' Parry gazed out over the single runway, everything shimmering in the great heat, the mountains in the distance lining the Empty Quarter. 'I know one thing.' He joined Lacey. 'This has to be the last place God made.'

'You can say that again.'

'I wonder how they're doing on the *Sultan*.'

'I'll call them later. Give them time to settle in.'

They entered the small terminal, where there were no passengers to be seen, just Arabs here and there who were obviously staff. The restaurant was open, and the smell was appetizing.

'My God, that does look good. Let's give it a try.' Lacey led the way.

The wind was blowing in from the land, warm and musky, with a certain amount of sand in it. Dillon and Billy sat among the diving equipment and got ready, and Billy was so eager he was first. He was wearing a green diving suit and clamped a tank to his inflatable and an Orca computer to the line of his air-pressure gauge. He spat in his mask and pulled it on, made an OK signal with a finger and thumb, and went over the rail backwards.

Dillon went after him, the complete bliss of it enveloping him, the great blue vault of the sea, the myriad of fish. He checked the dive computer, which told him his depth, how long he'd been down, how long he could stay.

The old freighter was clear below at ninety feet, covered in barnacles and marine growth of all kinds, fish passing in and out of portholes. Billy ventured inside through the jagged hole the German torpedoes had left, and Dillon followed, and they played a kind of hide and seek in those dark, sunken passageways, emerging by the stern and hovering over a mixture of sand, sea grass and detritus that was what was left of the ancient Phoenician trading ship. Billy had found a figurine there once, a temple votive figure of a woman with a swollen belly and big eyes. In Hazar he'd come as close to death as a man could, but he'd made it through because in his pocket was Sam, the name he'd given the votive figure. She was his good luck piece and yet, when an old boy at the British Museum had gone potty over her, Billy had handed her over. Still, he knew the glass display case she lived in, could see her whenever he wanted.

He turned away and pointed, a gloved hand on a rail. Dillon beckoned to him and they started up towards the keel of the *Sultan* and the diving platform at the bottom of the boarding ladder. As they surfaced, a large rubber boat swept past. Hamid was at the tiller, Hassim in the bow, an AK across his knees. Sara was seated in the centre beside Jasmine.

It had not been intended, the excursion round the bay, but Hussein and old Jemal had been called to what was called the South Port along the coast from where the freight ships for the Indian trade operated, the terminus for the single-track steam railway and the oil pipeline. They were late for an appointment, and when Sara asked if they could cruise the harbour the old man, half-deaf, was in a fuss and under pressure and relented, telling Hamid he had full responsibility and not to go far.

'On Wednesday morning I'm taking you to the mosque to meet the imam. Don't forget. Study your Koran. I want him to be impressed with you,' he told Sara.

'Of course, Uncle.'

The truth was that the business at South Port in which he and Hussein were mixed up was very delicate and involved arrangements for various illegal cargoes to be transported north to militias in Iraq. In any case, the young people set off in their boat, its powerful outboard motor pushing them very fast on a criss-crossing route in the harbour, and Sara became more demanding, urging them on. She'd observed the *Sultan*, the people on deck and those entering the water.

'They're diving,' she said. 'Circle around.' Hamid did so, and Hassim leaned over, cradling the AK, and peered down through the incredibly crystal clear water.

'You can see everything, Sara – the boat, the divers. Look, little cousin.'

He had spoken in English and she replied in the same language. 'Gosh, it's absolutely marvellous.'

On deck, standing beside Hal Stone, Caspar Rashid heard her voice and moaned slightly. One foot moved forward, but, cloaked in his desert robes, the fold of his turban hiding half of his face, there was no way she could recognize him. Hal Stone squeezed hard on his arm, felt Caspar pause, and then a sigh went out of him.

Now Sara said exactly the right thing. 'I wonder if you're Professor Hal Stone of Cambridge University?'

'Why, yes, I am, but how did you know that?'

'Oh, I've been told all about you and the old freighter down there on top of the Phoenician ship. I'm from the big house over there on the bluff. My name is Sara Rashid. It's a pretty romantic story.' At that moment Dillon emerged, followed by Billy, and they grabbed the edge of the diving platform.

Hal Stone, thinking very fast on his feet, took his hand out of the pocket of his bush jacket, palming two of the small photos provided by Roper.

'Fancy you knowing all that! Of course, it's not quite true. I *am* a professor at Cambridge, but home is 15 Gulf Road in Hampstead. It's awfully nice to meet you.' He leaned down, dropping to one knee, and pressed the palmed photos into her right hand as he shook it.

She frowned, and for a moment might

have ruined everything, but it was only a small moment, and Hal carried on, 'We'll be here for a while. Perhaps you could visit us properly. But what am I thinking of? I've offered you no hospitality. Caspar, iced water for our guests.'

Caspar Rashid responded with a nod, turned as if to go, and the strangest thing happened. Sara's face was wiped clean for the briefest of moments, and then she smiled, and it was the most wonderful smile Hal Stone had seen in his life.

Hamid said, 'Thank you for your offer of hospitality, but we must go now, Sara.'

'I hope to see you again, Professor. Are you diving again tomorrow? I can't come on Wednesday. I'm visiting the imam at the mosque.'

'Oh, yes, tomorrow you can see the divers at work. The water is so clear and we always hope to find something special.'

Caspar said, 'I think we already have.'

The boat turned away, Sara slipping her hand into her pocket. Her heart was beating furiously. She had to swallow hard. She said to Hamid, 'The Arab, who was he?'

'A Bedouin by his robes. Obviously the boat's caretaker. A real country boy from the look of him, from the Empty Quarter. Are you OK?'

'Fine, just fine, but I'm tired and I've had enough. Take me back.'

They did, and returned to her suite, where she took refuge from her women in the sanctuary of the bathroom. There she examined the photos. The first was the one of her in school uniform taken earlier in the year with her mother and father. The second showed Hal Stone, Dillon and Billy and her father in Bedouin robes, only in this one his face was not concealed by the flap of his turban.

Hot tears sprang to her eyes, and her hands shook a little. The photo of Stone and company she examined again and again, taking so long that Jasmine knocked on the bathroom door and called to ask if she was unwell. She had never felt better, suddenly full of energy, the life force flooding through her. Very carefully she cut the photos into pieces with little nail scissors, put them down the toilet and flushed them away.

The women were waiting. 'Are my uncle and Hussein back yet?'

'No, Sara,' Jasmine said, 'but supper is ready.'

'Then so am I.' Sara smiled. 'Let's go down to the terrace and enjoy ourselves.'

They did, and the servants lit the flares and candles, set the floor cushions and piled food high on the side tables. Two musicians sat cross-legged and plucked the strings of their instruments, the music plaintive on the evening air. Sara moved over to the balustrade and looked out across the harbour to the *Sultan*. Its deck lights were on and she had never been so excited in her life.

On the *Sultan*, seated in canvas chairs at a table in the stern, they discussed the situation. 'I must say it was a hell of a thing to do,' Caspar Rashid said. 'For a while there

I didn't know whether I was coming or going.'

Hal Stone said, 'Remember what Roper said about the whole thing being opportunistic? Well, what happened earlier was a perfect example. Everything just fell into place. It occurred to me that those two Arab boys couldn't have the slightest idea where she lived in London.'

'Good point,' Billy said.

'She's a remarkable young woman,' Dillon said. 'To field that ball and the mention of her father's name took some doing.'

'Slipping in her visit to the mosque on Wednesday was a nice one,' Hal Stone said.

'Yes, but we can't go in as a team,' Billy pointed out.

'I can go, see what the situation is in the mosque itself.' Caspar produced a pack of cigarettes and lit one. 'There's no need to worry about me any more, gentlemen. All my doubts are resolved, all passion spent. It's going to work, I know that now. The only thing is how.'

'I know one thing,' Hal Stone said. 'Her

visit to the mosque will do us no good. A family affair. Wouldn't you agree?'

'I'm afraid so. It's a kind of state visit to the imam, and my uncle and Hussein are bound to go.'

Dillon said, 'Roper was right. It all comes down to recognizing the opportunity and taking it.'

'What do you mean?' Hal Stone said.

'Billy and I weren't available, but you two were. All you had to do was shoot the two boys. Billy?'

Billy poured Dillon a Bushmills and handed it to him. 'I'm afraid he's right, gents.' He turned to Caspar. 'It's why we're along, to be worse than the bad guys. Don't kid yourself about those two nice boys with their Kalashnikovs. They've accompanied her from Baghdad. They've done their share of killing.'

Caspar took a deep breath. 'How would it be done?'

'We keep a look-out and hope for an approach. Billy and I can be in the water, just in diving jackets. Silenced Walthers are just as good in water.'

'And the woman with Sara?'

'Straight down the companionway and lock her in a cabin.' He looked across to the jetty. 'Turn up the speed, and we're there in fifteen minutes. Warn Lacey we're on our way, pile into the station wagon and it's the airport next stop. If by some odd chance Hussein turns up, we'll kill him too.'

'I'm going to the stateroom to call Lacey and Parry and bring them up to date. Then Ferguson. Then bed. See you all in the morning.'

Ferguson was himself in bed reading defence papers and having a brandy nightcap. Dillon brought him up to snuff.

'You really think you can pull it off?' Ferguson asked.

'If they visit us again like they did today, yes. I'll tell you one thing – Sara Rashid is no ordinary thirteen year old.'

'My dear Dillon, go to Shakespeare. Juliet was thirteen.'

'Jesus, General, that's all right then, we're

home and dry. Good night to you, as they say in Belfast!'

In a sense, the Broker was going to war. Ferguson would fall to Hussein Rashid. Now it was time to settle scores elsewhere: the Salters, both Harry and Billy. He knew all about the events involving Harry Moon and Big Harold, so he also knew Ruby Moon now ruled the bar at the Dark Man.

He brooded for a while. Besides the Dark Man, Salter had opened a highly successful high-end restaurant, he recalled, the kind of place that attracted only the best people. Trouble there would hit Salter hard.

He looked in his book and found Chekov's number.

'Who is it? I'm in bed and not alone. It's too damned late.'

'The Broker.'

Chekov was suddenly all attention. The Broker heard him say, 'Get some clothes on and get the hell out of here or I'll give you a slapping.'

He was back to the phone in a minute. 'What can I do for you?'

'You know Harry Salter and his nephew, Billy?'

'Who doesn't? He's a hard old bastard, that one. Why, what do you want?'

'I want them permanently removed. He and his people have caused serious distress to General Volkov and the President.'

'Well, we can't have that.'

'No. I think this is work for Stransky – Big Ivan. You know that fancy restaurant of Salter's?'

'I've been there. Harry's Place.'

'Destroy it. You know what to do.'

'And?'

'Salter started life as a river rat. Let him end there. Put him in the Thames along with his nephew and his hard men.'

'What about Dillon?'

'What about him?'

'He and the Salters are like brothers.'

'Then let them die like brothers.'

*   *   *

Chekov took a taxi to the Dorchester Hotel, where he knew he would find many members of the Russian community. Many of them were millionaires, and some billionaires, and they were a hard-drinking lot. When they wanted to avoid trouble of the violent or disruptive sort, they brought in Ivan Stransky.

He was six foot four, built like a brick wall, his hair cropped, and half his left ear was missing, left in Chechnya where he'd served in a Guards regiment. He was standing at the end of the bar, a black leather coat straining at his shoulders, a cigarette between his fingers, and saw Chekov at once.

A waitress was passing and Chekov said, 'Scotch whisky, my lovely, two large ones, and make it the cheap stuff.'

He took a seat in the corner, and Stransky sat beside him. 'What can I do for you?' said the big man.

'What do you know about Harry Salter?'

Stransky smiled without humour. 'A major gangster who's gone legit, they say – ware-house developments, casinos, apartment blocks. They say he's worth four or five hundred million.'

'But I bet he hasn't entirely given up his old ways, has he?'

'Of course not. Action is the juice of life to a man like him. It's the game that appeals. He's not rubbish, he's got balls and brains, and in his time he's killed. He's got a nephew, Billy, who's a younger version. So, what about him?'

'I want you to start giving Salter a bad time, as a favour to a broker friend of mine. Eventually we're going to eliminate him, but we're going to work up to it, let him think about it a bit. We'll start with that fancy restaurant of his, Harry's Place. A lot of rich people go there – they wouldn't like it if their cars got messed up, it would be very bad for business, you know what I mean?'

'When do you want this?'

'Right now. Sudden blitz, so that he knows whoever did it means it. A hunting party will do. Five or six top men.'

'My pleasure.'

Chekov finished his whisky. 'Have another.'

'No. I'd rather get moving. There are people I'll need to talk to.'

'Good.'

They hadn't mentioned money. It was not necessary. Stransky went out and Chekov called the waitress over. 'Large whisky, my love. I'll have the expensive stuff this time, the Highland Special that's eight hundred pounds a shot.'

Outside the hotel on the left-hand side private limousines were waiting, their chauffeurs chatting beside them, and Stransky's own Mercedes was there, his driver, a hard-looking young man called Bikov, standing by it smoking a cigarette. 'Get in.' Stransky opened the rear door.

'What's up, boss?' Bikov demanded.

'Café Rosa, quickly. Will Makeev and the boys still be there?'

'Sure. They're having a card school tonight.'

'I need five, maybe six of them.'

'Trouble?'

'No, to make trouble. You know Harry Salter?'

206

'Of course I do.'

'That restaurant of his, Harry's Place, Chekov wants it messed up good. Let's see if Bikov and his boys are interested.'

'For Chekov? You won't have to ask twice.'

Behind the bar at the Dark Man, Ruby called to Harry, who was sitting in a booth. Joe Baxter and Sam Hall were propping up the bar behind him.

'It's thinning out a bit, Harry. We can go if you like. Rita can close up.' Ruby came round the bar in a demure white blouse and a black velvet skirt and shoes to die for.

'Bleeding marvellous,' Harry said and turned to his minders. 'Isn't she?'

'Absolutely, Harry,' they chorused.

'Right, let's check how things are going at Harry's Place. Leave the Aston, we'll go in the Shogun.' He handed Ruby in and followed her.

'I'm really looking forward to this,' Ruby said. 'I was beginning to think you were going to ask Hamid to take me.'

'Don't be silly, girl, we just haven't had the opportunity. Anyway, you look like a princess. Doesn't she look like a princess, boys?'

'A Queen, Harry,' Baxter said.

'Get stuffed,' Ruby told him and leaned back. 'I wonder how it's going in Hazar.'

'We'll know soon enough, girl, but one thing's for sure. If anybody can handle it, Dillon and Billy can.' He leaned forward and said to Baxter, 'Are we tooled up?'

Baxter dropped a hidden flap. 'The Colt .25s, just like you said, boss, two of them.'

'Guns, Harry?' Ruby was shocked. 'Is that necessary?'

'There are funny people around these days, love. Russian Mafia, Albanians, fourteen year olds in knife gangs who'll stick a shiv in you as soon as look at you. I've got mates who are Italian Mafia and they're the good guys now.'

Sam Hall pulled in outside the warehouse Salter had transformed into Harry's Place, a red neon sign above the door and a queue outside. Two young black men in dinner suits had the door.

'The Harker twins,' Harry told Ruby.

Baxter and Hall took the Shogun to the car park, and Salter and Ruby walked along the side of the queue. They found five youths in black leathers pushing and shoving, alarming people ahead of them.

Ruby said, 'They're Russians, Harry. I used to serve a lot like that at the old pub.'

They were, in fact, Makeev and four of his friends, who'd been hired by Stransky as ordered.

'Here, you bleeding well cut it out,' Harry told them.

They jeered in good Cockney English, 'Who the hell are you, her father?'

He handed Ruby up the steps, where one of the Harker twins apologized profusely. 'Sorry, boss, real sorry, and more bad news. Big Ivan Stransky and another guy came in just before these guys turned up.'

Baxter and Hall arrived on the run and ranged themselves beside the Harkers, making a formidable barrier. Harry said, 'Don't let them in. We'll see what Stransky wants.'

He held out his hand. Baxter slipped a

Colt .25 in it and Harry took Ruby's arm as Fernando the head waiter appeared, full of apologies.

'Not needed,' Harry said. 'This is Mrs Moon. Take us to my table.' He added to Baxter and Hall, 'You come with us.'

The place was rather pretty, in an Art Deco style, with a cocktail bar, small, intimate tables, a dance floor, a trio playing music of the Cole Porter variety. Harry's table was in a booth with mirrors behind it, and Baxter and Hall stood one on each side.

A waiter in a white waistcoat with brass buttons who had responded to Harry's nod brought a large brandy and ginger ale for him and a champagne cocktail for Ruby.

'I thought you should have a champagne cocktail on your first visit.'

'It's lovely,' she said. 'What's that?'

'Brandy and ginger ale. They call it a Horse's Neck.'

'I wonder why?'

'Doesn't really matter, Ruby – it's a British thing. We're funny that way. Here's to you. You look lovely.'

He took his drink straight down and nodded to the waiter, then folded his arms as Stransky, Bikov behind him, came down the steps from the bar and crossed the dance floor towards them.

'Nice little place you've got, Harry,' Stransky said.

'Mr Salter to you. Now what can I do for you and the fairy prince here?'

Bikov's hand went in his pocket, his face tightened, but Sam Hall stepped close and slipped his hand in the same pocket. 'Gawd bless me, but someone's got a big one.' He produced a Smith & Wesson Bankers Special and put it on the table in front of Harry.

'A little old-fashioned,' Harry said. 'Bloody rude bringing it in at all, ladies present and so on.'

Stransky looked around. 'Ladies? I don't see any ladies.' He smiled at Ruby. 'Of course, I don't count the whore here.'

'She's got more class than you any day, you fat pig.'

Stransky stopped smiling. 'You'll be sorry

you said that, Salter, and when you're gone,' he laughed out loud, reached over and patted Ruby's face, 'we'll see.'

'Outside,' Harry told him.

'What an excellent idea. Come on, Bikov,' and they went.

'What do you think, boss?' Baxter said.

'They'll be up to no good outside with that bunch he brought along.' He sighed. 'I'm really getting too old for this. Let's go out and see what they're up to. You stay, Ruby love.'

'Not bloody likely.'

'All right, then, stay by the door. Just be a good girl. I told Billy I'd look after you.'

'What a liar you are, Harry Salter.' She took his arm and the whole group left. 'There was a story about you going the rounds year before last when the Franconi twins were running wild over half of London. The word was they got an IRA expert to put a bomb in your Jaguar.'

'God was on my side,' he told her cheerfully. 'The guy got the timer wrong and it blew up before Billy and I got there.'

'And is it true the Franconis are in cement on the North Circular Road?'

'Ruby, love, do I look like I'd do a thing like that?'

Outside, the queue had gone and it was quiet, only the sound of the trio playing 'Night and Day' drifting out. 'What's happening?' Harry asked the Harkers.

'The Russian punks cleared off, as far as I know, and Stransky and his driver went off to get his car.'

But Harry didn't believe it, and with Hall and Baxter he walked to the car park. Suddenly the Russians appeared, three of them with baseball bats swinging sideways into the cars, smashing windows, denting bumpers.

Harry didn't hesitate, took the Colt from his pocket and ducked under Makeev's flailing baseball bat, stuck the weapon against the Russian's right kneecap and pulled the trigger. The others, shocked, wavered, and Baxter picked up the baseball bat Makeev had dropped. He swung it side- ways, fracturing the side of a man's face, and then the other way, fracturing an arm.

The Harker twins arrived on the run, Ruby behind them, and Harry fired in the air.

The Russians froze. Makeev was writhing on the ground, moaning terribly. Harry reached out and pulled the nearest Russian over. 'You came in a car – which is it?' The man pointed to a white van. 'Get him in it, in fact all of you get in it, and deliver him to St Mary's. Of course, you'll stay shtum because I wasn't here, was I? I was elsewhere. Lots of people saw me. Who was the contract for?' he inquired of the driver. 'Better tell me, sunshine. I won't hold it against you.'

'Stransky said it was for Max Chekov.'

'Really?' Harry said. 'The oligarch? Interesting. Thanks very much.'

The van drove away, and Stransky, sitting in his car nearby, whispered to Bikov, 'We'd better go.'

'I'll have to switch on the engine,' Bikov said.

Harry's boys moved in their direction instantly and Harry himself tapped on the window on the passenger's side. 'Get the door open unless you want broken glass all over you.'

Stransky complied. 'Now look, Harry.'

'I thought you knew only my friends call me Harry. What have I done to Chekov to make him annoyed?'

'He was doing a favour for a friend, that's all I know. Some broker guy told me to mess you up.' He didn't bother telling Harry that wasn't all Chekov intended to do.

'Bizarre,' Harry said. 'But I like it. London's everybody's favourite destination these days, capital of the world, even for the gangsters. I feel it might be necessary for me to keep up the reputation of the *British* gangster.'

He reached inside the car, prodded Stransky's left kneecap and pulled the trigger. He couldn't tell what Stransky said, because it was in Russian, but the man howled like a werewolf. 'Go on, get out of here,' Harry said, and Bikov put his foot down and drove away.

Baxter and Hall applauded as he offered his arm to Ruby. 'God, you're a hard man,' Ruby said. 'I never realized.'

'Well let's go back inside. Champagne for everyone!'

The following morning, as Chekov was getting out of the shower in his sumptuous apartment off Park Lane, the front door bell sounded. Chekov cursed, because the maid didn't come in until nine o'clock. He went to the window, towelling himself. The flat was a duplex, and when he looked out a motorcycle was parked at the kerb and a man stood on the step wearing black leathers and helmet and a yellow waistcoat with Express Delivery emblazoned on it. He held a cardboard box and waited. Chekov pulled on a robe, went downstairs and opened the door.

The face was anonymous behind the black plastic. 'Mr Max Chekov?'

'That's me. What have we got here?' He took the box in both hands.

'Flowers,' the man said. 'Lilies.' He pulled at the end of the box, produced a sawn-off double-barrelled shotgun, rammed it against Chekov's left knee and pulled the trigger.

Chekov was hurled backwards. The man said, 'Have a nice day,' went down the steps to the motorcycle and drove away.

7

It was quiet at the airport at six in the morning, as Lacey and Parry kept up a semblance of working on the Gulfstream, the cowling of the port engine still off. A hawk of some kind swept in, dived on some creature in the brush on the other side of the runway, and Said appeared in a Land Rover.

'Have you fixed it?'

'Just about,' Lacey nodded. 'Started early while it's still cool.'

'I know what you mean. I'm going downtown early for the same reason.'

'Things don't look too busy.'

'As usual, it's like the morgue. There's an old Dakota on a transport run from Kuwait in around eleven o'clock, and today there's a British Airways flight. Due at three in the afternoon.'

'That should be lively.'

'Not really. I've seen the numbers. Seventy-three people. Hardly worth bothering with. I'll see you later. I'll need to be back for the Dakota.'

'I might be ready for that test flight later.'

'No problem. There's no traffic, so just go.'

He drove away and Parry said, 'That's nice of him.'

'Don't count your chickens. Now let's go and see if she's open for breakfast yet.'

About seven, Caspar and Billy ran the inflatable to the jetty where the station wagon was parked. Billy got behind the wheel and drove it a short distance to the garage and made certain the tank was full. When he returned, Caspar passed him three flight bags. Billy was wearing his green diving jacket, his eyes anonymous behind dark glasses. Caspar maintained his full disguise, the fold across his face. The harbour was barely stirring.

'It's going to be hot later,' Billy said.

'You could be right.'

They got into the boat, Billy turned on the engine and they moved away from the jetty.

'How are you feeling?'

'How should I feel?'

'Damn it, Caspar, you are her father.'

'True, but in such a situation as I find myself I realize I'm still a Muslim, and as we say, "Inshallah" – as God wills.'

'Maybe.' Billy pushed up to top speed and went out in a long sweeping curve towards the *Sultan*. 'And maybe not.'

On the dhow Hal Stone was sitting in a wicker chair, a cup of coffee on the table beside him, a pair of enormous glasses to his eyes, gazing towards the great house on the cliff.

'A number of gardeners working away. Activity already on the water, several fishing boats. Mainly on that side, things like motorboats, skiers. The beach over there attracts them.'

Billy took the glasses from him and looked. 'I see what you mean.' He handed them back. 'Where's Dillon?'

'In the galley seeing to bacon and eggs.'

'That's even better,' Billy said, and went down the companionway.

Dillon was whisking scrambled eggs. Like Billy, he just wore a diving jacket. 'I've left the weapons on the table in the saloon. You'd better take a look.'

'What about the woman?' Billy asked.

'She'll be frightened out of her wits if things go our way. I've put some stuff out that should take care of it.'

Billy went into the saloon. There were two Walther PPKs on the table, Carswell silencers screwed in place. He handled them both expertly, and two Uzi machine pistols that lay beside them. There were some plastic clip-on handcuffs and a roll of plastic tape.

Dillon looked in. 'Breakfast's ready.'

Billy turned, went to the kitchen behind him, picked up a laden tray and Dillon brought another. It was all calm and orderly, the sounds of traffic drifting across the water. They found the others at the table.

'What happens now?' Billy said as he ate.

'We finish eating, then we seem busy, just in case anyone is looking. Mess around with the diving equipment, stuff like that.'

Hal Stone said, 'The Uzis on the table in the saloon – I shouldn't think Caspar and I would need them.'

'Nice weapon – always liked them,' Dillon said. 'If you drop one, it stops automatically.'

'I remember very well,' the professor said. 'It's just that it's been a long time. What about you, Caspar?'

'My experience with any kind of firearms has been severely limited,' Rashid said. 'So, if things go according to plan, the woman with Sara will be handcuffed, dragged below and locked in a cabin?'

'Better than a bullet, which is what she'd get from some people. They'll find her whenever they come looking for Sara and the others.'

'A lot of places to look,' Hal Stone said.

'I think you'll find the women at the house

have already heard about yesterday's visit.' Dillon shrugged. 'Hussein Rashid is a special kind of man. Every sense in him is sharpened like some jungle animal. He'll work out what's happened here quickly. That's why we've got to move very fast indeed.'

There was silence. Billy went to the side table, got a bottle of Bushmills whiskey, poured half a glass and brought it to Dillon.

'Oh, if only I didn't hate alcohol . . . but here's looking at you,' Dillon toasted them and emptied the glass, then got up. 'Let's look busy, Billy.'

'I'm with you.'

Caspar loaded the tray. 'I'll get rid of this.'

Hal Stone said, 'Better bring the weapons back with you,' and as Dillon went over the side he picked up the glasses and focused them on the house on the bluff.

They didn't know it, but nobody at the house except Sara even wanted to go to South Port that morning. Sitting at a table on the terrace and reading an Arab newspaper, Hussein was enjoying a coffee after breakfast. His uncle had just been called away.

Sara, with Jasmine, stood on the upper terrace looking down on him, Hamid and Hassim behind them, smoking and talking.

Sara turned to them. 'Do you know if he's going to South Port this morning?'

'Well, he doesn't look like it,' Hamid replied. 'He hasn't said a word.'

She tried to stay calm. 'What a shame. I'd hoped to go and see them diving again.'

'I don't think so.'

At that moment, relief came from an unexpected quarter. Jemal appeared on the upper terrace a few yards away from them, leaned over and shouted to Hussein, 'We must leave at once. I've had a message from South Port. The loading of the *Kandara* has been disrupted.'

Hussein rose and started up the steps. 'What happened?' he called.

'The train was coming down from Baku with the last load two hours ago when one of the freight cars was derailed on that bend by Stack Four.'

'How bad is it?'

'It could mean the *Kandara*'s departure being delayed for some days.'

'That would be unfortunate. Our friends in Iraq need those weapons for the big push in Basra next month.'

'We must go at once. See if anything can be done.'

'Of course.' Hussein turned to Sara and the young men. 'You heard that. Bad trouble. We must get moving. Behave yourself, Sara.'

'Can we go out in the boat?'

'All right – the harbour only, Hamid.' He took his uncle's arm and helped him up to the entrance to the living room and they vanished inside.

'So – the boat it is.' Hamid looked through the Zeiss glasses at the *Sultan*. 'Yes, they're on the deck, the Bedouin and the old professor, and the two divers are getting ready to go down, from the looks of it.'

'We'll go and take a look.' Now that the moment had come, Sara was intensely nervous, her heart beating. If anything, she felt a little sick, but she tried to pull herself

together. 'Come on, Jasmine, let's get going.'
She picked up a parasol one of the women
had left on a bench and led the way down
to the inflatable tied up at the small jetty on
the beach below.

Hamid handed her in, then Jasmine.
Hassim sat in the prow, his AK across his
knees, and Hamid untied the line, stepped in
and sat in the stern.

Sara opened the parasol, Jasmine smiled,
and Hamid pressed the starter on the huge
outboard motor.

On the *Sultan* Hal Stone said, 'They're
coming. Sara's the one with the parasol. Her
companion is the same one as yesterday. The
boys are the same. How do we handle it?'

Dillon and Billy had discussed this already.
They came up from the diving platform.
Dillon pulled the zip of his diving jacket
down and slipped one of the Walthers inside.
Billy did the same.

'Caspar, you stand on the diving platform to take their line, Billy and I will jump

into the sea on the other side when they're closer, swim round underwater and deal with the boys. Hal, you just be ready for anything.'

Caspar said desperately, 'God forgive me, but it's as good as murder.'

'You want your daughter back, don't you?' Dillon said harshly. 'So pull yourself together. Come on, Billy.' He dodged round the mast to the other side of the deckhouse.

The sound of the inflatable's engine was somehow very loud and then it died. Sara's voice sounded, 'Good morning, Professor. Here we are again.'

Dillon and Billy dropped over the side, went four or five feet under the water and swam past the prow and towards the diving platform on its line, the inflatable beside it. Dillon gestured to the stern and went up, and Billy made for the prow. Hassim was leaning over. 'It's so clear, I can see the ship,' he said, and Billy's hand clutching the silenced Walther emerged. The first round caught the boy in the throat, the second between the eyes, hurling him back against Jasmine, who pushed at him with a shrill cry, sending him over into the water.

Hamid was quick, but not quick enough, for his AK was propped against the seat beside him. Realizing how hopeless it was, he flung himself over the stern as Dillon appeared, tearing at Dillon as he did so, leaving Dillon with no option but to pull the trigger several times.

Jasmine cried out again. Hal Stone leaned down at the side of Caspar and pulled her up.

'Oh, my God.' There was absolute horror in Sara's voice.

Caspar pulled the fold away, revealing his face. 'Sara – it's me.'

Dillon and Billy hauled themselves out of the water. Hamid floated up, rolled over, but there was no sign of Hassim.

'Daddy, it is *you*.'

'We've come for you, my darling.' He got down beside her in the inflatable. 'In a short while we'll be flying back to London in our own plane. Your mother's waiting for you.'

There was a vacant look on her face as

Hal Stone appeared and piled into the boat. 'Jasmine,' she asked. 'Where is she?'

'Quite safe in a cabin below, love.' Billy said.

Dillon nodded. 'When Hussein comes searching for you, they'll find Jasmine.'

He pressed the starter, the engine coughed into life and they raced towards the jetty.

'But not Hamid or Hassim,' she said dully. 'Was that necessary?'

'I'm afraid it was, my dear.' Hal Stone took out a bottle, shook a couple of pills into his palm and offered them. 'These will help to calm you, Sara.'

She turned to her father, 'Daddy?'

'Take them, darling.' She did so. He put an arm around her and she nestled against him, and a few moments later they swerved into the jetty and disembarked.

As they drove off in the station wagon, Billy at the wheel Dillon called Lacey. 'On our way. Fifteen minutes, no more.'

'Couldn't be better. Said isn't back yet and

I got his permission to do a test flight. Drive straight in the hangar. Parry will stand outside to show you which one. We'll load inside. Shall I notify Ferguson?'

'No, I'm superstitious. I'll do that when we're clear and on our way.'

It was so strange that the end of something which had been so difficult and painful seemed so simple. Minutes later they were loading the flight bags and boarding the Gulfstream. Parry closed the hatch and went and sat beside Lacey.

A quick word with an English-speaking Arab in the control tower who knew all about the test flight, and they were taking off. Lacey climbed steadily to 50,000 feet, then turned to Parry. 'Done it again, old boy. You take over and I'll go back and see how things are.'

So high in the incredible blue of that sky, Parry felt serene. He smiled as he veered to port to pass over distant Egypt and the Mediterranean beyond.

*   *   *

Caspar Rashid had taken off his robe and wrapped his daughter in it. She was very sleepy now, the pills taking their effect. At one moment, nestling in his arms, she said, 'What about Hussein? When he knows I'm gone, he'll be terribly angry. Hamid and Hassim were his men. It's a matter of honour.'

'He can do nothing,' Caspar said. 'Not now.'

'Some people would say he can do anything. He is the Hammer of God and he has killed twenty-seven soldiers. He has his friend, the Broker, to help him.' And then she was asleep.

They looked at each other. 'You have to admit the man's got an impressive track record,' Hal Stone said.

'Especially for somebody who was training to be a doctor before the war,' Dillon added.

Hal Stone frowned. 'I wonder who the Broker is?'

'A mystery man associated with Osama bin Laden,' Caspar said. 'When I was first approached, he was the man. A voice on a satellite phone, the kind you'd expect to hear at high table at any ancient Oxford college.'

'I'll let Ferguson know the good news.'

Dillon went and closeted himself at the other end of the cabin with his Codex Four.

To say that Ferguson was over the moon was an understatement. He demanded chapter and verse. 'Come on, everything, Dillon. The child's mother is going to be ecstatic, never mind Roper and Greta.'

So Dillon told him, leaving nothing out. 'It was a rough ride for Sara, especially being party to the shooting of the boys, but there was no other way.'

'I agree. A hell of a shock for Hussein Rashid.'

'You can say that again. Don't forget you were going to see his face plastered in every paper in the UK.'

'And every police station. By the time Blake Johnson's finished with him, the States will be off limits too. I wouldn't think his chances in Iraq would be very good. The girl hasn't said anything special about him, has she?'

'She was on pills, a bit woozy. She obviously thinks Hussein is hot stuff, and she mentioned his friend the Broker, then fell asleep.'

'The Broker again, which means Osama.

Roper will love the connection. So, ten or eleven hours. I'll see you at Farley.'

'Anything happened while we've been away?'

'Nothing much, apart from the Russian Mafia trying to do a number on Harry last night.'

'Good God. What happened?'

Ferguson told him. 'There's life in the old dog yet. Naturally he passed the whole thing to Roper for his intelligence pool and, believe it or not, the Broker came up again. And so did our old friend Chekov.'

'Maybe something should be done about that.'

'Taken care of. Harry sent an Express Delivery man round on his motorcycle with lilies.'

'Oh dear.'

'Oh dear indeed. I'll leave you now and spread the good word.'

Which he did. He told Greta first because, as usual, Molly was in theatre. 'I'd like you to pick her up and bring her back here. It's going to be about midnight when they get in. She'll want to see her daughter.'

'Leave it to me.'

Ferguson went into the computer room and found Roper. 'I think we deserve a drink together.'

'I agree with you.' Roper poured very large Scotches. 'To the team – great stuff once again.'

'And Harry didn't do too badly last night. He's dealt a sharp blow not only to the Russian Mafia in London, but to the Broker. That bastard is mixed up in everything.'

'Trouble is, we all know that but we don't know who he is. Nobody seems to.'

'Well, I'd say it's about time we found out.'

'By the way, I think you'll approve of this. Watch the screen,' said Roper. The picture that appeared was of Hussein Rashid, a good photo of him holding a pair of sunglasses. The one next to it showed him wearing the glasses. Underneath it said: *Hussein Rashid, known to be an associate of Osama bin Laden.*

There was more text beside it, the kind of stuff sub-editors would love to sink their teeth into, especially regarding Rashid's penchant for shooting soldiers. No mention of recent events.

'What are you doing with it?'

'It appears in most of the press in the morning, plus police stations, a certain amount of TV.'

'Well, let's hope the publicity kills off any hope of Hussein Rashid's turning up in England. He can go back to the struggle in Iraq as far as I'm concerned and get his head blown off. Good work, Roper. I'm going to my office.'

It was quiet, just the faint pings from cyberspace, the sizzle of static. Roper poured a Scotch and then he lit a cigarette and sat there looking at the man on the screen.

'You bastard,' he said. 'You're probably already on the way. Well, I'll be waiting.' He raised his glass and drank the whisky in a single swallow.

*   *   *

At the great house in Kafkar it had taken some time for anyone to realize that something was wrong. Khazid first became worried when the boating party failed to turn up for lunch at noon. When he had checked the *Sultan* through his glasses, there was no sign of anybody, or of any kind of activity.

He immediately called Hamid on his mobile phone. It didn't ring. Slightly worried now, he shouldered his AK-47, went down to the jetty, took one of the jet skis and drove off across the harbour towards the *Sultan*. There was a fishing boat a few yards away from it, two fishermen leaning over the side of the boat, pulling at something in the water.

When he got closer he saw that it was a body. Closer still, he switched off the jet ski motor and coasted in. Just then the body turned over in the current and he saw to his horror that it was Hamid.

He called the police, not that they had a reputation for efficiency. It took twenty minutes for the launch to appear because on the way from the jetty it came across the body of Hassim and stopped to pull it up out of the water as well. The two police officers were simple men, so Khazid, very young but his skills honed in the killing grounds of Baghdad, took charge. Ordering them to follow him, he approached the *Sultan* on the jet ski. By the time the police joined him he had searched the deserted ship, rescued Jasmine from the cabin and discovered from her the full horror. Not only that Sara had been abducted, but that the Bedouin in his robes on the boat had been her father. At that point he phoned Hussein Rashid on his mobile.

Hussein was a little way out of South Port beside the railway track, supervising the recovery of the derailed wagon. Stunned by the enormity of what he was hearing, he found difficulty in taking it in, but the facts were clear: two dead bodies and no Sara.

He pulled himself together. 'Clear the line. I want to make a call. We'll return as soon as possible.'

He phoned the airport and asked for control. It was Said who took the call. 'Hussein Rashid. Have you had a departure up there?'

'Yes, I'm still trying to work it out. I've been in town all morning. A Gulfstream belonging to the United Nations Ocean Survey has been here a couple of days. They had some engine trouble. Asked me if they could do a test flight, and as I was going to town I left them to it. They haven't come back. I'm getting worried. Where in the hell could they be?'

'Probably well over the Horn of Africa by now,' Hussein said and went in search of his uncle.

The old man was so shocked that he required the attention of his physician, who was waiting for them when they got to the house. It required servants to help carry the old man upstairs to his bedroom, and Dr Aziz accompanied him. He waved the servants away and checked the old man's heart. Hussein waited for the bad news.

Aziz turned, his face grave. 'It is not good. He's in a poor state of health anyway, much worse than you perhaps realized.' He opened his bag, took out a hypodermic and charged it. 'Hold his arm.' Hussein did so and Aziz gave the injection.

The old man groaned. His vacant eyes travelled the room and settled on Hussein. 'Why did you trust her?'

'Because she gave me her word,' Hussein said bleakly.

'They could not have done this thing, those who did it, unless she was willing. Her father, right under our noses!'

'The men from Baghdad – Dillon and Salter. It must be their work.'

'But her father, the apostate, the cursed one who turns his back on Allah! May every devil in hell wait for you, Caspar Rashid.' He shook his head. 'That he bears the name of our family shames me beyond belief.' He began to weep.

Aziz had retreated to the door to speak on the phone. Now he beckoned to Hussein. 'I've sent for an ambulance.'

'You think it's that bad?'

'Let me put it this way. It's a good thing Rashid Shipping invested in the development

of the hospital the past few years. We've got
the equipment to at least give him a fighting
chance.' He put an arm around Hussein's
shoulders. 'It's also good that your doctor is
Indian, and so are his nurses. There will be
no Muslim stupidities to make things difficult.'

'I think we've seen enough Muslim stupidities for one day,' Hussein said. 'Two friends
to bury, lads I soldiered with.' He shook his
head. 'Why did she betray me?'

'That's how you see it?'

'She was in shackles – I freed her. When
a dog named Ali ben Levi laid a hand on her,
I killed him. But more than that. I swore, a
hand on the Koran, that I would prove a true
husband to her in thought and deed when
she came of age. And no more than a couple
of hours before his death her grandfather put
her welfare in my hands when he placed her
in my care for the journey to Hazar. On my
honour, I swore to him to protect her always.'

'Can you be certain, my friend, it is not
just your pride which has been hurt?'

'Pride?' Hussein shrugged. 'What has this

miserable affair to do with such a shallow emotion?'

An approaching siren outside heralded the ambulance. Aziz went out to meet four porters in green hospital overalls carrying a stretcher, followed by two nurses in saris. Within a few moments the old man was manoeuvred on to a stretcher, drips were inserted, bottles held high as he was lifted.

'I'll come with you,' Hussein said.

'I'd rather you left it till later.'

The little column descended the stairs, accompanied by weeping women of the household, the servants visibly upset below. Hussein went down and moved among them. 'Pray for him, pray hard. Now attend to your work.'

Khazid stood by the open window, his AK hanging from his left shoulder. He looked sombre. They went outside on the terrace. Hussein took out a pack of American cigarettes, gave him one and a light. Khazid said, 'The look on Hamid's face. I think it was surprise.'

'Well, it would be. Come on, little brother,

you've seen enough of death to recognize it any way it comes. No shock there.'

'Not any more.'

'Well, then. You've been in touch with Said at the terminal. What did he have to say?'

'The Gulfstream, as you know, was UN. It turned up the other day, two pilots, this Professor Hal Stone, the archaeologist who has worked on this wreck in the harbour, and three men with him. One was your cousin Caspar Rashid, two were logged in as divers. Interestingly, the pilots had been here before – the other year.'

'And Hal Stone?'

'It would appear so. He came several times. They talked about it, the pilots, and the aircraft's insignia was definitely UN.'

'Which I don't believe for a moment. I'll tell you what I think. Dillon and Salter went to Baghdad, and we know what happened there. They then went back to London, probably having found out we were on our way to Hazar.'

'So?'

'You've been involved in enough of my

exploits in the past to know that the one essential ingredient is surprise. What greater surprise for them than attempting to snatch Sara from us virtually the moment we arrived? Who in hell would have expected it?'

'Yes, but there are still mysteries here. There must have been some sort of communication between them and Sara.'

'Possibly, but we'll never know without being told. Be a good soldier now. Go to the hospital and stand vigil for me.'

'And you?'

'You think it ends here, this business?' Hussein shook his head. 'Not if I can help it. Off you go and leave me to speak to the one man in the world who can truly help me.'

The Broker found little to comfort him at the news. Volkov had already called him with word about Max Chekov's unfortunate fate, and some of the best doctors in London were struggling to save his leg.

'What the hell is going on?' Volkov wanted to know. 'This could have a huge effect on our future plans.'

'You hardly need to make the point,' the Broker said, 'but it confirms what I suspected. Salter and his associates are totally ruthless men. Together with Dillon and Billy Salter, they pose a real threat.'

'Then I suggest you do something about it,' Volkov said. 'It's hardly the kind of news that will please President Putin,' and he ended the conversation.

The Broker sat there, brooding. An important kill was what was needed. Obviously to see Harry Salter stone cold dead in the market would be good, but Ferguson – that really would be something. But for that he needed Hussein more than ever. Even Putin would be impressed with Ferguson out of the way. He reached for his phone and called Hussein, only to receive the shocking news about Sara.

As Hussein spoke, he sat there, trying to take it all in, part of him unwilling to believe what had happened. When the account was finished, the Broker said, 'What do you want to do?'

'You wanted me to come to England anyway and deal with Ferguson. This would suit me very much. And not just for personal revenge. I refuse to leave Sara, wherever she is. I made a promise, a sacred oath to her grandfather. I intend to carry it out.'

'And so you shall. I will arrange things. General support in the UK will be from the Army of God network of spies and informers. I had meant to send Professor Dreq Khan to Hazar. I'll call him back at once to London and put him to work. He will be useful to you.'

'How do I come?'

'Plane to Paris, then the Channel Tunnel. You brought your special flight bag from Baghdad – the black one?'

'Of course.'

'Use the British passport. Hugh Darcy. I like that one. Get yourself a blazer. You'll look like an English gentleman who's been on holiday. The passport will support that. I'll arrange what happens to you when you reach London with Khan. When will you come?'

'Tomorrow if I can, but it depends on my uncle's health at the moment. This business has hit him hard.'

'I look forward to hearing from you.'

They disconnected, and the Broker called Professor Khan in Brussels, catching him at his hotel on his way out to dinner. He quickly filled him in on the situation in Hazar.

'My God,' Khan said. 'I can't believe that Caspar has managed to get his daughter back.'

'Helped by thoroughly ruthless men, which you would do well to remember. There is no point in your going to Hazar now. You are ordered back to London.'

'But Ferguson would move heaven and earth to get his hands on me.'

'Ferguson's got nothing to hold you on, you know that. He can't touch you. You'll book out of your hotel in the morning and catch the first flight to London. Is that clear? Osama himself has an interest in this affair.'

Which was enough. 'Of course. I'll do as you say.'

'And await further instructions.'

In the Gulfstream, everything had gone smoothly. After sleeping for five or six hours Sara had awakened, had something to eat and had talked a great deal with her father and Hal Stone, and later responded to some gentle probing from Dillon and even Billy.

She seemed very calm. Partly it was her nature, but Dillon considered it likely that to a certain extent it was also a kind of denial of what had gone before.

When you thought about it, the original circumstances had been extraordinary. The kidnap itself, the transfer to the war zone, the constant daily violence of Baghdad. Every impossible bad thing had been visited on her: the apparently genuine affection of her grandfather and yet leg irons, and then the final act in Hazar; the killing of Ali ben Levi when he laid hands on her; the sudden realization that Hussein was the Hammer of God, this

Arab fantasy figure from newspapers and television; the events which had developed with the *Sultan* and the shocking deaths of Hamid and Hassim, so close that there were bloodstains on her clothing. For an adult to cope with what had happened to her in the few months since the kidnapping would have been a near impossibility; for a young girl, little more than a child to most people, what hope could there be?

She dropped off to sleep again, and Dillon, turning in his seat to pour a Bushmills, found Hal Stone observing him.

'What do you think?' the professor asked. 'How in the hell is she ever going to get over what's happened?'

Her father was also dozing, an arm around her, and Dillon looked at them again. 'There's the mother, a pretty remarkable lady, but I don't know.' He shook his head. 'She's got a lot to cut free from.'

'Hussein Rashid, for one thing.'

'Oh, him most of all,' Dillon said.

Hal Stone nodded. 'At least there's a few thousand miles between them, and little likelihood of her ever having to see him again.'

'Let's hope so,' Dillon said.

Lacey's voice over the intercom announced, 'Farley Field in fifteen minutes. It's midnight right now, so that means we're moving into a new day, and if you're listening, Sara, God bless and welcome home.'

She sat up next to her father, slightly dazed as the plane coasted down. What happened next was all a strange confusion in which everything happened in slow motion: the Gulfstream landing, Parry opening the door, people outside, rain falling quite hard, then going down the steps ahead of her father and her mother crying out her name and throwing her arms about her fiercely.

They were all taken to the Holland Park safe house. Sitting across from Charles Ferguson, her arms around Sara, Molly Rashid said, 'What now?'

'You try to put some sanity into your lives again. At least you've nothing to fear from this man any more. We've seen to that. Here's the early edition of *The Times.*'

There was the photo of Hussein without his sunglasses at the bottom of the front page in the left-hand corner. The text read, 'Known associate of Osama bin Laden.'

Sara said, 'But that's Hussein.' There was panic on her face.

Ferguson said, 'You've nothing to worry about. With this photo in all the papers he'd never dare come to England.'

'Hussein Rashid, Hammer of God.' Sara's voice was suddenly very small, and she buried her face against her mother.

Several thousand miles away in the hospital at Hazar, Hussein and Khazid stood smoking on a balcony, the glass door open behind them to a corridor. Two nurses sat at a small table opposite, sipping tea, ready to provide back-up if necessary. A door opened, Aziz came out, and there was a glimpse behind him of Jemal festooned with cables and tubes, two more nurses at his bedside.

'How is he?' Hussein asked.

'We are in God's hands,' Aziz told him. 'That's all I can say.'

At that moment an alarm sounded, jarring, ugly, frightening. Aziz ran back in the room, followed by the two nurses in the corridor. The entire crash team was at work in seconds as Hussein and Khazid watched at the door. Not that any of it did the slightest good.

'Time of death –'

'Immaterial.' Hussein stood looking down at his uncle, then leaned over and kissed him on the forehead.

'See, my friend,' he said to Dr Aziz. 'They killed Hamid and Hassim to get Sara, now they kill my uncle. We can't have that, can we, Khazid?' He covered his uncle's face with the nearest sheet, turned and went out.

8

It was in Hussein's favour that his religion demanded so brief a period for the disposal of the body, no matter how important the individual. He needed action now, needed to get on with it, needed to channel the rage inside him.

The body was brought to the house and displayed in the entrance hall. The people who arranged such things worked through the night. The imam himself came to supervise, giving Hussein his blessing, of course, and not just because of his prowess in the war. He was, after all, not only the head of Rashid Shipping now, but of the clan itself, the possessor of great wealth, and his importance was shown by a new deference to him.

'So what will you do now about Sara?' the imam asked.

'As Allah wills.'

'You do not think her beyond hope?'

'Of course not. There were cruel influences at work.'

'What do you intend? A return to the war zone?'

'We'll see.' Hussein was keeping his own counsel. 'Let's bury my uncle first.'

The imam departed and Hussein went out on the terrace and lit a cigarette. Khazid, who had been listening, followed him.

'You wish to follow them to England, don't you?'

Hussein smiled. 'Now why would I do that?'

'Because it would be the most reckless thing to do. Can I come with you?'

'Why would you want to do such a thing?'

'Because we're friends who have been through hell together. Because I appreciate it could be a one-on-one mission but that you also need one person you can really rely on.'

'And you think that should be you?'

'It has been before. How do you plan to go?'

'Paris. Train to London.'

'I have both French and British passports, both excellent forgeries. And I speak French. Your alias?'

'Hugh Darcy, what the English call a toff. I used the passport last time I was in London and found the regimental tie of an English Guards officer tucked in my briefing case. It was the Broker's joke. The English still can't help touching their forelocks to a gentleman.'

'The Queen's son himself has served in such a regiment in Afghanistan,' Khazid said.

'There you are, then. OK, my friend, you can come as far as Paris. I'm not promising anything more. Now go and lie down. It'll be dawn soon, and we have three men to bury.'

'Something we're good at, something we've grown very used to.'

'Go on, little brother, good-night.'

Khazid went, and Hussein stood there thinking, then he went into the entrance hall where they had finished presenting his uncle.

He'd given the orders. No wailing women. At this stage, male servants only. Family members could join in on the morning, but for the moment, no.

He was restless, uncertain, and then he did an odd thing. He went into his uncle's small study, where there was a liquor cabinet for non-Muslim guests. He opened the lacquered doors and surveyed the contents, finally selecting a bottle of ice-cold Dom Perignon champagne that he found in the bar fridge. There was a strange excitement in him as he got a glass and walked out on the terrace. He stood there, thumbing the cork out.

Of course it was wrong, he knew that, but the night was dark and he had two comrades and his uncle to bury. Allah was merciful, Allah would understand. He raised his glass to Hassim and Hamid, then emptied the glass of champagne and threw the bottle from the terrace.

'Go to a good death, my friends, and watch over me in England,' he called.

*   *   *

Roper saw the local radio and television reports of the death of Jemal Rashid from a heart attack. There was television coverage of the cortège on its route to the mosque, Hussein leading the way. Roper recorded it and reported in to Ferguson, who was having breakfast at Cavendish Place.

'He won't like it,' Ferguson said. 'He'll blame us. The old boy died as a direct result of the affair.'

'Exactly.'

'What time did Doyle deliver the Rashids to Hampstead?'

'About three o'clock. We'll have to inform them.'

'I know. Dammit – I'll do it.'

At the house in Gulf Road, Caspar Rashid hadn't followed his wife to bed. She'd taken Sara. He couldn't sleep, and when the *Daily Telegraph* was shoved through the front door he found Hussein in a corner of the front page just like in *The Times*. And then the phone rang and it was Ferguson.

'Not very good news.' He told Caspar of the old man's death.

Caspar Rashid sat there taking it in. 'Dear God,' he said. 'Is there no end?'

Waiting at the airport in Paris, Dreq Khan bought a copy of *The Times* and nearly had a heart attack. He examined the papers on the newsstand and found Hussein's face staring out at him everywhere. He phoned the Broker at once.

'Have you seen the London papers?'

'Yes.'

'This must change everything. Obviously Hussein Rashid can't go to London. In fact, I wonder where he can go.'

'It changes nothing. You will still go to London and you will wait to hear from me. You still believe in the power of Osama?'

'Of course.'

'Now, get on your flight.' He switched his phone off and hesitated. No, Hussein would be busy with the funeral. He'd leave it till later.

*   *   *

A strange thing happened at the cemetery in Hazar. It rained suddenly, a real tropical downpour that prevented the wild exuberance that usually marked funerals. Hassim and Hamid had been wrapped in the green flag of Islam, as was proper for soldiers, the old man in something more subdued, and the rain fell and washed the dead, and Hussein and Khazid took their turns with a spade and shovelled dirt and said goodbye in their own way. Then it was back to the house for Hussein to receive condolences. Finally, about three o'clock in the afternoon, there was some peace.

Sitting on the terrace, having a coffee with Khazid, Hussein's phone went. It was the Broker.

'I knew you'd be busy with the funeral, so I didn't try to get you earlier.'

'What is it?'

'Trouble. Obviously Ferguson's used his power in certain quarters. Your face appears in a number of British newspapers, reported to be a known associate of Osama bin Laden, and possibly in Britain.'

'A clever bastard, Ferguson. This is to make it impossible for me to go. But it won't stop me.'

'If we try to put new plans into motion, it will be difficult and very awkward, not to say expensive.'

'Don't talk to me of expense. I know that Osama has great funds. I am a rich man myself from the death of my uncle. I'm going to England with you or without you, and I'm taking Khazid with me.'

'All right, all right. I'll get to work on it.'

'I can't wait, you must understand that.'

'I do. We'll get you to Algeria. There are many ways to move you around from there. Hold tight. I'll get back to you.'

At Holland Park, Roper sat at his computers and showed the TV footage of the funeral cortège in Hazar to Greta.

'What did Ferguson say?' she wanted to know.

'Poor sod.'

'Is that all?'

'Absolutely. He's gone to the Ministry of Defence for the rest of the day. Pass me the Scotch.'

'You're worse than a Russian with his vodka.'

'We drink for different reasons. What do you think?'

'About Hussein? Surely he's all washed up. Never mind coming to Britain, if he puts foot on a Baghdad street he's a dead man.'

'You think so?' He lit a cigarette. 'I'm wondering . . . After the Hannah Bernstein affair last year, when Igor Levin dumped his Russian masters and legged it to good old Dublin with his two sergeants, he phoned me and gave me his number.'

'A sort of challenge?'

'In a way. We couldn't track him legally in Dublin. I've spoken to him on the odd occasion, late at night, feeling cheesed off.'

'You never said.'

'I didn't think Ferguson would like it. The point is, I've told him about our current experience with our Russian friends and he's obliged me on occasion with his personal opinion. He knows quite a bit about what's been going on, with the Broker and all that.'

'Does he know who the Broker is?'

'I've told you – nobody does.'

'Does he know about Chekov?'

'Not from me – but I feel like telling him.'

'Well, don't stop because of me,' and she went and got herself a vodka.

Levin was sitting in the corner of Kelly's bar waiting for Chomsky when his mobile went and Roper said, 'It's me, homing in like Spock from cyberspace.'

'Tell me what happened in Baghdad. Did it get anywhere?'

'Let me give you a quick recap.' When he had finished, he added, 'What do you think?'

'I think you've got trouble, my friend. He'll be on somebody's doorstep before you know it. It's good to know Dillon and Billy can still cut the mustard.'

'More to the point, so can Harry. Greta's standing right next to me. Let her tell you.'

'Hey, lovely,' he said. 'So you're speaking to me?'

'I didn't know I could, you rogue.'

'Do you still love me?'

'Naturally.'

'So what's this about Harry?'

She told him, and he was thoroughly amused. 'Chekov on sticks. So much for the Moscow Mafia in London. Chomsky has just joined me. He sends his best.'

Roper had put the call on the speaker. 'Dillon and Billy aren't here. They've gone to see Harry at the Dark Man. He's put Ruby Moon behind the bar. Remember her?'

'How could I forget? Now I've got something interesting to tell you. Remember friend Popov? He now works for Michael Flynn at a firm called Scamrock Securities.'

'Yes, used to be chief of staff of the Provisional IRA years ago. A bit of a bruiser. What's your point?'

'This Broker, the mystery man who fronts for Osama, is apparently also heavily involved with Michael Flynn, who, it would seem, is in the mercenary business.'

262

'I could have told you about the mercenary bit.'

'But not the Broker, who is involved with Volkov. I don't know what's going to happen at Drumore with Belov International, but they will need a decent bunch to keep our soldiers out.'

'The decent bunch being ex-Provos.'

'I think you'll find Flynn is after the work.'

'Interesting.'

'And I happen to know that Volkov got Popov the job at Scamrock, and as we've said, Volkov means the Broker and the Broker means Osama.'

'Did Popov tell you he got the job from Volkov?'

Chomsky's voice was heard over the speaker, 'No, he didn't, the bastard. I've got my ear to Igor's phone, Roper. I'll deal with Popov.'

It was Greta who cut in, 'No, don't be stupid, Chomsky. You wait, see just what his involvement is before making a move.'

'Sorry, Major,' Chomsky said. 'You're right.'

'Of course she is,' Levin said. 'Take care, my friends. And call again.'

Roper switched off. 'Well, that was interesting, you must admit.'

'Yes, very much so,' Charles Ferguson said from the doorway. 'The things the help gets up to when one's away.'

'Oh dear,' Roper said.

'Well, it could be.' Charles Ferguson smiled. 'But I always wanted to get my hands on Levin, as you well know. He's too good to be sitting around on his backside.'

'Well, there you are then. As for me, I need a break. If Sergeant Doyle is available he can run me to the Dark Man.'

'And I'll go with you,' Greta said.

'All right, you talked me into it.'

Doyle phoned ahead, and when they got to the pub there was a booth waiting for them. They crowded round two tables, Ruby supervising things, Baxter and Hall as usual propping up the wall.

'My goodness, you did well in the car park

affray,' Ferguson said. 'For you, Harry, it's a return to your old form.'

'It never went away,' Billy said. 'It was just like the old days.'

'Yes, I was a very naughty boy in my youth,' Harry said. 'Let's have a drink, my love. Champagne all round.' He made as if he would slap Ruby's bottom, but managed to stop himself in time.

She smiled. 'That's a good boy, Harry,' and went off for the champagne.

Roper lit a cigarette and Greta said, 'What will you do when they ban the cigarettes?'

Roper shrugged, 'I'll figure out something. By the way, General. Item of news from Heathrow which may interest you. Professor Dreq Khan is back. Flew in from Brussels today.'

'That is interesting.'

'That bastard is untouchable,' Dillon said.

'And he knows it,' Roper put in.

'Makes you wonder why he's come back,' Greta said.

'If that means could there be a purpose to his return, I'm sure there is,' Roper said as

Ruby arrived with the champagne on a trolley.

At Ali Hassim's corner shop on Delamere Road, Professor Khan drew up in an Audi and went inside. Ali himself was behind the counter with a young girl in a smock, a niqab covering her entire face except for the eyes.

'Professor,' he said in Arabic. 'What a surprise.' He nodded to the girl. 'Come on,' he told Khan and led the way into the small back room. They sat opposite each other at the table.

'I thought you were to go to Hazar?' Ali said.

'Yes, but the news from Hazar is bad.'

'I've heard wild rumours. Can it be so?'

'Absolutely.'

'So the Rashid girl is once again at the house in Gulf Road.'

'The father, assisted by devils from hell, abducted her from Hazar. She'd gone there with her cousin and future husband, Hussein Rashid.'

'The Hammer of God himself. Praise be his name.'

'Praise indeed. They had left Baghdad, where her grandfather was killed by a car bomb in his Mercedes planted by Sunni dogs.'

'Curse them,' Ali said. 'What happened in Hazar?'

Khan gave him as close an account as he was capable of.

'So what happens now?' Ali inquired. 'Hussein Rashid is what he is and a great man, but there aren't just newspaper photos. One of my sweepers had to go to Hampstead police station for the new business, and there were two photos on the big noticeboard in the Most Wanted section. He could never come to England now.'

'So it would seem.' Khan got up. 'I must go.'

Ali accompanied him to the street door and stood by the Audi. Khan said, 'You never heard a word from Abu?' In fact he knew perfectly well that Abu was dead, shot by Greta Novikova, for Jamal had told him, but there had seemed little point informing Ali

Hassim. There were more important considerations, and he had sworn Jamal to secrecy.

Ali Hassim was remarkably calm in his reply. 'I think they murdered him. It is the only explanation. If he was alive somewhere he would have let us know by now.'

'May you meet in Paradise. I'll be in touch.'

As he got in the Audi, Ali said, 'Things go badly, am I right?'

'No. It is just a minor setback. Hold true to your faith in Allah and in Osama.'

'Always that.' Ali closed the door for him and Khan drove away.

Not long afterwards there was an emergency at the hospital and Molly Rashid was called. In an effort to return to some sort of normality, the three of them had intended to go to the cinema together, but the child in question at the hospital was only seven, heart valves were involved, and Molly really was very good at that.

So off she went, and when Caspar

suggested just the two of them going to the cinema Sara said she'd rather not. He tried talking to her as they worked their way through the light salad Molly had left for supper, but he got little response.

Later, in the main drawing room by the fire, he tried to make conversation and failed miserably. When he tried to discuss the future, it had disastrous results. His hesitant mention of school drew a totally negative response. She actually came alive.

'Do you really think that would be appropriate, Daddy? School blazer, jolly hockey sticks?'

'But look, love, you'll have to go to school. The law demands it.'

'The law!' There was a kind of fire in her eyes. 'What's that? All I saw for months were people shot, saw it on a regular basis. Your mother was killed along with seventy-two people in a market bombing in downtown Baghdad, your father in a car bomb by Sunnis.'

'I know, darling.' He tried to take her hand. She pulled away. 'You say Sunni as if you hate them.'

'Why not? At the villa, including servants we had over forty people, because those who lost their homes brought their families. People lived in tents in the grounds, and every week without fail somebody was killed. There were always three or four. One week was bad – ten in another market bombing.' She shrugged. 'And the dead were replaced by more refugees. It was a cycle. It never stopped. There was no time for school. I don't think I'll ever find time for it again.'

'Don't talk like that.'

She said, 'I think I'll go to bed.'

'Are you sure you're all right?' he asked.

'Oh, yes, you've got to look on the bright side.' She actually managed a smile. 'I've just thought of something good. At school we do our A-levels in a few years. Just think, I could probably do Advanced Arabic right now and get an A. Goodnight.'

He sat there thinking about it, and the terrible thing was that in spite of his learning, his degree, the books he had written, there was nothing he could do.

He stood quietly in the hall for a while,

then went upstairs and tiptoed to her bedroom door. She was crying, he could hear that well enough.

As he went back downstairs, he'd never felt so helpless in his life.

Hussein, frustrated and angry, hired a private jet from a company in Kuwait, a Citation X, a twin-engined plane requiring two pilots. The owners of the company were good Muslims, so it wasn't just a question of money when they realized who he was. The aircraft was reputed to be the fastest commercial jet in the world since the Concorde's departure. It was due the following day, but, like everyone in the Broker's world, he had no means of getting in touch with him and could only wait.

At last the call came and he took it, angry. 'What in hell is going on? I've already booked a private jet, it's coming tomorrow morning.'

'Excellent. I have a destination for you.'

'Where?'

271

'Algeria, just as I said. You, of course, did your combat training there in the camps. So did Dillon thirty years ago when he was nineteen and first joined the IRA. Do you know an area called the Khufra, on the coast?'

'No, I was in the desert two hundred miles west. It had a bad reputation. Why would we go there?'

'In a way, it's a message from me to Major Roper that I'm on to him. Ferguson's people had a hard time of it there last year. They're still wanted by the Algerian police for several murders. Anyway, it's a bad place, hundreds of miles of marsh, creeks, lots of boats and a hotbed of smuggling and drug-running. There is an airstrip, old hangars, a basic control tower.'

'And where do we go from there?'

'You will be met by Major Hakim Mahmoud of the Algerian Secret Police. Taking a bribe is second nature to him.'

'So there is no moral aim to anything he does?'

'Money talks, Hussein.'

'I've nothing against a thief, but he must

be an honest thief. I have no time to find this out by experience.'

'Well, my experience has been satisfactory.'

Hussein thought about it. 'Another thing, this business of leaving all communication on your side has to stop. I need to be able to communicate with you if things go wrong.'

'No – my privacy is non-negotiable, even for you. It has always been so, and so it will remain.'

'Then I'll make my own arrangements.'

'You won't be able to.'

'Look, let's discuss this. With my face plastered all over the papers I'm not very hopeful that I can get to England from France by any known airline or train. You must have some sort of plan for the final approach.'

'Yes, a small boat under cover of darkness from a port called St Denis in Brittany. There's a man named George Roman, English, used to be in the Navy. He specializes in high-priced clients who need to get into England the hard way.'

'Will he have weapons?'

'I presume you'll carry pistols, but any

heavy stuff you need you'll get in England. It's all provided for there. A man called Darcus Wellington. He was an actor for years, he still pops up in old British black-and-white films on television, but his homo-sexuality sent him to prison for a few years. That was his downfall, and crime followed. He also has a flair for make-up, which you'll find very useful. I'm hoping he may be able to disguise you in some way.'

'Excellent. Now how do we get from Khufra in Algeria to St Denis in Brittany?'

'Mahmoud is sorting that out now. He intends to place you as passengers on a small plane making a smuggling run to France. The drop will be at a private airfield where a car will be provided. You can drive to St Denis. If Roper checks Hazar, when he sees a Citation X booked he'll suspect it's for you. If he traces it to Algeria, it will simply fly away again.'

'Leaving us to our anonymity?'

'You've described it exactly, so there's no need for concern.'

'I suppose not.' There was reluctance in Hussein's voice.

'There you are, then. You may download all this on your laptop.'

'Of course. Anything else?'

'Yes, your special flight bag, the black one you brought from Baghdad.'

'What about it?'

'When you open it, you will find hidden in the lining of the bottom right-hand corner a gold and enamel brooch. Rather pretty. It slides open, and a button is inside. If you press it I will always call you straight back. You alone have such a device.'

'You bastard.'

'I've been called that before.' The Broker switched off.

ALGERIA

FRANCE

9

The Citation arrived on schedule, bearing two pilots named Selim and Ahmadi who came down to the house after they arrived and sat on the terrace with Hussein and Khazid and drank coffee.

'You know who I am?' Hussein asked.

Selim did the talking. 'Yes. We are here to serve you. It is an honour. Are you familiar with the plane?'

'No, but I hear great things about it. I am a pilot myself.'

'Excellent.' Eager to please, Selim added, 'You could try the controls. It's an experience flying this plane, I can tell you.'

'I'm sure it is, but there's no time to play. Your job is to get us to our destination, drop us off, and then you clear off. Is that understood?'

Ahmadi, the younger one, looked disappointed, but Selim was all business. 'And the destination?'

'Algeria.' Hussein opened a file on the table. 'All the details are there. I'll leave you to work out your flight plan.' He walked away, Khazid following him.

They went in the study, sat on either side of the desk, and Hussein opened a drawer, produced a couple of Walthers plus silencers and pushed one across. Two Colt .25's followed from the drawer, and they started to load them.

'You said you would promise me nothing beyond Paris,' Khazid said.

'So I did.'

'Now my future seems an inevitability.' Hussein had downloaded his laptop and discussed everything with him.

'So it would appear. Is there a problem?'

'Not at all. I am proud to serve.' Khazid finished loading one of the Colts. 'But I was thinking ahead to England and heavy artillery.'

'I've given you all the details. This Darcus Wellington will be taking care of our needs.'

'Darcus Wellington – such a ridiculous name. I marvel that such a person could involve himself in someone like the Broker's business.'

'Oh, I don't know. In a way it's rather like his playacting in films, I suppose, only in this case it's serious business.'

'And real bullets.' Khazid slammed the magazine into the butt of the Walther. 'What next?'

'Finish your packing. Travel light. I'll have a word with the pilots. Let's say we leave in one hour. Does that suit you?'

'Absolutely.' They walked out into the great entrance hall. 'Here we go. Into the war zone again,' Khazid said. 'Why us?'

Hussein put an arm about his shoulder. 'Because, little brother, Allah has ordained it. Though, to be honest, I can no longer look at religion in the same way I once did. It provides no solace for me.'

'So the business of war? Why do we take part in it?'

'Because it is our nature.'

'And is that all?'

'I'm afraid so. Now go and get ready.'

At his computers, Roper had inserted a trace element on aircraft movement at Hazar, though it was no big deal since traffic was so light. He was being served bacon sandwiches and tea by Sergeant Doyle when the signal sounded.

'Get Dillon for me,' he said.

'He's in the dining room with the Major.'

Doyle cleared off and Roper checked into a series of screen images. Dillon and Greta appeared.

'What's the good word?' Dillon demanded.

'Citation X left Kuwait under charter to Rashid Shipping, landed at Hazar three hours ago. It's departed under a flight plan taking it to Khufra in Algeria.'

'Not that dump. What in the hell does he have to go there for?'

'Let's look at this. If he's on his way to anywhere, you can bet the Broker has organized it. Chartering the Citation was a way of Hussein saying: "It's me. What are you going to do about it?" because he and the Broker know we must be watching.'

'But why Khufra?' Greta asked. 'Look what we went through there last year.'

'The Broker knows that and he knows I'm monitoring him, so it's his way of mocking me. And I know that you know that kind of thing. Khufra, by its nature, is a hotbed of smuggling and drug-running, by boat as well as air, and it's a perfect place for Hussein to drop out of sight. My bet is the Citation leaves him there.'

'And what happens to him?' Greta asked.

'Across the water, Spain is convenient. Who knows?'

'One thing is certain,' she said. 'He can't be coming to England, not with his face plastered all over the place.'

'Well, he isn't going to stay in Algeria, there wouldn't be any point. As for France, that's a possibility.'

'Actually, some of the papers on the Continent picked up the picture too,' Roper said. He tapped some keys and page four of the previous day's *Le Monde* appeared, with Hussein's photo. 'There you are, page four, but it's enough.'

'So what's his next move?' Dillon asked.

'I think he'll keep his head down,' Greta said.

'No,' Dillon said. 'There is one thing I'm sure of. Hiring the Citation, flaunting it with the trip to Algeria, it has to have reason to it. He has a purpose, and sooner or later it's bound to become clear what that purpose is. We'll just have to wait.'

At the Hampshire house, Molly and Caspar, in the kitchen, discussed Sara. They could see Sara in the garden on a bench on the terrace reading a book.

'She's pretending,' Caspar said. 'You can tell.'

'Have you discussed school with her again?' Molly asked.

'For God's sake, it's far too soon for that. She'd need a new school anyway, fresh faces, another environment, perhaps a boarding school.'

'Whatever it is, it's got to be faced, this situation.' Molly reached for the coffee pot and poured another cup. 'And appropriate treatment found.'

'You're talking about her as if she's a patient,' Caspar said. 'But that's what doctors do, I suppose. Personally, I think we need to make a firm decision.'

'And what's that supposed to mean?'

'Tell her we've decided she needn't go back to her old school and needn't go back to any school for six months. Let her vegetate, find her own feet.'

Beyond his wife through the window, he saw that Sara had gone from the bench. She was, in fact, in the hall, but he didn't know that.

Molly said, 'I don't think that's any good at all. To be frank with you, I had a long chat on the phone this morning with Professor Janet Hardcastle. She was very interested in the case, and has offered to take her on.'

In spite of the fact that the lady in question was one of the most eminent psychiatrists in the country, Caspar was not impressed. 'Dammit, Molly, psychiatrists now. What about some simple loving kindness? We should stop trying to understand until she understands herself, because she is capable of that. She's a hugely intelligent girl.'

Sara appeared at the door. 'Oh, that's all right. I don't mind playing word games with Professor Hardcastle, but I'm still not going back to school. I feel like a rest now. I'll go to my room.'

She put the book she had been reading on the side and went out. Caspar picked it up, glanced at his wife and held it out to her without a word. It was the Koran in Arabic.

Roper had enjoyed his chat with Igor Levin, the former boy wonder of the GRU, for Levin also had medals from all those dubious Kremlin wars, had sweated in Afghanistan, had got close enough to a Chechen general to cut his throat. Roper remembered him as a so-called commercial attaché working for GRU Head of Station, Colonel Boris Luzhkov, in London, so now, on a whim, he contacted Luzhkov on his private number at the Embassy of the Russian Federation situated in Kensington Gardens.

Luzhkov answered at once in Russian, and Roper, who actually spoke rather decent Russian, said in English, 'Cut that out, Boris.'

'Who is it?' Boris asked.

'Roper.'

'My God – to what do I owe this pleasure?'

'Nothing special. I was just talking to Igor Levin in Dublin and that put me in mind of you.'

As every attempt made by Luzhkov to contact Levin had been rebuffed, he was intrigued. 'How is Igor?'

'Just enjoying life. As for his pals, Chomsky works for lawyers and Popov is with a security firm. But then you know this.'

'Do I?'

'The thing is, I'd have thought that futile attempt to knock off Blake Johnson would have taught you Russians a lesson. So what was all this nonsense with Stransky and his goons at Harry's Place? And Chekov? I'm shocked. Have they succeeded in saving the leg, by the way?'

'My dear Giles, I have no comment at this time.'

'I bet you haven't, and what's with Giles? How did you discover that? It's a closely guarded secret!'

'Like any good spy, I have my sources. May I also make a comment? There are people who to think that Boris Luzhkov is a stumblebum – an old buffer long past his best, if there ever was a best. But Ivan Stransky has a brain the size of a pea, and as for Chekov, his brain is between his legs. To anyone with half a brain the size of Harry Salter's property empire and bank balance should have given pause for thought all by themselves.'

'I for one never fell for your act, Boris. Anyway, is there going to be a new chief executive officer at Belov International? Because the one you've got now can't do much more than go over to Drumore Place and sit on the terrace in a wheelchair, an umbrella over his head. Mind you, he'd be all right for the weekends. It only rains five days a week in Ireland.'

Luzhkov finally managed to stop laughing. 'God, but you've cheered me up.'

'So who's going to run the show? You can tell me.'

'Of course. They've managed to save Chekov's leg, but real recovery will take a very long time. I might as well tell you, because you'll find out anyway. General Volkov will assume command for the moment.'

'Surprise, surprise, the President's right-hand man.'

'Exactly. Anything else?'

'Yes – for Volkov's ears, and perhaps for his friend, the Broker.'

Luzhkov's voice changed slightly to careful. 'Yes?'

'You've seen the press releases in the news-papers on Hussein Rashid?'

'I could hardly miss them.'

'How about the full story on the other Rashid –, the thirteen-year-old daughter kidnapped by Army of God fanatics for the grandfather in Iraq? It's Hussein who's supposed to marry her when she comes of age.'

'I've heard certain whispers.'

'Well, Hussein took the girl down to Hazar and Dillon and Billy and the child's father swooped down, stole her from right under his nose and flew off to good old Blighty, leaving two of his best men dead.'

'Oh dear. Let me put my supposedly stupid mind to this. These photos in the newspapers – they are supposed to keep Hussein out of Britain?'

'Something like that, just for the moment, and to make the family feel secure.'

'I'm not so sure it will work.'

'Why not?'

'Because he's the Hammer of God. He won't want to let his audience down.'

'That's what I think too,' Roper said.

'Do you mind if I share all this with Volkov?'

'That's why I told you.' At that moment Greta came in. 'Greta sends her best. She's thriving.'

'My God, how I miss that girl. Such a beauty.'

Roper switched off and Greta said, 'Who was that?'

'Luzhkov.' Roper smiled. 'I was feeling lonely.'

The Citation crossed Saudi Arabia, Egypt, then northern Libya, following the coast at enormous speed and most of the time at 50,000 feet. Selim invited Hussein to take the controls when they were over Libya, and, changing his mind, Hussein did so for a while, revelling in it.

Later, as they approached their destination, Selim came back to consult him. 'I'm worried about fuel. Oran is only a couple of hundred miles away from Khufra. I think we should stop and refuel there.'

Hussein thought about it. Private planes like the Citation were used only by the rich and always received preferential treatment. They should be safe enough.

'All right.'

So Oran it was. He used the British passport and Khazid a French one in the name
of Henri Duval. They got out to stretch their
legs. Ahmadi took their passports to the
office for them, but he was waved away.

'So simple,' Khazid said.

'Yes, but not to be taken for granted,'
Hussein replied. 'There could be a time when
they're all over us.'

'As Allah wills.'

'Perhaps, but what if it's all actually in our
own hands?'

'I am a simple man, my friend. I accept
what I know and do what I'm told.'

'And I prefer you that way.' Hussein
climbed back in the plane, Khazid followed,
then they soared again into an evening sky,
climbing to no more than 10,000 feet. Later
they saw the marshes of the Khufra sprawled
on the desert below, the creeks stretching out
to the sea, here and there a dhow, sails
bulging in the wind and sometimes motorboats and the odd freighter.

They descended to 1,000 feet and Selim
saw the runway to the left of them, the

control tower and two hangars, but oddly there was no contact from the control tower. Selim circled again and passed over the town and small harbour. There was a jetty at one point, an old Eagle float plane tied up beside it.

Selim said, 'An Eagle Amphibian. You can lower the wheels beneath the floats and taxi out of the water onto shore. Years old, but sturdy. They were built for bush flying in places like Canada.'

He slowed right down and they almost seemed to hang there suspended. 'Strange, still no response from the tower,' Hussein pondered, every sense alert. 'This is what you do. Land, go to the far end of the runway and turn for your take-off. We'll get out. Ahmadi closes the hatch, and we wait. If the right people are here, they'll come for us. If there is a problem, I fire a shot and you get the hell out of here.'

Selim immediately protested. 'We can't leave you. It would bring great shame upon us.'

'I order it, my friend. This is our business.'

He put an arm around Khazid. 'We're very good at it.'

'Then I obey you with deep regret,' Selim said.

They circled the runway, but nothing moved. It was strange, the two hangars with doors open, but no sign of life, and it was getting darker by the minute.

'Down we go,' Hussein said. 'You take both flight bags.'

'Good thing we travel light.' Khazid smiled.

'You need a suit, you buy a suit, that's my motto. Here we go again, little brother.'

The Citation dropped in and rolled along the runway. It turned at the far end, the reeds around the airstrip turbulent in the jet stream. Ahmadi turned the handle, thrusting the hatch out as the steps fell. Khazid went down, crouching in the blast. Hussein followed, turned to glance up at Ahmadi, and there was a roar as two Land Rovers emerged from one of the hangars at full speed and turned onto the runway.

'Close it!' Hussein called, and Ahmadi did as he was told, slamming the hatch shut.

Hussein pulled out his Walther, firing into the air. Selim boosted power and roared down the runway, forcing the Land Rovers to swerve to each side. The Citation rose and lifted in the air at the end of the runway.

Khazid was preparing to shoot. Hussein ordered him, 'Into the reeds – go now. Keep in touch with your mobile. I'll hold them off.' He took careful aim and shot the front offside tyre of the leading vehicle. It swerved violently, throwing the man next to the driver out. The other swerved past and came on, four men in some kind of khaki police uniform.

Hussein fired again, this time at the second Land Rover, splintering the windscreen. He turned and plunged into the reeds, and immediately fell foul of a rusting cable hidden in the undergrowth. He went headlong and they were all over him, boot and fist everywhere. He was pulled to his feet, and someone found his Walther, but not the Colt. He had left that in his flight bag with Khazid.

An overweight, bearded captain appeared to be in charge. One of the men gave him the Walther. 'Nice one. I appreciate your gift.'

'Ah, a cool customer. You are here to see Major Hakim Mahmoud of the Algerian Secret Police?'

'If he's available.'

'Oh, yes. You must be an important man. That was a wonderful plane.' One of his men emerged from the reeds. 'Any sign of the other one?'

'No, he's gone, Captain.'

'Never mind.' The three men in the other Land Rover were fitting the spare tyre. 'I'll be in the office, but hurry up, I want to get back to the fort. They say it's going to rain.' He turned to Hussein, 'I am Captain Ali. I'm sure we'll get along.' He patted his face. 'You are a handsome young man.' Hussein got in the Land Rover between two policemen and they drove away.

Behind them, well hidden in the reeds, Khazid had heard everything and watched them go, leaving the three men wrestling with the damaged tyre. One of them was a sergeant, the one who had been thrown out of the vehicle. Khazid got his Walther out, unzipped his case and found a Carswell silencer. Quickly he screwed it in place just as the two men on the tyre had it fixed.

'Good,' the sergeant said. 'Let's go.'

Khazid put down the flight bags and stepped out of the reeds, Walther in hand. He whistled, they all turned, and he shot the sergeant between the eyes. The other two were completely shocked.

'The captain said he was going to the office. Where is that?'

'The bottom of the control tower,' one man said.

'Excellent. Now this fort he mentioned?'

The second man was shaking with fear, so it was left to the other again. 'The old Foreign Legion fort a half a mile down the road to the left.'

'Thank you.'

Khazid shot both of them dead, not because of any conscious cruelty, but because he had no choice in the matter if he was to rescue his friend in one piece. He put the flight bags in the passenger seat, pausing only

297

to pull up the canvas roof of the Land Rover because it would give him some sort of cover. He drove along the runway towards the control tower, taking his time, but when he got there the other Land Rover had gone.

It was dark now, with no need for caution. The door was unlocked, he opened it and found a light switch. It was a reception area. He went behind a counter, opened the door marked office and turned on the light.

The man behind the desk was seated in a swivel chair, and from the state of him had obviously had a bad time of it, his hands handcuffed behind his back. His final end had been a bullet in the head. He was presumably Major Hakim Mahmoud. He looked around him. There was a large torch on the table, which worked when he tried it. He left it on, switched off the light and went out to the Land Rover. Now for the fort.

It was cold, surprisingly cold, and Hussein shivered as three of the policemen manhandled him out of the Land Rover. There

was a fort, he could see that. The green and
white flag with the red crescent and star, the
flag of Algeria, flared in the lights from the
battlements over his head, and there were
two lighted braziers on either side of the gate
they passed through, a sentry with a rifle
beside each brazier.

They paused at the bottom of some steps
leading up to the battlements and got Hussein
out. Captain Ali was seated on a stone bench
drinking whisky. He was obviously that kind
of Muslim. Hussein felt only contempt. The
man resembled a disease you wanted to
stamp out.

'Major Hakim Mahmoud was a bad man
– an evil man. He traded with drug dealers,
all things evil, always his hand out for money.
So, if you dealt with him, you must be both
very wicked and very rich.'

'Not really.'

'I want to know who you are, and who
are your companions.'

'It's against the rules.'

'Rules? So you want to play games? You
think you must now brace yourself to bear

some physical force, don't you? Well, it's not necessary. In the old days they trained Foreign Legionnaires here, hard men who needed to be controlled, but the French were very practical people. They had the Hole over by the wall there. Very uncomfortable.'

'I'm sure it is.'

'I mean, rats – you either like them or you don't.'

'Very intelligent creatures, rats,' Hussein told him.

Above the Hole was a windlass coiled with rope, and a turning handle. 'One of you, bring a light and we'll let him see what he's up against.' Another policemen was already holding a robe.

They made Hussein put his foot in a kind of stirrup and lowered him. It was cold and damp, and he landed in two feet of water. It was raining, and water was running down the sides of the hole. They tossed the robe down to him and he put it on. There was a scurrying sound. The rope was pulled back up.

He sat on a stone shelf, switched on the

light and found two rats, eyes glinting in the beam. They seemed curiously friendly.

'Now behave yourselves,' he said in Arabic.

The rain increased its force, and he shook his head. 'Khazid, where are you?' he said softly.

Khazid drove down the road in the heavy rain, grateful for the canvas roof. He could see the fort up ahead, the flag hanging limply. There wasn't a sentry box, just a stone alcove from the old days, a sentry sitting smoking a cigarette, another one standing beside him. They looked at Khazid curiously. The one who was standing came forward. 'Who are you? What do you want?'

'Secret police. Where would I find Captain Ali and the prisoner he just brought in from the airfield?'

The policeman raised his rifle a little. 'Secret police? I don't know you.'

The Walther and the silencer were on the seat beside him. Khazid picked it up and shot the policeman between the eyes. The other man cried out and leapt to his feet.

Khazid said, 'Stand still, I don't want to miss you.' The man was terrified and dropped his rifle. 'So tell me.'

'He put the prisoner in the Hole. It's on the battlements. I don't know where he is himself. He may be in the fort.'

Khazid got out and left the Land Rover where it was. 'This place, the Hole,' he said to the sentry. 'Lead the way.'

The man did so, mounting the stairs to the battlements. There was no sign of Captain Ali, but there were lights down in the barracks, and laughter. The Hole was self-evident, with its windlass.

'Are you in one piece, brother?' Khazid called.

'Other than the rats trying for the odd nibble, I'm fine,' Hussein called. 'I've missed you, little brother.'

'I'm sure you have.' Khazid nodded to the policeman. 'Lower the stirrup.'

The man exerted himself on the ancient handle, the rope went down and Hussein called, 'That's fine,' and said to the rats, 'Goodbye, my friends.' The windlass creaked again, the man pushing against the weight, and Hussein emerged.

'I stink like an old sow.'

'But you're in one piece, which is more than I can say for the late Major Hakim Mahmoud.'

'May he rest in peace. Remind me to let the Broker know.'

'He should have known.'

A door banged. A moment later there were footsteps at the other end of the battlements and Captain Ali appeared, looking rather incongruous, an umbrella over his head. He was humming to himself and looking down, but not for long.

'It's you,' he said stupidly.

'Yes, it is.' Hussein patted his pockets and found the Walther.

Strangely enough, fat Ali didn't show fear, although that could have been because of the bottle of whisky in his left hand.

'I knew you were somebody special, just from that plane. If you're going to shoot me, at least tell me who you are.'

'My name is Hussein Rashid. They know me in Baghdad.'

'Merciful heaven, they know you everywhere in the Arab world.'

'I should kill you, but I was trained in Algerian camps.'

'Which makes us brothers in a way,' Ali said eagerly.

'Anything but. Down you go. The rats are waiting.'

'My thanks. You are a great man.'

Ali stuck his foot in the stirrup. It took all the policeman's strength to control the weight, and Khazid had to help.

Ali's voice echoed up. 'I see what you mean. I don't know what you are up to, but go to a good grave, my friend.'

'Let's get out of here,' Hussein said to Khazid. He nodded at the frightened policeman. 'Bring him with you.'

They went down to the Land Rover. The policeman was terrified, expecting death at any minute.

Hussein said, 'Which way to town?' The man pointed. 'There's been enough killing for one night. Run like hell,' Hussein said, and the man took off.

Khazid said, 'I'd say we're in a bad fix. We need to get out of here fast, and Brittany is a hell of a long way off.'

Hussein got in beside him. 'I've had an idea. What about flying out?'

Khazid started the engine. 'But we haven't got a plane.'

'Who says we haven't?' They drove quickly away.

There was a board on a building at the end of the jetty which said *CAN-AIR*, whatever that was supposed to mean, but no lights showed at any of the windows beneath it and everything was quiet. Here and there was a light in some of the craft moored in the harbour, and occasionally the sound of faint laughter drifted from the cafés in the web of narrow streets, but they didn't care about any of that.

Khazid had the torch he had taken from the control tower and they used it to examine the pod enclosing the fuel tanks. It was so old-fashioned there was a dipstick. It registered about two-thirds full.

'Not bad,' Hussein said.

'You still haven't told me where we're going.'

'The Balearic Islands. Majorca, the largest, would be best. The airport at Palma operates international flights, dozens a day, awash with tourists. There are flights to almost anywhere.'

'Are you saying we take a chance on a direct flight to England?'

'No, that would be too much of a risk, but there are plenty of flights from Majorca to France, crammed with holiday-makers going home. That's a different proposition.'

On the far side of the harbour a police car turned onto the far jetty and two officers got out. A moment later, another came down from the town and parked behind it.

'Do you think that could be trouble?' Khazid asked. 'Maybe the captain is covering his back. We did leave several dead men.'

'I've no intention of waiting to find out. Get in.'

He got the door open, Khazid slipped the line, pulled it in and joined him. They strapped themselves in and Hussein fired the engine and let the plane float away. He started to taxi through the darkness towards the harbour entrance, which was well lit. He moved near the pier, and beyond was only darkness.

Khazid was looking out and saw one of the police cars racing round. 'I think we've managed to attract some police attention.'

'Well, whatever they want, it's too late now.' Hussein turned into the wind and boosted power. He pulled back the column at exactly the right moment and the Eagle climbed effortlessly over the darkness of the sea. Here and there they could see the lights of boats below.

'How long to Majorca?' Khazid asked.

'I'll take my time. I'll use less fuel if I don't push this old bucket too hard. Besides, I like it. Maybe three and a half hours – something like that. Then we'll check the plane situation at Palma. I've got a good feeling. It all worked out. It could have been much worse.' He levelled off at 5,000 feet and put the plane on automatic. 'God, I stink.' He looked down at the soiled suit. 'I don't know what Armani would think.'

'You're the man who said, "If you need a suit, you buy a suit." You'll be OK at the airport.'

'Yes, Palma's sophisticated enough. I expect the airport's full of boutiques. Open my flight bag for me. In the bottom right corner there's a brooch in the lining.' Khazid found it. Hussein slid back the top and found the button.

'Our lifeline to the Broker.' He pressed it and put the brooch in his pocket.

It was amazing how quickly the response came, and the Broker listened quietly to Hussein's story.

'A pity about Major Mahmoud. A valued ally.'

'You'll replace him soon enough.'

'So what happens now?'

'We'll park the seaplane when we get there, then we'll go to the airport. You check on flights for us, and call me back.'

A half hour later, the Broker did so. 'There

are a lot of flights to French destinations, including a number of cheap basic flights to provincial airports – the kind of flights where they pack you in and don't even offer a cup of coffee, but they don't give a damn who you are. One such destination is Rennes, which is less than fifty miles by train from St Malo on the Brittany coast. St Denis is only twelve miles outside St Malo. That should be your best bet. The booking is your affair.' He rang off.

'The insolence of this man is unique,' Khazid said. 'With his so-called perfect world showing signs of cracking, his condescension is breathtaking.'

'Don't let it get to you.' Hussein put things back on manual. 'Try and get some sleep. I'm going to fly the plane.' He took the control column, leaned back and started to enjoy himself.

At four o'clock, a half-moon giving everything a faint luminosity, they came in from the sea at 500 feet, turning parallel to the coast looking for just the right sort of place. It was

Khazid who finally noticed one, a small crescent-shaped cove beneath a steep headland at the north end of the island. There were many opulent villas on the coast on either side of it, and a lonely jetty, no boats tied up.

'I think people will think an item like a private aircraft properly belongs to somebody in a rich man's area like this.'

'It does have a certain logic.'

Hussein landed on the sea beyond the cove and taxied in, his engines reduced to a muted rumble. They coasted in and he cut the engines, allowing small waves to edge the plane against the jetty, then opened the door and got out, followed by Khazid with the curved rope of the line in one hand. He tied up, then got the two flight bags, passing his to Hussein. There was a line of steps and a decent path beyond.

There was a pine wood at the top of the hill and the path led them through it to an extensive vineyard beyond. There were villas here and there, cottages, but it was a scattered sort of landscape.

'Coats off,' Hussein said. 'Try to fit in, look casual.'

310

The sky was pink, then gold; the sun rose, and they occasionally saw people in the distance. It was all incredibly beautiful. Reaching the main road, they came to their first village, and already life was stirring.

'Well?' Khazid said. 'What next?'

'I don't know.' At that moment they came to the end of the village and found an inn with a pleasant garden, a young woman brushing a terrace.

She smiled and said good morning in Spanish, and Hussein answered in English. Khazid followed, putting on a slight French accent.

'Good morning, mademoiselle. I see no sign of a bus service.'

'Not until noon. Do you have you a problem?'

He said smoothly, 'Our problem is a hire car which gave up the ghost on us, I'm afraid, and I've tried the company's number but there is no reply.'

'And we have a plane at noon,' Hussein added.

'Oh, I see. So you need to get to Palma?'

'As soon as possible.'

'As it happens, my barman, Juan, is going to town in the truck for supplies after he's had his breakfast. I'm sure you could come to an agreement with him. I'll go and have a word. Perhaps you would like some coffee and rolls while you're waiting?'

She went out and they sat at a small table. 'We do have another problem,' Hussein said. 'The plane we didn't get, the one doing some sort of drug run from Khufra to France, was going to drop us off illegally – which meant that we could still keep our weapons.'

'So no guns,' Khazid said.

'And none from Roman. Everything we need will be provided by Darcus Wellington, that's what the Broker said.'

'OK. Let's get it over with.' Khazid transferred the two Walthers and the Colt .25s into his pockets. 'It breaks my heart, but if it must be done . . .' He shrugged. 'I'll go and find a drain.'

He moved into the vineyard beside the garden and disappeared. The girl returned with coffee, rolls and marmalade. She wrinkled her nose. 'What happened to you?'

'I was trying to fix the car, and fell into a ditch beside it.'

'If you want to use the washroom, feel free. It's the door next to the bar. There's a shower.'

So in he went, saying hello to a young man, presumably Juan, cleaning the bar top. In the washroom he examined himself, a sorry sight, then stripped his clothes and showered and towelled himself vigorously, which made him look better, although the clothes were still dreadful. When he went back, Khazid was flirting outrageously with the girl and drinking red wine she had supplied.

'Come on, mon ami,' he said. 'Try a glass. It's good for the heart.' And Hussein, knowing what he was trying to do, took the wine down manfully.

Juan appeared, goodbyes were said and they got in the rear of the open truck, their backs against the driver's cabin, and departed.

'Nice girl,' Khazid said. 'Just think. A

couple of real desperadoes like us, and she never knew.'

'Better for her, I think, much better.' Hussein leaned back and closed his eyes in the early morning sun.

At the airport, they gave Juan fifty dollars, then searched the numerous shops and selected a men's boutique. Hussein kept his flight bag, but gave Khazid his British passport on the off chance they'd allow him to get both tickets. No one knew better than he did how slipshod matters of security could be, especially when dealing with large numbers of people.

In the boutique, the proprietor and an assistant who was obviously his boyfriend tut-tutted when he explained about the accident and set about clothing him from head to toe. Underwear, socks of silk, shirts, white and blue, an expensive tan summer suit from Armani and tan brogues finished things off. He stood and examined himself in the mirror. Yes, it would do for now. He noticed a khaki trenchcoat on a rail, bought that, too, and was just paying for it all when Khazid returned.

'My goodness, but you look stylish,' he said.

'Flattery is the last thing I need. What about the tickets?'

'Easy. The girl was French, and I do French well. Two tickets in row E, taking off for Rennes at eleven-thirty. We're returning holiday-makers.'

'Good. Hide those extra passports in the special compartment in your flight bag. We'll buy a suitcase and put both flight bags inside so they can go in the hold. I'm going to speak to the Broker.'

Which he did, calling him in with the panic button, sitting in the corner of the airport lounge when they spoke.

'We had to dispose of our guns, an unlooked-for problem.'

'There's nothing I can do about that, but you'll be all right when you reach England. Darcus Wellington may surprise you.'

'You'll confirm to George Roman we're on the way?'

'All taken care of.'

The Broker departed, and Hussein said to Khazid, 'A decent meal, I think, is what we need now.'

'I couldn't agree more.' They made their way to one of the restaurants.

IRELAND

LONDON

10

It had been the previous day, twenty-four hours before Hussein and Khazid reached Majorca, when Roper had astonished Boris Luzhkov with his candid conversation. Obviously Luzhkov couldn't speak to the Broker, but Volkov was a different matter. Luzhkov phoned him on his secure line at the Kremlin.

'I've got something for you – rather interesting.'

'Well, that makes a change.'

'I've just had a conversation with Roper at Holland Park.'

'Have you, by God? Tell me everything.'

It couldn't be quite everything, for at that stage of the game Hussein had just buried his uncle and his two friends. Admittedly, the

photo planted by Roper in the British newspapers had just appeared, but the Broker hadn't
made any mention to Volkov of Hussein's
determination still to travel to England.

'What do you think?' Luzhkov said. 'Is
Roper a loose cannon?'

'No, everything he does has a purpose,'
replied Volkov. 'So he tells you Greta is
working for Charles Ferguson. We suspected
that anyway. He talks of Levin in Dublin. We
know very well that Levin is in Dublin, and
his sergeants. This Rashid business, the girl
in Hazar, is interesting, though hardly
surprising with Dillon and that wretched
Salter involved. Personally, the idea that
Hussein would for any reason come to
England now confirms to me that it would
be stupid. In my opinion, any hopes of using
his services for any of our own problems must
go out of the window. But we've still got to
do something about Ferguson. This unholy
alliance with Dillon and Harry Salter and all
his criminal connections is unacceptable.'

'And so we see even the Moscow Mafia
confounded.' Luzhkov laughed. 'Now that

Chekov is out of the picture for a while, what do you intend to do?'

'I'm not certain, but it must be something, and soon.'

'It needs to be something to make people sit up and take notice,' Luzhkov told him. 'Physical violence may be old-fashioned, but Stransky and Chekov certainly got the point.'

'A great many people, not only in our line of work, but in the criminal underworld, got the message that Harry Salter is back in business.'

'If he ever went away.'

'He's doing a very clever thing, Boris, and even the police reluctantly approve. The things he does, he does to bad people, unpopular people.'

'Like Russians in London,' Luzhkov said. 'Billionaire oligarchs and foot soldiers in the Mafia. So they got a rough passage. Why should ordinary Londoners care?'

'I'd love to take Salter down,' Volkov said.

'You'd never get near him, just the way you'd never get near Ferguson.'

'I don't know,' Volkov said. 'I've always believed that if you want to shoot someone, it's perfectly possible. Look at that idiot who shot President Reagan.'

'"Honey, I forgot to duck," he said to his wife.'

'Yes, he had a great sense of humour.'

'For a man intent on destroying Communism and the Soviet Union.'

'Thank you for reminding me. Let me remind you that when Igor Levin was given the job of disposing of that Chechnyan general he got close enough to cut his throat in the hotel they were using as command headquarters.'

'Yes, Levin was a true artist.'

'Roper, of course, only talked to you so that you would talk to me. I wonder why.'

'Stirring the pot perhaps.'

And with that, they hung up.

Who is he ringing now? Luzhkov wondered, and indeed Volkov was already calling Igor Levin. It was eleven o'clock on as wet a morning as Dublin could provide. Levin was at his apartment, with his great view of the Liffey obscured by the grey curtain of rain outside.

Levin answered, always aware that a call on his encoded phone meant someone important, and was surprised to find Volkov on the other end, considering how short a time it had been since their last conversation.

'General, what a surprise. What can I do for you?'

'I won't beat about the bush. When I spoke to you from Paris the other day I told you I wanted you back. I also said I'd spoken to President Putin and he told me to tell you that Russia needs you and that he needs you.'

Levin burst out laughing. 'What a load of balls. Who do you want killing?' He laughed again. 'There are plenty of killers in Dublin. Shall I find you one?'

Volkov was furious and frustrated. 'You Jewish ingrate,' he shouted.

'Only half-Jewish, thanks to my mother of blessed memory. And may I remind you that in his time my father was a much-decorated colonel in the Red Army.' He wasn't seething at the slur, he wasn't even angry. 'Hey, General, I've served Russia well.'

At the other end, Volkov breathed deeply a couple of times and moderated his tone. 'My dear Levin, forgive me for what I have said. As for your father, he was indeed a great man. And you've just given me an idea. Excuse me.'

He hung up and immediately phoned Michael Flynn at Scamrock Security, who was further along the Liffey, sitting at his desk, dictating to his secretary Mary O'Toole, the young woman Popov had been taking out recently.

'Mr Flynn, it's Volkov. We need to talk.'

'Certainly. Is it important?'

'Vitally – to both of us.'

'Just a moment,' Flynn said. 'Mary, take your tea break. I'll call you later.'

'Certainly, Mr Flynn.'

What transpired was unfortunate for Flynn. Mary had received the kind of attention a man in his late fifties may well give a pretty girl in her twenties. As usual, the affair hadn't lasted, leaving Mary, as girls often will in such cases, feeling aggrieved, especially as she was from a Fenian family and had been proud of her association with a pillar of the original Provisional IRA. Being a security specialist, Flynn had a number of recording devices servicing the room, some operated from the secretary's office outside. It was only recently that Mary had taken to listening in. She did so now.

'Drumore Place and the Belov International complex. Are you still interested in the security job there?' Volkov asked.

'By God, I am.'

'Then it's yours. I'll see your firm gets an official contract. You'll be responsible for all the security at the house and complex. You've heard of Max Chekov's unfortunate problem in London?'

'Bad news travels fast. We know how to handle that sort of thing in Dublin. A damn shame.'

'I'm taking over. Frankly, I'm wondering if you might be the one I am looking for to take over all the security services for Belov International.'

Flynn couldn't believe it. 'By God, I'm your man, General.'

'You are, of course, able to recruit old comrades from your days in the Provisional IRA?'

'You mean you're after mercenaries?'

'Call them what you like. Men who are used to the gun and won't flinch at using it. Don't let's beat about the bush. You know exactly what I am, and I know what you were. Say I had work for you in London. Would you be able to provide suitable people?'

'To do what?'

'There's a General Charles Ferguson who heads a special intelligence unit, and is a great thorn in my side. I know you're already familiar with some of his associates, like Sean Dillon, and Harry and Billy Salter.'

'I've known Ferguson for nearly thirty years. Dillon as well, though differently in those days. A good comrade, but if he got in my way now I'd shoot him without hesitation. Where is all this leading?'

'Would you accept contracts on Ferguson, and on Harry Salter, who is responsible for what happened to Chekov?' Volkov asked.

'Absolutely. Believe me, there are old IRA hands in London who can still do the business, bomb or bullet. The Irish quarter, Kilburn, never goes away. You want sleepers working in the city or in publishing or on some newspapers: I can supply them. The Muslims think they invented it – they only discovered it. When do you want it sorted?'

'Tonight would be fine.'

'Good God.'

'But not absolutely necessary. There is one thing you could do as soon as you like. Kill someone in Dublin. He's an ex-agent of mine called Igor Levin. Your man Popov was his sergeant. I should warn you, he's a highly dangerous man.'

'We eat dangerous men for breakfast.'

'Terms to be agreed in all cases.'

'Levin will be my gift to you, General, this very day.'

'I expected nothing less. We'll do great things together.'

Flynn hadn't been so excited in years. He spoke on the intercom to Popov and called him in. Mary watched the Russian brush past her, face flushed, and continued to listen.

'I'm taking over all security services at Belov International, so you'll be working for General Volkov again. He's in charge of things now. Max Chekov had an unfortunate accident.'

'That's marvellous – the General, I mean. Is there any way I can be of help?'

'You can help right now. This friend of yours, Igor Levin?'

'Ah, yes, we worked together in the GRU.'

'I'd like to have words with him. It's a confidential matter. I might be able to throw a bit of work his way.'

'I don't know about that. I should tell you he's quite rich. A bit difficult.'

'Well, you know what they say in the Mafia: I'll make him an offer he can't refuse.'

Popov agreed reluctantly. 'What do I do?'

'Tell him I'd like to see him on business. Take him down to Riley's Bar in Crown Street by the river. It'll be closed, but just knock on the door and tell him I'll be waiting. Leave him there and you clear off. Say you'll be at the café at the end of the street. Call him now. Go, use your mobile. I'll see you later. I've things to do.' Popov gone, he murmured into his own mobile, 'That you, Riley? I'm sending a disposal. Deal with him. The usual people will pick the body up.'

Alone in the computer room, Flynn called the Green Tinker, a good Fenian pub in Kilburn in Irish Lane run by Jimmy Nolan and his cousin, Patrick Kelly, both comrades from the old days who'd served time with Flynn in the Maze Prison. He enjoyed a business-like chat with Jimmy, which was received with great enthusiasm.

'Ah, we know that bastard Ferguson from the old days in Belfast. Dillon too, though what the hell he's doing mixed up with bowsers like Ferguson I'll never know. Salter's your average gangster. He probably started off sticking up off-licences as a kid, then graduated to a gun in his pocket and thought he was a big man. People like that are criminals, Michael, not like us at all.'

'I'm just tapping some photos and background info into your computer. There you are. Call me when you come up with something. There's real money in this. A hundred thousand pounds, my word on it. Don't screw up, Jimmy.'

Levin got the call that changed everything from Mary O'Toole before Popov arrived at his flat. She was determined to do what was right. Yes, Flynn had used her, but it wasn't just that. From a fiercely Irish Republican family, her father shot dead by British paratroopers when she was seven years of age, she was proud of her connection with the IRA, and Flynn, whom she had worshipped in the past when he was Chief of Staff, had let her down spectacularly. So she phoned Igor Levin, whom she had met a time or two when she was with Popov, told him what had happened and what she could remember.

Levin was not only grateful, he believed her. He immediately phoned Chomsky, found him in his car in the city centre and told him everything.

'Are you going to go? You're being set up, that's obvious. And this stuff she's told you about – Dillon, the Salters, Ferguson – this is serious business,' Chomsky told him.

'As we who served in Afghanistan and Chechnya know, Sergeant, and isn't it great? I've been sitting on my backside too long.' The bell went for the front door. 'Sounds like Popov now,' Levin said.

'I'm in my car only five minutes away. I'll crash the party.'

Levin opened the door, expressed surprise on seeing Popov and listened to his story with simulated interest. 'I wonder what he wants. Maybe it's something to do with a job in the firm.'

Popov said, 'I told him I didn't think you'd be interested. I mean, you know, not with your money.'

'Come in. Let me finish dressing.' Levin led the way into the sitting room. 'Get yourself a drink.'

He went into his bedroom, found a tie and tweed jacket, then went to his desk in front of the bow window with the river view, opened a drawer, felt in the back and produced first one Walther, then two, both with silencers. He put one in each pocket and went back to the sitting room as the doorbell rang again, and opened the door to Chomsky, who stood there in his raincoat. Levin slipped a Walther into one of Chomsky's pockets.

'Hello, there. You've just caught us. Popov and I have to meet a man called Riley – Riley's Bar, Crown Street.'

'I was passing,' Chomsky said, 'so I thought I'd check to see if you were free for lunch. Why don't we all go?'

Popov looked put out. 'I'm not sure.'

'Oh, come on, it'll be good,' Levin told him. 'We can talk over old times after I'm finished with Flynn,' and he took his arm and led him out. They got in the car and Chomsky drove away. 'We think I might be getting a job offer. Security work,' Levin said.

They were already down by the river, turned into a maze of streets with what looked like old warehouses lining them and came to Crown Street. Chomsky parked behind a lorry. There wasn't much choice.

'The café must be at the other end,' Levin said.

'I'm supposed to wait down there,' Popov protested.

'But we'd miss you,' Levin told him. 'And here we are.'

There was a wooden door, paint peeling, shutters at the windows, a narrow alley down one side. Chomsky said, 'Excuse me.' He disappeared down it.

Levin said, 'Go on, open the door.'

Popov said, in a panic, 'It's locked.'

'No, it isn't,' Levin turned the knob, opened the door and pushed Popov in.

Halfway along the alley Chomsky found a door, opened it and found himself in a kitchen with a table, chairs, another door. He pushed it gently. Further along at the bottom of some stairs a man in blue overalls was holding a silenced pistol and looking towards a green curtain at the far end. There was the sound of a voice and the man fired twice, a dull thud each time. Popov came through the curtain headlong and fell on his face.

Chomsky shot the man in the left shoulder, spinning him around, then shot him in the heart and he went down. He jerked twice, then was still.

Levin checked Popov. 'Our old friend seems to be dead.'

'No old friend of mine. This bastard's had it, too. What do we do?'

'Unfortunately shootings are common occurrence in Dublin these days. People think it's because of old IRA hands who can't get out of the habit. So this, alas, will be just two more. Off we go, nice and steady up the street, and away.'

It was absolutely pouring. They got in the car and Chomsky drove off. 'Now what?'

'Back to my house to pick up a few things and dispose of the weapons.'

'Why?'

'Well, we can't take them to London. I

mean, the security people don't like that these days, even if you fly in privately.'

'Is that what we're going to do?'

'I'd say so. There's a flying club I know at Killane, executive planes, just right for millionaires like me. We'll call at your place too. Don't forget your passport,' and he leaned back.

Roper received the call from Killane at one-thirty. He was having a conference meeting with Ferguson, Dillon, Billy and Greta. Doyle and Henderson stood against the wall.

Ferguson had just said, 'Right, people, I want to bring you all up to speed on the present situation.'

The phone went and Roper flicked it on to open transmission. Levin said, 'Roper, it's me, Levin. Can we talk?'

'If you don't mind the entire firm hearing. Everybody's here.'

'Fine by me. Very convenient, actually. Volkov tried to stitch me up royally, with the assistance of Michael Flynn.'

'Stitch you up how?' Ferguson demanded.

'Oh, the coffin lid being slammed down firmly. Would you be interested to know that Flynn is going to take over all security services at Belov International?'

'Yes, I damn well would,' Ferguson replied. 'Tell me more.'

Which Levin did. Everything that Mary O'Toole had told him – the Popov betrayal, the shootings at Riley's Bar.

Dillon broke in, 'So you've two bodies lying there. Does that give you a problem?'

'No. It seems that in Flynn's original discussion with Riley, Flynn told him the usual people would pick my body up. Now they'll have two. I always thought Popov would come to a bad end.'

'Damn Judas,' Dillon said. 'Why do you think Mary O'Toole told you everything?'

'Interesting, that. She said that for a man who had been Chief of Staff of the Provisional IRA he was a disgrace. Then I recalled Popov telling me once that her father was IRA, killed in a gunfight with Brit paratroopers in Ulster.'

'God save us, but that kind of Fenian female can be harder than an Orange Presbyterian. Make sure she's safe. You owe her, big time.'

'I will, be sure of that.'

Roper said, 'So where are you now?'

'A flying club at Killane outside Dublin. Under the circumstances, Chomsky and I have decided to come over.'

It was Greta who broke in now. 'Does that mean what it sounds like?'

'Greta, my love, I'm bored. Dublin is totally charming, one of the world's great cities, but I pass my days in idle pleasure.'

'I would say that sounds unlikely, based on what you've told us,' Ferguson said. 'But if what you're trying to say is that you and Sergeant Chomsky are seeking employment, I welcome you with open arms.'

'Are you sure of that, General?'

'All sins forgiven. You're booking a plane from Killane?'

'That's right.'

'Do bring your British passports. I know you have a selection, but I'd prefer it, and tell your pilot to call his details ahead and he'll be welcomed at Farley Field.'

'We'll see you soon, General.'

The death of Riley had not yet become known, and Flynn had not returned to Scamrock Security. Mary O'Toole pulled on her coat, picked up her handbag and made for the door, when the phone rang on her desk. She picked it up.

'Mary O'Toole? It's Levin.'

'I was just leaving. Flynn's not back.'

'I trust you're leaving for good. You saved my life, Miss O'Toole, but as long as you've disposed of any evidence of your involvement you should be safe enough.'

'I've left my notice on his desk. To be honest with you, I think he'll be glad to be shut of me. We had an affair, I was his leavings, but that wasn't the reason I did what I did. When I thought of my dad and what he stood for, and Flynn and his scheming and rottenness, I had to tell you.'

'Very quickly: Do you live alone?'

'Yes – I rent a flat only fifteen minutes' walk from the office.'

'Do you have a passport?'

'Of course I have.'

'You have done me the greatest favour in my life, and I must repay the debt. I'm at Killane, twenty minutes outside the city at the Aero Club. Chomsky and I are going to fly to England in a private plane. I think you'd be better out of things for a while, just in case. You're perfectly welcome to join us. London's a big place. Easy to lose yourself.'

'Do you really mean that?'

'Absolutely. Do you have money for a taxi?'

'Of course I do. There's a rank outside the office. I'll get a driver to take me home and wait for me.'

Levin put his mobile away and, standing at the counter of the small bar, Chomsky ordered two vodka shots He raised his glass. 'To a nice girl called Mary O'Toole, who did the right thing.'

'And thank God for it,' Levin said.

They moved out into the entrance and

found Magee, the chief pilot, standing under the canopy out of the rain, smoking a cigarette and chatting to a young pilot named Murphy. They stopped their conversation.

'Have you sorted it out yet?' Magee asked Levin.

'Three passengers – destination, Farley Field, in Kent, just outside London. It's all fixed up. We're expected.'

'I don't know that one. Check it on the screen, Murphy.'

Murphy returned in a few moments. 'It's there all right, and classified restricted.'

'Did you send our names?' Chomsky said, the efficient sergeant taking over. 'Look again. I'll come with you.' And it was there on the screen. Captain Igor Levin and Sergeant Ivan Chomsky.

Magee said, 'My God, you must have some pull for a place like that. I think I'll do the flight myself. You can come with me,' he told Murphy. 'A couple of nights in London will do us good. We'll take the King Air.' He turned to Levin, 'Turbo prop, but it gets you there nearly as fast as the jet, and the seats are bigger. What about the other passenger?'

'A lady. She'll be here soon.'

'Is she on the classified list?'

'Thanks for reminding me. Are you?'

'As we both served in the RAF, I expect so.'

Roper answered at once. Levin said, 'The girl, Mary O'Toole. I've decided to get her out of here fast in case of any trouble from Flynn, so we'll give her a lift. Will that be OK?'

'Certainly. I was talking to Harry. He says he really owes you one. If you hadn't come up with the story, he could have had Jimmy Nolan and Patrick Kelly visiting with maybe a bomb and certainly guns.'

'Yes, but I wouldn't have known if it hadn't been for the girl. If he wants to do anyone a favour, he can help her get a job.'

'Yes, that makes sense. I'll see you at Holland Park.'

'You mean I can't stay at the Dorchester any more?'

'Look on it as a debriefing. Anyway, the safe house is a bit like a hotel these days.'

A little later Mary was delivered in her taxi. She had only one small suitcase and a handbag. She was excited. 'I'm travelling light.'

'Any sign of Flynn?' Levin asked.

'Not when I left.'

'Let Ivan have your passport. He'll put your details through.'

She went off with Chomsky, leaving her case by the door. Murphy picked it up. 'That's women for you. There could be a bomb in there. They never learn.'

'No, they never do,' said Levin with some irony. He took Mary's case from him and went to join them.

Magee was finishing some sort of documentation at the desk and suddenly they were all together. 'OK, folks, follow Murphy. I'm right behind.'

They went out to the runway, and the King Air was there in the rain. Murphy got a couple of golfing umbrellas from a stand by the door and they walked under their shelter together towards the plane. Levin was smiling, and so was Chomsky when he glanced at him. It was behind them, what had been. What was ahead was a new chapter, and that could mean anything.

Called by two of his collectors, as he thought of them, to Riley's Bar, Michael Flynn was confronted by the bodies of Riley and Popov and couldn't believe what he saw. Riley was a creature of almost Dickensian evil. He had murdered many times, both men and women, available to whomever was capable of paying him; a butcher, allowed to exist by the IRA in the hard times because of how useful he was. Even his presence had terrified people, and here he was with two bullets in him. His collectors were a couple on the same level as Riley. 'Can't believe it, Mr Flynn. Riley murdered. I never thought I'd see the day.'

Flynn would hardly have described Riley's death in quite that way. 'He's finally dead, and that's it. Get him in the body bag.'

'And the other? His papers are here. Funny name.' One of them handed over Popov's empty wallet.

Flynn said, 'I've told you before. Keep the cash, but not credit cards or any identity stuff. I'll dispose of those.'

The man gave them to him. 'It's lucky we had another body bag in the van.'

'Where will you put them?'

'Oh, you wouldn't want to know that, Mr Flynn.'

'No, I wouldn't.' He took a bulging envelope from his pocket, stuffed with Euros.

'It was supposed to be one, Mr Flynn. Riley was extra.'

'So I'll give you extra next time. Now get on with it,' and Flynn left them.

He found his car and drove away. It was unfortunate for Popov, but God alone knew what had happened to Levin. He'd have him checked out. He was annoyed with himself that his first attempt to do Volkov a good turn had ended in failure, but there was no need to tell the Russian for the moment.

At the Green Tinker at about two-thirty, the snug was down to old Bert Fahy behind the bar and two ageing men enjoying a beer. Nolan and Kelly had been making calls, and the result was two cars turning up outside and four men entering the snug, one after the other.

They were all from Kilburn, the Irish quarter for over 150 years, which is why its inhabitants were known as London Irish and hard men. Hard and wild, where Danny Delaney and Sol Flanagan were concerned. They were the same age, twenty-five, wearing loose, flashy suits in the Italian style, their hair just a little too long. In both cases drugs were a priority, and they had a mad, dangerous look to them and a history mainly involving armed robbery.

James Burke and Tim Cohan were very different, members of the IRA since their youth, veterans of the long struggle that the Irish had always called the Troubles. Both were in their late forties, hard, calm faces giving little away. It was the first time they'd met as a group, and there was a hint of contempt in the way the older men looked at the younger. One thing was certain. The days of the IRA holding London in thrall were over, there was no disguising that by brave talk.

Danny Delaney said, 'Jimmy Nolan told me he was bringing you in on this. Burke and Cohan.' He laughed, the slightly nervous giggle of somebody who was on something. 'Sounds like undertakers.'

Flanagan said, 'I heard you were with the crew who knocked off that Muslim travel agency in Trenchard Street the other week. These Pakis have real cash in those places.'

Delaney said, 'I heard twenty grand.'

The two older men didn't say a word, and Bert Fahy spoke up as the customers left their beers and made for the door. 'What's it to be, gents?'

'Let's just make it Bushmills all round, large ones,' Delaney said. 'If we're talking business, I like to keep a clear head.' He put a line of coke on the bar in an abstracted way, whistling cheerfully, and sniffed it and drank the glass of Bushmills that Fahy offered him.

'Now that's what I call good stuff, man. Go on, have a go.'

Flanagan did, also pausing to down his whiskey. 'That's so great, man. Let's do it again.'

Burke looked on with obvious disapproval. 'Rots the inside of your nose, I hear.'

'If you indulge enough,' Cohan observed.

Delaney was really on a roll. 'Your travel agency. Reminds me of that Paki store we turned over the other week in Bayswater. Big bastard with a beard. Wouldn't open the safe. Young girl was wearing one of those things on her face with only the eyes showing. I pulled it off, the veil. Real good looker. I mean, I'd have given her one if I'd had time.' He took a pistol from his pocket, a silencer on the end. 'Put her over the counter and shot her in her right bum cheek. She never even screamed.'

'That was shock, you see,' Flanagan said.

'But he got the safe open bloody quick after that,' Delaney said. 'And there was only eight hundred quid in it. Must have been to the bank. I'd have given him one, too, only we had to get moving.'

Burke turned to Cohan. 'The great days

are behind us indeed, Tim, if this is what
we've come down to.'

'So it would appear.'

'You wouldn't know how to have a laugh
if you saw one,' Delaney told him.

'And you wouldn't know how to handle
serious business if it hit you in the face,
Sunshine.'

Delaney giggled again. 'Last of the old
brigade, a sort of Dad's Army of the
Provisional IRA.'

Burke grabbed him by the lapels. 'Don't
take the piss out of the IRA, boy. I did a
stretch at Long Kesh, the Maze Prison itself.
In five minutes you'd have been on your
knees in the shower room begging. And I've
got one of these, too.'

He produced a silenced pistol from his
pocket and held it up. Delaney pulled away,
higher than ever. 'But is it as big as mine?'

The door to the office opened and Nolan
appeared. 'Cut it out. Get in here.'

Kelly was sitting on one end of the desk.
On the wall behind was the material Flynn
had sent on the computer. A row of photos,

an information sheet under each one.

Ferguson, Harry Salter, Billy, Dillon and Roper in his wheelchair. There was nothing on Greta Novikova, but Harry's minders, Joe Baxter and Sam Hall, were represented.

'They look like nothing much to me,' Flanagan said.

'I agree.' Delaney nodded.

Burke said, 'I recognize that bastard, Ferguson. Years ago he was a colonel in Derry when they lifted a bunch of us.'

'Major General now. He's the prime target, and I can tell you boys there is big money in this for all of us, you have my word on it.'

Cohan said, 'How much?'

'A hundred grand, and my client is good for it, believe me.'

'But we've got to deliver the goods before we see any of that?' Delaney frowned.

Kelly, who had been silent, said, 'So we do. Let's have some plain speaking. I hate time wasting. If the terms aren't satisfactory, there's the door.'

'No need to be so butch,' Delaney said.

'We might as well have a go. Nothing else on at the moment.'

Cohan said, 'So what are we talking about?'

'The main targets are Harry Salter – and a lot of people will heave a sigh of relief if you manage to kill that one – and Charles Ferguson. The others are minders, back-up people, but Salter and Ferguson go down any way we can.'

'Any suggestions?' Burke asked.

'A bullet in the head is as good as anything.' Cohan nodded. 'I wouldn't hesitate to shoot Ferguson in the back if I saw him in the street on a wet night.' He looked at the photos again. 'God save us, Sean Dillon himself. The Small Man, some called him.'

'Looks like rubbish to me,' Delaney said.

'Chief enforcer in the Movement for twenty years. Killed more men than you could imagine, boy.'

Cohan said, 'He never got his collar felt once by the Army or the RUC.'

Delaney said, 'You knew him, then?'

'Only by reputation.'

Nolan cut in. 'Have any of you been to the Dark Man, Salter's pub in Wapping?' Nobody had. 'That's OK then. It's Friday night so it should be busy. Go down there, mingle, get the feel of the place, the area. It's on Cable Wharf. The pub is the first place Salter owned. There's a development next door. It seems he's turned an old warehouse into luxury apartments. He even keeps a boat along the wharf.'

'Anything else?' Cohan asked.

'Drive past Ferguson's pad in Cavendish Place, just to have a look, and Dillon's in Stable Mews. That's walking distance from Cavendish Place. Feel it all out, but carefully at this stage. We'll speak again.'

Delaney said impatiently, 'So what's the point?'

Burke said, 'To use the military term, so you're familiar with the killing ground, stupid, and know what we're talking about.'

'All the people on the board meet at the Dark Man on a regular basis. I'm betting

351

most of them will be there tonight,' Nolan pointed out.

Kelly said, 'And so will we. See that you are. Now away with you.'

'Thank God for that,' Delaney said. 'Come on, Sol,' and Flanagan followed him.

Cohan said, 'Are those two for real? Is this what we've come down to, working with scum?'

'They kill without hesitation,' Nolan told him.

'It's the only point in their favour.'

'And have to be drugged up to the eyeballs to be able to do it,' Burke said.

Cohan shook his head. 'Not Delaney, he's naturally evil, that one, and born that way.' As he followed Burke out, he paused at the door. 'Christ, is this what it was all about? The great days we knew, and it comes down to this?'

'Those days have gone,' Nolan said, 'and won't ever come back.'

'Enough bloody nostalgia,' Kelly put in, then opened a drawer in the desk, took out a pistol and silencer and three clips, which he pushed across to Nolan, then took out the same for himself. 'We'll go for a drive, check out Ferguson's gaff and Dillon's.'

Nolan loaded his weapon, a Colt automatic, and Burke and Cohan watched him. 'That sounds sensible. Do it like the movies.'

'To hell with that. I remember when we *were* the movies. The biggest bombing campaign seen in London since the Luftwaffe,' Burke said. 'The bowsers had to virtually wall off the City, the Bank of England, the lot. God, you had to keep your head down at that time.'

'There was a bar called Grady's in Canal Street. A left-over from Victorian times. There was a canal running down to the Pool of London, with a bridge over it. I stayed there more than once in the great days when I was on the run.' Kelly nodded as if to himself. 'Grady died years ago, but a fella told me the other week his wife, Maggie, still runs it. She must be seventy-five if she's a day.' He turned to Nolan. 'Let's check out Grady's, for old times' sake.'

Nolan said, 'That's a great idea. Spend some time there before the Dark Man.'

Kelly turned to Burke and Cohan. 'Why not join us, say about six, give the Dark Man the chance to warm up? We'll have a couple of glasses to start the evening off.'

'And why not?' Cohan said. 'We'll see you there. Come on, Jack.'

Nolan took down a reefer coat from a peg, whistling tunelessly. He loaded his Colt, screwed on the silencer, and Kelly said, 'Come on then, Jimmy.'

Nolan swung to look at him, eyes wild, and from somewhere deep inside it all burst out. 'What in the hell happened to us, Patrick?'

'It's simple, Jimmy. We lost the war.' Kelly patted him on the shoulder. 'Let's go, old son, and make the best of it.'

They went out to the snug, where Fahy, who had been listening at the door to all the comings and goings, was suddenly busy polishing glasses behind the door.

'We'll be out for the day,' Nolan said.

'That's fine, Jimmy. I'll see to things.'

354

They went out, and Fahy, his face grave, poured himself a whiskey and filled his pipe.

11

It was a little earlier that a council of war at Holland Park had examined the situation. 'The real threat in all this,' Ferguson said, 'is Russian. By taking Flynn on board, Volkov has thrown down the gauntlet.'

'So he must have Presidential backing,' Roper said. 'I'm sure Putin has felt for some time that something should be done about us, General.' He glanced at Harry. 'And anyone who's on our side.'

'But the thing at the moment is Nolan and Kelly and that contract and what to do about it,' Roper pointed out.

'If we were police, you couldn't touch them,' Ferguson said, 'because they haven't done anything, but I have implicit faith that you'll find a way of dealing with it. I have a meeting in one hour with the Prime Minister. I'll call in later at Holland Park and I'll greet our friends from Dublin then.'

'I admit I've got things to do at the development,' Harry said. 'I mean, we can't let stupid threats interfere with business.'

'I admire your spirit, Harry,' Ferguson said. 'But I think we can leave the activities at the Green Tinker to these three.'

He and Harry went out. Dillon said, 'Where's Greta?'

'She was going to call in at Gulf Road, see how the Rashids are coping. Hal Stone has hit the highway this morning for Cambridge and the halls of academia,' said Roper.

'My God, the students would flock to his lectures if they knew only half of the things that fella gets up to. Do you think Hussein will come?'

'Only time will tell, but now to the matter at hand. Jimmy Nolan and Patrick Kelly, his cousin. They own the Green Tinker pub in Kilburn. Both active in the Republican movement, and not only in Ulster. Nolan was down as a suspect for that mortar attack on John Major's cabinet during the Gulf War, but we discovered it was someone else.'

Billy looked at Dillon. 'And we know who.'

'Still, he was seven years into a fifteen-year prison term when it was all over, so he was released from prison according to the terms of the peace agreement. Kelly got pretty much the same deal. British citizens, born in London, they inherited the Green Tinker from Nolan's father. Served their time, clean as a whistle, both of them.'

'Like hell they are,' Billy said. 'I think Dillon and I will go and check the beer out.'

'Stay calm, Billy.'

'With a couple of guys who've accepted a contract on my uncle?'

'Well, leave your Walther at home.'

'Roper, old son, I'd remind you that as an agent of Her Majesty's Secret Services I actually have a licence for it. We'll go in my car, Dillon.'

'I thought so.' Billy had just taken delivery of a scarlet Alfa Romeo Spider and was obviously proud of it. 'Very nice,' Dillon told him. 'I'm impressed. Now, as to business, I don't recall these two from my IRA time, so they're both a blank page to me except for what Roper had to say.'

'So what? There's only one way to handle this.'

'You noticed the prison photos on Roper's screen were about twenty years old. You wouldn't even recognize them now.'

'Let's just see.'

They parked outside the Green Tinker and went in the saloon bar. Three old men sat at a table by the window playing dominoes. An unshaven young man in a black T-shirt with short sleeves and lots of muscle stood behind the bar reading a newspaper. The snug door was open and old Fahy was filling a pipe. He took one look at them and an expression of horror appeared on his face. The barman glanced up. He wore a black patch over his right eye. From the expression on his face, he wasn't impressed by what he saw.

'Yes?'

'I'll have half a bottle of still water,' Billy told him.

'And a glass of your strongest for me.' Dillon smiled. 'Bushmills, if you have it.'

'And we'd also like to see Nolan and Kelly,' Billy said.

The man put Dillon's whiskey into a shot glass. He gave it to Dillon, pushed another glass at Billy and picked up a jug of water from behind the bar. 'Will this do, sir?'

Billy reached for the glass. 'Why not?' The man started to pour the water into the glass, then moved all the way up the sleeve of Billy's trenchcoat.

Old Fahy called, 'I wouldn't do that, Michael,' but Billy was already pulling the man across the bar, punching him heavily in the face several times.

The old man stopped talking. Billy pulled Michael up, jerked the left arm out straight, the edge of his own right hand descending like a chopping axe. He eased him down into a chair.

'I think you'll find I've broken it. Now, Nolan and Kelly? Who's going to speak up?'

Old Fahy said, 'You'd better come in the office. I expect you'll force your way in anyway.'

They stood and looked at the photographs of themselves on the wall, read what was said about them.

'I think yours is quite good,' Dillon said. 'I'm not sure about mine.'

'It's called the older man look,' Billy said. 'You know, been places, done things.'

'Is that it?' Dillon passed his glass to Fahy. 'I'll have the same again.'

'The Bushmills as usual. I know that well.'

He poured a large one. Dillon said, 'And how would you know?'

'Because he heard you order one from the prick next door,' Billy said.

The old man shook his head. 'I'm from Derry. I saw you three times with Martin McGuiness there. I had my moments with the IRA, but ten years inside finished me off and I came to Kilburn. Remember a pub called the Irish Guard? I was pot man there. Gerry Brady was the publican. Did me a favour and found me a job. I remember the first time you came in and asked for Gerry, only you weren't calling yourself Sean Dillon.'

'Well, I wouldn't be.'

'But I knew you. February ninety-one it was, the time somebody mounted a mortar attack on the Prime Minister and the War Cabinet at Downing Street.'

Dillon smiled. 'We won't get into that one. Have a Bushmills and tell us what you know about this lot on the wall.'

'And what bleeding Nolan and Kelly are up to,' Billy said.

Fahy poured himself the Bushmills. 'Now do I look like an informer?'

'You'd look a damn sight worse if I put you on sticks,' Billy told him.

'For you, then, Mr Dillon. Jimmy got all this stuff on his computer, photos, pages and so on, from a man called Flynn in Dublin.'

'You listened in?'

'The walls are terribly thin here. They were being offered a contract, that's the upshot of it. A hundred thousand pounds. That's why they put everything up on the board.'

'The bastards,' Billy said. 'So they intend to do all of us.'

'The Ferguson fella and Harry Salter are the prime targets, that was the phrase used.'

'And how was this to be achieved?' Dillon asked.

'Nolan and his cousin Patrick run this place.'

'We know that,' Billy said. 'Do they intend to do it themselves or put a crew together?'

'They've got Danny Delaney and a worm called Sol Flanagan. Drugs, booze – they're off their heads most of the time.'

'What's their game?'

'Armed robbery, shops, particularly Muslim stores of any kind. Delaney is crackers. He really hates those Pakistanis and he shoots without hesitation.'

'And Flanagan?'

'Cut from the same bolt of cloth.'

'And never been nailed for any of this?' Dillon asked.

'Oh, they've been pulled in, appeared in court on occasion, but you can't get a conviction without witnesses, can you?'

'Who else?' Dillon asked.

'Different breed altogether. James Burke and Tim Cohan. London Irish, the kind who slipped off to Ulster to join the Provos when they were kids. They did the lot, including the Maze. They know you, Mr Dillon, and were distressed to see you in bad company.'

'Who did they particularly dislike?'

'Ferguson. Burke said he was lifted along with some others when Ferguson was a colonel in Derry. Cohan said that if he passed him on a wet night in the rain he'd shoot him in the back without hesitation.'

'Never mind all this,' Billy said. 'Where are Nolan and Kelly now?'

'They went out about forty minutes ago. They were both armed, and they aren't coming back. Their conversation was all about filling the time until this evening. They were going to drive past Ferguson's house, check out your place, Mr Dillon, then later visit the Dark Man. Something about the movies was mentioned – maybe they intend to kill time there until it's late enough.'

364

'So the bastards intend to show up at the pub?' Billy said.

'Well, it is Friday night, so don't tell me you won't be busy. He said the word was that most of you on that board had a habit of getting together at the Dark Man of an evening. The idea is they go along, familiarize themselves with the place, the surroundings. They've also been ordered to check out Ferguson's house, and yours, Mr Dillon. Obviously, Jimmy and Patrick do the same.'

'And then what?' Billy demanded. 'Who gets it first?'

'Jimmy said after they've done all that I've told you about, they'd speak again. Oh, there is something else. Burke and Cohan – they're like a lot of the boys are, the great days gone.'

'And they don't like it?' Dillon said.

'They don't care for the company they have to keep. They once had pride, and now it's gone.' He tapped out his pipe. 'Would there be anything else?'

'You've told us a lot,' Dillon said, 'and I suspect it's all true. Why?'

'I've always admired you, Mr Dillon. A

great man and great for the Cause. But I haven't done it for you. My reasons were purely selfish. Your friend here looks like the kind of fella who'd have beaten it out of me one way or another, and I'm getting too old for that.'

'Yes, you are, you old bastard.' Billy turned to Dillon. 'Stick him in the back of the Alfa and take him to Holland Park. Put him behind lock and key until this is over.'

'Good on you, Billy.' Dillon patted Fahy on the shoulder. 'Does it suit you? A comfortable safe house?'

'Well, I certainly won't be safe here.' He led the way through the snug, pausing to take his coat from behind the bar. 'I'll just check on Michael.'

He led the way into the saloon bar, which was empty. He called, but there was no reply. 'Maybe he's gone to get his arm fixed.'

'Not your problem,' Billy said. 'It's the safe house for you. You'll love it. Better than a hotel.'

* * *

Dillon reported in to Roper. 'Are Harry and Ferguson still occupied elsewhere?'

'They haven't contacted me yet. What have you discovered? Should we be worried?'

'See what you think,' and Dillon gave him a brief account of what had happened.

When he had finished, Roper said, 'I'll put them all through my computer, pull out photos and general information. Anything I can find. It could be fun.'

'So you're in favour of letting these six guys do some nosing around tonight and we don't do anything about it?'

'I didn't say that. From what your informant has told you, they are not supposed to do anything except size the situation up. What we've got to decide is what we do if things get out of hand. I'll try and contact the General and Harry. After all, they are the main targets. I'd remind you the flight from Dublin is due in an hour. What do we do about that?'

'We'll call in at Holland Park, drop Fahy off and take one of the people carriers to Farley.'

'Greta got back an hour ago. She's having

a drink with me now. I think she'd like to greet her compatriots. It must be some Russian thing.'

There had been headwinds, which had slowed them down, but the King Air had performed well, and Levin, Mary and Chomsky, having discovered a bottle of champagne in an ice box, had consumed it between them.

'So what do you fancy putting your hand to, Mary?' Chomsky asked her.

'I'm beyond caring. Mind you, I have a degree in business studies and computer technology.'

'Well, in the world of today you'll never starve,' Chomsky told her. He turned to Levin. 'Don't you agree?'

Levin nodded. 'All you need is the right connections, and you've certainly got those. You not only saved my life but that of Harry Salter, and considering how much of the Thames Waterfront he's developed, I think he'll find you something.'

'As long as you don't mind being employed

by one of the most prominent gangsters in London,' Chomsky said.

'This is nonsense,' Levin told him. 'A girl with her background would fit particularly well in Harry's world.'

But now they were dropping through clouds, and there was London below. They drifted across and then they were descending to Farley Field and a perfect landing.

They rolled along the runway towards the terminal building, Magee following instructions. He switched off the engines. Murphy opened the door, and Magee followed. He said to Levin, 'I was right about this place. Three RAF planes and two helicopters. You really are somebodies.'

'But you'll never know who,' Chomsky said cheerfully, and followed Mary out.

The people carrier stood beside the terminal building, Greta, Dillon and Billy beside it. Greta ran forward and flung her arms around Levin first, and then Chomsky.

'You wonderful bastards,' she said, and there were tears in her eyes. 'I never knew it would be so good to see you.'

'And if it wasn't for this girl I wouldn't even be here. Meet Mary O'Toole,'

Levin told her.

Billy moved in quickly. 'I'm Billy Salter, Harry Salter's nephew. I think you'll find he'll show you his gratitude big time.'

Dillon took her hand. 'Sean Dillon.'

Her eyes widened. 'Mother Mary, that I should see the day. I've heard of you since I was a young girl.'

'Well, you've seen me now, so let's get in and we'll be away.'

Billy was at the wheel. As they drove off, Dillon told Levin what was going on.

When they reached Holland Park they found Harry and Ferguson had arrived. Mary was introduced and Harry said, 'You're coming back with me, love, to my pub, the Dark Man. Our Ruby can look after you for a while until you decide what you want to do. Lots of opportunities in my personal empire. We've just got a few things to sort out here.' He turned to those assembled in the computer room. 'Let's see it again, Roper.'

Roper paraded Flynn's crew across the big

screen. The photos had been obtained from police files, those of Burke and Cohan being several years old. They had a certain rugged dignity that came with men who had believed they were fighting for a cause.

Delaney and Flanagan were a different proposition, cocky, smirking and in most photos obviously on something, drugs, alcohol or probably both.

'Give us your lecture, Major,' Ferguson instructed Roper.

'Delaney and Flanagan, shoot at will. They've got away with a string of armed robberies through intimidation of witnesses.'

'And Cohan and Burke?'

'IRA foot soldiers for years, total professionals, and that means damned good at killing. Any psychological profile would tell you they don't like robbing corner shops for a living, but, pushing fifty, men like that don't have much choice.'

'It's a point of view,' Ferguson said, 'but I have little sympathy for them. You play that kind of game, you take the consequences when all is lost. Having said that, I intend to get out my nylon and titanium waistcoat, which fitted quite snugly under my shirt when I last wore it. Guaranteed to stop a .45 magnum round at point-blank range. I recommend those who have one to wear it until we have this matter sorted.'

'I agree,' Harry said. 'It's up to you, Dillon and Billy, of course. You can pull in Baxter and Hall as foot soldiers.'

'And as Captain Levin and Sergeant Chomsky have already been involved in the circumstances leading to all this, I'm sure they would be willing to assist.'

'No problem, General.'

'I'd like you and Chomsky to stay here for a few days for a thorough debriefing with Major Roper. After that, Harry's suggested you move down to the warehouse development of his at Hangman's Wharf which you'll remember from your visit last year.'

'I remember it well.' Levin smiled. 'Quite convenient for the Dark Man.'

'Well, you would. I wouldn't recommend you going for a swim in the Thames with your clothes on again. Wrong time of year.'

He went out briskly. Harry followed with Mary and Billy, who said, 'I'll hand her over to Ruby at the pub and join up with you later.'

'Fine,' Dillon said, left Levin and Chomsky to Sergeant Doyle and went back to Roper, who had Greta with him. Dillon helped himself to a Scotch.

'You've got a problem,' Greta said. 'I can tell.'

'What would it be?' Roper inquired.

'Bert Fahy, the old man I brought in. He gave me a good story and I'm prepared to accept that it was true, but only as far as it went. It was a bit too pat. I didn't quite buy what he said Nolan and Kelly would be doing.'

'Really? Well, we can't have that.' He called up Sergeant Henderson. 'Bring our new guest in. Mr Fahy.'

He was produced within five minutes, and the pleasant surprise the comfort of his quarters had given him disappeared rapidly when he found himself in a pool of light looking up to them.

'Fahy, you lied to me,' Dillon said. 'The idea that Nolan and Kelly would go to the cinema before visiting us tonight is unbelievable.'

Roper broke in, 'Which means you were concealing something else they intend to do.'

'God help me, sir, would I lie to Mr Dillon?'

'All right, I won't waste time. I will issue a warrant for your detention under the Anti-Terrorism Act, at Wormwood Scrubs Prison.'

Fahy almost had a bowel movement at the thought of incarceration in that dread institution. 'No, sir, have pity on an old man. My memory plays tricks on me.'

'Try again.'

'Well, Major, there's the bar called Grady's close to the Pool of London.'

When he had finished telling them what he knew, Henderson took him back to his quarters. Dillon said, 'This could be a real break. I'm going to go and have a look. Are you busy?' he asked Greta.

'Not until tonight. Molly Rashid's on a night shift and she asked me to keep Sara company. The girl's having difficulty relating to her father.'

'Maybe it's the other way round. We'll go in your Mini Cooper. I'll see you in the car park – and you later,' he shouted to Roper.

He went straight to his room, found his favourite Walther and joined Greta, who was already at the wheel of the Mini Cooper.

'I remember all this when I was a kid with my father growing up in London,' he said as they made their way downriver. 'The Pool of London, the docks, ships crammed in every-where, hundreds of enormous cranes. I don't know if it was the biggest port in the world, but it should have been.'

'But you were Irish,' she said. 'Why were you here at all?'

'My mother died, my father ran out of work in Ulster.' He shrugged. 'The Irish always had a big connection with London. Michael Collins was a civil servant in the Post Office here before he decided to change the course of Irish history.'

'It all seems very different now,' she observed.

'That's development for you. A lot of the

warehouses are apartment blocks like that one of Harry's on Hangman's Wharf, but there are still some streets and buildings that haven't been touched.'

She had entered Canal Street into the satellite navigator in the Cooper, and they soon arrived there. There was a section of the docks in decay, a canal flowing quite fast into the river, an ironwork footbridge leading across it, and on the other side decaying working-class terrace houses, mostly boarded up and awaiting demolition. There was a pub on the corner with a sign that said Grady's Bar. The door was half open and an old lady with very white hair and an apron over a long black dress was polishing a brass knocker. Over the door was the usual board with the licence details of the publican. It said Margaret Grady. She was perhaps seventy-five, her voice faded as if she wasn't really there, the merest hint of an Irish accent.

'Can I help you? I don't open till six o'clock. We're a free house.'

'That's all right,' Dillon said. 'We weren't looking for a drink.'

Greta joined in. 'We were searching for Canal Street, but we've obviously found the wrong one.'

'Oh, there must be a lot in the telephone directory.'

'An interesting place,' Dillon said.

'In the old days it was quite thriving, with the ships and so on, but when they went the life went out of everything. They've pulled down all the properties up there. We're like an oasis. Another six months and that's it. We were a lodging house for years.'

'I'm sorry to hear it,' Greta said. 'Do you get any customers?'

'Now and then, but there are days when there's nobody. Still, the Council have promised me a place in an old folks' home.'

There really wasn't much to say. 'We won't hold you up any more.' Dillon smiled, and he and Greta went back across the bridge, down to the car and drove away.

'Back to Holland Park, quick as you like.'

'So you're going to trace them, are you?' she asked.

'No, Greta. If things work out, I hope to

dispose of them. A few old IRA hands who've met a bad end, and Scotland Yard will close the files with quiet satisfaction.'

'But Volkov will get the message.'

'And the Broker, which means Al-Qaeda and the Army of God. Greta, we've gone beyond negotiation. In the world of tomorrow that's emerged in the last few years, we fight fire with fire or go under. You may think that strange, coming from a man who was once an IRA enforcer, but that's the way it is.'

'I don't think it's strange – I think it's ironic, that's all.'

'Excellent, so keep driving and I'll call Roper.'

By the time they got back to Holland Park it was just after five o'clock. Roper had called in Billy, Levin and Chomsky.

Greta said to Roper, 'I've got this thing with the Rashids. I'll call in later.'

Dillon said, 'Number one, I don't want you on board, Chomsky. You did your bit in Dublin and proved your worth. You go down to the Dark Man. They may need an extra gun.'

'You're the boss.' Chomsky shrugged.

378

Dillon said to Roper, 'You've thoroughly briefed them on this?'

'Absolutely.'

Dillon faced Levin and Billy. 'There are four good men, with years of experience with the IRA, the revolutionary movement that invented revolutionary movements. The object is to kill all four. To the authorities, the explanation will be some sort of IRA feud, old scores being settled and who gives a damn. I've just been to the bar on Canal Street. You go up by the canal, cross a Victorian iron bridge and the pub is almost the only building standing in a demolition area. They've no idea we're on to them and it will be dark when we get there.'

'And bleeding raining again,' Billy said. 'Are you tooled up, Igor?'

'Thanks to Sergeant Henderson.' He took a silenced Walther from his pocket. 'Just like you, Dillon.'

'OK, my car. Let's do it,' Billy said and led the way out.

*   *   *

When Maggie Grady unlocked and opened the door at six, it was dark, but she'd switched the light on overhead and Kelly and Nolan stood there smiling at her.

'Mother Mary, is it yourself, Patrick?'

'And no other.' He kissed her on the cheek. 'I've brought a pal – Jimmy Nolan. We thought we'd have a drink with you. I've a couple of boys working with me at the moment. They'll be along presently.'

The little bar was neat and tidy, a coal fire in the grate, old Victorian iron tables and chairs scattered round the room. Bottles stood ranged against a mirror behind the bar.

She got over her shock soon enough, even excelled herself by joining them in an Irish whiskey, just the one. In the middle of a story from Kelly the outer door opened and Burke and Cohan entered.

'We've found you at last, praise be to God, and a grand sight it is with the fire and all.' The drink flowed, and even old Maggie was tempted to another.

Burke said, 'So this is the good woman

who looked after you when you were on the run?'

'A queen among women,' Kelly told him. 'A lodging house as well as a pub, it was then. Sailors ashore from ships in the Pool. You've never seen anything like it. Every nationality on God's earth – Indians, Blacks, Lascars – and if you dressed the right way you got swallowed up by them.' He looked at his watch. 'Damn me, it's seven already. We'll have to get moving.' He gave her a hug and a peck on the cheek. 'God bless you, my darling. Here's one man who'll never forget you.'

They were laughing as they went out, and she closed the door, tired and sad. Making a sudden decision, she shot the bolt, crossed the bar, turned the light out and went upstairs very slowly, for she was old and past things now, that was the truth of it.

Outside, it was very dark in the decaying street, for just a single lamp hung from a bracket on the far side of the canal. The group started down to the bridge and rain was falling, glistening in the feeble light.

Dillon and Billy came up the steps side by side, each with a Walther in his hand.

'Who the hell are you?' Kelly cried.

Dillon's hand swung up and he shot Kelly between the eyes, the sound of his silenced weapon only a dull thud, knocking him back against Nolan, who was struggling to get his gun out, pushing Kelly's corpse violently away from him so that it went over the rail into the swirling waters of the canal and was instantly swept away.

Nolan almost got his gun out, but Billy was faster, shooting him in the left shoulder, turning him round and then shattering his spine with a second. Nolan fell across the bridge rail and hung there.

Burke went straight down on one knee, avoiding a return shot from Billy, and shot him in the chest. Behind him, Cohan turned to run back to the pub but Igor Levin stood up from behind a pile of bricks and shot him in the head. Burke, with nowhere else to go, vaulted over the rail into the canal, went under, came to the surface and was instantly gripped by the current, but Levin, running fast, fired several times, driving him under the water.

When he turned to rejoin the others, Billy and Dillon were carrying Cohan between them to throw him in the canal. The current swept him away into darkness.

'All the way down to the Pool and the Thames, and maybe even the open sea,' Dillon said.

Billy had opened his raincoat and was feeling inside his shirt.

'Are you all right, Billy?' Levin asked.

'Well, you heard what Ferguson said. Titanium and nylon waistcoat. If you've got one, wear it.'

He produced a damaged round which had stuck in the waistcoat. Levin said, 'I'm wearing one, too. General Volkov gave it to me as a present for saving him from an assassin.'

'Let's move it,' Dillon said. 'Mission accomplished. Now back to Holland Park.'

At the safe house they found Roper and Ferguson. Levin helped himself and Dillon to whiskies from the Major's private stock.

'All four?' Ferguson shook his head. 'Remarkable. Reminds me of Ulster in the old days.'

Roper said, 'It was exactly like Ulster in the old days. You did the job like you said you would, Sean.'

Ferguson turned to Levin. 'What can I say about you? Sterling service indeed. You've served us well.'

'I'll see the right kind of whisper gets through to Flynn and Volkov, just so they get the point,' Roper said. 'The Thames is a tidal river, and bodies don't often turn up if you look at the statistics.'

'What happens now to Delaney and Flanagan?' Levin asked.

'Well, I must admit I'd prefer closure,' Ferguson said. 'We'll have to see. They should be rising to the surface at the Dark Man soon, unless they decide not to arrive at all. Billy and Harry, Baxter and Hall and our new friend, Sergeant Chomsky, should be perfectly capable of dealing with them.'

'I'd say so,' Dillon agreed.

'So let's go and watch them do it.'

'Why not?' Levin said.

'Well, if you lot are going, I'm going,' Roper announced. 'Doyle can fetch the people carrier. I'll be ten minutes.'

'Excellent. I'll travel with you. I have never accompanied you in that contraption. You have your own automatic lift, I've observed.'

'We'll follow in my Mini,' Dillon said. 'You can lead the way.'

He and Levin hurried out through heavy rain and got in the Mini. As they waited, Dillon called Billy. 'What's happening?'

'The joint, as they say, is jumping. Lots of punters, no aggravation, and so far we haven't seen a sign of the two ratbags we're looking for.'

'OK. We'll see you soon. Roper, Ferguson, Doyle and me. I'd say we'll be about twenty minutes.'

Delaney and Flanagan had spent two hours in an establishment called Festival, where the music rocked and regular visits to the toilet were solely for the purpose of drug taking. By six o'clock they were out of their heads on cocaine, and the amount of vodka they'd taken with it was lethal. They had both reached that state where they viewed the world with a false belief that it was theirs and that anything was possible.

The car they were in was a Mercedes stolen earlier that day before their visit to the Green Tinker, and Flanagan was driving it with total indifference to everyone else on the road. He scraped three cars, one after another, and narrowly missed a police officer, who raised a hand and then had to jump for his life. Delaney roared with laughter, pulled out his silenced pistol and fired into several shop windows as they passed, then vanished into a warren of back streets leading down to the Thames.

'This is Wapping, man, I know it is,' Delaney said. 'The Dark Man, Cable Wharf. Hah, you punched it in right, man.' He pointed at the satellite navigator. 'We're there.'

The Dark Man was ablaze with lights, there was music on the night air, cars parked all along the wharf, a few boats tied up, and at the end of them Harry Salter's pride and joy, the *Linda Jones*.

They swerved into the car park at the side of the wharf just past the pub. 'So this is it,' Flanagan said. 'What do we do?' The rain increased suddenly.

'Shoot the place up, man.' Delaney took a half-bottle of vodka from the glove compartment and opened it. 'Here's to us.'

He swallowed, then passed it to Flanagan to take a pull, and at that moment the people carrier arrived. It stopped, the back opened and Ferguson walked round just as Roper was delivered in his wheelchair. At the same moment the Mini arrived with Dillon and Levin, and paused a little distance away.

'Christ,' Delaney said. 'The guy standing beside the wheelchair – it's Ferguson.' He pushed open the passenger door, stepped out and fired his silenced pistol wildly at the van, but Ferguson had turned to speak to Roper, leaning forward. Delaney's rounds simply hit the vehicle and Ferguson and Roper went down together in a tangle.

Levin jumped out of the Mini and fired at the Mercedes, but it was a difficult shot with Delaney on the far side of the vehicle hurling himself back inside. Dillon put his foot down and rammed the other car's rear. Flanagan, in a blind panic, accelerated along the wharf past the *Linda Jones* and went straight off the end into the Thames. They watched the back end as it tilted and went down to the bottom. They waited, but nobody appeared.

'That's it,' Dillon said, 'It's forty feet deep around here. Put your gun away. Let's see about Ferguson and Roper.'

Back at the Dark Man, Harry, Billy and Chomsky were there, with Doyle righting the wheelchair and helping Ferguson up and Roper into the chair.

'We're fine,' Ferguson told them. 'Whoever it was missed us. What's happened to them?'

'Bottom of the Thames.'

'I'm so sorry,' Ferguson said sarcastically.

'Chomsky was on the door,' Harry said. 'He was aware of the shooting, but with silenced pistols you couldn't hear a thing in the saloon bar, just the noise of the cars colliding. That's brought a few out.'

Behind them, some of the punters were watching, glasses in hand. Ruby came out anxiously, Mary with her, and at the same moment not one police car, but three pulled in and a young police sergeant came forward. 'Oh, it's you, Mr Salter. We've been chasing a Mercedes over half of Wapping with gunmen shooting at shop windows on the way by.'

'Disgusting. Don't know what the world's coming to,' Harry said. 'Collided with my friends' vehicle and went straight down the wharf.'

'And into the Thames,' Dillon said. 'We saw it go down, and no one came up.'

'Christ,' the sergeant said.

'We'll leave you to it and get the Major here inside,' Harry said piously. 'I mean, with his war record, it's disgusting that he should be subject to this kind of treatment in his own city.'

Inside, Baxter and Hall had cleared a

couple of booths. Ruby served champagne, and Mary helped her.

'All in all, I'd say that was more than satisfactory,' Ferguson said.

'I should bleeding think so.' Harry chuckled. 'Talk about clearing the decks.'

'Volkov can chew on that.' Roper nodded as the police sergeant came in.

'What can I do for you, Sergeant?' Harry said.

'Just to let you know. A recovery detail's been booked for tomorrow, and a series of reports indicate the people in the Mercedes were a couple of hoods with very bad reputations. They'd stolen the car, spent a few hours at the Festival getting coked up and, as I told you, shooting half of Wapping up on the way. I don't know what they intended. Names of Delaney and Flanagan.'

'Never heard of them in my life, Sergeant. A lot of rats around these days.'

The sergeant departed and they all relaxed. 'That's it then, all sorted,' Billy said.

'Except for the question of Hussein Rashid,' Ferguson pointed out.

There was a pause while they thought about it. 'Maybe he won't come. What do you think, Roper?' Dillon asked.

'You know what I think. Now if you don't mind, I could do with getting back to Holland Park. I'm bruised all over.'

BRITTANY

ENGLAND

12

The low-budget flight to Rennes was crammed with passengers and had resembled a refugee flight from some war zone. The train to St Malo, on the other hand, was excellent. A taxi from there took them to St Denis. According to the details the Broker had given Hussein, Roman lived on a boat, the *Seagull*.

'This is the best I can do, monsieur,' the taxi driver said.

Khazid handled it in rapid and fluent French. 'That's OK. We'll find it.' He over-tipped the man, who drove off, leaving them looking at a half-empty marina.

'Let's start searching,' Khazid said in Arabic.

Hussein lectured him quietly. 'No Arabic,

395

just in case. You might as well make it English. My French is poor at the best of times.'

'As you wish.'

There was a walkway, boats of many kinds moored on each side, but it looked like it would take a long time to check them all, so Khazid paused and shouted, 'Ahoy, *Seagull*.'

Nothing happened for a while and Hussein said, 'You fool.'

A young woman came out of the wheel-house of a motor cruiser and looked towards them. She was pretty enough, denims and a black sweater, and there was a gypsy look to her.

She spoke in French. 'What do you want?'

Khazid handled her. 'We're looking for a man named George Roman.'

'He's at the bar on the jetty. I'll show you.'

Both her English and French had strong accents. As they went back along the walkway, Khazid said, 'Where are you from?'

'Kosovo.'

'So you were in the war, little sister?'

Hussein managed to kick his ankle, for if

the girl was a refugee, which seemed likely coming from Kosovo, she was almost certainly a Muslim.

'The war was a long time ago.'

'And your name?'

'Saida.'

Which confirmed it. At the end of the walkway she paused, took a packet of Gitanes from her pocket and a lighter. She put a cigarette in her mouth and Khazid took the lighter from her. 'Allow me.'

'Thank you.' She took the lighter back, and inhaled and said in heavily accented Arabic, 'I don't know who you are or what you're doing here, but take care with this man. He's English Royal Navy, but rotten to the core.'

Hussein said gently, 'You are Muslim?'

'And the war stank. Allah bless Tony Blair for sending the British Army and RAF to Kosovo to save us from the Serbs.'

'It is true he did such a thing,' Khazid said. 'But what of Iraq?'

'Agreed, but life is learning to live with the good and the bad.'

'What a wise girl,' Hussein commented.

'My father was a teacher of children at the mosque in our small town. When the Serbs came, they hanged him. They hanged boys, too.'

All this was delivered in the most matter-of-fact way as they came to a café called the Belle Aurore. There was a terrace at the front with tables, waiters in white jackets, not particularly busy. The man they were seeking was at a corner table reading a copy of *Le Figaro*. He wore a reefer coat and a seaman's cap; he was perhaps sixty, with a florid face and a cruel mouth. He reached out for a glass and continued to read.

Saida said, 'George, these gentlemen are looking for you.'

Hussein said, 'Mr Roman, I'm Hugh Darcy.'

Roman looked him over. 'It's Commander Roman, and it won't do you know. Sit down.'

'Why won't it do, Commander?'

'This is yesterday's paper. We always get it late in this neck of the woods. Lot of people here who would run a mile and shout for the gendarmes if they knew who you are. Page four.'

Hussein sat down and stared at his photo. In that minute everything so carefully contrived turned to ashes.

Saida, reading over his shoulder, gasped. 'You are him.'

Khazid said, 'Come, brother, let's get out of here'

'No need to panic,' Roman said. 'It's just a question of being practical about things. Of course the only problem is I can't contact the Broker – he contacts me. Can you get in touch with him?'

'Yes,' Hussein said.

'Excellent. This drink is marvellous. Brandy and ginger ale. Takes me back to my Navy days. You should try one.' He laughed. 'But then you can't – I was forgetting.'

'No, but Hugh Darcy could.'

'Yes, by God, you're right. You don't look like a raghead at all.' He shouted at the waiter. 'Pierre, two Horses Necks – no, three.' He glanced up at Khazid. 'Got to play the game, eh?'

'If you say so.'

'Good boy.' Roman slapped Saida on the bottom. 'Go and get the groceries and divest yourself of those appalling jeans when you get back on board. I've told you, I like little cotton skirts so a man can have a decent feel. Nothing like it.'

The waiter had just brought the three drinks. He put them on the table and the girl picked one up and threw it in Roman's face. He wasn't in the least put out, and licked his lips.

'Delicious.' He reached for a napkin and wiped his face. 'I'll have to chastise you for that, but I'll have great pleasure in taking care of it on the voyage.'

She was stunned. 'On the voyage? You'll take me?'

'England,' Roman said to Hussein. 'People are desperate to get there, especially refugees without permission. She turned up months ago with an Albanian, but when push came to shove he dumped her on the waterfront when we left, and she was still here when I returned.'

'Each time he does another English run he promises me a trip,' she complained. 'I'll go for the groceries.' She paused. 'But I've hardly any money.' She shrugged and walked away.

Hussein nodded to Khazid, who went after her.

Roman said, 'You don't like me very much, do you?'

'If I may borrow one of the great Humphrey Bogart's best lines: If I thought about you at all, I probably wouldn't.' He opened his flight bag, felt for the brooch and pressed the button. He closed the case. 'Now we wait.'

Khazid caught up with Saida. 'Don't worry. Get anything you want. I'll take care of it.'

'Your friend,' she said. 'Even I have heard of him. The Hammer of God.'

'A great man and a great soldier,' Khazid said.

'And you also are a soldier in the war?'

'Of course. In Iraq it's bad, believe me.'

'I see that on television. The Americans, the British.'

'No, it's more than that. It's a blackness, a disease that touches everyone. The brothers are killing each other – some weeks more than a thousand. Women and children die in the crossfire.'

'And how does it end?'

'Maybe never. But where are you going? The supermarket over there?'

'Yes.'

'Carry on. I'll join you in a little while.'

They had just passed a cutlery shop and he walked back to inspect the window full of knives of every possible description. With his French background he was aware that the authorities were more open-minded about certain types of weapons than other countries. He entered and found a white-haired old man behind the counter.

'Monsieur, what can I show you?'

'I seek a folding knife, substantial and preferably automatic.'

Fifteen minutes later he left after purchasing a horn-handled flick knife with a seven-inch, razor-sharp, double-edged blade that jumped eagerly to his command at the

touch of his thumb. He crossed to the supermarket and joined her.

'Have you got what you wanted?' she
asked.

'Oh, yes,' he said. 'There's nothing like
being prepared for anything in this life, and
I don't like the Commander. Does that make
me a bad man?'

'Anything but.'

'Good, then let's make sure you've got all
your groceries.'

For once, the Broker had been badly caught
out. The appearance of the newspaper in the
small French port with Hussein's photo was
unexpected, the reaction of Commander
Roman unfortunate. For the moment he had
to meet Roman's price if Hussein and Khazid
were to make the next move in their progress
to England. That he would be able to punish
the man for his blackmail in the near future
was certain. Al-Qaeda would see to that. He
guaranteed the substantial additional funding
Roman demanded, to be transferred to

Switzerland in a matter of hours. When he had finished, he insisted on speaking to Hussein.

'Take a walk. I don't want that creature to get any hint of what is happening.'

'Fine.'

'Our plans haven't changed. I admit the other side has had some successes. Harry Salter disposed of a substantial outfit produced by the Russian Mafia. A contract on Ferguson and Salter involving six IRA operatives did no better. Two of them, common street gangsters, made a feeble attempt on Ferguson and Roper and now reside at the bottom of the Thames awaiting police recovery. Drugged to the eyeballs, they shot up half of Wapping.' He sighed. 'So now it's all up to you. Good luck with your crossing. I'm confident Darcus will be helpful, and Dreq Khan. Use him and his Army of God sweepers and the Brotherhood in London. But remember this is not just a personal crusade concerning the Rashids and the girl. Ferguson must be a target, if possible, and Salter. The others are *not* prime targets.'

He cut off, preventing any further discussion, and Hussein went back to the table. Khazid and Saida had gone back to the boat.

'I think your friend fancies her,' remarked Roman. 'Could be giving her a good shag now. We'll get along to the boat and see if we can catch them.'

'You know, when I said that if I thought about you at all I probably wouldn't like you? Well, I don't,' Hussein told him.

'Oh, I'm a reasonable chap when I want to be. I've offered the girl a free trip with you, unless you object.'

'Casting her ashore with no papers and no money?'

They were moving along to the boat. 'If she walks into the nearest police station, they arrest her and deliver her to the welfare authorities. She'll be placed in reasonable accommodation and given substantial payments to keep her going, and it's highly unlikely she'll be sent back. England's like that these days, mosques in every city. Not fair, old man. Try finding a church in Mecca or Medina, and what about Iraqi Christians?

Chased out of the country in their thousands.'

Hussein ignored him. 'When do we leave?'

Roman glanced at his watch. It was five-thirty. 'I can't see much point in hanging around.' He had a half-bottle of some wine or other, and poured it down. 'I checked on the weather. Could be rain squalls, and there'll be fog in the morning.'

They came to the *Seagull* and paused. 'A nice boat,' Hussein said.

'You can say that again. Thirty foot, built by Akerboon, twin screws, twenty-five knots, automatic steering if you want it, and I've got an inflatable with an outboard motor. Plenty of booze.' He laughed. 'Damn me, I was forgetting about you.'

'And you'll take the girl?'

'I suppose so. Peel Strand is our destination, the Dorset coast quite close to Portland Bill. We anchor offshore, I take you in using the inflatable. I've got a sketch of your route inland. There's a cottage by a marsh pond called Folly Way. I've never met the guy, and with a name like Darcus I doubt I'd want to. But enough conversation. Let's get on board.'

Which they did. 'Where the bloody hell are you?' he called to Saida.

'I'm in the galley getting supper ready. Henri is in the saloon.'

'Henri, my arse. Make the meal, then leave it ready. We're going.'

She came out of the galley and stood at the bottom of the companionway looking up. 'Does that include me?'

'Yes, though I don't why I bother. You've not changed your jeans. I'm really going to have to take you in hand.'

She ducked out of sight. Khazid brushed past her and came up to join them in the wheelhouse. 'When do we go?'

'Within half an hour. Might as well get started.'

'How far?' Hussein asked.

'About a couple of hundred miles.' He checked the instruments and said to Hussein, 'I set the course, which I know like the back of my hand, but I keep Admiralty charts out for the whole Channel crossing, just in case. Of course you can also switch over to automatic steering.' He turned to Hussein. 'It would be useful if you could take the wheel for a while and spell me. Do you know much about boats?'

'No, but I'm a qualified pilot, so I'm an expert navigator, can set a course, read charts and so on.'

'Yes, well, if you look at the Admiralty chart, I've marked our course to Peel Strand. That's it, the red line.'

'Is there a village there?'

'No, the village has the name, but it's a good half a mile inland. I've never been. I've spoken to this Darcus guy many times on the ship-to-shore radio. The Broker got him one the other year when he started doing this as regular work. I know his background. He sounds like an old fruit to me. Anyway, let's move it.'

He pressed the starter, the engine rumbled into life and he called to Khazid to cast off, which he did. They eased away from their mooring and moved slowly out to sea, the light beginning to fade. As they slipped out of the harbour entrance he switched on the navigation lights and increased the speed.

'Wonderful – a joy. Never fails.' He took a half-bottle of brandy out of his reefer coat, opened it one handed with his teeth and took a deep swallow. 'Go below, enjoy yourself. Come back later.'

Hussein descended below, looked in on Saida in the galley preparing the food and went in the saloon. There was a cabin aft with two bunks and a small toilet and cramped shower. The cabin forward also had two bunks. There was a centre table, and Khazid was seated at it with a glass of wine.

'As you can see, I'm acting my role and rather enjoying it. Do you want one?'

'No, thanks, and not because I'm becoming pious. Religion seems to mean much less to me these days,' Hussein told him.

'That's strange. No one has done more for the struggle than you.'

'But I've been fighting for my country, for Iraq, not so much for Islam.' Saida could hear in the galley, and without asking she brought him a coffee. 'My parents died in the bombing in the Gulf War. I didn't like

Saddam, but I didn't welcome invaders, either. It's all a mystery to me.' Hussein turned to Saida, 'What about you?'

'Religion?' She shook her head. 'I don't know. The Serbs who killed my father and most of the men in my village were Christian, but hardly very good Christians. I think religious differences that lead to war are just an excuse to kill. These days it's so barbaric and cruel.'

Hussein signed. 'You've got a point. I think I'll have that glass of wine after all.'

Saida went to a cupboard, got a bottle out without comment and filled a glass. Khazid held out his for a refill, and they toasted each other.

'What do we drink to?' Khazid asked.

'To us, my friend, for the only good thing to come out of war is comradeship.' He emptied the glass. 'I'll go up top and see how things are.'

The boat ploughed on, the waves increasing somewhat, and rain dripped off the stretched awning in the stern. The deck lights were switched on.

'There you are,' Roman said. 'Try the wheel.'

He moved out of the way to make room for Hussein, then took the half-bottle of brandy out of his pocket and had a huge swallow. 'Jersey to starboard, just coming up, the good old Channel Islands. Guernsey up there in the distance, beyond that Alderney, and north from there ending up with Portland Bill, the English coast and our destination.' He swallowed again. 'Dammit, the bottle is empty. I'll go and get another.'

He went out and Hussein felt the wheel kick with a sense of pleasure. The windscreen wipers were on, the radio crackled and occasionally voices came through the static with weather details and sometimes ship movements.

He felt relaxed, comfortable, not really thinking of anything in particular, and then the sea started becoming very lively, waves bursting over the prow, and it was exciting. Roman returned.

'Force five – could make six.' He took out a fresh bottle and got it open. 'You'd better go down and get something to eat. I grabbed a sandwich.'

Hussein went below and found Khazid and Saida eating salad sandwiches made with unleavened bread and drinking tea. He joined in, suddenly discovering an appetite.

'I think I'll have another. They're good.' Khazid took the flick knife from his pocket, sprang the blade, leaned over and spiked a sandwich.

'Very nice. Where did you get it?' Hussein asked.

'Cutlery shop by the marina. I felt naked. It's been a long time since I had a gun in my pocket. This makes me feel better. I'll go and take the wheel for a while.'

He went up the companionway, and a few minutes later Roman slipped and fell down the last three or four steps. Hussein went to help him out. Roman struggled and struck out at him, thoroughly drunk. Hussein put his hands up in a placating way. 'Get away from me,' Roman said, and gave the girl a violent shove. 'Go and get me another drink.' He lurched down on the bench seat.

Hussein said, 'No booze. Coffee – lots of coffee.'

He went up the companionway and found Khazid wrestling with the wheel, the boat plunging all over the place. 'I'll take over,' he said, and did so just as there was a scream from below and Saida called out, 'I can't take it any more.'

The boat was veering all over the place. It was very dark, with only white streaks of foam, the deck wet and slippery, as the girl emerged from the companionway, Roman behind, reaching to grab her.

'Come on – let's be having you.'

'Never – never again,' she said and tried to get away from him, sliding on the wet deck to the stern. He slid after her, that drunken laugh again, and went straight into her, knocking her over the rail. In a strange way, it was the most shocking thing Khazid had ever known in spite of the violent life he had led. One second she was there, the next gone.

Hussein switched off the engine at once and the boat rolled from side to side. Khazid managed to throw a life-belt over, but to what? A small pool of light from the deck lights, and only darkness beyond.

Roman, on his hands and knees, shouted, 'Silly bitch.'

Khazid kicked him as hard as he could in the ribs. 'You murdering bastard.' Roman managed to get up, scrambled for the companionway, Khazid put a foot in his backside and Roman slid down the steps.

'I'll turn the engine on again,' Hussein called to Khazid.

'What for? She's gone,' Khazid replied. He moved along the deck to the stern. He heard Hussein cry out and there was movement behind him. He turned and there was Roman, swaying drunkenly, an old revolver in his hand.

'See this?' He fired, narrowly missing Khazid. 'You stinking wog. Put your hands on me, would you?' He stepped close.

In an instant Khazid's hand came out of his pocket, the blade of the flick knife jumped and sheared up under Roman's chin into the roof of his mouth.

'How does that suit you?' He swung him round and pushed him over the rail. The body was visible for a moment, then gone. At the same time Hussein switched on the engine and the *Seagull* surged forward.

It was its own world in the wheelhouse, rain dashing against the windscreen, foul weather indeed, and so it had been for an hour since the madness that had cost two lives. It was after midnight when Khazid came up from the galley with an old-fashioned swinging can. The wind howled as the door opened and closed again.

Hanging on to the wheel, Hussein didn't even turn. 'Coffee?' Khazid poured half a cup and Hussein managed to grab it for long enough to get it down.

'Another?'

'I think so.'

Khazid poured, then took one for himself. 'Good,' he said. 'Damn good. I needed that.'

'You didn't reach for the Scotch then?'

'Yes, that too. I was in shock. I've killed

before, as nobody knows better than you, but not that way.'

'No need to feel guilty. If you hadn't bought that knife in St Denis you'd have been over the rail yourself with a bullet in you. The way he treated that girl was an affront to Allah.'

'So what do we do?'

'Why, carry on. Don't worry. As I told Roman, I may know nothing about boats, but as an aircraft pilot I can navigate, read charts, and plot a course soundly enough to find Portland Bill and Peel Strand.'

'Even in this weather?'

'I've already checked the weather reports on the radio. It will moderate the closer we get. There will be fog in the morning, but we'll cope with that as it comes.'

'Anything else? Do you want some sand-wiches? Saida left a stockpile in the fridge.'

'I'll have some when I come down, which I will now actually, because I must contact the Broker. You can take over here for a while.'

*   *   *

The Broker said, 'For God's sake, isn't it possible to control that boy?'

'What he did was totally justified,' Hussein told him. 'George Roman was a foul man and the world is well rid of him, so no apologies are necessary.'

There was not only steel in his voice, but a calm indifference which gave the Broker pause for thought.

'Can you cope?'

'With the boat? Of course I can. There will be considerable fog in the vicinity when we get to Peel Strand. I'll take advantage of the concealment it offers to sink the *Seagull*.'

'Is that necessary?'

'I imagine someone would inform the Coast Guard after a while if it was just left there at anchor. We have a perfectly good inflatable with an outboard motor, so we'll get inshore, no problem.'

'Have you any idea when you'll be in?'

'About four o'clock, something like that. Dawn will be coming up. Roman had an Admiralty chart of the area in the wheelhouse. There is the Strand, some shingle beach indicated, fading into saltings. Wellington lives in the old marsh warden's cottage.'

'Good. I'll contact him, tell him to meet you.'

'What will you say? That there was an accident?'

'I think not. I'll say Roman turned back close to shore because he was afraid of running aground in the fog.'

'And the inflatable?'

'He told me to say that he could keep it.'

'I'm sure Darcus will be pleased. It would seem the panic button has been of use.'

'So it would appear,' the Broker said.

'What about Professor Khan? When can I contact him?'

'Whenever you consider it appropriate. It's up to you.'

Hussein went back to the wheelhouse. Khazid seemed happy enough, hands still firmly on the wheel. 'How did it go?'

Hussein told him what the Broker had said and filled him in on what he had been told earlier at the café in St Denis.

'So not only have the Salters dealt with the Russian Mafia in London, but the IRA mercenaries have been stamped on. Six of them taken out. This is beginning to sound like serious business,' Khazid commented.

'We've handled serious business before.' Hussein smiled. 'I'm going to go and lie on a bunk for an hour. Wake me.' He went below.

Darcus Wellington, at Folly Way on Peel Strand, came awake with an angry moan and scrabbled for the bedside telephone, knocking over a half-empty cup of cold coffee. He sat up in his tumbled bed and reached for the light.

'Who in the hell is it?'

The answer galvanized him into action and he swung his legs to the floor, an old-fashioned nightshirt riding over his knees.

'Your visitors are arriving soon,' the Broker told him. 'A rotten morning, I think you'll find. It would be a nice thought if you took a walk down to the Strand about four-thirty and extended the hand of welcome. And, remember, these are special people.'

'With Hussein's face in all the papers, they would be.'

'Don't start moaning. I'll be in touch.'

He clicked off and Wellington sat there for a moment breathing deeply. His head was bald, his face sagged, but over sixty years in show business had to stand for something. He got up and drew the curtains. Although there were undeniable signs of early dawn, the fog crouched at the window as if trying to get in at him.

'Dear God Almighty.'

He went into the bathroom, turned on the shower, stood looking at it and changed his mind. He returned to the bedroom, where he removed his nightshirt and dressed in a denim shirt and brown corduroy trousers and buttoned up a sweater with a shawl collar. His dressing table provided a plentiful supply of make-up and he sat down, rubbing cream into his face, a little rouge to his cheeks and liner around his eyes. It undeniably worked in a theatrical kind of way, one had to admit that. Finally he picked up the auburn wig that curled discreetly and eased it over his bald pate. Satisfied, he stood up and made his way out through a rather charming, old-fashioned sitting room to the kitchen.

Like the other rooms, it had beamed ceilings, but everything else was state of the art, a kind of temple to a person who adored cooking. He turned on the kettle, humming to himself, got a bowl of muesli, and milk from the fridge, and ate without any obvious enjoyment. When the kettle boiled he made green tea and went and peered out for another look at the fog.

He checked his watch and saw it was just after four. 'Oh, well,' he said softly. 'I suppose I'd better make a move.'

He fetched a pair of rubber boots from the cloakroom, went out to the hall and sat down to pull them on, reached for a heavy anorak with a hood, and ventured outside.

The fog swirled and there was a drizzle of fine rain. There was the pond and the special smell you only got from saltings. He followed a track along a dike, passing through a bleak landscape of silted-up sea creeks and mud flats. Climate change and the rising sea level had had their effect on what had been a rather special place. Even the birds seemed to be hiding from it. He reached a very ancient, decaying sea wall of stone, beach pilings beyond it, the shingle dipping down, disappearing into the fog, and the noise of the approaching engine was loud.

'Hello – over here!' he called.

Hussein had taken advantage of the boat's depth sounder as he took the *Seagull* in. A hundred feet seemed appropriate. He switched off the engine.

'Pull the inflatable round from the stern, untie her and get in.'

'What about you?' Khazid said.

Hussein was removing the engine hatch. 'I'll operate the sea cocks.' He disappeared into the cramped engine room, found what he needed almost straightaway, did what was necessary and scrambled out.

He joined Khazid in the inflatable and drifted away with a push. They continued drifting and sat there watching the boat settling in the water. Hussein found his cigarettes, lit one and passed it to Khazid, then lit one for himself. The sea was swirling across the *Seagull's* deck, the boat settled much more and then completely disappeared.

'It's supposed to be sad to see a ship of any kind sinking,' Khazid said.

'Why would that be?' Hussein pressed the starter button on the outboard and the engine kicked into life.

'It's like someone dying.'

'Is that so?'

A small wind curled across the water, not much, but enough to stir the fog. There was a vague suggestion of land, and then the sound of Darcus Wellington calling to them. Hussein throttled back the engine and they drifted in.

'Where's Roman and the *Seagull*?' Darcus asked.

'He didn't fancy his chances much in this fog,' Hussein said. 'It's an absolute peasouper all over the bay and he started worrying about the boat. In the end he decided we must come in the inflatable. He said you could keep it.'

'Did he now? Well, that's nice of him. I'll walk along the beach about fifty yards. There's what's left of an old stone jetty. You can disembark without having to wade. Pull the thing ashore for me.'

A matter of minutes and it was done, the inflatable ashore and the two Iraqis standing beside it.

'Darcus Wellington, that's me, and you'll be the Hammer of God, according to the newspapers. Who's your friend?'

'My name is Henri Duval,' Khazid said.

'Darling,' Darcus told him cheerfully, 'if you're Henri Duval I'm Prince Charles.'

They had started to climb to the dike and Khazid said, in his perfect French, 'But I assure you, mon ami, I am who I say I am.'

Darcus was impressed. 'Well, that's a show-stopper, I must say. You can certainly speak the lingo.' The rain increased in a sudden rush. 'Come on, hurry up or we'll all get soaked.'

He started to jog and the fog was clearing now so that they could see the house before they got there. He flung open the front door and led the way in. 'Folly Way,' he said. 'That's what they called it when Bernard and I bought it. He was my partner. It was a sea marsh then, creeks gurgling with water, wonderful plants, lots of bird life. Then a few years ago, after Bernard died, I'd come back from touring and find it had altered, changed a little bit more. Something to do with sea levels and silting up. Anyway, welcome to the end of the world.'

'Why do you call it that?' Hussein asked.

'Because every time I go away and return, I think it's died just a little bit more. But never mind that. Take off your coats, come in the kitchen and I'll make you a nice breakfast.'

13

The breakfast was remarkable by any standards. Darcus poached haddock, scrambled eggs, sliced onion, found a packet of unleavened bread in his freezer and defrosted it. There was yoghurt and fruit in plenty, and green tea.

'Cooking's my passion. I've worked as a chef in my day, but I lost my temper with the staff too easily. I expected too much.' He started to gather in the crockery and put it in the dishwasher. 'I've been in show business all my life since I first saw a circus when I was thirteen. There's nothing I haven't tried. Cabaret, theatre, film. Having a settled home to come back to was always a problem. That's why Bernard and I bought this place. I mean, it seemed a good idea at the time. We were in summer cabaret at Bournemouth – that's a seaside town near here. We went for a drive one Sunday and came across this place, a bloody sight different from what it is now, I can tell you. Folly Way just about sums it up.'

He talked endlessly, much of it amusing, and yet there was a certain malice when he touched on people. 'Talent, love,' he said to Hussein, 'is a curse. It's something your fellow actors can never forgive. Of course, some things are beyond teaching. Take you. You've got an enormous talent.'

'What for?' Hussein asked.

'For killing people. I mean, it's not a very easy thing to do. You do it remarkably well. You're a true revolutionary, dedicated to a cause. Che Guevara – that's who you most resemble. A romantic hero with balls. You even look like Che with that beard.'

'Hey, that's good,' Khazid said. 'I mean, I actually think there could be some truth in that.' He said to Darcus, 'There are kids in Baghdad who are proud to wear T-shirts with "Hammer of God" on them.'

'But not his face, love?' Darcus was aghast. 'I mean we couldn't have that.'

'One day,' Khazid said, 'when Iraq is free again, his face will be known to all men.'

'Well, he wouldn't be the first revolutionary to end up president of his country. What about George Washington?'

'Exactly,' Khazid said.

Hussein, uncomfortable with all this, said, 'Let's get down to important matters. What about the weaponry?'

'God knows I've got enough of that, not that I've ever fired a gun in my life. This way, gentlemen.'

He led the way to his study, in the centre of the house. The panelled walls of yew were lined with scores of framed photos of the theatre, film and television.

'My life in performance, and what a performance! I deserved an Oscar.'

'But what's this got to do with weaponry?' Hussein asked.

Wellington smiled and kicked in the bottom of the end panelling, producing a sharp click, and a hidden door moved a couple of inches. He pulled it right back, stepped inside and switched on a light, revealing guns and accessories of every kind. 'Behold my treasures.'

Hussein noted several Walthers, Carswell silencers, Colts, machine pistols such as the very latest model of Uzi, three AKs, a box of hand grenades and even Semtex and a box of pencil fuses, neatly numbered. 'My God,' he said. 'You really are going to war.'

'Not me, love. Like I told you, I've never fired a gun in my life. You two have a good look and work out what you want. I'll be in the kitchen doing my chores. Take your time.' He left Hussein and Khazid sorting through the weapons.

'The usual gear,' Khazid said. 'Tools of the assassin's trade.'

'You're being dramatic,' Hussein replied. 'They do the job, and in unfortunate circumstances they're easy to get rid of. The jobs ahead of us won't lend themselves to a sniper.'

'A grenade perhaps?'

'Pointless. No need for it. It's two individuals we want, not passers-by.'

'OK if I take an Uzi, with folding stock, if it fits in my flight bag?'

Hussein, exasperated, said, 'Have it your way. Check the weapons here at the study table. Ammunition, of course, but you needn't overdo it. We could always call on Khan in London for more.'

At Holland Park, Dillon was finishing an early breakfast when Roper called him on the intercom and asked him to come up to the computer room.

'What have you got?' Dillon demanded.

'My contact in the Spanish Secret Service has been in touch. A float plane stolen in Khufra has turned up dumped in Majorca. Even more interesting, his informant in the police at Khufra tells of a Citation jet the other night dropping off two men. It seems there was some sort of shoot-out.'

'Then they stole the float plane. Hussein's an expert pilot. It has to be him. But who's the other man?'

'He left Baghdad with three men. Hamid

and Hassim, whom you and Billy shot, and a man named Khazid. And before you ask, let me put those security photos from Kuwait up, but they're not good, nothing on Khazid.'

'Have we got anything on this Khazid at all?'

'Hussein's third cousin, and another Rashid. A highly experienced foot soldier. Some sort of cousin to Sara, I suppose, and something in common with her.'

'What would that be?'

'Another half-and-half. His mother was French.'

'Was?'

'Got killed in the first Gulf War with his father, fleeing from Kuwait on the Highway of Death in a car.'

'So – what does it mean?' Dillon said.

'Hang on, there's more. International airport at Palma, flights to all sorts of destinations. The Spanish have been rather clever. The police checked around the cove where the float plane came in and it was heard landing. If you then calculate how long it would take to make the airport, we could say about noon, and for men desperate to get the hell out of there that narrows the time of departure.'

'Which means the Spanish didn't have to painstakingly work their way through the tapes for hours.'

'Well, see for yourself.' Roper brought it up on screen, Hussein walking through security, pausing to take off his sunglasses briefly while his boarding ticket was being checked. The man behind him was obviously Khazid, because they were talking, but his face was half-turned away.

'You have the plane?'

'It was one of those low-price efforts, crammed with tourists. There were some empty seats. They've gone to Rennes in France.'

'A staging post to England?'

'Absolutely. Brittany means the Channel Islands, and once on Jersey it's British soil. Daily planes to Britain and the South Coast. That's only conjecture, mind you, but I'd say he's on his way, and we know what that means.'

Dillon sat there thinking about it. 'Right, we pass the word round to everybody. Use all the press contacts to keep his photo going and the line that he could be in the UK.'

'Yes, but the emphasis is on that word "could". We're at a dead stop here, waiting for something to turn up.'

'The only thing that's going to turn up is Hussein with Khazid. You know it and I know it, and we know what the target is going to be: the Rashids in Gulf Road, Hampstead.'

'So what do you suggest?'

'It's up to Ferguson to decide that. Maybe keep them here at the safe house,' Dillon told him.

'Dr Rashid won't like that.'

'It could be she hasn't got much choice in the matter. You'd better speak to Ferguson.'

By the time Ferguson had arrived in the Daimler, Roper had called in Billy and Greta, Igor Levin and Chomsky. They all listened gravely as Roper explained the situation.

When he had finished, there were grave

looks. He added, 'Of course, this is just a "maybe" situation. We can't be sure of anything.'

Billy said, 'Only of one thing: the bastard's on his way. I know that, and I think everybody else here knows that. The question is, what do we do about it?'

'Move the Rashids from Hampstead, that's essential. Right out of town and away from everything while we hunt him down.'

'Molly won't like that,' Greta said. 'Through everything, she's stuck to the idea that her work is of prime importance. She won't want to leave it.'

'I think she'll have to,' Ferguson told her.

There was a silence, then Greta said, 'One thing I still wonder about. What exactly does Hussein intend? To kidnap the girl and take her back?'

'How would he do that?' Levin asked.

'Exactly!'

Billy said, 'Maybe he wants to knock off Caspar for his part in saving her?'

'Which would still leave him with the Sara problem.'

Roper said, 'Perhaps he doesn't know himself. We don't need to go into his background, you all know it. The deaths in his extended family alone would be a sufficient cause for revenge to many people, and it's certainly enough to make him a driven man.'

'And one of the world's most successful assassins,' Levin put in.

There was another silence, and it was Billy, a gangster and streetwise since his youth, who said, 'It might be a lot simpler than we think. Maybe he's just striking out, hasn't thought it through.'

'God help us if that's what it is,' Ferguson said. 'If he doesn't know himself, what chance do we have?'

'None,' Dillon said and turned to Ferguson. 'What did you mean when you said the Rashids should be moved from Hampstead and away from everything?'

'We have a country house called Zion Place in West Sussex and close to the coast and marshland. It was donated to the Ministry of Defence in the Second World War and used to train SOE agents. Over the years it's been

435

used by the Ministry for training purposes, but at the moment it's in a caretaker situation, watched over by half a dozen uniformed security men, all ex-military police run by Captain Bosey.'

Dillon said, 'This marshland, what would be the situation there?'

'It's owned by the National Trust. The bird life is unique. Curlew, redshank and brant geese from Siberia, that sort of thing.'

'Are bird-watchers a problem?'

'Zion Place has unique features. High-security fencing on top of the wall, and if you tried to get over that you'd fry.'

'Sounds a bit harsh.'

'Warning signs everywhere, security cameras. We can't do more. There's never been a problem with any attempts at unlawful entry in the twenty or more years that I've been responsible for it.'

'Sounds good to me,' Dillon said. 'Anything else?'

'There's a concrete airstrip there at the side of the marsh from SOE days. We could fly the Rashids down from Farley, and any of you lot.'

'It would certainly clear the decks,' Dillon said. 'Who would you send?'

'Greta has good contacts with the family. If Levin and Sergeant Chomsky went with her for starters, that would make it a Russian affair.'

There were nods all round. 'Sounds good to me,' Dillon said. 'Let's get moving, and sort it with the Rashids.'

'You and Greta come with me, the rest stay. Roper in charge.' Ferguson led the way out.

They sat in the sitting room at Gulf Road with Caspar, Molly and Sara, and Ferguson explained patiently what the situation was. Greta stood by the window.

'So what are you trying to tell us?' Molly Rashid demanded. 'That Hussein is here in England?'

'We believe very strongly that he's on his way,' Ferguson said. 'Hazar to Algeria, stealing the float plane to Majorca, then Rennes in Brittany. Look at it on the map and it speaks for itself.'

She sounded desperate. 'He'd be mad to come, and what for?'

Sara stood up. 'If you'll excuse me, I'll go into the garden. Whatever you decide suits me. Zion Place sounds fun.'

'This does concern you, darling,' Caspar said.

'Not really,' Sara said calmly. 'Hussein won't do anything to harm me.' She went out, and Greta followed.

Molly Rashid started again. 'I think you have to realize, General, we're trying to live as normal a life as possible for Sara's sake.'

Dillon got up. 'Your decision. I'll just go out on the terrace for a smoke. It's up to you, General.'

Sara was moving slowly around the garden. Across the road, a sweeper in yellow had noted the arrival of Ferguson's Daimler and its occupants and managed a shot with a special camera donated by Khan.

Dillon lit a cigarette and approached Sara and Greta. 'Hello, Mr Dillon, what do you want?' Sara asked.

'I'm interested in what you said about

Hussein. How can you be so certain? He's a very violent man.'

'I suppose you mean all this Hammer of God thing.' She shrugged. 'In Baghdad it was in the papers and on television, but not with photos, so I didn't know it was Hussein. He always looked after me. Made sure people treated me properly.'

'Did he change then?'

'Not really. At the oasis at Fuad in the Empty Quarter, when the bandit Ali ben Levi manhandled me, Hussein shot him.'

'How did you feel about that?'

'Ben Levi was a truly evil man. He was whipping a priest for being a Christian. I told him that so was I. That's when he treated me as he did.'

Dillon smiled bleakly. 'In those circumstances I'd probably have shot him myself. Tell me, I've no business asking you this, but what about this Muslim thing and being promised in marriage when you're of age?'

'That's nonsense,' she said. 'I never took that seriously, and I told Hussein so.'

'And he accepted that?'

'He was told. I could do no more.'

Dillon took a deep breath. 'You're a truly remarkable young lady.'

Caspar came out on the terrace and called, 'Come on, Sara, it's all decided. We're going to Zion Place, flying down.'

His wife appeared. 'For a week – seven days only, so come and pack.'

The girl joined them, they went inside and she went upstairs.

Ferguson appeared. 'I'm going back to Holland Park. You two stay while they pack. I'll send the people carrier to pick you all up and take the Rashids to Farley. I'll arrange for Levin and Chomsky to meet you there.'

He went off and Dillon said, 'Sara's quite a girl.'

'What do you expect? She's half Bedouin,' Greta remarked. 'Come into the kitchen and we'll have a coffee.'

In his shop near the corner of Gulf Road, Ali Hassim was acting as middle man for

Professor Khan, overseeing a network of sweepers, hospital porters, minicab drivers and even young girls, office personnel at the local hospitals. The sweeper assigned to the Rashid house phoned in.

'They've had visitors. Two of them were on the photos Professor Khan showed us. The General and the man Dillon. There was also a woman. The General left in a Daimler car. I've got pictures. Dillon and the woman are still there.'

'Any sign of the family?'

'Only the girl, Sara. She was in the garden talking to Dillon.'

'I'm going to send Jamal on his motorcycle just in case they go somewhere. He'll be with you in minutes.'

The sweeper waited and then the people carrier turned up, pausing at the electronic gates until they opened. It moved inside and the sweeper caught a glimpse of the front door, Caspar Rashid with two suitcases emerging, his wife behind him, then Sara, Greta and Dillon.

At that moment Jamal arrived on his

motorcycle. He rode down by the canal and into the trees. 'What's happening?' he called.

'They're leaving. It looks to me as if they're all going. I saw suitcases. You must follow.'

'That's what I'm here for, you fool.'

Jamal waited, his engine turning over. The gates opened and the people carrier emerged and turned right, and he followed in traffic so heavy it was possible for him to get really close on more than one occasion so that he soon established who was inside.

At Farley Field he had to turn into the public car park as the van paused at the security entrance and was admitted, but he watched its progress to the terminal building, saw them get out and meet Levin and Chomsky.

A sign at the gate said 'Ministry of Defence, Farley Field, Restricted Area', but in the car park it amused him to see plane-spotters. Probably any kind of security breach would have been classed as a violation of their human rights. 'Only the English,' he said to himself. 'That's why we will win.'

He took out a pair of Zeiss glasses. The plane was an old Hawk, though he didn't know it, but he did get a photo.

On the airfield Dillon waited for the plane to take off, then got back in the people carrier and told Sergeant Doyle to take him to Holland Park.

Jamal waited until it had gone, then mounted his motorcycle. There was nothing he could do except return to Ali Hassim at the shop.

Ali hauled him into the back room. 'You're sure they have gone?'

'Definitely. The suitcases mean for some time, and the plane means they're going somewhere far away.'

'You had no means of finding out the destination?'

'No way of getting in. I've told you, it's a restricted area. Security guards everywhere. You wouldn't even get through the gate.'

Ali was upset. 'So we really have no idea where they've gone?'

'Only that they *have* gone. I saw this with

my own eyes, and their house is empty. Tell Professor Khan that.'

Ali sighed. 'He won't like it. Anyway, go and make yourself a coffee in the kitchen while I give him the bad news, and leave your camera so I can check the photo for the type of plane.'

It didn't take long and he found it quite quickly in a handbook of small planes: a Hawk, eight seater, twin engines.

He started to go through a number of photos taken by the sweepers watching the comings and goings at the Rashid's house since their return, not that there had been many. The most interesting was the man who had turned out to be the archaeologist from Hazar, Professor Hal Stone. Friends to the Brotherhood, academics at London University, had confirmed his identity. He was a Fellow at Corpus Christi College in Cambridge. He had called at the house in Gulf Road in a taxi, which had waited for him and taken him on to King's Cross station. Jamal had followed him and watched him board a train for Cambridge. Obviously returning to his work.

All in all, not good news, and he phoned Khan and told him so.

Hussein sat in front of the make-up table in Darcus Wellington's bedroom, naked to the waist. The mirror was very bright with all those small bulbs around it, and the profusion of make-up itself was something alien to Hussein and he found the smell of it distasteful.

Khazid was sitting on a settle by the window, smoking a cigarette. Hussein said, 'Open the window, then go and find something to do.'

'But I want to watch.'

'And I don't want you to. Go away.'

Khazid went reluctantly and Darcus put a large towel around Hussein's shoulders. 'The mark of a true actor, love. Make-up is such a private affair. Not something to share. Knowing who you are, that's the thing.'

'And who am I?' Hussein asked himself. 'Hussein Rashid or the Hammer of God?'

Rain fell heavily outside the open window, bringing the smell of rotting vegetation, and Darcus went and closed the window. 'If you don't mind, love, it smells as if the whole world's dying.'

'Perhaps in some ways it is,' Hussein said.

Garish in his auburn wig, Darcus stood there, arms folded, chin on one hand, and observed him. 'The Che Guevara look. Was that a conscious decision on your part?'

'Not that I know of.' Hussein was beginning to feel uncomfortable.

'A true romantic, Guevara. He really looked the part. In a way he gave people what they expected. It was all in the look, love. Was that what you tried to do, give the people what they expected?'

'Where would this be leading?'

'It's also a question of knowing what you are and still liking yourself. Most actors, of course, would rather be someone else.'

'I am what I am. What I need from you is a new face.'

'Frankly, I have a suspicion that I can achieve that best by removing the mask that's already there.'

Hussein said, 'If that means goodbye Che Guevara, so be it.'

'And what else must go with that?'

'I don't know. We'll have to see.'

The corridor door was slightly ajar, and Khazid watched in a kind of horror as the man he had served for so long changed before his eyes. Darcus worked at the hair, cutting, thinning particularly, shaping into an entirely different style and making it much, much shorter.

Then he lathered the entire face and took a cut-throat razor to it, shortening the sideburns, thinning the eyebrows and very carefully removing the fringe of beard and the moustache.

'I'd like you in the bathroom now, love. Don't be alarmed, you just need a shampoo.'

Khazid dodged into the kitchen and Darcus led the way.

Afterwards, back at the mirror and using a hair dryer, he shaped the hair more carefully, took the scissors to it again, then turned Hussein in the swivel chair, did some more work on thinning the eyebrows and applied a little dark pencil.

Hussein sat staring at himself, yet not

himself. 'God Almighty, you look so young,' Darcus told him. 'How old are you?'

'Twenty-five.'

'And now you look it, and that's the difference. Put your shirt on.'

He scrabbled around in various drawers and finally found what he was looking for: a pair of horn-rimmed glasses, not prescription, but clear glass. 'Try these.' Hussein did. 'Good, it gives you a hint of the intellectual. You could be a schoolteacher or something.'

'Not the Hammer of God.'

'See for yourself.' Darcus opened a copy of *The Times* with the original photo in it. 'Who could possibly recognize you from that as you look now?'

'Even I don't,' Hussein said slowly and walked through to the kitchen.

Khazid was waiting for the kettle to boil, standing there, looking out at the rain. He turned, and his sense of shock was obvious.

'Merciful heaven, where have you gone?' He shook his head. 'I'm not sure it's you any more.'

'And maybe it isn't.' There was a strange

smile on Darcus's face. 'Who knows? Remember Pandora's box?'

'What do you mean?' Khazid said.

'Greek mythology,' Hussein told him. 'When the box was opened, it released all sorts of unpleasant things.'

Khazid, uneasy, frowned slightly and Darcus said, 'I'll make some coffee.'

'And I'll phone Dreq Khan,' Hussein said to Khazid. 'Work out our next stop.'

'Hampstead?' Khazid asked.

'It would seem obvious. After all, as no one knows we are here. One should seize the moment.'

'If you say so, but I think we need to talk, and privately.'

'Of course.'

'You can use the study.' Darcus said, but they went outside on the porch, the door open, the rain pouring down.

'Is there a problem?' Hussein asked.

'Hampstead, Sara, her parents. Surely our primary task, the most important to our cause, is the assassination of General Ferguson, and this man Salter if possible. If we go to London with that in mind we could succeed, because, as you rightly point out, the authorities have no idea that you're in England. In light of this, I'm in favour of us going to London, but not of a visit to Hampstead. Sara and her parents are a side-show, cousin. What would you do, shoot her parents? I shouldn't imagine she'd thank you.'

'Don't be a fool,' Hussein told him.

'Or break in the house, kidnap her? Then how would you smuggle her out of the country?'

'Professor Khan, the Army of God, the Brotherhood, they would all offer their ser-vices. Between us we would find a way.'

'Do you honestly think the fate of this young girl is of the slightest importance to these people? No, but Ferguson's head on a platter, the British Prime Minister's most valued secu-rity advisor – that would be a triumph.'

Much of what he said made sense, but Hussein was unable to let go. 'I'll phone Khan now and see what the situation is, then it will be my decision.'

*   *   *

In answer to Ali Hassim's call, Khan had gone round to the shop to discuss the latest development, and it was there that he received the call that he had, if truth be known, been dreading for some time.

He put a hand over his coded mobile and whispered to Ali Hassim, 'It's him, Hussein Rashid himself, and he's in England.'

'Allah be praised,' Ali said.

Khan returned to the phone. 'Where are you?'

'Dorset – Peel Strand, with one of the Broker's people. A cottage called Folly Way. Khazid and I landed this morning. We intend to come to London.'

'Can this be wise? Your face is in so many newspapers.'

'That's been taken care of. No one will recognize me. Trust me in this. Now tell me what the situation is with the Rashids.'

'We monitored them closely, my network of sweepers and informants, even used a motorcycle unit so that cars which left their house in Hampstead could be followed. Because of this I have the address of the enemy's safe house in Holland Park. We know where Ferguson and Dillon live, which would obviously be of importance to you.'

Hussein cut in on him. 'Get to the point. You appear to have some bad news for me. Spit it out.'

So Khan told him the worst.

Hussein said, 'They've gone, spirited away you don't know where, and the circumstances indicate only security-classified travel?'

'I'm afraid so.'

'You didn't mention the plane.'

'Ali looked it up. A Hawk.'

'A good old workhorse of a plane. I flew one in the badlands in Algeria. I think if they'd been venturing very far, say cross-Channel, they'd have used more than that. I would say the Hawk indicates relatively local travel. Somewhere in the countryside, a reasonable distance from London.'

'Which would be impossible for us to discover,' Khan said.

'So Ferguson and Dillon visited the house in Gulf Road. Anyone else?'

'Yes, Professor Hal Stone.'

'The archaeologist from Hazar. I wonder what he wanted.'

'I think he was saying goodbye. One of my men, Jamal, followed him to King's Cross, where he caught a train to Cambridge. He's a professor at Corpus Christi College there. It's now turned out he's Ferguson's cousin.'

'Is he indeed? He's been involved in this affair intimately. I'll bet he possesses all the information we need.'

'You could be right.'

'I think I am. Ali Hassim – tell me about him.' Khan did, and when he had finished, Hussein said, 'Is he to be trusted?'

'Completely. Few people actually know how important he is.'

'Then I'll have his address. He may expect me at any time.'

'What is your intention?'

'I'll visit this Hal Stone at Cambridge University today. Bournemouth is close to where I am. We'll go by train.'

'To Cambridge? You'd have to change in London. Is this wise?'

'My dear Professor, even I don't recognize myself. I'll be in touch.'

He turned and found Khazid watching him, face troubled. 'I'll explain it all later when we're on the train,' he said. 'But I must speak to the Broker.'

He lit a cigarette after pressing the panic button and waited, calm and in charge of himself again. The Broker called him instantly. Very quickly, Hussein explained the situation and his intentions.

'Do you approve?'

'I must say I do. I can't access the departures from Farley like I used to be able to. It has a special security system. I can only wish you luck in Cambridge. Are you sure of your safety in travelling? Is Darcus that good?'

'Yes is the short answer to that. Goodbye.'

He brushed past Khazid and found Darcus in the kitchen. 'We need to get to Bournemouth. I presume there's a reasonable train service from there?'

'Yes, excellent. When would you be leaving?'

'As soon as you like.'

'Not me, love. I've got prostate problems you wouldn't want to hear about. Our doctor only looks in twice a week, that's up in Peel Strand village. It's only half a mile, so I usually walk.' He looked at the time. 'Ten o'clock, and he doesn't arrive until after lunch.'

'So what's the alternative?' Khazid asked.

'You can take my car, leave it in the car park at Bournemouth station and leave the key in the glove compartment. I can't say fairer than that. I think you'd have to change in London to get to Cambridge, though. Anyway, it's been great meeting you. Makes life so much more interesting.'

'And lucrative for you?' Hussein said.

'Of course, love. We all need to earn a crust.'

They were fully clothed, flight bags in hand and on their way within fifteen minutes. An old Mini awaited them in the rain by the garage.

'The key's in. Good luck,' Darcus shouted and closed the door.

Hussein got behind the wheel and Khazid slipped off his wristwatch, put it in his rain-coat pocket and leaned down. 'Sorry – I left my watch in the bathroom. I'll just be a minute.'

Darcus had told them as part of his goodbye chatter that they'd have to change trains in London for Cambridge, but the only mention of Cambridge had been in Hussein's supposedly private conversations when he and Khazid had been in the study, which meant Darcus had been listening.

Khazid stepped into the porch, opened his flight bag, took out a Walther and screwed on the Carswell. He eased open the door to the hall, aware of the voice whittering on.

'My goodness, Charlie darling, if you knew what I've been up to.'

Khazid whistled softly. Darcus turned. 'Oh, my God.' He put the phone down.

Khazid said, 'Naughty, Darcus, very.' He shot him between the eyes and turned away.

He threw his flight bag in the back of the Mini and got in, putting on his watch.

'OK?' Hussein asked.

'Never better,' and they drove away.

*   *   *

The flight from Farley had been placed in the hands of Lacey and Parry by Ferguson's direct order for the obvious reason that they knew everybody. Levin and Chomsky needed introducing to the Rashids, and Greta took care of that. Sara responded well to Levin and Chomsky, but the one person who wasn't happy at all was Molly Rashid.

She and her husband were sitting together in the two rear seats. Their conversation was at first just a murmur, but it became increasingly fraught.

'Where on earth is it getting us all?' Molly asked.

'It's for our own good. Just a week until we see how things develop,' replied Caspar.

'I've my work to consider, some of the most important of my life.'

'But the colleagues who've stepped in for you are first-class people.'

'That isn't the point. The Bedford child, for example. Absolutely ground-breaking stuff. I should be hovering over her every day of the week, and where am I? It won't do, Caspar.'

'The Bedford child has got good people hovering over her, seeing to her every need like we're doing with our child.'

Sara smiled solemnly at Levin and raised her eyes, then she turned, kneeling on her seat, and said, 'Is there any way you could treat this like a holiday in the country, so that we can all get along together, because that's what I intend to do.' She didn't wait for an answer, just swivelled round and said, 'Tell me some more about the Kremlin, Igor. I think it sounds fascinating.'

Her parents, embarrassed, were reduced to silence, and a moment later Lacey said, 'Our short flight is coming to an end, folks. That's the Sussex coastline over there. You'll notice quite extensive salt marshes. There's a village of Zion, but Zion Place is three miles outside it and close to the marshes. We're going down now.'

They descended and moved in at 500 feet. The house looked like everything it should be, with gracious gardens, and stone walls surrounding it, some sort of wire running along the top. There was a guard house at the gate. The marsh was very near to the house, huge reeds springing out of the water, leading to a dike, the landing strip on the other side of it.

'Is that what they call a grass runway?' she asked Levin.

'No, it's concrete. Have you done this before?'

'Oh, yes, in the Empty Quarter. We had to land in the sand at Fuad. There was oil seal trouble in the port engine. Oil was spilling out and burning. You've never seen such black smoke. It was lucky Hussein was doing the flying. He's a wonderful pilot. He let me do the navigating.' She leaned back as they touched down. 'I'm really going to enjoy myself here.'

And to that, there was little that anyone could say.

They bumped down on the concrete runway. There was no hangar, just a wooden hut. The man waiting for them wore a navy blue uniform and a clipped moustache, his cap under his left arm, all very regimental. There was a van beside him.

As they approached, he said, 'Captain Rodger Bosey. I run things here. You're all very welcome. What about you chaps?' he asked the pilots.

'We're under General Ferguson's command,' Lacey said, 'and he wants a quick return. Things are a bit fraught, so we'll take off straightaway. See you all soon,' and he and Parry got back in the Hawk.

There were introductions, then they all got in the van and watched the take-off. 'Here we go then. I'll take you all up to the house and settle you in.'

They turned along a dike, and through a fringe of pine trees, the great reeds of the marsh close, trembling in the wind. A little way off there was a group of people in anoraks, sitting on a bank, eating sandwiches.

'Bird-watchers,' Bosey told them. 'We get a few of those.'

'Any problem?' Levin said.

'Not really. Sometimes if some rare bird turns up, the numbers increase. They're completely harmless from my point of view.

Some do make a bit of a holiday out of it, stay at a bed and breakfast in Zion village, and there's a place that hires caravans. Harmless eccentrics, in a way.'

'Why do you say that?' Sara demanded.

'Well, I remember one of them telling me in the pub that the rooks in the village came from St Petersburg in October, the winter there for them being too cold. Starlings, too.'

'Why would that make them eccentric?' Sara asked.

'Doesn't seem all that likely.'

'The Russians ring birds, too. I'm sure they could do that in St Petersburg. Don't you think so, Igor?' Sara asked.

'Ask Greta. She comes from St Petersburg.'

'Yes, they do ring rooks there and they do fly away to avoid the Russian winter. I learned this as a little girl.'

'Well, there you are then,' Sara said, and they pulled up at the gate. A man in a similar uniform to Bosey looked out, then operated the electronic barrier, which rose.

'Hello,' Sara called cheerfully, and he grinned and saluted. 'Wasn't that nice? I feel like the Queen now. You run a good outfit, Captain Bosey.'

Her mother muttered, 'For goodness' sake, Sara.'

But Bosey, totally charmed, flushed with pleasure, although he couldn't think of a thing to say.

In a way it was rather like the old days in that kind of house, for they were greeted on the wide steps by a middle-aged lady whom Bosey introduced as Mrs Bertha Tetley, the housekeeper, who lived in, as did her support staff, Kitty, Ida and Vera.

'If you follow me, I'll show you all your rooms. Luncheon will be served soon. This way.' She took them through to the vast hall and led the way upstairs.

'I'll see you in a moment and we'll discuss things,' Levin said to Bosey, who nodded.

When Levin and Chomsky came downstairs they found Bosey in the library. He offered them a drink and they settled for vodka. 'Have you been here long?' Levin asked.

'Ten years, and not just for General Ferguson, but I've handled jobs for him on a number of occasions, so I've come to know him well.'

'You were an army man?'

'Military police.'

'An excellent recommendation. What do you know about this business?'

'General Ferguson told me all I need. We're providing refuge for the Rashid family, who are apparently under some terrorist threat. A period of one week, longer if needed. I understand that you gentlemen and Miss Novikova are members of General Ferguson's security outfit, and that's enough for me. We have weaponry on the premises, but don't usually carry it.'

'Good man, and it's Major Novikova. She outranks us all.' At that moment she came in. 'Just in time for a drink, Major,' Levin said. He winked at Bosey, who smiled and reached for the vodka bottle.

'Thank you, Captain.' She toasted them. 'To a pleasant stay and all our troubles over.'

There were voices on the stairs outside, Sara's, and then Caspar and Molly followed her into the library. Sara was in excellent spirits.

'This is nice,' she said and ran to the window. Caspar looked hunted and his wife unhappy. 'Is lunch ready?' Caspar asked.

'There's something we have to get clear first,' Levin said, 'and this comes directly from General Ferguson. The house phones are only for use internally. You can't call London. If we communicate with the outside world, it must be through Captain Bosey and his coded mobile system in the communications room. The staff are not allowed personal mobiles on the premises.'

'What on earth are you talking about?' Molly exclaimed.

Her husband said warily, 'A call from a mobile phone can be very easily traced.'

'What nonsense! It's preposterous.'

'At the moment no one knows where you are,' Greta said patiently. 'We'd prefer to leave it that way.'

'So I am not allowed to phone a hospital to check on my patients?'

'For God's sake.' Caspar took a mobile phone from his pocket and slammed it down on the table. 'It's only for a week.'

Molly took a deep breath and seemed about to explode, and then the breath went out of her. She opened her handbag and took out not one, but two phones. 'If you must, and Sara's, of course.'

Sara said, 'Cheer up, Mummy. We're going to have a lovely time. Now let's eat.'

After lunch Molly went up to the bedroom and checked the luggage, which included her doctor's bag. She opened it, pulled her stethoscope out of the way and revealed the spare mobile and its charger she always kept in there in case of a hospital emergency. At least she could still check on the progress of the Bedford child, but it could wait.

14

Hal Stone had a mews cottage in Chapel Lane, Cambridge, even though his position at Corpus Christi entitled him to rooms at the college. The cottage was somewhere to hide from the incessant demands of students when he was writing a book.

It was a Victorian cottage consisting of three bedrooms, a study, a kitchen and a lovely sitting room, its old-fashioned French windows opening onto his great pride, a garden surrounded by flint walls with a door that led to a back lane.

He was in the kitchen making tea when his phone rang. He answered it, declaring, 'Hal Stone has gone away.'

'No, he hasn't, you daft bastard,' Roper said. 'You've just got back.'

'Ah, Roper, is that you? You're not wanting me for anything active again? After Hazar, I need a rest. Indiana Jones I'm not.'

'Don't worry, old boy, I'm just bringing you up to speed on what's happened. Just listen.' He went through everything: Hussein's departure from Hazar with Khazid, what had taken place in Algeria, the stolen float plane to Majorca, the security film at Palma, the plane to Rennes.

'Well, I see where you're coming from. It looks like a stage-by-stage progress to England.'

'Where else? No point in bringing the French in because of that plane at Rennes. He would have been out of France to wherever long ago.'

'I still can't see it, him coming to England. It would be suicide. I mean, his face has been all over the place. Somebody somewhere would be bound to recognize him. He's hardly had time for plastic surgery.'

'God knows, it's beyond me, but at night alone in front of the computers and fighting my own personal pain with more whisky, I look at him on the screen and think he's on his way.'

'So what are you doing about it?'

'We've persuaded the Rashids to vacate the Hampstead house and fly down to the depths of West Sussex for a week in a safe house. Zion Place.'

'Now that does sound interesting. Tell me more.'

Roper did, everything, including the report he'd just had in from Levin. 'Molly Rashid's a tough one. Likes her own way too much. The business about her mobile, all that fuss. Too damn much.'

'She's a truly fine surgeon, and people like that are obsessive. They think that what they do is more important than anything else. Unfortunately, it often is.'

'Anyway, now you know the present score,' Roper said. 'To a great extent we're in Hussein's hands.'

'And I think he won't come at all.' Hal Stone laughed. 'After all, he's a Harvard man. He'd have more sense.'

'Try telling them that at Yale,' Roper told him.

'I wish you luck, my friend. Take care.'

'So long.'

Hal Stone shook his head. Crazy, the whole business. He returned to making his tea.

At that moment Hussein and Khazid, having arrived in Cambridge without incident on the train from London, were in a shop specializing in academic gowns, college scarves and the like. Khazid, under Hussein's orders, purchased a short gown of the type worn by undergraduates, but not a Corpus Christi scarf.

'I expect the porters pride themselves on knowing their own students.'

Khazid went down the list and chose a New Hall scarf and a dark beret, and they left. Entrance to the college was no problem, students passing in and out through the gates – students everywhere, or so it seemed. They moved up a floor and Khazid, in his Henri Duval persona, stopped a passing female undergraduate and inquired for Professor Stone in English heavily laced with French, his beret helping establish his nationality.

She was obviously amused, but waved towards the other end of the corridor. 'Down there, but he's never in.'

'Then where would he be, mademoiselle?'

'Don't ask me. Try the phone book.'

She hurried away. Khazid shrugged. They reached the end of the corridor and found a wooden sign hanging on the door saying simply, 'Hal Stone Is Not Here Today.'

Khazid tried the door, but it was locked. 'Now what do we do?'

'The obvious,' Hussein told him. 'We do what the girl suggested and look in a phone book.'

'And what if he's not in?'

'You're a pessimist, my friend. He's a famous man at one of the great colleges, a professor of the University of Cambridge – of course he'll be in the phone book. Now let's find one.'

At Zion Place, Caspar was exploring the garden with his daughter and found some of his cares slipping away. The three Russians sat on the terrace and watched.

'That girl is really quite amazing,' Greta said. 'She can be a child and adore childish things one minute, and the next she's like a mature woman.'

'But then if you consider what she's been through,' Levin said, 'the death, the destruction at such a young age . . .'

Chomsky said, 'In Chechnya, one could see the same look a hundred times on the faces of children that on occasion I have seen on hers. The face goes blank to conceal what lies inside.'

'God help her survive it all. I'll do everything I can to help,' Greta said.

'But the mother,' Levin said, 'is something else.'

'A brilliant surgeon.' Greta nodded and said the same thing as Hal Stone. 'An obsessive who is convinced that what she does is more important than anything else in her life.'

'Good for her ego, but lousy from a relationship point of view,' Levin pointed out.

Upstairs Molly Rashid was proving him

right to a certain extent, locking herself in the bathroom and calling the hospital where she'd operated on the Bedford child, on the direct mobile number of a Dr Harry Sampson who, to a great extent, had taken over for her. She caught him on the ward itself, a private one.

'It's me, Molly Rashid,' she said. 'How is she?'

Although the news was mixed and there was much to say, finally he got personal. 'How are you?'

'Oh, well, I think. We had a problem with Sara, but a rest in the country is doing her good and I'll be back in a week, definitely. But never mind that. It's Lisa Bedford I'm concerned about.'

'Can I have the number in case I need to contact you?'

'We're moving around a bit, Harry. It's not my phone.'

'No, please don't go. I'm really concerned about little Lisa Bedford. You did a wonderful operation and I've got to give this my best shot. It would be good for me to be able to check with you if things do take a turn for the worse.'

In the end, she was trapped, by both her feelings and the situation. 'Dammit, Harry, when you've taken a call you can call me straight back on a mobile. You know that. I said it wasn't my phone, but it is. Call me back any time you want. I'll switch off the sound and leave it on vibration.'

He was concerned. 'Look, are you all right?'

'Oh, everything's in a mess,' she burst out. 'I'm here with Caspar and Sara, at this sort of country retreat in West Sussex. Zion Place.' Instantly regretted, but it was too late.

'You mean some sort of clinic?'

'Oh, God, I don't know what I mean. Goodbye, Harry.'

'Zion Place,' he murmured, put his mobile down on the table and started writing up his notes.

The nurse on duty was a young Muslim woman named Ayesha who had been ordered by Ali Hassim to swap shifts to get on the

Bedford case, precisely because of the connection with Molly Rashid.

'What was that you said, Doctor?'

He looked up, slightly abstracted. 'It was Dr Rashid, wanting to know how the child is getting on. Said she was somewhere called Zion Place in West Sussex. She'll be away for a week. Her daughter's had some problem or other.'

The loudspeaker crackled, calling him on an emergency, and he ran out, leaving his mobile. She pressed the return call button, copied Molly's number and went into an empty room. Since there was no other nurse there she was able to phone Ali Hassim on her own mobile.

When he answered, she said, 'Dr Rashid phoned up to check on the child. She said she was in West Sussex at somewhere called Zion Place. I've also got her mobile phone number for you.'

'Excellent, girl. You have done well.'

'I have only done my duty. I'm sure you can find this place on the internet.'

She was right, of course. Ali immediately

phoned for the assistance of a member of the Brotherhood, giving him the facts and telling him it was urgent. An hour later the man appeared at the shop with his laptop and Ali took him in the back room.

'There are several mentions. The marshland about the place is National Trust. The house itself is mentioned a number of times in an official history of the Special Operations Executive, which who used to train agents there during the Second World War. Since then it's been in the hands of the Ministry of Defence. Apparently there are various restriction orders in place. There is also a concrete runway. Then I've found mention of it in general West Sussex tourist guides. Zion village is three miles from the house, with a medieval church called St Andrew, two pubs, several bed and breakfasts, a caravan site.'

'Brilliant,' Ali said.

'No it's really very simple. These machines can do anything you want them to. You should learn. I'll go now. I must earn a living, you know.'

He left, and Ali sat there trying to think who he should call first.

They found the cottage in Chapel Lane easily enough. There was another message on a board hanging from the front door: 'Students Definitely Not Welcome.'

'A humorist,' Khazid said.

'I knew professors just like that. It's an academic thing. However, if he means it, we don't get in. That's a voice box on the door. If you touch the call button, it usually puts you on screen. Look, there's a camera up there.'

'So what do we do?'

'Let's explore.'

There was a narrow flagged path down one side of the cottage that turned behind the back garden wall. There was a stout wooden door, which was locked, and the top of the wall was crowned with ancient Victorian spikes.

'What do we do?' Khazid asked. 'Try and climb over?'

'If he's there in the kitchen or sitting room he'd be certain to see us and reach for the nearest phone.' Hussein shook his head. 'That notice probably means what it says. There are times when he values his privacy. On the other hand, a young undergraduate in gown and scarf with a beret on his head and a very French accent, seeking advice, might interest him. Go and give it a try at the front door. If it works, take him prisoner. Don't harm him in any way, and let me in through this door.'

'I'll give it a try.'

'No, make it a performance. Go.'

Hal Stone was in the sitting room, reading a rather indifferent thesis, the French windows open to the garden, when he heard the buzz of the entry phone. Irritably he put the thesis to one side, went into the hall and found Khazid on the small screen.

'Who on earth are you?'

'I am Henri Duval of New Hall, Professeur. I am an archaeology and anthropology student. I seek your assistance.'

'Well, as a student at Cambridge you must

be able to read English, and my notice is on the door, so clear off.'

Khazid excelled himself with a stream of very fluent French. 'I beg you, with all my heart. My first year exams are coming up, and I have to write a paper. I genuinely need your advice.'

Hal Stone paused before replying in the same language. 'What's your thesis subject?'

Khazid was feeling more into his role and returned to fractured English, 'The influence of Spartan mercenaries on the wars in Persia.'

Hal Stone laughed out loud. 'That's a tall order, but a glamorous one, which I suppose is why you chose it. All right, I'll give you twenty minutes.'

The door clicked open and Khazid stepped inside, dropping his flight bag and trench-coat to one side, but still wearing the beret and short undergraduate gown. He clutched the silenced Walther in his right hand against his leg and opened the inner door into the hall. Hal Stone was waiting, a smile on his face, which faded instantly as Khazid covered him with the Walther.

'Just do as you're told or I'll shoot you in your left kneecap.'

'Who the hell are you? Is this some kind of joke?'

'We have a debt to settle.'

'I've never seen you before in my life.'

'But I've seen you.' Khazid was so absorbed he'd virtually forgotten about Hussein waiting. 'At Hazar I used to watch you on the deck of the *Sultan* through Zeiss glasses as I stood on the terrace at the great house at Kafkar. You and your people murdered two of my best friends.'

'Dear God,' Stone said. 'You're not Hussein, so you must be the other one, Khazid.' He shook his head. 'Come for your revenge.'

'And I intend to have it,' Khazid told him. 'Your world is a world of books, Professor, but in mine one sword is worth ten thousand words, as it is taught in the Koran.'

'To hell with your damned ideology. What do you want with me?'

'We intended to call on Sara and her parents at their house in Hampstead, but

Ferguson has had them spirited away. We want to know where.'

'And you think I know?'

'You've been involved in the whole business since the beginning, and you're Ferguson's cousin. I'm sure you do.'

'Actually, I don't. And even if I did I wouldn't oblige you.'

'Be it on your own head. Get into the sitting room.'

Stone turned, opened the door, then swung it behind him and ran through the open French windows and made for the garden door. Khazid fired twice. The first shot hit Stone below the left shoulder, driving him against the door. He managed to reach for the large bolt at the top of the door and pulled it to one side, and Khazid shot him again in the lower back. Hussein, waiting impatiently, pushed on the door, sending Stone staggering to fall flat on his face.

The body twitched and went still. 'What in the hell are you playing at?' Hussein demanded.

Khazid said, 'He tried to make a run for it.'

'Why? What did you say to him?'

Khazid, calmer now, was reduced to a certain dishonesty as regards the facts. 'He said I was the other one. He knew my name. All I did was try to get the information about where the Rashids have gone from him. He said he had no idea and wouldn't tell me if he could.'

'And you threatened him?'

'What did you expect me to do, pat him on the head? I told him I'd start with his kneecap. He slammed a door on me and made a run for it.'

'You should have waited for me.'

Hussein knelt on one knee. Hal Stone's face was turned slightly to one side, blood seeping through his shirt. Hussein felt the neck. He shook his head. 'He's dead.'

'Are you certain? Another in the head, perhaps?'

'I studied medicine, fool. How many times have you been glad of that in the past two years?' He stood. 'Leave him where he is and let's get out of here.' He pushed Khazid before him. 'Hurry, I tell you. Straight to the railway station and back to London.'

'As you say, brother.' Khazid dumped his gown and scarf, put on his trenchcoat again and followed Hussein. They left the cottage, walked up to the main road and turned to the railway station. They got there with fifteen minutes to spare.

Once the train was moving, Khazid lay back in the seat, exhausted. 'Now what?'

'Give me time to think about it.' Hussein turned to stare out of the window, wondering what was happening. His lie to Khazid, the still beating pulse in Hal Stone's neck that his fingers had felt. Why had he done that? There was no answer, and for Hal Stone life or death was a matter for Allah.

Ali Hassim had been impressed when Khan told him Hussein would be in touch with him for any help or aid that Ali could offer. For him, Hussein was the great warrior, the Hammer of God, a liberator for the people from Allah himself. He remembered his shock on first hearing Hussein's voice on the radio news programme from the Middle East, and then in the middle of his Arabic rhetoric Hussein describing himself in a simple English phrase, 'Hammer of God'. It was a gesture of contempt for his enemies, but that name was now known to millions of Arabs in the Middle East who were not familiar with the English language at all.

So, thinking over his problem about who to first tell about Zion Place, he realized that he had found a new and worthier allegiance. But he needed to make everything perfect, so he called in another member of the Brotherhood, a young accountant in a financial firm in the City. A short chat over the phone, the suggestion that he could be of great service to the Brotherhood, produced the man he wanted within an hour, and he also sent for his laptop expert, and waited.

Sam Bolton was actually Selim Bolton, his father English, his mother Muslim. He had been raised in an English culture until his first year at London University studying business and accountancy, and then his father had died of cancer. An immediate consequence of this was that his mother was restored to Islam.

There were those in the Brotherhood who saw great possibilities in individuals with a similar background to his, and he joined their ranks as a sleeper, a handsome young man in a good suit and a university tie, accepted anywhere.

He turned up at the shop and discovered Ali waiting with the laptop expert. Ali said, 'Listen carefully while our brother explains,' and the laptop man told him everything regarding Zion Place.

Bolton took it all in. Finally he said, 'So what you really want to know is the feel of things generally, the attitudes of the villagers, perhaps, to Zion Place?'

'Exactly. What's special about it.'

'I think you mean what its purpose is, if any.' He stood up. 'I might as well get on with it. I called in at the flat, so I've got an overnight bag in the Audi.'

'So you accept this assignment?'

'Of course.'

'You could not do our cause a greater service.'

'I'll be in touch.'

The laptop man left and Ali nodded to himself. He was doing the right thing. No phone call to Khan. He had set things in motion and could afford to wait to hear from Hussein.

Hal Stone's cleaning lady, a widow named Amy Robinson, usually only worked mornings, but she had her own key and his laundry to deliver, so she called in at the cottage and discovered him in the garden. She had once been a nurse and was still expert enough to establish that he was alive. It was roughly an hour and a half since Hussein and Khazid had left.

She dialled 999 and called for ambulance and police, stipulating gunshot wounds, then she went out with a rug and pillows and tried to make him comfortable. She was kneeling beside him, stroking his hair, when his eyes opened. He looked at her, bewildered. 'Amy?'

'Don't fuss, love, lie still. There's an ambulance on its way. Who did this to you?'

'My cousin, General Ferguson – you met him when he visited the other year. My address book's on the desk. His private mobile number. Call him for me.'

'Don't upset yourself, love. I'm sure he'll be contacted in time.'

'You don't understand.' He clutched at her with a bloodstained hand. 'Tell him they were here, both of them. They are here in England. The other one shot me.' He closed his eyes and opened them. 'I didn't mention Zion.'

He lost consciousness again and there was a sudden confusion outside as the ambulance arrived.

She went to the front door and admitted the paramedics, who followed her as she showed them into the garden. And then, of course, the police came, first one car, then two. She waited, bewildered by it all, and then a man in civilian clothes arrived, who she was told was a Chief Inspector Harper. He had a quick look round the cottage and

486

went outside. When he returned, a police sergeant was taking a written statement from Amy.

'He did say something strange when he came to for a moment.' She told him what it was.

Harper, coming in through the French windows, heard. 'Did you say General Ferguson?'

'Yes, Professor Stone's cousin. He's very important in one of the ministries.'

'You can say that again, if it's who I think it is.'

'The Professor said the General's personal number was in his address book on the desk.'

Harper rushed to find it, and so it was that Ferguson, who had just arrived at the Holland Park safe house to discuss progress, heard the dreadful news.

The train was just twenty minutes out of King's Cross when Ali received the call from Hussein. 'We're just arriving from Cambridge.

A waste of time. We'll come round to your shop. We'll need somewhere to stay.'

'I've been waiting to hear from you. I have discovered where they have taken the Rashids.'

'But where does such information come from? Khan, I suppose, and presumably he would have got it from the Broker?'

'No, neither Khan nor the Broker know about it. It was the action of the Rashid woman, the doctor, which came to our aid. She was concerned for the welfare of a child she had operated on and telephoned the surgeon who has taken over the case. He wanted to be able to get in touch with her if there was a change in the child's condition. One of the nurses, a member of my network, was on duty and obtained the address for us.'

'This is truly unbelievable. They are still in England then?'

'West Sussex, a house called Zion Place. Not only can I show it to you on a laptop when you get here, I've also sent a trusted agent straight down there to scout the place out for you. I've impressed on him the urgency of his report.'

'It is hard to imagine that Ferguson let them make phone calls.'

'She probably broke the rules,' Ali said.

'And must pay the price. It would suit me very well for the enemy not to know that we are here. If you mention your discovery of Zion Place to Dreq Khan, he will in turn inform the Broker.'

'And that one you distrust?'

'He has had his uses, but he has his fingers in too many pies. You must not take this as an attack on Osama bin Laden, whom Allah protect, because on the ground he represents Osama in certain matters. In those affairs he is simply serving a great man's needs, and he must remember his place. Sometimes such men see themselves as being more important than they are.'

'Professor Khan, for example?'

'It is difficult for some people to remember that the cause they represent is more important than themselves,' Hussein said.

Ali said calmly, 'Khan will not be told of

489

Zion from me. I look forward to receiving you.'

'We shall be seeing you soon,' Hussein told him. He turned off his phone.

Khazid said, 'What was all that about?'

'Brother, Allah is on our side. Ali Hassim has discovered where the Rashids have been taken.' He proceeded to tell Khazid as much as he needed to know.

'Perfect,' Khazid said. 'With the Professor dead, no one in Ferguson's organization even knows we are here.'

'Of course,' Hussein said, a faint shadow on his face as that wavering pulse came back to haunt him. He took a deep breath. 'Nothing can go wrong now.' A few minutes later the train arrived at King's Cross.

At Holland Park, Ferguson was speaking to Harper again. 'Chief Inspector, I'm invoking the Terrorism Act to put a blanket on this for the moment. Some very nasty people are involved.'

'We are dealing with terrorists here, sir?'

'I have a special warrant from Downing Street on this one. I also have an official request to your Chief Constable that you act as my liaison there.'

Harper's spirits lifted. 'Very good of you, sir. Happy to be on board.'

'I've borrowed a police helicopter from the Met, thanks to the Commissioner. They're lifting me from a school football field just down the road from here.'

'Stone's hanging on by inches, General, that's what the surgeon in charge informs me. The scans show two bullets, one under the left shoulder that's apparently fragmented much of the shoulder blade, and there's a major artery close by that will give a problem.'

'And the other?'

'Low in the back. It's done a lot of damage to the pelvic girdle. What I'm telling you is what the scans show. I expect the surgery will reveal much more.'

'Thanks very much. I'll see you soon.'

Roper said, 'What a bastard.' Dillon and Billy looked grim.

Billy said, 'What did he say to the cleaning lady?'

'He said to tell me they were here, both of them, they were here in England. "The other one shot me. I didn't tell them about Zion."'

'It was them, all right,' Dillon said. 'Has to be.'

'And the other one, the bastard who shot him in the back, was this Khazid guy.' Billy was angry.

'I think that's obvious,' Ferguson said. They could hear the chatter of the helicopter passing overhead to the football field. 'Sean,' he said to Dillon, 'Hal is the closest relative I have left. Would you come with me?'

It was a direct appeal that couldn't be refused. 'Of course I will.'

'Good luck,' Roper called as they went out of the door.

The noise of the helicopter was with them for about ten minutes and then the aircraft lifted and moved away. Roper reached for the Scotch.

Billy said, 'Knock it off. At a time like this a man needs friends to drink with.'

'That's the best idea you've had for some time.' Roper started his wheelchair and Billy followed him out.

On his way to Zion, Sam Bolton had stopped in Guildford and visited the Army & Navy store, where he purchased an anorak, a jumper, a waterproof bush hat and trousers to go with it, and some boots. He then cast around for a pair of binoculars and found something suitable in a camera shop. He also purchased a canvas carrying bag from a nearby shop, then went in a convenient hotel and found the gentlemen's toilets.

He changed clothes in one of the cubicles, putting his smart suit, tie and shoes into the bag. When he emerged he was wearing everything else he had bought, and the binoculars were slung around his neck. 'Nothing like looking the part,' he said softly, examining himself in the mirror. 'But what do you really know about birds except the female variety?'

He returned to the Audi, drove around looking and found a bookshop. Within minutes, he was emerging with a suitable item covering the coastal areas of England. It was a magazine type of book with an illustrated cover. Good to carry under your arm to let the uninformed know what you were. Pleased with himself, he got back in the Audi and continued his drive towards the coast and Zion.

He arrived in the middle of the afternoon, put the Audi's top down and had a look round. What he saw was a typical English village: one pub called the Ploughman, and another down the street named the Zion Arms, old cottages, a church. He parked the Audi and went into the Zion Arms. Everything you expected from an English country pub was there, from logs burning on the hearth of a stone fireplace to the beamed ceiling, the mahogany bar, the mirrored shelves. The stout late-middle-aged lady behind it, with rosy cheeks and wearing a floral dress, seemed too good to be true. There weren't many people – a party of three, a young couple talking in low voices, a very ancient-looking man on the wooden settle by the fire, alone, a half-empty pint of beer in front of him.

Selim Bolton he might be, but it was Sam Bolton who approached the bar. In previous adventures for the Brotherhood he had seldom used an alias. He was himself, a university graduate and a middle-ranking executive in a private bank in the City of London. Anyone who wished to query him, even the police, would discover that quickly enough and look elsewhere. He even had a company card with Sam Bolton engraved on it.

Outside the village he had pulled into a lay-by and looked up Zion in the bird book. He had an extremely good memory; he noted Zion Marsh, the fact that it was National Trust, and a brief mention that the house was not open to the public.

'Ah, you'd be staying here for the bird-watching?' the bar lady said as he placed the book on the counter. 'Plenty of people come here for that.'

He'd concocted his story in advance. 'I work in London in finance. Sometimes you feel trapped, you just want to get away for a few days. I've got friends further along the coast, Aldwick Bay on the other side of Bognor Regis. Lovely shingle beaches up there. I'm making my way back to London, taking my time, and I'd noticed in the book that Zion Marsh is a bit special.'

'People seem to think so. What will you have?'

'A pint, please.'

The old man by the fire emptied his glass and spoke up. 'I was eighty-seven last month and I've lived here all my days, mainly working the land farming. When I was a lad, birds were just birds, part of life you took for granted. Now we have the bird-watchers like you, people who take it seriously. Last year we had people turn up in coaches to try and catch sight of some lapwing in the marsh. Supposed to be special. God knows why.'

'I see your point. I don't take it seriously. I work hard in an office most of the time. I like to get out in the fresh air, but I like to have a reason, so I've started on birds. Could I buy you a drink? I see you've run dry.'

'A pint wouldn't be a burden. That all right with you, Annie?'

'Shame on you, Seth Harker. You're an old cadger.'

She pulled the pint and Bolton paid her and took the glasses over. 'All right if I join you?'

'Why not?'

'Good health.' Bolton drank some of his beer. 'Do they cause a problem, bird-watchers, on the marsh?'

'National Trust, that. No, they're a harmless lot, and it's good for the economy. These days any kind of tourist is welcome. Creates jobs for people. There's the caravan site, bed and breakfasts.'

'All from birds.'

Harker chuckled. 'That's a fact, when you think about it.'

'I passed a stately home when I was approaching the village. I checked in my book and it said visitors weren't allowed. Zion Place, was it?'

'Oh, you can't go there. Owned by the government, and has been as long as I can remember. I wasn't allowed to go into the army in the Second World War – farming, you see, reserved occupation – so I was here right through.' He nodded his head. 'All sorts of dodgy things went on at Zion Place. Planes in and out from the runway, a lot of it at night. All highly secret.'

'Is that so?'

Seth Harker nodded. 'The thing is, the Ministry of Defence still runs it like that. High security, guards in blue uniforms.'

'Jobs for the villagers?'

'Oh, no, the guards are all outsiders. The housekeeper, Mrs Tetley, lives in, and she's got three young women on staff who help with the catering and other duties. Looking after guests, really. Kitty, Ida and Vera. Nice girls, but not from around here. They keep themselves to themselves.'

'You said guests. Is it some kind of hotel?'

'Where the guests never show themselves?' Harker cackled. 'And don't visit the village.'

'Yes, but you must see them arrive. Surely they visit the pub?'

The bar had emptied and Annie was in the back. Seth Harker was reasonably drunk by now. 'Ah, but they always come in by plane. There's a concrete runway by the house. That was the way it was in the war, and still the way it is today.' His glass was empty, and he looked at Bolton's. 'You're not drinking.'

'Well, you know how it is. I've got the car, the driving to think of if I carry on back to London. You know what the police are like these days.'

'Pity to waste it.' Bolton pushed it across, and the old man drank deeply. 'My cottage is on a small rise overlooking things. Fern End, it's called. You get a good view of the runway from there. I've watched people come and go for years. I've got a pair of old binoculars. There was a plane in at round about half-eleven this morning. It dropped off two women and a girl and three men. They were picked up by Captain Bosey, head of security, and taken up to the house.' He patted the side of his nose with a finger. 'Not much

I don't know. Mind you, I think I could do with the necessary.'

He took Bolton's arm to stand and was surprisingly steady as he crossed the bar and went into the lavatory. Annie came in from the back. 'Has he been a nuisance?'

'Certainly not, he's a real character. Is he fit to get home? He told me about his cottage.'

'Oh, he'll be fine. If he wants a snooze he can use the room in the back. When he does that someone will give him a lift home. Can I get you anything else?'

'I'm fine, actually. I'll be off, I think.'

'Well, if you decide to stay, we do have four rooms for the night, and there's always the caravan site. I own that as well.'

She went into the back again and Seth Harker returned. 'Ah, going are you?' He eased himself down.

'I must.'

Harker was definitely under the influence now. 'What we were talking about, security. All balls really. There's always a way. Take Zion Place – walls, electric wiring, cameras. All for nothing if you could go under.'

'What on earth do you mean?'

'In 1943, during the war, there was only a grass runway and small planes used it on a nightly basis for flights to France. Bad weather of any kind – rain, flooding from the marsh – sometimes made it unusable. So they dug a tunnel that started in the wood, continued it under the wall into the garden.'

'What was the idea?'

'A network of clay piping under the grass from the runway that would drain into the tunnel. By putting the other end in the garden, they had the idea of linking it up with ordinary drains from the house.'

'Who told you about this?'

'RAF lads based at Zion Place, and they also had some Royal Engineers. It was done on the quiet, and then some RAF Group Captain inspected it and said it was a lousy idea and ordered them to just concrete the runway so planes could land even if it had water on it.'

'And the tunnel and drainpipes?'

'They ordered a stop to that work, blocked off the end in the wood with a big manhole cover and used grass sods to cover it. It's a creepy sort of place. There's a granite pillar there with some lettering that doesn't made sense. Rubbed away with time.'

'Did you ever take a look?'

Harker smiled. ''Course I did. Over fifty years ago, a bit after the war. It was there all right. Iron rungs to help you down, and you had to paddle in water then. God knows what it would be like now.'

'And the garden end?'

'There was another manhole cover there, too, which I couldn't budge. What they covered it with, I've no idea. I never went down there again, but I always thought it a bit of a laugh over the years, with all their security improvements.'

'And nobody knew about it?'

'It was the war, you see. Top secret stamped on everything. Who on earth cared when it was over, and who would care after so many years? Any mention of it was lost in RAF files years ago.'

'Yes, I can see that.' Bolton got up again and held out his hand. 'You are a fascinating man, Seth.'

'And what would your name be, boy?'

'Bolton – Sam Bolton.'

There was a kind of knowing look on Harker's face, a touch of cunning. 'I hope you got what you came for?'

'I met you, didn't I?'

He went out, and behind him Annie came in with a long tray of glasses and put them on the bar. 'He's gone, has he? What a nice young man.'

'A good listener,' Seth said. 'I'll have another pint.'

Bolton followed the road past Zion Place, noting the electronic gates at the entrance and the uniformed security guard outside his hut smoking a cigarette. He carried on past until he came to a large signboard saying 'Zion Marshes and Wildfowl Protection Area. National Trust.' Beyond it was the car park. The wood ran parallel to the wall of the house at that point, stretching towards the marsh and the runway.

Late in the afternoon of a gloomy day the car park was empty, and it started to rain, but that suited him. He hurriedly raised the roof of the Audi, opened the back, found the toolkit and pulled out the steel tyre lever.

The rain increased as he walked along the edge of the wood, pausing to look at the concrete runway. At that point you could see over the wall into the garden; with binoculars you could also see the terrace at the back of the house. He turned and walked into the wood at what seemed to be the point the old man had meant. And there it was, the granite stone, just as he had been told, tilted slightly to one side.

The grass was long all around. He started prodding into it with the tyre lever, bending over, moving backwards, reaching to the left and then the right, persevering as the rain increased; and then it came, the clang of metal on metal.

He knelt there in the pouring rain, secure in his waterproof clothes, and hacked away at the grass and soil beneath, holding the lever in both hands, and gradually a patch

504

tore away. He scrabbled with his hands, and found a portion of a cast-iron manhole cover. He felt for a part of the circular edge and forced the lever under it, hoping to lift it. It was hopeless. It needed the right tools, but that wasn't his problem. He looked around him. A crowded thicket of bushes and undergrowth surrounded the spot, and the trees were close. It was certainly private enough.

He went back through the rain, immensely cheered by the way things had turned out, especially his extraordinary good fortune in meeting Seth Harker. He got in the Audi and called Ali Hassim on his mobile. There was an instant answer, for Ali was entertaining Hussein and Khazid in the back room of the shop.

'Where are you?'

'Zion, of course. I'm coming back. I'll see you in about three hours.'

'Why aren't you staying overnight?'

'Because I've completed the task you gave me. Zion Place has a purpose. I believe it to be a high-security safe house. People only arrive by plane. It has its own runway. A plane came in at eleven-thirty this morning with two women passengers, a young girl and three men. I haven't the slightest idea who they are, but I suspect you do.'

'This is incredible,' Ali told him.

'What *is* incredible is the fact that in spite of all their security I've found a way in.'

'If that is so, truly Allah is on our side.'

'I thought you'd say that.' Bolton drove away fast.

At the shop, Ali turned to face Hussein and Khazid and told them everything.

15

At the Dark Man, Harry and Billy sat in their usual booth, Roper beside them in his wheelchair, Joe Baxter and Sam Hall leaning against the wall and talking in low voices. Sergeant Doyle, who had brought Roper down in the people carrier, was sitting in it outside, reading a book as usual. They all looked troubled. Harry had just swallowed a large Scotch and called to Ruby, who was tending the bar with Mary O'Toole.

'We'll have another, love, me and the Major.'

'All right, Harry.' She poured the drinks. 'I've not seen this from Harry before, the black rage. He frightens me in a way.'

'Did he know this Professor Stone well?'

'According to Billy they worked quite

closely with him when the outfit had some sort of bad time in Hazar two or three years ago.'

'Ruby, what's keeping you?'

Mary picked up the tray. 'I'll take it for you.'

Harry accepted it in silence, staring into space, his face like stone. Ferguson had phoned Billy and told him that the surgeon, a Professor Vaughan at the hospital in Cambridge, unhappy with Hal Stone's condition, was holding back on the operation.

Billy shook his head in a kind of controlled fury. 'I wonder where those bastards are now.'

Roper swallowed his Scotch. 'Well, only they would know that.'

Harry seemed to come alive. 'Yes, but they must have some plan. I mean, this Hussein is a clever bugger. He wouldn't do anything without back-up.'

'You're right,' Roper said. 'He wouldn't have dared come to England without knowing there were extremist organizations who would back him to the hilt.'

'Well, we all know that,' Harry said. 'Fanatics who get away with preaching terror everywhere from television to the London streets.'

Billy said, 'Yeah, but there's their human rights to consider. We know what they are, but can't do anything about it.'

'Well, I bloody well can.' Harry turned to Roper. 'This guy with the funny name, Professor Dreq Khan, and his Army of God thing?'

'He's untouchable. Covers his back constantly.'

'Bloody disgraceful, why hasn't he been nicked?' Harry demanded.

'His work with the UN gives him diplomatic immunity. We know he's guilty as sin, but proving it legally is another thing. Even if Ferguson gave evidence it would be laughed out of court, and with Khan's UN status he'd probably be allowed to do a runner anyway,' Roper told him.

'Well, I'm not happy about that, and I think I'd like to discuss it with him. I presume you've got an address?'

'The Army of God is a registered organization,' Roper told him. 'It's in the phone book.'

'I was thinking of something a little more private than that.'

Roper smiled. 'I should say, "Are you sure you want to do this?" But you know what, Harry? Khan is a very bad man. Like you, I've had enough.' He called Holland Park, gave Khan's name into the automated connection in his computer. A recorded voice gave him an answer in seconds. 'Huntley Street Mansions,' he said.

Harry started to move and Billy stood up. 'This is my gig, Harry. The boys and I will get him.'

'You've got to think of your position, Billy.'

'As a member of Her Majesty's Secret Intelligence Services? Harry, I don't give a toss. I'm as pissed off as you two.' He turned to Hall and Baxter. 'Are you available?'

'Too bloody true we are,' Baxter told him.

Harry said, 'OK, I'll see you on the *Linda Jones*, and you, Major, I think you've got things to attend to at Holland Park.'

'You mean I'm not up to it?'

'I just don't want you involved.'

'He's right,' Billy said. 'Come on, boys.' Baxter and Hall followed him out to the Alfa Romeo parked by the people carrier.

'Major Roper's coming out,' Billy called to Doyle, behind the wheel with his book, and piled into the Alfa with Baxter and Hall. In a second they were away.

Roper emerged in the wheelchair, Harry following, and the rear door of the people carrier came down as the lift descended at Doyle's touch. Harry put a hand on Roper's shoulder. 'I'll be in touch.'

'Try not to kill him,' Roper said. 'Sometimes I've had enough of that, too. It's been a hell of a life, Harry.'

'I know, old son. I'll try and oblige you.'

The lift took Roper up and inside. Doyle drove away.

Ruby appeared. 'Everything all right, Harry?'

'Just going down to the *Linda*, love. I've got a bit of business to handle, phone calls to make. I don't want to be disturbed, OK?'

'Just as you say, Harry.'

She went back inside and he walked slowly along the wharf.

Khan was at the desk in his study, working on some papers, when the buzzer sounded from the entry phone in the hall. Billy had given the matter some thought on the way. That Khan was involved in the whole affair was obvious, which meant he might have seen photos of the Salters and Dillon. So it was Baxter who held up Billy's warrant card when he pressed the buzzer.

Khan looked at him on the entry screen. 'Yes?'

'Professor Khan? Sergeant Jones, CID Paddington Green. Young Muslim lady was assaulted. A patrol car has brought her in, but her English isn't too good. She mentioned your name. I'm really asking for assistance here.'

'I'm always happy to help the police.'

Khan pressed the button, took a few steps to the door, which burst open. Baxter moved fast and punched him in the stomach, Billy and Hall crowded in behind. An overcoat was taken down from a hall stand, his arms were thrust into it, a dark trilby hat rammed on his head. Baxter and Hall walked him out to the Alfa, sat him between them in the back, and Billy drove away.

Harry was sitting in the stern of the *Linda Jones*, under an awning, light spilling out from the deck lamp into the gathering darkness, a glass of Scotch in his hand. Baxter and Hall held Khan in front of him. Billy leaned against the rail, watching.

Khan had recovered himself, but he did recognize Salter and was genuinely terrified, yet he tried bluster. 'What's going on here?'

'I'm Harry Salter, you are Dreq Khan. I'm going to ask you some questions, and if you don't answer me I'll kill you and we'll throw you in the river.'

Khan almost had a bowel movement. 'What is it you want?'

'Hussein Rashid and his chum Khazid. We

know they were on their way to England. I'd like your confirmation that they've arrived.'

'What nonsense is this?'

'Don't mess me around. A good friend of mine in Cambridge, Professor Hal Stone, just back from Hazar after helping Dillon and my Billy here to bring Sara Rashid home, was shot twice today in his garden and left for dead. We figure it must have been Hussein and Khazid. What do you think?'

'I've no idea what you are talking about,' Khan said desperately.

'He's wasting our time, Billy. Try the hoist.'

Baxter and Hall pulled off Khan's over-coat and jacket, forced him down and Billy reached for the hemp line suspended from a hoist and looped it round the ankles. Baxter and Hall heaved on the rope and pulled Khan up, head down.

'Simple question,' Billy said in his ear. 'Are they in England, and have you heard from them?'

They swung him over and dropped him in the Thames. He went under, crying out. As his hands were untied, he managed to move his arms about. When he stopped struggling, Harry nodded and they pulled him up. He floundered on the deck, coughing and spluttering, and there was nothing left in him.

Harry said, 'Let me make it quite clear. If we have to put you over again, we leave the river to take you away.'

'No, for pity's sake.' Khan sat up, reaching for a rail. 'They are here. I had nothing to do with it. It was handled by the Broker, Osama's man, and don't ask for his phone number. He contacts you when he wants. You never contact him because you can't. Hussein and Khazid came in a boat by night from France to England. His phone call was a total surprise to me. Hussein said he was at a cottage called Folly Way at Peel Strand in Dorset. He didn't mention the name of the person he was staying with, I swear it.'

'Go on.'

'I tell you the truth when I admit that the Army of God has a network of spies who are just small people. I had the Rashids' house watched and one of my men reported they had left the house. He followed them to

Farley Field where they flew away to an unknown destination.'

'Was Hussein angry when you told him that?'

'Yes. He said we had to find out where the Rashid family had been taken. I told him that was an impossibility for us.'

'And then what?'

Khan lied desperately. 'He said there was one person he could visit because the Broker had mentioned that Professor Stone, who had been part of the whole affair in Hazar, was Ferguson's cousin. Hussein said they would pay him a visit in Cambridge.' There was a pause while Harry considered the matter.

Billy said, 'Bleeding liar.'

Harry shook his head. 'The fact that Hussein has no idea where the Rashids are must be true, otherwise why bother to go to Cambridge? His assumption that Hal Stone would know something makes sense.' He got up, went into the salon and poured Scotch.

Billy followed and closed the door. 'So you believe the bastard?'

Harry said, 'Remember what Hal said?

That they were here, both of them, "the other one" shot him, and he didn't tell them about Zion.'

'That's right,' Billy said. 'Ferguson admitted he'd told Stone about Zion.'

'The reason they tracked Stone down was because they had no idea where the Rashids had gone. They must have told him that was the purpose of the visit. His saying he hadn't told them about Zion confirms they've still no idea where the Rashids are.'

'Stone probably made a run for it and got the two bullets in the back,' Billy said. 'So what about this asshole outside? Do we finish him?'

Harry opened the door and stepped out. Baxter and Hall had seated Khan in a chair. He looked as if he'd come to the end of his tether.

'What's your idea on where Hussein would be now?'

'I don't know,' Khan said wearily. 'He's a crazy man. With his photo all over the newspapers, it was madness his coming to England in the first place.'

'That's the strangest part of the whole deal,' Billy said. 'He should have been lifted within hours of arrival.'

Khan suddenly remembered the phone conversation with Hussein and came out with one special piece of information. 'When he was talking to me from Peel Strand and mentioned going to Cambridge, I told him that he'd have to change trains in London and wasn't that unwise because his face was in so many papers.'

'And what did he say?' Harry demanded.

'That it had been taken care of and that no one would recognize him. He said: "Trust me in this." Nothing more.'

Billy said, 'Rubbish. He couldn't have had time for plastic surgery.'

'Well, as he hasn't been lifted, something must have happened to him.' Harry turned to Khan. 'Mr Baxter and Mr Hall are going to take you home where you'll get a change of clothes, money, credit cards, passport – whatever. They will then escort you to Heathrow and see you leave on the first available plane.'

Khan was stupefied. 'You mean you're not going to kill me?'

'Not now, but if you ever return to England I'll know, and you'll be dead inside a week. Get him out of here, boys.'

Khan was for the moment stunned. They got his jacket and overcoat on and marched him along the wharf, and it was then that he found he was experiencing the greatest feeling of relief in his life. There was also a certain satisfaction in the fact that by crediting the Broker for guiding Hussein to Hal Stone at Cambridge, he'd been able to let Ali Hassim off the hook.

Back on the boat, Billy said, 'Have you turned into a big softy or something?'

'Roper asked me to go easy on him. Anyway, we've managed to establish without doubt that Hussein has no idea where the Rashids are, so let's go and see Roper.'

Roper listened to what they had to say. Harry said, 'You think I did the right thing? Will he stay away?'

'The question is, will the people in the larger world he's been involved with allow him to? We've known for a long time about the Al-Qaeda influence on the Army of God. What Osama will think of a man who's done a runner is anyone's guess. The Broker won't be too happy either. These important men in the world of terror obviously don't like any indication that things are falling apart.'

'I don't give a toss about Osama and his people,' Harry said. 'We've got to stand up and be counted.'

'I agree, but the Al-Qaeda leaders in Iraq would dearly love to have another spectacular in Britain. Big Ben would be good, or Buckingham Palace. The possibilities are endless.'

'That would really be out of order,' Harry said.

Billy put in, 'They'd be happy if the Queen was at home when they did it.'

'Bastards,' Harry said.

'I could show you intelligence reports indicating that at least a couple of hundred Britons have served in Al-Qaeda's foreign legion in Iraq. These are the things the public doesn't know about. And it's not just regular bombs they'd like to set off, but dirty bombs.'

'Several plots involving such weapons in the UK have already been foiled,' Roper noted. 'We're at war, and that's the fact of it.'

There was a pause and Billy said, 'Which leaves us with Hussein. What are his intentions?'

'He's never been a bomb man,' Roper said. 'My bet is assassination.'

'You mean the Prime Minister or someone at that level?' Harry asked.

'Let's look at it this way. His intentions regarding the Rashids have been thwarted, at least for now, so he's got to find something to do. And he's changed his appearance in some way – Khan told us that. It was worth dumping Khan in the Thames to learn it.'

His phone went. It was Ferguson, and Roper put it on speaker. 'How are things?'

'He's out of surgery. Professor Vaughan says it was bad and it will take time, but he's going to weather the storm.'

Harry and Billy cheered, and Roper said, 'Have you managed to speak to him?'

'Just a few sentences. Apparently it was Khazid who held him at gunpoint and wanted to know where the Rashids were. Hal refused to say, and made a run for it to the door in the garden. Khazid shot him the back as he pulled the bolt. He lost it then, was vaguely aware of another person rushing through, but didn't see him.

'A pity,' Roper told him. 'Harry put the screws on Khan earlier this evening. Rather interesting.' He told of Harry's exploit with Khan and the results.

Ferguson said, 'Christ Almighty, so we no longer know what the bastard looks like?'

'Or his intentions, or where he is now. The only thing we can be certain of is that he doesn't know where the Caspar family are,' Roper said.

'And thank God for it.'

'We do know one thing,' Roper told him. 'When he made that original phone call to Khan, he said he and Khazid had landed by boat and were with one of the Broker's people at Peel Strand in Dorset, a cottage called Folly Way.'

'Right, I'll contact the chief constable of the Dorset constabulary now. Anything else?'

'The Caspars at Zion. They need to be informed of the attempt on Hal Stone's life.'

'It will frighten Molly Caspar to death. They can't be reached, that's the important thing, so we can leave it for the moment.'

'And the others?'

'I'll speak to Levin. I think he, Chomsky and Greta deserve to know. We'll make a decision later on whether I should fly down tomorrow. I'd prefer to tell the Caspars personally. Dillon and I will leave in the helicopter in thirty minutes. See you soon.'

In the back room of the shop, Hussein and Khazid sat at the dining table with Bolton and went over the details again and again. They'd also had a CD prepared for them by the laptop man, covering every possible aspect of the village and the house, even a list of useful bird names.

Khazid had found that amusing. 'The most intelligent birds are crows. They can communicate with each other, and count. Does that establish my credentials?'

Bolton said, 'Just be yourself, as I did, and look the part.' He turned to Ali. 'I'll go now and purchase the same garments, boots and so on that I used. What about a vehicle?'

'Taken care of by a member of the Brotherhood in the motor trade. It's a Caravanette, with a bunk on either side in the rear, and cooking facilities. A family sort of thing, popular with campers. He will also supply some tools that with luck should meet all our requirements. They will be delivered to us in a little while.'

As Bolton stood up, Hussein said, 'One thing I must ask. You mentioned being able to look from the edge of the wood over the wall into the garden itself and to the rear of the house, a terrace and so on. Did you see anyone?'

'No. The weather was poor, heavy rain, and my binoculars were nothing special.'

Hussein looked at Ali. 'May he remedy

that and find me a pair of Zeiss glasses with top magnification?'

'Of course.' Ali said, and nodded to Bolton. 'You know who to call.'

'I'll take care of it.' Bolton glanced at Hussein. 'A privilege to serve.'

He went out, and Hussein said, 'A good man.'

'One of the best. Can I do anything else at the moment?'

'I think not. If Khan phones, simply say I haven't been in touch with you and you have no idea where I am.'

'Whatever you say.'

'I'll deal with the Broker.'

'As you wish.' He got up to go and there was a knock on the door. He opened it and the girl assistant passed him the *Evening Standard*. The stop press had a brief report that the police were pursuing inquiries into the shooting of Cambridge Professor Hal Stone, who was doing as well as could be expected after successful surgery.

'Perhaps you should read this.' He put it on the table without a word and went out.

Khazid read it first and exploded. 'You said there was no pulse! You should have let me finish him!'

'Things happen.'

'Sooner or later he'll be able to talk.'

'So what? He can't report on my new persona because he didn't see me, which is one good thing. Another is that Ferguson has no idea we know about Zion. This will work, cousin, I feel it. Our astonishing good luck with Selim Bolton finding a way in, for example, can only be looked upon as the will of Allah himself.'

'Be practical, cousin. We don't even know if our simple tools will move that manhole. We don't know what's down there if we can remove it, and what about the other end? It could be under six feet of earth, a garden rockery, anything.'

'A reconnaissance then,' Hussein said. 'And how many times have we had to do that in the last two years of the war, cousin, and succeeded in our purpose?'

'But what is our objective? Let's say we can force a way through this tunnel into the garden. Do we sit in a shrubbery, waiting for Sara to come out to play, and if so, what do you do, shoot her?'

'Don't be absurd.'

'OK, so you hope she's alone, knock her out, fling her over your shoulder, drag her through the tunnel and drive away.' Hussein sat there staring at him, and Khazid said, 'Of course, if anyone was with her we'd have to shoot them. Even if it was her parents.'

Hussein's face was sombre. 'I gave Sara's grandfather my most solemn oath before Allah to protect, her, honour her in every way. I failed miserably in all respects. Death followed at every turn. Our comrades died at the hands of Dillon and Salter, my uncle – struck down with the shame of it – was dead before his true time. You are right in everything you say. I do not know what to do or even what I would say if I were to look upon her face again. Allah was the one who chose this path for me.'

'I think the truth is you never knew where everything was leading from the beginning.' Khazid got up. 'If we had only pursued our worthwhile targets, Ferguson and the others, there would have been some point, but now . . .'

'There will be a purpose to everything, and Allah will show what it is. I must go to Zion. I have no choice.'

'And neither do I.' Khazid sighed. 'I finally accept that for the past two years as a soldier in the war in Iraq I've been commanded by a raving lunatic. All of a sudden I don't find any comfort in the idea that I'm in the hands of Allah.'

'So you will desert me?' Hussein sat there, his face bleak. 'So this is what it's come to?'

Khazid managed a smile. 'Do I look like that kind of man, cousin? No, I'll go down to hell with you if that's what you want.'

Ali returned. 'So, now we wait. I have arranged for Jamal to drive up to the public car park at Farley Field in a BT van. He'll wait there and observe, just in case the Hawk plane gets some use. He is familiar with most of Ferguson's crowd and will phone me the moment he has something, and I'll contact you.'

'Good idea,' Khazid told him, and Hussein's special mobile sounded.

'It's me,' the Broker said. 'Cambridge didn't go well, I hear.'

'It was unfortunate and led nowhere. We have no idea where Ferguson has the Rashids.'

'Forget the girl,' the Broker said. 'Turn to more worthy targets. Have you been in touch with Khan?'

'No.'

'Strange, I get no response from him however I try.'

'I can't help you.'

'Where are you?'

'A safe house. That is all I can tell you. Goodbye.' Hussein looked at Ali and Khazid. 'So much for the Broker. Can we have some coffee?'

In the library at Zion Place the Russians sat having a drink in the corner, trying to absorb the bad news about Hal Stone. Caspar and Molly were watching a film in the television room, and Sara was playing Patience.

Levin said, 'What an absolute bastard.'

'Two in the back.' Chomsky shook his head. 'A hard thing to cope with, even with a great surgeon.'

'Sara looks lonely,' Greta said. 'I'll go and chat to her.' She sat down on the other side of the table. 'How's it going?'

'A bore, really. How's Professor Stone?'

Greta was shocked. 'How on earth did you know?'

'It's my guilty secret. I've got really good hearing. I can hear people speaking two rooms away. I can hear the conversation in a cell phone in your hand across the table without putting it to my ear. At my school the girls called me Gestapo Bitch, because with me they had no privacy. Anyway, Professor Stone. At least he's come through surgery.'

'That's true.'

'And it was Khazid who shot him.' It was a statement and not a query.

'I'm afraid so.'

'Where do you think Hussein and Khazid are now?'

'We've no idea, but we do know for certain that they don't know that you and your parents are here.'

'Really? The Hammer of God seems to be slipping, and that would be a first. Speaking of telephones, by the way, my mother must have had another mobile. I've heard her phoning Dr Sampson at the hospital about the Bedford child several times.' She shook her head. 'Very silly.'

Greta said gravely, 'I'll have to let Ferguson know.'

'Of course.' Sara got up. 'I'm ready for bed. I'm not going to tell them. I leave that decision to you.'

She went out and Greta moved back to the others and told them. Levin called Ferguson at once, caught him with Roper at Holland Park and gave him the bad news.

'What a stupid thing to do,' Ferguson said. 'But don't say anything to her. I'll handle it myself. I'll fly down in the morning with Dillon and Billy. More bad news. That address in Dorset at Peel Strand, cottage called Folly Way? The Dorset police checked

it out. Found the owner, one Darcus
Wellington, shot dead.'

'Good God,' Levin said.

'Good God indeed. They've traced his car
to Bournemouth railway station from where
they obviously caught a fast train to London.
Our boys have been busy. You see, Igor, it
all starts to fit.'

At Holland Park, Ferguson sat in the
computer room with Billy and Dillon. Roper
had his Scotch in his hand.

'Well, here's to Dr Molly Rashid, great
surgeon and humanitarian.'

'The trouble is, her work's the most important thing in her life,' Dillon said. 'It's so
important it sweeps everything else aside.'

'What on earth are you implying?'
Ferguson demanded of Roper.

'That if I was, for example, Al-Qaeda, I'd
let the word go out to sympathizers that any
news of even the briefest contact with Dr
Molly Rashid and where she was would be
welcome.'

'Stop it, Major,' Ferguson said. 'Bloody nonsense. All the same, we'll fly down from Farley at nine sharp.'

The Caravanette was packed with everything they needed, and Ali, Hussein and Khazid sat in the back of the shop for a little while in silence.

After a while, Hussein said, 'Bed, I think. We'll depart at six a.m. With three hours on the road, we'll reach there about nine.'

'It should have been a weekend,' Khazid said. 'More bird-watchers.'

'The fewer the better,' Hussein told him, and stood up. 'You will wake us, my friend?' he asked Ali.

Khazid said, 'I had a good friend called Hassim. They killed him in Hazar, Dillon and Salter. Could he have been kin to you?'

'I think not. May he rest in peace.'

Hussein went upstairs, Khazid following. Ali had given them a small bedroom each. They stood on the landing, looking at each other, then parted without a word.

Khazid put his flight bag on the bed, took out his silenced Walther, the clips, and the Uzi machine pistol with its spare magazine. He doubled them up with Scotch tape so that he could reverse load when under stress. Everything was ready, including the hand grenade he'd slipped in without telling Hussein. He lay on the bed, closed his eyes and went to sleep quickly.

Next door Hussein checked and loaded his Walther, put it back in his flight bag, knelt on the floor and said his prayers, as he had done since childhood. He closed his eyes. He was in the hands of Allah now. He had never been more certain of anything in his life.

16

At Holland Park Roper dozed in his wheel-chair in front of the screens, as he often did through the night. He usually awakened after an hour or so, checked the screens, then dozed off, and usually opened his eyes again when the pain become hard to bear. His ravaged body was long past doctors' prescriptions, but of course the cigarettes and what he called the whisky sups helped.

Sergeant Doyle, on night duty, had peered through the small window in the door, as he did frequently, observed that the Major was awake and went to the canteen and made him the kind of bacon and egg sandwich that Roper enjoyed and took it to him. It was just before five o'clock in the morning and he put it down in front of Roper.

'There you go, Major. I didn't bother with tea, I knew you'd just let it go cold. Have you had a good night?'

'Sit down and join me for a while, Sergeant.' Roper wolfed down the sandwich. 'Between midnight and dawn is the strangest time of all to be on your own, because all you've got is the past and you know you can't alter that.'

'Would you want to, Major? I've spent twenty years of my life as a soldier and I've never known a finer one than you, or a braver.'

'Hunched over all those bombs in good old Ireland until I made the one careless mistake over a silly little parked car?'

'You were doing your duty, getting the job done. We all accept what soldiering means. It comes with the Queen's shilling and the first time you put on the uniform.'

'Let's look at that,' Roper said. 'You did Irish time?'

'Six tours.'

'Then you know that members of the Provisional IRA considered themselves soldiers. How do you react to that?'

'Not particularly well,' Doyle said, 'as I was frequently shot at during my tours of duty by bastards who didn't wear a uniform.'

'Neither did the French Resistance in the Second World War. The guy who made the bomb that got me was called Murphy. When he ended up in court he refused to recognize it. Said he was a soldier fighting a war.'

'What happened to him?'

'Three life sentences in the Maze. He died of cancer.'

Doyle thought about it. 'Where's this going, Major?'

'Like I said, between midnight and dawn, the past going through your head. I saw some film on television showing a British-born Muslim swearing allegiance to Al-Qaeda. He also said he was a soldier fighting a war.'

'I saw that,' Doyle said. 'Where does it end?'

'I'd say with our present problem, Hussein Rashid. Put it to him, he'd say exactly the same thing as all of them.'

'Then maybe it's just an excuse, a cop-out? At least you were blown apart wearing a uniform, Major. That bugger Murphy wasn't.' He stood up and shrugged. 'There's no solution to it, really. I'm going to make tea now. Want some?'

'Actually, I would.'

Doyle went to the door and paused. 'I didn't tell you it's started raining outside and the wind's building up. You might find the Hawk can't get off at Farley.'

'I'll keep an eye on it.'

He checked the weather report on television and it wasn't good, then he accepted the mug of tea from Doyle and poured a whisky sup in it when he was alone. He pulled Hussein's photo on screen. It stared back at him, that Che Guevara look.

'Yes, I know that isn't you any more, but where the hell are you?'

Closer than he would have dreamed possible, in the shop on the edge of West Hampstead, Ali Hassim was tapping on Hussein's door, a cup of tea in his hand. He put on the light and went in. Hussein was awake.

'It's earlier than you said, but the weather is not good.' He put the green tea down at the side of the bed.

The window rattled in the wind. Hussein said, 'My thanks for the tea, but I must pray for a while. I'll be ready to leave at the time agreed. If you would turn off the light.'

'Of course.'

Ali went out, tapped on Khazid's door and went downstairs.

Roper dozed again and came awake to find it was just seven o'clock. At the same time the Caravanette pulled in at a Little Chef outside Guildford. There was a strong wind and the rain was relentless, but Hussein and Khazid were impervious to it, thanks to the outfits Bolton had purchased. The three-quarter-length anoraks in olive green were hooded, with capacious pockets large enough for the silenced Walthers they carried, including spare clips of ammunition.

Waterproof bush hats, leggings and heavy boots made short work of the weather.

There were a dozen or so customers scattered around the café, mainly truck drivers from the look of what was in the car park. Hussein and Khazid sat in a corner away from anyone else.

'What do we eat?' Khazid asked.

'Look at the menu. The popular choice is the full English breakfast with a mug of tea.'

'Which includes bacon for a start.'

'In the circumstances Allah will be merciful. So, go to the counter and in your best broken French give the order. To be practical, I'm hungry and we have a long day ahead of us.'

Khazid went and spoke to the young girl on duty and returned and sat down. 'What do you think of the Caravanette? It's hardly a getaway car, the engine throbbing when you put your foot down.'

'It could be argued that it would be perfect for such a purpose. What police are usually chasing is the faster traffic, not the vehicle in the slow lane.'

'A debatable point,' Khazid said.

The girl brought the breakfasts and teas on a tray, put everything on the table and departed.

'My chief instructor in the camp in Algeria had a saying: "Walk, don't run, whenever possible." Now eat your breakfast, little brother, and shut up.'

It was eight o'clock when Dillon and Billy joined Roper, and his news wasn't too good. 'I've had Lacey on. He and Parry have arrived at Farley. It's not too nice. He certainly thinks it's not on for a nine o'clock departure. They'll just have to wait for a window of opportunity. I've spoken to Ferguson. He's suggested we have a quick breakfast. He'll be here for an eight-thirty departure.'

'That's fine,' Dillon said. 'Are you going to join us?'

'I don't think so. I'd a bad night, and then this weather.' He shook his head. 'I think I'll check with Zion Place while you eat. See you later.'

Dillon and Billy left him for the canteen and Roper called Levin.

In the dining room at Zion Place, Levin, Chomsky and Greta sat at a corner table as rain rattled against the French windows, the terrace outside streaming with it as it fell on the garden all the way to the wall and into the wood beyond.

There was a certain amount of mist that made everything look a little mysterious. Various trees, masses of rhododendrons, willow trees, an old summerhouse, sheltered pathways running through shrubberies.

Greta, who was drinking coffee and looking out, said, 'Rain, bloody rain, but it suits the garden.'

Sara came up behind. 'I heard that. It's like something out of *Jane Eyre*. Dark and brooding.'

'Would you like to join us?' Greta asked.

'No, I'd better go and sit in the far corner. The parents are coming down. I'll see you later.'

She moved across, waving cheerfully at Captain Bosey and Fletcher and Smith, two of his guards, who were eating together. A little later Caspar and Molly arrived and joined their daughter. Kitty took their order and went off to the kitchen.

Levin's phone went. It was Roper. 'How's the house party proceeding?'

'Rain and even a little mist. Makes the garden look romantic.'

'What about the runway?'

'I can't see from here. Hang on and I'll go to the terrace.' Which he did, going out to the hall and helping himself to an umbrella he found behind the door. He opened it and stepped out, giving Roper a running commentary. 'There's no way this rain is going to stop, that's for sure, but I can see the runway. There is some mist there, certainly. What's the word from your end?'

'Well, Lacey doesn't seem to think nine o'clock's likely. He'll await a window of opportunity, was what he said.'

'OK, I'll keep in touch.'

Levin returned to the house to report to the others.

At Farley Field, Jamal had set himself up in the public car park. He parked in a spot from which he could see the arrivals. The Hawk was already parked on the other side of the terminal building.

The grey van had 'BT' on the side. He raised the rear door like a flap against the rain and sat there from half-past seven and waited. He was surrounded by coils of wire, a large tool box was open, and in his yellow oilskins with 'BT' on the back he looked perfectly acceptable.

Ali Hassim, who had phoned several times, tried again at half past eight. 'Still nothing?'

'I'm afraid so. I will contact you the moment I see anything.'

He opened a lunch box and took out a carton of yoghurt, ate it slowly with a spoon, then unpeeled a banana, watching. Time ticked by. Suddenly the people carrier from Holland Park, the vehicle which he had followed on his motorbike when it had taken the Caspars and the three other people to Farley, arrived. He watched it park at the end of the terminal. Three men hurried for shelter. He knew one was Ferguson because Hassim had shown him a photo.

He phoned Ali instantly. 'They've arrived, Ferguson definitely and two other men. They were too fast for me, hurrying through the rain.'

'Allah be praised. Phone me again the moment they take off.'

'It may be a while. The weather is not good.'

'So wait and watch.'

In the terminal building Ferguson talked to Lacey. 'What do you think?'

'I don't hold out any hope of nine o'clock. The flight down there takes an hour, a little more, depending on the wind and whether it changes direction. Maybe another half hour. That would give an estimated time of arrival at about ten-thirty. We'll just have to see. I suggest coffee, General.'

'Oh, very well.' Ferguson wasn't pleased. He phoned Levin.

'Nine o'clock and waiting. Lacey still has hopes. I'll call you.' He shrugged and said to Dillon and Billy, 'Can't be helped. Let's find that coffee.'

At Zion, the Caravanette had arrived twenty minutes earlier and passed through the village with Khazid at the wheel, following Bolton's instructions, passing the house and the electronic barrier at the estate entrance with the guardhouse beside it.

Further along, they came to the sprawling country car park surrounded by high hedges and the wood on the other side. There was one thing that Bolton had failed to mention: a brick public convenience. As for the car park, at that moment there wasn't a single vehicle parked there.

Khazid got out. 'I have an idea.'

He went to the public convenience, looked behind it and returned. 'I think I could squeeze the Caravanette round the back of it.'

'No, we won't do that,' Hussein said. 'Remember what I said? Walk, don't run. We are harmless eccentrics who prefer to be out in the pouring rain watching birds to sitting at home. We've nothing to hide. Just park us there by the wood. The gate guard can't see down here anyway.'

His phone went. It was Ali, who described the situation at Farley. Hussein took the news quite calmly. 'Call me the moment the Hawk leaves.'

'Where are you?'

'Where we are supposed to be. Now don't bother me until you have news.'

Khazid said, 'What's happening?'

'Jamal at Farley has seen the Hawk waiting and Ferguson and two men arrive, probably Dillon and Billy Salter. He will inform Ali the moment the Hawk takes off. I know that plane, I've flown one. I'd say in good weather it would be here at Zion in an hour, may be a little more today.'

'Allah preserve us,' Khazid said in awe. 'Ferguson himself on the terrace of that house? The British Prime Minister's head of security, a man with huge links to the American President. What a target! This changes everything. Our place in heaven is assured.'

'It changes nothing,' Hussein told him. 'First we need to get into the grounds, fool. So, orders. The large pockets in our anoraks will carry our weapons and additional ammunition with no problem, even your Uzi with the stock folded. We leave the flight bags locked in the Caravanette. You can carry the canvas bag with the toolkit, I will have my Zeiss glasses around my neck, and then into the wood with us.'

'To watch birds,' Khazid answered.

'Of course, and if any bird-watchers as crazy as us turn up in this weather, remember you're French.' He led the way along the side of the wood towards the runway end, checking his watch and finding it was just after nine.

Bolton's instructions had really been very good. Hussein turned into the fringe of pine trees at that point and said, 'Stop. I want to take a look.'

He focussed the Zeiss glasses that Bolton had procured. They were excellent. He scanned the garden, then checked the terrace extending the whole front of the house, the main door in the centre. At that moment the French window opened and Sara came out, holding an umbrella over her head. Caspar stood in the French window, obviously urging her to come in out of the rain. She stayed for a moment, then turned and went in. The French window was closed.

Hussein said hoarsely, 'I've just seen Sara on the terrace, and Caspar behind her. They've gone in again. Have a quick look.'

Khazid did, handed them back, and Hussein said, 'Let's get to it.'

Within a few minutes, thanks to Bolton's briefing, they forced their way through the thicket and found the stone.

'Excellent.' He stamped around, kicking in the grass, and Khazid unfolded the canvas toolkit. There were two small steel spades and two lengthy crowbars ranged along the bottom of the bag, a sledge-hammer and a torch. There was also a dark green waterproof cape, to hide an open hole if necessary.

Remembering what Bolton had told them he had done, Hussein tapped around in the turf and heard the clang of metal on metal.

'Now the spades,' he said. 'Come on, both of us.'

They attacked savagely and the pointed steel blades tore into the turf, turning it over, soon revealing a circular iron manhole. It was worn with the years, pitted, but it was still possible to read the manufacturer's name: Watson & Company, Canal Street, Leeds.

They looked at it in silence. 'Amazing,' Khazid said. 'After all these years.'

'Try moving it,' Hussein told him.

There was a steel handle in a cup setting in the centre. Khazid pushed one of the crowbars through and heaved. Nothing much happened, and at that moment Hussein's mobile sounded. He answered at once and found Ali there.

'Jamal has just called me. Although the weather is still poor here, the Hawk has just departed. It's nine thirty. Does everything go well?'

'We've found the entrance, but I've no time to talk.' He slipped the phone in his pocket and took the other crowbar from the bag, inserted it and they heaved together without success.

'Take some of the smaller tools, the screwdrivers, and we'll scrape round the edges of the circle. That was Ali. Jamal reports the Hawk departing at nine thirty.' He scraped away furiously, as did Khazid. 'That would mean an ETA of ten thirty plus the drive from the runway. I'd say they'll arrive at the house at about ten forty-five. Now put your back into it, little brother.'

The manhole cover moved with a strange kind of groan, tilted and broke free. They carried it further into the thicket and dumped it in the long grass.

'You first,' Hussein said to Khazid and pulled the cape from the toolbag. 'I'll pass it to you. There seem to be rungs down into this thing.'

Khazid did as he was told, the torch in

one hand. His voice echoed up. 'It's about five feet in diameter. Drop the bag.'

Hussein did so, spread the cape on the ground, went a few steps down the rungs and reached up to pull the cape over the hole. It was green in colour, and with any luck it could be undetected for a very long time.

The beam from the torch in Khazid's hand picked out the tunnel ahead. Its curved sides were concrete and very wet, and the drip of water could be heard.

'Must be leakage of some kind,' Khazid said.

He moved ahead, bending over slightly, oblivious in his stout boots to the sludge under his feet. There was a smell, but it wasn't unpleasant. Rather like walking through a wood in the rain, earthy and damp.

In his head, Hussein moved in slow motion as if in a dream. The sight of Sara under that umbrella had shocked him. It was the reality of her presence after the things that had gone before, the journey from Hazar, so much violence and death. Now she was near and there was little doubt what Khazid would expect him to do.

And Khazid was right to expect such a thing. They *were* soldiers, fighting in a war, one of the worst of modern times, which one way or another had cost the lives of many thousands of his fellow Iraqis, including his parents. It would be the worst kind of dishonour to fail them all now, even at the cost of his life. He saw all this so clearly. He was the Hammer of God and he had never failed in his duty.

There was the same kind of ladder in a brick wall ahead of them. He said to Khazid, 'Mount a few rungs with a crowbar and see what you can do. I'll brace you.'

Khazid put down the lantern, mounted to the right level and got to work, as Hussein took his weight. He was having difficulty, but a crack was obvious at the left-hand side of the manhole cover, the decay of the years.

'I can get the end of the crowbar in there. I'll hold it with one hand while you get the hammer and swing it against the end.'

Hussein did exactly that and everything happened in a rush, two or three bricks tumbling down. He jumped out of the way, then pushed his hands into Khazid's back, holding him firmly, while the manhole cover seemed to slide to one side and a considerable amount of earth showered in.

Hussein shook it off. 'Go through, see where we are,' he ordered.

Khazid mounted the rungs further, pushing the lid right to one side, and emerged, heavy rain pouring down, in the middle of a mass of rhododendron bushes surrounded by willow trees and close to a summerhouse styled in the manner of a pagoda. He was hidden from any kind of view, although a narrow path was near at hand, a walkway through the heavy foliage. There was the house, and the front door, the terrace on either side, a glimpse of someone passing the french windows. Although he wasn't to know, it was Kitty and Ida, setting the dining-room tables for lunch.

Khazid slid down into the tunnel and told Hussein what to expect. Hussein mounted a few rungs, paused a moment, then came down.

'Perfect.' He glanced at his watch. It was ten-twenty and the air was filled with the noise of the Hawk landing on the runway. 'Ten minutes early. I got it wrong.'

'But we are just in time for Ferguson, is it not so?'

'Absolutely.' Hussein took out the silenced Walther and checked it.

Khazid did the same with his, leaving the Uzi in the other capacious pocket, already loaded with the taped magazines. He left in his breast pocket the hand grenade he had taken from Darcus Wellington's collection without telling Hussein.

'So, Sara is no longer a problem?' he said. 'It will be Ferguson?'

Hussein nodded slightly. 'Yes, Ferguson, because it must be so. I see now I was very wrong where Sara was concerned. My duty lies elsewhere.' He smiled. 'Sometimes you see truth more easily than I do. A hard lesson for me to learn.' He kissed Khazid on each cheek. 'I will meet you in Paradise, little brother.'

'And I you.' Tears stained Khazid's face, and he gave his leader a fierce hug.

'Go to a good death,' Hussein told him, waited for Khazid to go up and then followed him.

Captain Bosey was by the runway, umbrella ready to shield Ferguson from the heavy rain. Dillon and Billy followed behind him, and Ferguson turned as Squadron Leader Lacey peered out of the hatch.

'We'll certainly be here for a few hours, so you and Parry might as well come up to the house.'

'That's kind of you, sir, but we've got things to do.' He turned to Bosey. 'Could you come back for us in an hour?'

'I'll see to it.' Bosey held open the Land Rover door for Ferguson, and Dillon and Billy bundled in.

'What a bleeding day,' Billy observed.

'Takes you back to Belfast on a wet Saturday night,' Ferguson added as Bosey drove away. 'I must say Lacey and Parry did a fine job.

There were times when I flinched.' He turned to Bosey. 'How's everything at the house?'

'Perfect, General, no problems. The Rashids have settled in well, and your people seem perfectly happy.'

'Excellent,' Ferguson told him. 'Pity about the weather, but I'm sure you have a nice lunch arranged.'

'Oh, you can rely on Mrs Tetley for that, General.'

The sound of the Hawk had touched every-body at Zion Place with a kind of antici-pation, especially Molly Rashid, who was feeling even more unhappy than usual.

'Thank God they've got here. I thought it might be cancelled by this dreadful weather, and I need to have words with General Ferguson.' She was sitting on a sofa beside Caspar and Sara, and the three Russians were chatting in the corner. She stood up. 'I'm just popping upstairs for a moment.'

'What for? A phone call, Mummy?'

'Yes. I'll only be a few minutes.' There was

instant dismay on her face as she realized her error. The Russians stopped their conversation and Molly, horrified at being caught out, fled.

Caspar said, 'What on earth's going on?'

'Why don't you ask her?' Sara stood up. 'You know how much I like the rain. I'm going for a walk in the garden.'

'You'll get soaked,' he told her.

'No, I won't. I shall borrow Igor's trenchcoat and take an umbrella.' She turned to the Russians as she walked out. 'Taking your trenchcoat, Igor. I'm just going for a stroll.'

'Do you want any company?' Greta asked.

'Suit yourself,' Sara said.

'I'll be right with you.'

A few minutes later they went out the front door, Greta also in a raincoat, linked arms for a moment and paused at the balustrade. Hidden in the rhododendron bushes by the pagoda, Hussein and Khazid saw them emerge, and Hussein raised the Zeiss glasses.

'It's Sara and some woman.'

At that same moment the Land Rover entered the main gate and started along the driveway. Sara said to Greta, 'Oh, damn, here they are. I'm not ready for it yet. Let's go, just for a few minutes at least.'

'If you like.'

They hurried down the steps and branched off on a path bringing them through to the end of the garden. They paused close to the pagoda. They looked back and saw Levin and Chomsky standing at the front door in welcome as Ferguson, Dillon and Billy got out of the back of the Land Rover. There were words exchanged up there. Ferguson turned to the balustrade and peered down, looking for them.

In the bushes, Khazid couldn't contain himself. 'It's Ferguson – perfect.' He stepped out of the bushes and found himself face to face with Sara and Greta.

Sara stared at him. 'It's you, Khazid.' She was stunned. 'I can't believe it.'

Hussein stepped out and took off his bush hat. 'Hello, Sara. It's a long way from home.'

She stared at him. 'Good heavens, Hussein, what have you done to yourself?'

'Everything changes, cousin.'

She said, 'I don't know how you got here, but I've no intention of going anywhere with you.'

'So the Hammer of God has fallen so low?'

And she said the strangest thing. 'Oh, Hussein, you're such a good man, in spite of yourself.'

'Enough of this nonsense,' Khazid said, took the grenade from his pocket, and hurled it up towards the balustrade, where it bounced off the steps, rolled back into a flower bed and exploded.

There was total confusion, everyone ducking, weapons appearing in their hands. Greta, who was carrying her own Walther in her raincoat pocket, drew it. Khazid grabbed her wrist, but she discharged twice, slicing his left shoulder, the second shot catching Hussein in the stomach as he stood to the side.

Khazid shot Greta at point-blank range in the body and she was hurled away to fall on her back. He went completely berserk, pulled out the Uzi and ran wildly up through the garden, calling out Ferguson's name at the top of his voice. Dillon and Billy pumped one round after another into him.

Sara shouted wildly, hands up. 'No more! Stop it, now!'

Her parents had emerged from the house and Molly tried to run forward, but Ferguson called, 'Cease firing.'

Sara looked at Greta, then called, 'Come and get Major Novikova at once, but no violence, please.' She turned to face Hussein, old beyond her years, aged by experience. 'What now, cousin?' she said. He was leaning against the pagoda and turned inside, a hand to his stomach, blood oozing. 'How did you know where we were?' she asked.

'An unwise call to your mother's hospital, a nurse sympathetic to our cause who overheard. But no matter. This is our final meeting, Sara. May Allah bless you all your days, but go now. Obey me in my last request.'

'No more killing,' she said. 'It is enough.'

She turned as Dillon, Billy and Levin arrived and walked past them as Levin knelt over Greta. She went calmly up the steps and her mother grabbed her.

'Are you all right?'

'Oh, yes, but no more phone calls, Mummy. They cost too much. Telling Dr Sampson where you were was a lousy idea. It got into the wrong hands.' She walked into the hall and went upstairs.

There was a kind of horror on Molly's face as she realized the implication. Caspar said, 'What on earth did she mean?'

'That somehow what has happened here was my fault. I rang Dr Sampson at the hospital a number of times on an extra mobile I keep in my bag. I couldn't help myself.'

'How could you do that?' He shook his head. 'So stupid.' She turned wearily and went inside. He sighed, and went after her.

Hussein was still in the pagoda, fumbling at his anorak, the blood oozing more than ever between his fingers, but when he finally stood up and lurched outside the Walther was in his right hand.

'Mr Dillon, Mr Salter.' They faced him, weapons ready. His hand swung up and each of them shot twice, throwing him backwards, the Walther flying to one side.

He was instantly dead. Billy picked up the Walther, inspected it and turned to Dillon as Ferguson appeared. 'It was empty.'

Dillon's face was bleak. 'Poor bastard, he'd nowhere else to go.' He turned to Ferguson. 'Greta?'

'Levin thinks she'll be all right. Ambulance on its way.'

'And the bodies?'

'The usual disposal team. I'll send in the order to Roper now. Hussein Rashid and this chap Khazid cease to exist. It never happened.'

Dillon nodded. 'Do you ever wonder what it's all about?'

'No, I've no bloody time. It's the world we live in, it's what we have to do to survive these days, with enemies like the Broker and Osama, Khan and people like him. So let's get back to London and get on with it.'

He turned and walked away as an ambulance drew up on the terrace and three paramedics piled out, came down the steps and hurried to where Levin crouched over Greta.

Dillon turned to Billy, 'OK, you heard the man,' and they followed Ferguson up to the terrace and into the house.

Bad Company

Jack Higgins

Wartime secrets threaten to topple a President – in the heart-stopping new adventure from the incomparable Jack Higgins.

In the waning days of World War II, Hitler entrusted his diary to a young aide, Baron Max von Berger. Over the years, von Berger has used his inheritance to become one of the richest men in the world, developing a secret alliance with the Rashid family – long-time foes of Major Ferguson of British Intelligence, his undercover enforcer Sean Dillon and their American colleague Blake Johnson. Now the ultimate confrontation is drawing near. The diary and its explosive revelations of a secret wartime meeting between emissaries of Hitler and Roosevelt will destroy the US President Jake Cazalet . . . unless Dillon can find it first.

'A Master craftsmen at the peak of his powers . . . first-rate tales of intrigue, suspense and full-on action.'

Sunday Express

0-00-712718-9

Dark Justice

Jack Higgins

It is night in Manhattan. The President of the United States is scheduled to have dinner with an old friend, but in the building across the street, a man has disabled the security and stands at a window, a rifle in his hand.

The assassination doesn't go according to plan, but this is only the beginning. Someone is recruiting a shadowy network of agents with the intention of creating terror.

Their range is broad, their identities masked, their methods subtle. White House operative Blake Johnson and his opposite number in British intelligence, Sean Dillon, set out to trace the source of the havoc, but behind the first man lies another, and behind him another still. And that man is not pleased by the interference. Soon, he will target them all: Johnson, Dillon, Dillon's colleagues. And one of them will fall....

'Open a Jack Higgins novel and you'll encounter a master craftsman at the peak of his powers . . . first-rate tales of intrigue, suspense and full-on action'   *Sunday Express*

0-00-712723-5

Without Mercy
Jack Higgins

In Jack Higgins' acclaimed bestseller *Dark Justice*, intelligence operative Sean Dillon and his colleagues in Britain and the United States beat back a terrible enemy, but at an equally terrible cost. One of them was shot, another run down in the street. Both were expected to survive – but only one of them does.

As Detective Superintendent Hannah Bernstein of Special Branch lies recuperating in the hospital, a dark shadow from their past, scarred deep by hatred, steals across the room and finishes the job. Consumed by grief and rage, Dillon, Blake, Ferguson and all who loved Hannah swear vengeance, no matter where it takes them. But they have no idea of the searing journey upon which they are about to embark – nor of the war which will change them all.

'Higgins is a master of his craft'   *Daily Telegraph*

ISBN 978-0-00-719945-7